For Elizabeth,
With much love,
Phyllis

Anglo-Jewish Women Writing the Holocaust

Also available by Phyllis Lassner

BRITISH WOMEN WRITERS OF WORLD WAR II

COLONIAL STRANGERS: Women Writing the End of the British Empire

ELIZABETH BOWEN

ELIZABETH BOWEN: A Study of the Short Fiction

For Elizabeth,
With much love,
Phyllis

Anglo-Jewish Women Writing the Holocaust

Displaced Witnesses

Phyllis Lassner

First published 2008 by
PALGRAVE MACMILLAN
Houndmills, Basingstoke, Hampshire RG21 6XS and
175 Fifth Avenue, New York, N.Y. 10010
Companies and representatives throughout the world

PALGRAVE MACMILLAN is the global academic imprint of the Palgrave Macmillan division of St. Martin's Press, LLC and of Palgrave Macmillan Ltd. Macmillan® is a registered trademark in the United States, United Kingdom and other countries. Palgrave is a registered trademark in the European Union and other countries.

ISBN-13: 978–0–230–20258–0   hardback
ISBN-10: 0–230–20258–6   hardback

This book is printed on paper suitable for recycling and made from fully managed and sustained forest sources. Logging, pulping and manufacturing processes are expected to conform to the environmental regulations of the country of origin.

A catalogue record for this book is available from the British Library.

A catalog record for this book is available from the Library of Congress.

10   9   8   7   6   5   4   3   2   1
17   16   15   14   13   12   11   10   09   08

Printed and bound in Great Britain by
CPI Antony Rowe, Chippenham and Eastbourne

To the next Lassner generation
Julia, Brody, and Tyler

Contents

Acknowledgements

I'd like to express appreciation to all those who have given permission to quote from their writing. In addition to permission to quote from Karen Gershon's poems, her daughter Stella Tripp also helped me locate her mother's video, *Strangers in a Strange Land*. For permission to quote from the video, I thank South West Film and Television Archive. Ester Golan granted permission to quote from her mother's letters. I am very grateful to Peter Lawson who shared Gershon's unpublished manuscripts with me as well as discussion about her work. I thank the Manchester Jewish Museum for permission to reprint the photo image that forms the cover of this book. Elaine Feinstein's generosity in sharing bibliographies and granting permission to quote from her manuscripts and poems, as well as ongoing support for my writing about hers, is matched by the friendship we have now shared for many years. I would also like to thank Diane Samuels and Julia Pascal for permission to quote from their plays as well as Oberon Books, Pascal's publisher. Readings from their plays at a conference on Post-War British Jewish Writing in Mainz, Germany, became the inspiration for this book. Later, when they talked with me in London, their insights helped me to find a focus. Every effort has been made to trace rights holders, but if any have been inadvertently overlooked the publishers would be pleased to make the necessary arrangements at the first opportunity.

I am grateful to Northwestern University for the Hewlett grants that funded my research-based courses on Holocaust representation as well as my travels to England, all of which happened because of Bob Gundlach's constant support and teaching wisdom. I would also like to express appreciation to audiences and their questions at conferences here in the US, in England, at Ben Gurion University in Israel, and in Belgium, as well as to Paul Goring who invited me to speak about my work at the Norwegian University of Science and Technology. My colleagues and friends in the Space Between Society and invitations from Alan Rosen, Keren Goldfrad, Jenny Taylor, and Marina MacKay to write on other Holocaust stories have given me so many opportunities to think, rethink, and revise my work on this very difficult subject. I am infinitely grateful for Elizabeth Maslen's generous friendship and wise responses to my ideas and writing.

I wish to express thanks to Paula Kennedy, my editor, for her enthusiastic interest from start to finish. And, as ever, there is Jake Lassner, who has always fully understood the often overwhelming power of writing about the Holocaust and who spurred me on with his own passion for the continuity of Jewish culture.

Introduction

> I was interested in the concept of survival, having been born in the wake
> of the Holocaust. There is so much guilt about surviving and this was my
> drive to write it.
>
> (Diane Samuels, in Sonja Lyndon, 'Speaking Out' 24)

Why is the Holocaust still being written? Unlike survivors, those who were
'born in the wake of the Holocaust' and its memory do not feel the pressures
of time. Unlike the Second Generation, they do not struggle with the inherited burden of a Holocaust identity. If, as so many have argued, the Holocaust
presents so many obstacles to representation, why do writers today still struggle with this near impossible mission?[1] Especially, as so many critics note, in
addition to aesthetic and historicist concerns, there are ethical risks in Holocaust representation. As Sara Horowitz points out, 'there is a high degree of
discomfort with the idea of an aesthetic project built upon actual atrocity,
as well as a proprietary sense of what belongs properly to the domain of the
historian' (*Voicing* 8). Such 'discomfort' calls our attention to so many objec-
tions: how the startling variety and totality of Nazi atrocities are fertile ground
for sensationalist plots, pornographic images, and narcissistic projections and
appropriations. In contrast to such Holocaust hype, more oblique postmodern narrative experiments can be viewed as equally disturbing. Experiments
in intertextuality and self-referential forms can easily be accused of submerging Holocaust historicity and veering all too close to Holocaust erasure. Such
ethical concerns about Holocaust representation apply as well to interpretations that universalize or apply the memory and meanings of the atrocities
to other genocides or sexual abuse and other forms of brutality and suffering. Yet despite strong criticism of exploiting the Holocaust to questionable
ends, there can be no doubt that controversial art exhibits and fictions will
continue, especially as the testimonies and sensitivities of survivors recede
into the past and leave a wide-open representational space.[2]

If the substance of Holocaust representation is cause for concern, so is
overexposure to Holocaust stories and images that could inure audiences to
the ethical urgency of remembering. In this vein, many deplore the efforts

1

of Holocaust writers, artists, and critics who offer upbeat moral pieties that obfuscate the horrors. Or offering the opposite – what has been called grief pornography. Holocaust scholars enter this fray by insisting on the necessity of providing Holocaust education to offset its denial and a kind of negation that, as Geoffrey Hartman notes, 'does lead to amnesia' or an *'anti-memory* – something that displays the colors of memory, like the commemoration at Bitburg cemetery, but drifts toward the closure of forgetful ritualization' (*Longest* 10, Hartman's italics).[3] Abigail Morris, artist director of the Soho Theatre Company that first produced Diane Samuel's 1993 play, *Kindertransport*, reflects on the complicated state of Holocaust representation today:

> We have a need to tell and re-tell the story; we need to remember, to remind others, to grieve and to try and make sense of all those deaths. On the other hand, we have to face the possibility that some of these feelings may never be resolved. This means there is a danger that we will imprison ourselves in a relentless, unconstructive pattern of repetition. And if we are not very sensitive to the danger of this treadmill, the images we create may be sentimental and thus actually lessen the importance of the event. Not only is this unhelpful and unhealthy for us as a people, who must create ourselves in the now and for the future, but it also creates a problem for non-Jews, who can misunderstand our painful psychological treadmill as a claim to be uniquely hurt and damaged. ('Beware')

These paradoxical issues about the need for and problems of the continued production of Holocaust representation are complicated even more by national memories and cultural mythologies. With historical memories of the abhorrent events of sixty years ago subsumed by commemorations of one nation's heroism or another's suffering, issues of national identity come into play.[4] One writer whose persona and work combine to dramatize this specious contest is W. G. Sebald, who sheds important critical light on the World War II roles and cultural histories of Germany and Britain. Born in 1944 and son of a German soldier who never spoke of his experiences, Sebald first learned about the war from his father's photo album where he found pictures of the September 1939 Polish campaign. Eric Homberger observes,

> He sensed that something in the grinning German soldiers and boy scout atmosphere of the campaign, ending with the torching of villages not unlike his own Bavarian home in Wertach am Allgäu, hinted at the meaning of the destroyed buildings, silences and absence of memory around him. ('W. G. Sebald')

Sebald broke through these silences and absences when he moved to Britain where he taught and wrote for over thirty years. His novels are revolutionary, not only because of his experiments with literary and pictorial forms, but because he finds the Holocaust bleeding its effects across the entire western hemisphere – from Manchester to New Jersey and back to every corner and train station in Europe.[5] Sebald deplored the category 'Holocaust Literature' on the grounds that 'it's a dreadful idea that you can have a sub-genre and make a specialty out of it; it's grotesque' (quoted by Maya Jaggi). But as his wandering characters search obsessively for their origins, identities, and meaning amid the detritus of European history and the stability promised by Britain, Sebald implies that all of modern culture is implicated in and has been soiled by the Holocaust. As his characters study the European monuments, travel to the United States, and live as disconnected and emotionally isolated creatures in Britain, Sebald insists that the inability to heal the scars of the Holocaust may be traced not only to the perpetrator nations but also to those which fought to defeat Nazism. Like some kind of dark justice in his writing, the Holocaust has taken an irrevocable toll not only on survivors but also on the character and fate of the West.

The fact that Sebald spun his Holocaust fables in German while living in England also adds a touch of irony to any consideration of Holocaust writing today. Whatever his own reasons for choosing England as a writing base, his position there as a German writing about the Kindertransport in his novel *Austerlitz* and about a British Jewish artist in *The Emigrants* highlights questions about British memories of the Holocaust. Although this book will not discuss Sebald's writing, his German-British position writing the Holocaust calls attention to the connections forged by Anglo-Jewish women writers between Britain's responses to the Holocaust and its European history. Despite its acclaimed Holocaust exhibition and wartime heroism, among all those people and places producing Holocaust literature and art, Britain has received the least attention. While it is true that there are fewer survivors, testimony projects, and Holocaust exhibitions in Britain than elsewhere, its writing is powerful and significant. And yet, even the most recent American anthologies and surveys of Holocaust writing omit the contributions of British memoirists and imaginative writers of the Holocaust and its aftermath. One reason may be that, until fairly recently, those who escaped to Britain have not been considered among those we identify as Holocaust survivors. Neither the refugees who came as individuals or families nor those on the Kindertransport suffered the ghettoes or camps. They are not among the children who were hidden with non-Jewish families or in convents, and they did not pass as Aryans with forged identity papers. They escaped the Holocaust before the round-ups and deportations began. More complicated yet is the position of those British writers with no personal or community connection to the Holocaust. Twice removed from Holocaust experience and memory, they nonetheless feel and write the pressures of Holocaust memory and its effects on those who were saved by Britain. Together, the writers considered in this book attest to the importance of including their remembered and imagined stories in the international Holocaust narrative.

As the autobiographical and imaginative writing I study here attests, those who were saved by Britain did not escape the effects of the Holocaust. Most lost their immediate and extended families and, as Jewish refugees in a nation desiring unity at the moment of its greatest threat, their experience of a safe haven was often compromised by their being considered enemy aliens or unassimilable. Now, so many decades later, a body of literature is emerging that, as Nicholas de Jongh notes, 'probes a closed, vanishing refugee world' (491). In addition to the external, social, and political opprobrium felt by the refugees, a powerful element in their new world was the tension they felt between veneration for those who had experienced the Holocaust and their own displacement. Although this literature makes no claims to represent any events within the world of Holocaust atrocities, it occupies a telling space between that world and the one that became the refugees' safe harbor. The losses of family and personal and cultural identities left an emotional void that refugee writers transform into an imaginative space. They fill this emptiness with portraits of remembered people and places as they imagine them so many decades later. Marita Grimwood asserts that 'it is the very absence of [the Holocaust] experience that is often an uncanny presence' in the writing of the Second Generation (3). Refugee writers create an 'uncanny presence' by fusing memory and imagination in writing that cannot recapture their lost people and places. Families, friends, and communities are there and not there, alive in memory and imagined reconstruction or even in fantasies and allegorical fairy tales, but always disappearing once again in the folds of new realities. In the writing of those like Elaine Feinstein, Julia Pascal, and Diane Samuels, who are neither refugees nor survivors, an uncanny presence persists in the haunted memories and spaces of their characters' lives. Working with interviews and documentation, they create arguments for the urgency of weaving stories of betrayal and rescue into Britain's World War II saga.

While the 'vanishing refugee world' obviously includes men, my justification for focusing on women writers began with discovering fiction, poetry, memoirs, and plays that formed compellingly interrelated patterns of representation and interpretation. Women writers became firmly implanted as my subject because of their intriguing narratives that expressed the imposed and willed silences and passionately vocalized explorations of loss as well as refugees' conflicted relations with their own and foster families and even within themselves. Significantly for the study of Holocaust rescue and its survival, these struggles also work as tropes representing the manifold tensions that shaped or contorted adaptations to a new language, cultural identity, and home. Because of the ages of many protagonists, these tensions would include the emotional vicissitudes of adolescence, including ambivalences about independence and attachments to substitute families and turbulent sexual feelings. A hallmark contribution of these women writers is their concern with gender identity and the relationship between Jewish women as bearers of Jewish identity and issues about Jewish continuity.[6] Writers such as Sue Frumin, Lore Segal, and Karen Gershon among others examine their characters' remembered and constructed responses to the gender identities and roles British cultural and social codes prescribed. Julia Pascal's plays and Elaine Feinstein's novels dramatize links between sexual passion, women's domestic roles, and historical crisis.

The complications of the World War II refugee experience in Britain have produced a literature that adds significantly to our knowledge of the Holocaust as an event and as an effect. While much attention has been given to Denmark's role in saving Jews and to the intrepid help of such diplomats as Raoul Wallenberg and Chiune Sugihara, the focus has been on rescuers, not the rescued. Since writing by and about refugees has emerged, however, so has a relationship that complicates the story of heroic rescue. In particular, this study of Britain's rescue of European Jews highlights the urgency of debates about relationships between the cultural identities and historical memory of both the rescuer nation and the rescued. As historical and personal investigations tell us, despite a vaunted tradition of tolerance, British wartime fears about fifth columns and economic austerity contributed to the unease with which European Jews were received on British soil. Not only could the Jewish refugees not share the nation's historical consciousness and its traditions, but everything about Jews' differences made them seem foreign and often suspect. At the same time, so many refugees were treated kindly by individual host families and those Jewish and non-Jewish organizations responsible for their rescue. In turn, Jewish refugees were infinitely grateful for a safe haven and many became eager to be acculturated.

If the chapter by and about Jewish refugees in Britain has been neglected by non-British scholars, wide recognition has been given to literature about the Holocaust by well-known British writers. The best-known works, however, are by already acclaimed writers and deal with the Holocaust in obliquely postmodern terms, as in Martin Amis's *Time's Arrow*, or in Anita Brookner's subdued novels.[7] Other writings, in genres such as plays, memoirs, poetry, novels, and literary criticism, highlight issues about representation, as well as responsibility and culpability for the destruction of European Jewry. A discussion by major Jewish and non-Jewish British writers and critics about the problems of Holocaust representation considers such issues as the role writers of fiction play in 'giving voice to the partial and the uncertain' (Amis et al. 12). Bryan Cheyette calls for writers to express their self-consciousness about 'the limitations inherent in representing this history', while David Cesarani notes the difficulty of dealing with Holocaust fiction because it has 'a peculiar form of authority' (Amis et al. 15). In the case of Britain's role in the Holocaust, it is history as a context and as a subject that presents limitations and difficulties about fictional authority. As we have seen in the last two decades, however, and as this book will demonstrate, there are Anglo-Jewish women writers who address these difficulties and limitations within their work. Their powerful writings explore how the nation's story of its wartime heroism and stoicism is glossed by a relationship between the definitive rescue and irresolute integration of its Jewish refugees.

In 1938 and 1939, between Kristallnacht and the onset of war, the British government, with help from Jewish and Quaker organizations, rescued 10,000 Jewish and non-Aryan children from Germany, Austria, Poland, and Czechoslovakia.[8] Commemorated in sixtieth-anniversary exhibitions all over Britain, this rescue continues to represent an uplifting reminder of the nation's moral rectitude in the face of Europe's capitulations.[9] In terms of its modern historical narrative, the story of a singularly humanitarian Britain has been especially important to the nation and Empire's sense of itself as we can see in a parliamentary statement. By 1933, when German Jews were already caught in the Nazis' tightening vise, Commander Oliver Locker-Lampson, MP, introduced a Bill on 26 July which would create citizenship opportunities 'in Palestine for Jews deprived of citizenship elsewhere', reminding the House 'that it is un-English, it is caddish to bully a minority' and suggesting that the British Empire should 'stand by Jewry in its trouble' (quoted in Sherman 39). Holding the higher moral ground has remained important to Britain as it has had to reconstitute its national pride ever since the Empire ended, world power fell to the United States, and the European Union emerged as a competing voice and economy. And now, with the devolution of Great Britain, and the prolonged birth pangs of an integrated multicultural population, Anglo-Jewish women writing the Holocaust insist on the inclusion of their stories in the evolving national narrative. Their writing argues that, as part of its national identity, Britain must reconsider its complicated relationship to the Holocaust and Jewish culture. While there is no doubt that the British deserve unequivocal recognition for the Kindertransport (known officially at first as the Movement for the Care of Children from Germany, and then as the Refugee Children's Movement) and other rescues, the memoirs and fiction inspired by these humane efforts attest to traumatic effects that should be integral to Britain's historical identity.

The stories of traumatic effects borne by the rescued also serve as a significant coda to the trauma experienced by Holocaust victims and survivors. Though originating in radically different circumstances, the Kinder's experiences of loss, cultural disorientation, and uncertain fates produced cognitive and emotional disjunctions that would not be resolved by the tremulous safety or security that Britain provided. Instead, what may have been most consistent in the experience of rescue was a continuous disjunction between memories of a stable self that were now unsustainable and a timorous selfhood in the present. Most Jewish refugees eventually adapted and went on to live highly productive lives, but, as so many have recounted, the emotional road to success and stability was chiseled out of feelings of abandonment and self-doubt. Considering the extremes of Holocaust experience, the term trauma has been considered very useful to analyze how these shocks continue unabated in Holocaust memory and how they are expressed in Holocaust representations. Although all the autobiographical writing I consider is written retrospectively and therefore appears to achieve mastery over the cognitive confusions that mark traumatized memory, it also registers doubts about this mastery. As I will argue, this writing and that which imagines Holocaust memory demonstrates a psychological space between trauma and mastery, between the shocks of personal and communal loss and the painful adaptations to an ambivalent rescuing nation. Dominick LaCapra's work on Holocaust trauma is particularly helpful here. He distinguishes the 'existential' traumas of ordinary human development, such as the psychological separation of child from mother, from the 'historical' trauma of war and genocide.[10] The writers considered in this book narrate combinations of these traumas by exploring the forms of expression that display immediate, not deferred, and conscious, not repressed, understanding of them.

If we consider that the Kinder were between three and sixteen years old, then the experience of being wrenched away from their parents combines both the normative psychic jolt of developmental separation and the disturbing historical fact that most would never see their parents again. These children and adolescents are among those child survivors Susan Rubin Suleiman has identified as the 1.5 generation whose 'shared experience is that of premature bewilderment and helplessness... [Their] specific experience was that the trauma occurred (or at least began) before the formation of stable identity that we associate with adulthood, and in some cases before any conscious sense of self' ('1.5 Generation' 277). Their extenuating circumstance was that loss of family was absolute; there was to be no psychological and social process of renegotiating parent–child relations as these children grew to adulthood and individuation. Regardless of whether it would have been psychologically possible, no emotional compensation was available in the experience of searching for emotional attachment, consolation, and relationship in the Kinder's foster families or group homes. Despite the best intentions of host families and groups, because the rescue was predicated on a temporary stay and because of cultural mismatches, misperceptions, and misunderstandings, the establishment of emotionally intimate and secure relations was rare. In order to feel accepted by their foster parents, the Kinder had to abandon cultural norms and social conventions that had been ingrained as a result of the various degrees and types of Jewish observances and identities. For the more reflective and older children, this meant a conscious and difficult choice, for they learned that they had to be grateful to those who sheltered them while abandoning much of which they held dear.[11] In contrast, as Andrea Hammel points out, it was generally assumed at the time that most of the children were 'too young to remember any trauma or, at least, it was considered easier for them to integrate into a new society' (65-6). By the time the war ended and the facts about most parents' deaths in the camps and ghettos emerged, it was too late to express feelings of abandonment of and by the lost parents. There were those, however, who would harbor such feelings without resolution. Furthermore, unlike survivors who had experienced the Holocaust's tortures directly, there were no targets toward which their emotionally logical responses of outrage and hatred could be aimed. As they were told and internalized, they had grown up in the six years of rescue and were already embarked on building new lives as Britons.

The Kindertransport and Holocaust writing I examine represents a challenge to the morale-boosting wartime myths of a united British identity and culture. While the home front muddled through with traditional allegiances to liberty, the law, and the community, wartime myths were solidified in the rhetoric of the British Empire standing alone against the Axis imperial alliance. As revealed in a 2005 *Daily Telegraph* survey, these myths have remained an integral part of British identity.[12] Fifty-nine percent of those who answered the question, 'What defines British', concurred that it was 'Britain's defiance of Nazi Germany in 1940' (Anon., 'National Identity' 14). The ethos of that defining moment prevailed even after the war, through austerity and waning global power. Britain's sense of national purpose was nurtured by a perennial insistence on Britain's exceptional moral and political profile, an image of liberalism that distinguished it from Europe's past and continuing struggle with totalitarian persecutions and antisemitism. Confirming a history of Britain's distance from European antisemitism was the fact that no Dreyfus case had ever erupted in England, and although there were violent antisemitic outbreaks in South Wales in 1911 and in the East End in the thirties, none of these resembled the pogroms of Eastern Europe. Even if an illiberal British antisemitism has persisted as polite social patter in upper-class drawing rooms and salons of the cognoscenti, its diluted form has been accepted as a benign trifle. Cast more positively, this diluted antisemitism is seen as a sign of irreversible progress from the medieval history of Jewish expulsion and modern history of the Aliens acts. Anthony Julius explains the languid nature of modern English antisemitism: 'The English anti-Semite... tends to regard anti-Semitism as vulgar and extravagant. It is taken to be characteristic of a certain kind of continental sensibility – excitable, immoderate, ideological' (59).

Britain's pride in its political and cultural differences from Europe has included its defense of its liberal principles and practices. From 1933 onwards, rather than betray xenophobia all too similar to that of fascist Europe, Britain welcomed its immigrants by encouraging them to become acculturated. And then, as proof of the nation's abiding commitment to preserve the rights of all its citizens, even under the threat of invasion, in 1940 the government imprisoned Oswald Mosley, leader of the British Union of Fascists.[13] Tony Kushner explains the official response to Mosley's fascism: 'political antisemitism' was considered 'a threat to law and order' ('Paradox of Prejudice' 85). The most dramatic sign of affirming Britain's liberalism may very well have been its rescue of Jewish refugees from Hitler's Europe, most famously, the Kindertransport.[14] And despite the nation's difficulties integrating the wartime refugees, its persistent racial divides, and today's postmodern doubts about liberalism, British belief in the efficacy and constancy of its liberalism appears to continue unabated even when questioned or challenged.

Even in the light of so much historically corroborating evidence, the story of Britain's rescue of the Jews is strained by the responses of both British officials and the Jewish community. Colonial injunctions prevented endangered Jews from entering Palestine and other colonies, and domestic restrictions kept most parents from joining their Kinder in Britain.[15] Even as Jewish refugees were adapting economically and culturally, the Jewish community complied with official expectations to insist that the refugees remake themselves in a British image by revising their European Jewish identities and styles of being.[16] This revision, however, would not prove to be easy. Expressed as secrets in the plays *Theresa* by Julia Pascal and *Kindertransport* by Diane Samuels, a hidden message was woven into Britain's welcome mat: no matter how well they might adapt, Jews and their cultural differences were not part of its design. This absence was expressed as a silence wherein none of the welcoming documents ever alluded to Jewish identity or culture. The documents only implied that if Britain was earning its reputation as a liberal and tolerant state, it was also demonstrating crucial differences 'between tolerance and acceptance' (Kushner, *Persistence of Prejudice* 93).[17] How this absence served a vulnerable British pride can be inferred by viewing the silence as representing a complex British ambivalence about supporting refugee immigration. After all, a European Jewish influx might be discomforting on at least two counts: it could contest the cohesive and continuous thread of Britain's national history and threaten the myth of a homogeneous, authentic England.[18] Resulting in a double bind for refugees, that myth included the cultural imperative to keep the racialized Others paradoxically integrated and separate.

The boundaries of this imperative served as a warning to refugees about real possibilities for 'acceptance'. Social welfare agencies issued booklets with lists of dos and don'ts to acquire British manners, but not necessarily citizenship. Anglo-Jewry's responses to Jewish refugees were driven by official British ambivalence and a history of antisemitism. Despite cooperation between the Jewish and non-Jewish communities on behalf of child refugees, apprehension about reigniting antisemitism with its own activism prevailed in the Jewish community.[19] This anxiety is apparent in the defensively cautious instructions issued by the Jewish community for Jewish immigrants that mirrored or mimicked British attitudes. Anticipating the government's lack of support, the Jewish community played down the extent to which Hitler had already begun victimizing the Jews before Kristallnacht. The community could not forget that from the moment the Nuremberg Laws were passed in

1934–35, the Reich began robbing the Jews of their economic assets, professional and business positions, and education. As though British antisemitism could also emerge with official sanctions, the Jewish community focused on offsetting the refugees' cultural differences or economic dependence on the welcoming nation by promoting only those who were 'young, self-supporting, skilled, and assimilated' (Bolchover, *British Jewry* 49).[20] Anglo-Jewish defensiveness is only too apparent in a booklet issued by the German Jewish Aid Committee in conjunction with the Jewish Board of Deputies: *While You Are in England: Helpful Information and Guidance for Every Refugee.* For example, note the first word in the title, *'While'*, which assumes the refugee's stay is only temporary. Moreover, as the following proviso indicates, the agency's urge to be 'helpful' is matched by broader impulses to keep the refugees in their designated place as forever alienated but grateful:

> Do not criticize any government regulations, nor the way things are done over here. Do not speak of 'how much better this or that is done in Germany'. It may be true in some matters, but it weighs as nothing against the sympathy and freedom and liberty of England which are now given to you. Never forget that point.[21]

This final edict carried the message that although integration was not expected of the refugees, acculturation, loyalty, and gratitude were. This instruction encoded its expectations of immigrants and their acculturation in double messages that would be very difficult to crack, especially for many refugees struggling with basic English, and even for those already somewhat fluent. Take, for example, the tone and address of the above sample. Its register is authoritative and impersonal, as a set of instructions to the collective 'you'. But if, and I'm sure this is the case, the 'you' would be taken as addressed to the individual reader, the voice is admonishing, assuming the reader is about to commit inappropriate behavior. Considering that the pamphlet is authored by a Jewish organization, its voice may strike us as perplexing. Instead of the empathy or support we could assume of a community organization addressing its beleaguered exiled brethren, we hear a carping paternalistic scolding. This voice does not, however, originate without a context. Compounding the coherence of refugee guidance was the not-quite-perfect fit of Anglo-Jewry and British cultural style and values. Unlike the general populace who, despite class clashes, felt unified in their resolve to defend themselves against a common enemy, Anglo-Jewry had to expend 'scarce resources and time to combating antisemitism in Britain during the war' while worrying about the refugees as well as those left behind, not to mention their own fate if Hitler should invade Britain (Kushner, *Holocaust and the Liberal Imagination* 131). One message conveyed to refugees by the government and the Anglo-Jewish community was that the children of the

Kindertransport would be treated to all the political and cultural benefits of a humane society. British schools and homes would educate and acculturate them. The system would embrace them.

At the same time, however, instead of being invited to join the battle of the British Empire against the Reich, adult refugees would be mistrusted as itinerants for lacking a nativist loyalty, and for imposing on national security and economic opportunity. As Barry Turner reports, 'Anyone with a foreign accent, including refugee children, were labeled as potential saboteurs' (*Policeman Smiled* 145). Boys and girls of sixteen and older were in danger of being interned while many boys were included with those men deported to Canada and Australia as enemy aliens once France fell and the British feared a German invasion. One of Karen Gershon's interviewees remembers the perplexity of being rescued and then interned:

> To be told that the country of my birth was the declared enemy of the country of my adoption was hardly conducive to the settling-down process. Not that my loyalties were divided: I was definitely for England and against Germany. I learned very quickly to omit any reference to my nationality when being introduced to people, and I adopted the same attitude to my religion. At this time I wanted above all to be 'accepted' and that meant pretending to be as average and English as possible.[22]

The presence of foreign Jews and their history of estrangement would also create a disturbance in Britain's narrative of national continuity and identity. A social survey in October 1940 revealed that of 'all comments concerning oppressed people, 47 percent were directed towards the Jews, yet only 18 percent felt Jews were deserving sympathy' (Kushner, *Persistence* 117). The fact that the Jews were considered victims could be seen as reflecting the humanitarian spirit of the many non-Jews who raised money for the rescue and took children into their homes. But this also meant that the children would be identified as needing cultural and social rescue in addition to nurturing their physical well being. There was scarce recognition of them as people with an identity that possessed its own authenticity and integrity. As Ann Parry sees this condition, it 'is the effacement of singularity involved in [the] discovery that the only group to which [the refugee] "belongs" is that of the victim, a group which is everywhere, but belongs nowhere' ('Lost' 9).

Having escaped their toxic fate as despised and feared objects of the Reich, refugees were now suspicious objects of British benevolence. For example, many of the Kinder came from upper-middle-class homes where higher education and professional occupations had been the norm. Whatever transition into British society and even the acquisition of Englishness the Kinder might have expected was dashed, however, by their newly acquired status. Thus, one contributor to Karen Gershon's collective memoir reports, 'When I came to England I thought that now I would be like everyone else, that my life would be normal. When I asked what I wanted to be I said a doctor. The woman who was filling the form in said: "I can't put that down – you must remember that you are a refugee" ' (*We Came as Children* 40). Though there were many instances of nurture and support among Jewish and non-Jewish host families, and some children qualified for higher education scholarships, this unsettling response contributed to the refugees' feeling that their Jewish cultural subjectivity was being denied. Although nothing in the social welfare booklets indicated that refugees should reject their Jewish identities, there were too many signs in the Jewish and non-Jewish communities of the regnant class-ridden and Anglo-Christian character of the nation.

In turn, the government exploited the anxieties of the Jewish community with the reminder that a sizeable Jewish immigration could lead to an antisemitic backlash.[23] Even those who could more easily become self-sufficient found themselves isolated in large part from Anglo-Jewish life when they arrived, for the Jewish community demonstrated its distance by supporting the government policy of interning Jewish refugees over the age of sixteen.[24] Finally, instead of being integrated into Britain's major Jewish communities, those who were not interned and those who were later released were dispersed around the country and instructed 'to keep a low profile, so as to avoid the impression of a substantial and menacing Jewish body within England' (Bolchover, *British Jewry* 50). Refugees were instructed that they occupied a precariously in-between space in British society, always learning to be innocuous but recognized nonetheless as different in ways that could never fit any British cultural setting or cultural category.[25] Because Britain's pride also rested on a notion of a culture that was already complete, the nation presented itself as a gated society, closed to the habits of being and relating that expressed the refugees' identities and cultures. Dependent and therefore entwined with the host nation, the Jews' differences severed them from Britain's cultural traditions. Despite its generosity towards the refugees, the Anglo-Jewish community did little to bridge this chasm. Its insecurities produced responses that were more puzzling and disturbing, for being Jewish.

The liminal space occupied by these Jewish refugees – neither open nor closed yet both – invited neither reinvention nor hybridity. Their identities would remain hyphenated: the Anglo and Jewish ends would reside in uneasy proximity to each other, inspiring acute anxieties emanating from their contradictory social, political, and cultural positions. Sara Horowitz's discussion of 'the in-betweenness' and 'shifting borders' of the performance of Jewish identity in contemporary Jewish American fiction offers an anthropological approach and insights applicable to representations of the refugees' negotiations with Jewish and British identities ('Mind' 253). '[D]uring times of social change that challenge traditional ways of viewing cultures and cultural membership, people become more aware of the impermanence, perhaps even arbitrariness, of identity and the instability of communal boundaries' ('Mind' 244). We can see the wartime rescue mission and efforts to integrate the Kinder and other refugees into British society as producing a startling awareness of the instability of cultural boundaries that had been considered sacrosanct. As refugees stumbled through their performances of adaptation and integration, they highlighted the ethical and ideological underpinnings of British manners. As Horowitz observes of cultural boundaries,

> In that sense, performance challenges what are perceived as fixed norms, destabilizing the boundaries between self and other, insider and outsider, belonging and exclusion. In resolving liminal states, the dynamics of performance may reassert firm boundaries, reshape cultural norms, and open up new cultural possibilities that then become the norm. At some level, these dynamics denaturalize the sense of wholeness of both communal and individual identity, revealing complicated sets of interactions between individuals within a community and between individuals and their communities. Even while reasserting a perception of cultural stability, liminal performances also reveal the provisional nature of inside and outside, challenging such binary categories. ('Mind' 246)

The confusions inscribed in this complex weave of insider/outsider relations, of rescue and rejection, only exacerbated the insecurities of Jewish refugees. As Victor Seidler reminds us, Jewish refugees from Nazi persecution 'could not feel so confident in the hopes and aspirations of a liberal culture, for they had experienced the revoking of their rights in Germany and Austria, which had supposedly cherished the ideals of an Enlightenment modernity' (4). At the same time, however, the complications of a British Enlightenment, including its insistent homogeneity, inspired the Jewish refugees to respond with their own rational interpretation: a retreat from their cultural origins. They clung to the 'feeling that they could give to their children the precious gift of "becoming English"... for to be English was to be "safe"', especially from the contemporary confirmation of their irremedial state of exile which to many at this moment must have been felt as perpetual (Seidler 4). In gratitude for this safe harbor, those very refugees, with identities forged deeply from many different European nations, pressured their children 'to become invisible', to keep a low profile and only express their Jewish cultural and religious identities privately (4). We see how these pressures persist into the present in the character of Judith, in Pascal's play *The Dybbuk*, who wails, 'Keep your head down. Be British, be cool, be part of the crowd' (*Holocaust Trilogy* 106).[26] Such an attitude conforms not only to stereotypes of British reserve, but also to a marginal British identity with which the Anglo-Jewish community had complied and that represented its insecurity. Richard Bolchover notes, Anglo-Jewry overall was 'acculturated, not assimilated' (29).[27]

Although Anglo-Jews took pride in the many differences of their religious identity and practices, they expressed them almost apologetically. In effect, they presented themselves as inseparable from their paradoxical historic status, as emancipated but still considered only marginally desirable and potentially perfidious aliens. Despite the increasing material successes of the Jewish communities, their manners and codes of respectability had developed and remained in the shadows of antisemitism. Sue Frumin, daughter of a Czech refugee, wrote her play *The Housetrample* in response not only to her mother's experience but to the antisemitism that has 'been fairly and obviously prevalent' in her own life (107). Frumin 'felt it was important to write a piece which might make people aware of their own antisemitism, and which created a sympathetic and non-stereotypical picture of a Jewish woman' (107). Though British Jewry never failed to express appreciation for British tolerance, the community also reacted to European refugees as though the Jews' expulsion centuries earlier and modern British social and economic restrictions were intertwined. This 'politics of fear', according to Bolchover, led the Jews of Britain to believe in an 'emancipation contract' between the state and the Jews that kept them enthralled to reticence, a British style of relating that erased their own. The Jews would not ask Britain to accept them as equals in their 'full self-proclaimed identity', but to forget and ignore their 'separateness' (*British Jewry* 119).[28] For example, Second Generation survivor Anne Karpf reports that her parents' refugee experience in Britain was tinged with the fear of an antisemitic 'backlash' if their Jewishness attracted attention (*War After* 13). When Karpf published a diary entry about Yom Kippur in the *Sunday Times*, her parents 'expressed a mixture of pleasure and anxiety at this public coming out' (*War After* 13). Such a public display was problematic because for Anglo-Jewry, there was 'little visible alternative public secular culture of our own' (*War After* 50).

As so many Anglo-Jewish writers have attested, Britain has no equivalent to the acclaimed tradition of American Jewish literature. Elaine Feinstein views Anglo-Jewish literature as occupying the position of outsider:

> No Jewish literature in England is perceived as interesting and exotic, as for example Asian poetry and Black poetry tend to be. We're not perceived as *exotic*, although we remain *other*. And that wouldn't matter at all if there were an interest within the Jewish community itself... ('Way Out in the Centre' 65; Feinstein's italics)[29]

Even today, producer/director Abigail Morris speaks of being a Jew in that hallowed tradition of British theater as follows:

> It's very different here. You've got to be integrated, you can't just be seen to be 'doing Jewish'... It's a prejudice that seems to cut both ways... in London... Jews themselves don't like to see things that are specifically

Jewish, until they've been reviewed in the national non-Jewish press. When a Jewish play has become something that's legitimated by the non-Jewish world, then they love it. Till that moment they don't want to see it. (22)

Although there is now a vibrant and celebrated young generation of Jewish writers in Britain, it is not clear that this has inspired Jewish confidence in constructing an Anglo-Jewish literary and cultural tradition.[30] Career concerns are still deeply implicated in considering the place of Jewish identity in Britain. Bryan Cheyette, who has built his academic career studying the construction of the Jew and Jewish writers in modern Britain, asks: 'What is it about Englishness that is so deforming?' ('Moroseness' 22). He points to the position of British Jews as outsiders to an 'English national culture . . . made up of a peculiarly homogeneous unchanging idea of the past' ('Moroseness' 23). His own position is that Anglo-Jewish writers are 'most interesting' when they are 'transcending their Englishness' ('Moroseness' 23). As though in response to these judgments, the writers I study address the question posed by Natasha Lehrer of 'how to engage explicitly as a Jewish writer with English culture without being confined to the margins of that very culture as a result' (75).[31] To which this book responds, with British memory of the Holocaust.

For those Jewish refugees who stayed on after the war, becoming British would not mean assimilating to British culture but submerging their own history and culture under the weightier if tremulous traditions of Anglo-Jewry. The refugees would create a functional, acceptable Jewish identity, but, according to Elaine Feinstein, it would be shadowed by Britain's imperial influence on Anglo-Jewish identity:

the white, English middle or upper-middle class people, who went out and formed an empire . . . would have been very careful to keep out anyone perceived as alien from what might be called the mainstream . . . I was only able, if you like, to enter the English consciousness, much later than I might have been able to, when the mainstream became permeable. ('Dark Inheritance' 59)

According to Feinstein, refugees 'had to absorb enough English culture for them to be – half and half . . . they would be using post-colonial English, essentially' (59). So often, especially for children and adolescent refugees, the syllabus for learning Anglo-Jewish social codes included abandoning the past responsible for shaping them. Kindertransportee Hans Schneider testifies,

A past in a different country is a burden on a teenager attempting to make a new life for himself or herself, and it leads to (I am tempted to say 'requires') memory loss of one's previous life. Silence, unless with others similarly placed, is needed by a young outsider for fitting into a [homogeneous] society – a silence which becomes deeply ingrained. (Review 116)

One such expression of silence resulted from being isolated from survivors and from concrete information about the fates of those left behind. Some Kinder, like Martha Blend, felt that her

> adolescent shoulders were simply not strong enough to bear the burden of such a vast atrocity which, as I later discovered, had destroyed dozens of members of my parents' large extended families. This meant that my hold on reality was brittle and my identity blurred. (*Child Alone* 143)

Despite Britain's rescue efforts, so many refugees write that the burdens of their reception exacerbated a persistent sense of imminent danger. Warned that after two or three years they should expect to move on, refugee writers conjure up the image of the wandering Jew who is unwelcome everywhere. This wanderer is unlike the new cosmopolitan or transnational subject celebrated in contemporary cultural studies who crosses borders and scoffs at the idea that national identity offers pathways to selfhood, safety, and security. More closely associated with the old rootless cosmopolitan, the Jewish refugee resembles the impermeable image of the Jew who has little to celebrate. With no sense of belonging, embodying and juggling several cultural identities, including spoken and body languages, dress, and other customs, Jewish refugees are often figured by themselves and by others as uncanny and unstable, even grotesque. This Jew cannot settle down and become integrated into any British community, Jewish or non-Jewish, no matter how many years and how acculturated he or she might become. Whatever models of British affiliation are purveyed and followed, their normative position remains one of unsettling the local culture. A result of this mutual insecurity becomes especially apparent in Charlotte Eilenberg's play, *The Lucky Ones*, where the middle-aged Kinder, having lived in England for decades, bemoan their accented English and awkward repertoire of acceptable English gestures and body language. Moreover, as though the fate of European Jewry is written on the refugees' personae, they appear to be not completely living beings, to be unnatural, as though they are not quite human or totally alive, but rather a living form of lamentation for the dead.

The unstable liminal space occupied by these Jewish refugees is represented in so much writing by and about them as narrative discontinuity. Although James E. Young applies this term to representations of violent Holocaust events, it also describes the literature dramatizing the emotional violence experienced by the refugees. Young interprets the effects of narrative structuring on the representation of Holocaust violence as losing the 'particularity' of its '"violent" quality' through narrative resolution and being integrated into a 'cultural continuum' (*Writing* 15). The inadequacies of language and literary forms seem to conspire against the possibility of representing horrific events factually and authentically. The frustration, even desperation, felt by writers to bear witness thus led to what we could call a crisis of Holocaust representation. Certainly, as Young argues, victims and survivors who have managed to record their experiences have often abandoned forms of literary realism even as they 'assumed that the more realistic a representation, the more adequate it becomes as testimonial evidence of outrageous events' (*Writing* 17). The ten thousand children saved by Britain would not be motivated by imminent danger to bear witness, but many were driven to write their memoirs when their fiftieth reunion confronted them with the passage of time, receding memories, and their shared sense of a prevailing silence about their refugee experiences.

As so many of these memoirs reveal, Kinder and other refugee writers also confronted the disjunctions between mostly ordinary middle-class childhoods and the uncertainties and losses of emigration and growing up without family. Writing decades later, from an inquiring perspective on events and relationships that they barely and rarely understood as children, many were encouraged to search for a narrative form that would suggest the discontinuities and incoherencies of their experiences. As Vivian Patraka observes of those writers who 'have no direct knowledge of the Holocaust', they

> foreground the question of knowledge... rather than offer knowledge of the Holocaust. Eschewing realism, they do not present a story of the Holocaust as if they were recapturing it or offering 'the truth'. Instead... they reject realism's inscription of the subject as complete, coherent, and rational. There is for [these] writers no disruption in the landscape of the Holocaust that is containable within the borders of realism and, in terms of form, no social order to which to return. (*Spectacular Suffering* 62)

These writers would also question whether a narrative about such a dramatic rupture between past and present can be unified – or is it unified by its fragments of social and emotional realities?

Even when memoirs follow a chronological structure, scenes from a past overshadowed by belated knowledge suggest fable more than realistic form. What the characters don't understand guides the narrative rather than the pathway to knowledge and adult experience. Like those writers who experienced the immediacy of the Holocaust, these authors have turned to 'archetypal and mythological representations' to narrate their jagged processes of growing up (Young, *Writing* 17). Instead of subscribing to the linear model of the *Bildungsroman* to show how they face adult disillusionments, their writing critiques it by turning it inside out or upside down. References to or mini-fairy tale allegories give expression to the terror of familial rupture or abandonment, the fear and reality of Nazi danger, as well as the encoded double messages about British integration. These fairy tale snippets do not court verisimilitude by relating the jumble of unconscious fantasy to the chaos of external threats. Instead, their spectral figures and body parts perform an indecipherable reality. Unlike the fairy tale books carried by so many Kinder, these tales are not meant to comfort. Nor will they serve as memory cues many years later. As we will see in examining Diane Samuels's stand-in for the Pied Piper in her play, *Kindertransport*, anxiety outruns the possibility of comfort or relatedness. The child's book must be buried to assuage unresolved fears of betrayal.

Such an interpolation of childhood reading addresses our desire for reconciliation, resolution, and recovery by frustrating it. In all their guises, the uses of fairy tales challenge such desire with fresh insights into the lingering effects of the traumas instigated by the refugees' experience of rupture. As Ruth Gilbert notes, 'fairy tales are the perfect narrative device for representing the painful and primary memories' because they 'are fragmented, cyclical, orally based stories, punctuated by astonishing moments of cruelty' ('Ever After' 30). The struggles of fictional and real characters to adapt to their new nation insist that the reconstruction and construction of Holocaust experience cannot be reified as historical knowledge of a revealed past. Instead of comforting us with a character's understanding that we can share, these texts confront readers with the necessary failure of Holocaust stories to do so. While many of the writers in this book rely on historical research to substantiate their memories and imaginations, they also participate in ongoing debates about the roles of memory and emotional and moral imagination in historical narratives. Like historians, they provide multifaceted perspectives and evidential arguments about the Holocaust subjects of their concern, but they also intervene in the tendency of historical discourse to dull the edges of argument and to make evidence ever more problematic.

These writers express concern about a danger that presides over the passage of time and the fading of historical memory – that historical debate will overwhelm the moral and psychological parameters of what took place. Instead, the memoirs, plays, and fictions by Anglo-Jewish women writers attempt to bring into full view the moral and psychological crises that accompany the Holocaust and rescue experiences they narrate. This literature does not function as historical guides. It also cannot be considered a memorial service or a celebration of stable new starts and the regeneration of Jewish culture in a new homeland. Instead of eulogies that offer the solace of closure, instead of a burial that would resound with memories of internment and erasure of the Jewish past, Anglo-Jewish women writers ask us to bear the unrelieved burden of our persistent but uncertain knowing beyond their writing.

1
Other People's Houses: Remembering the Kindertransport

In the Labyrinth of the mind
resides the Minotaur, the merciless mythical beast
who will find and devour me
in a furious feast
but before my demise
I am compelled to recognize
my own repulsive reflection
mirrored in the feature
of the insatiable creature
I try to elude in the maze

(Schieber, 'Labyrinth')

Unlike Holocaust memoirs shaped by the crises of mass deportation, incarceration, and extermination, those which recount the Kindertransport and other refugee experiences in Britain tell a different story of discontinuity and disorientation.[1] The events of which the Kinder were a part resulted from emergency efforts by Jewish and other charity organizations as Nazi persecution intensified. The success of these efforts, including the leadership of Sir Nicholas Winton and £500,000 raised in a radio appeal by former Prime Minister, Lord Baldwin, meant that the Kinder experienced none of the suffering associated with the Holocaust itself. For a long time, however, in fact until the 1989 Kindertransport reunion in Britain and the opening of the Imperial War Museum's Holocaust exhibition, many refugees did not even consider their stories sufficiently connected or pertinent to the history and moral lessons imparted by Holocaust memoirs. Moreover, unlike diarists and memoirists of the camps and ghettos, who worried about the empirical value of their testimony, there was nothing the Kinder witnessed or could offer as testimony that would serve to further the cause of justice sought in the War Crimes Trials or that would fit the newly designated crimes against humanity. Mediated by parents' protective evasions and rationalizations, persecution was felt most directly in children's expulsions from non-Jewish schools, recreation, and friendships. Their experience of the Holocaust extends only to the prologues to roundups and deportations. Then, as the young refugees struggled to integrate into British society, their links to the atrocities may have seemed even more remote, reinforcing the sense that their experiences and responses were peripheral. This marginalization was exacerbated by the fact that even the core events that shaped the refugees' experiences, as well as their reactions, often receded into lost or blurred memories. This was especially true for the younger children. Then, when so many learned that their families had been killed, their stories of escape were overwhelmed by grieving, further adaptation, and continued migrancy. For all these reasons, for a long time, the children's stories did not become part of efforts to add complexity and comprehensiveness to knowledge of the Holocaust.[2]

Yet, even as these children found safe harbor, so many lost their parents, siblings, and extended families, as well as the homes, homelands, and cultural identities which they had believed were theirs. It all started once the Nuremberg laws took hold in 1934–35 and Jews were expelled from all public spheres, including work. The Kinder then witnessed and absorbed their parents' intensifying panic about their families' possibilities for escape. Parents believed they were protecting their children from the anguish of their frantic and frustrated efforts to be added to quota lists and to acquire transport visas, but fear broke through their silences. The trepidations that had been seeping through unanswered questions and whispers were ironically only aggravated by the announcement in 1938 of the Kindertransport. In a week or even the next day, the children would need to be ready to board trains to take them to England. Because only the barest facts about the rescue were available, the reassurances parents could provide confirmed the children's worst fears about their collective fate. Kindertransport memoirs chart the anxiety filled frenetic movements that led to planning the escape, the wrenching separation from family, the journey across Europe to England, and the often transient and mixed foster experiences that shaped their adaptation and integration into British society. Sometimes these were stories of abject failure. With the publication of individual and collective memoirs about this journey, we have learned more about Nazi persecution as well as British immigration policies and attitudes towards Hitler's Jewish victims. As this chapter and the next will demonstrate, women's Kindertransport memoirs also address concerns about Holocaust representation by connecting the writers' already constructed sense of the past to the memory work of the present.

A narrative challenge for refugee and Kindertransport writers, and one that is shared with Holocaust memoirists, is the attempt to convey their complex and barely understood experiences with precision and conviction. Although the rescue of ten thousand children cannot compare to the 1.5 million who perished in the Holocaust, the Kindertransport number is sufficiently large to lead to a problematically homogenized understanding of their experience, especially as one can easily detect generalized patterns of loss and adaptation among the children. James Young addresses these problems of representation:

> But if the function of literary testimony then becomes to establish facts or evidence, it grows apparent first of all to the writer that he may be demanding of narrative an impossible task. For the diarists and memoirists intuit that in asking literature to establish the facts of the Holocaust – or evidence of events – they are demanding not just that words signify experiences, but that they become – like the writers themselves – *traces* of their experiences. Their impossible task is then to show somehow that their words are material fragments of experiences, that the current existence of their narrative is causal proof that its objects also existed in historical time. (*Writing* 23).

Looking back from the perspective of fifty years later, even after establishing herself as a successful writer, Lore Segal notes the persistence of uncertainty about whether writing can communicate the '*trace*' of the events and experiences that drove her to become a refugee. Convinced at the time that her British Jewish hosts 'were not properly imagining what was going on in Vienna and what might be happening to my parents', she fills an old bound notebook

> from front to back with my Hitler stories. It was my first experience of the writer's chronic grief that what was getting down on paper was not right, was not all that there was to say. As poor J. Alfred Prufrock puts it, 'That is not it at all. That is not what I meant, at all,' and so I added several sunsets. ('Bough' 242)

Despite their experiential distance from the actual Holocaust, the Kinder's writing of displacement and adaptation adds a significant dimension to analyses of Holocaust representation and reception. As many have testified, the invitation to attend a fifty-year reunion reignited memories and feelings that for many had lain dormant in efforts to avoid the pain of profound loss and the frustrations of adaptation in order to build their lives anew. As Lore Segal learned, while the facts of the Holocaust were readily available to the general public by the 1950s, the story of the Kindertransport was not: 'And so I understood that I had a story to tell' ('Bough' 245). Published Kindertransport memoirs attest to a complex spectrum of experiences, including moments of departure, the children's reception in Britain, and their continuing adjustment to a new language and culture. And just as Holocaust memoirs humanize the victims of mass slaughter and survival, so Kindertransport memoirs offer us a glimpse into the emotional climate that formed the backdrop as well as aftermath of the Holocaust. As part of this humanization, the memoirs and fiction about the Kinder's experiences share a narrative complication with memoirists of the ghettos, of hiding, and of the camps. For example, one significant issue that emerges from Kindertransport memoirs is their complicated relationship with readers. Precisely because the youngsters escaped and most thrived, readers may find it easier to relate to this Holocaust experience and even to identify with the protagonists. As a result, the writer's past and presence may get lost in the readers' experience and responses.[3]

There is also a problem in reverse. To read these memoirs as documentary testimony may avoid the pitfalls of personal relatedness, but the memoirs are not written as historical discourse. Instead, as we shall see, what women writers document are their negotiations with extant genres, forms, and readers' expectations that for them and for readers present a canonical rhetoric of Holocaust representation. If, for example, the Kinder experienced their adaptation favorably, they might easily feel their stories don't meet readers' expectations of Holocaust deprivation and suffering. On the other hand, the story of a difficult or conflicted experience might not be received well by the nation that saved their lives. Ambivalence could all too easily be seen as a sign of ingratitude, especially in light of the first Kindertransport histories which celebrated how the children were welcomed and integrated into the Anglo-Jewish and British communities.[4] For the Kinder who stayed on after the war, social and economic success depended on submitting to the pressures embedded in this welcoming narrative. The delays in communicating their stories could therefore be explained in part by the feeling that it may not have been wise to publish and therefore publicize painful stories of their transports. Their dramas of complicated and even troubled personal and bureaucratic relations would have challenged the mythic or propagandist uses of the Kindertransport. Instead, however, many women's memoirs would question Britain's Janus-faced reception that expected unceasing gratitude in return for an unclear and unstable status as fully integrated Britons. This internalized conflict between emotional actuality and social ideology registers in the oblique and allusive narrative forms of Kindertransport memoirs rather than an attempt at overt expression or representation of the writers' emotional responses. For example, Ruth David's observations draw attention to the indirect forms of emotional expression that mirror the integration process of the young women refugees. This process involved a form of social suppression that was designed to produce 'ladylike' deportment, wherein even whispering was considered 'vulgar' (74, 75). One can only imagine how such an interdiction would not only suppress the public sharing of painful feelings but also could have a lasting silencing effect on women's psyche and self-expression as well.

This highly complex set of liminal circumstances and responses was compounded by the fact that many Kinder had come from highly assimilated, non-observant or intermarried families. The issue of a distinct Jewish identity, which had become diffused in prewar Europe until Hitler's Nuremberg laws, had now surfaced once again to haunt the refugees in Britain. At an official level, the British stamped those refugees who were sixteen or older with the designation of enemy alien. More generally, neither the bureaucracy nor the English populace showed an understanding of what it meant to be German Jewish as opposed to a German citizen of the Third Reich or merely to claim an identity that was different from the majority English culture. If these exigencies seemed to mirror the discrimination that drove the refugees away from Europe, adaptation and acceptance in Britain shaped a very different future. Yet as so many memoirs show, despite the passage of decades, with their incumbent life cycle events of careers and/or marriage and family life, endings remain open, with promises of forging an ever evolving and occasionally surprising future. This pattern is necessarily different from Holocaust memoirs that often stop with the liberation of the camps and emergence from hiding or speed to the celebration of building and sustaining new lives, rarely elucidating the lasting effects of their losses on their hopes for the future. Hardly ever do Holocaust memoirs depict the jagged trajectories of personal development, but rather move forward either to the circumstances that led to rescue and to recovering the self from the moment when personal development was thwarted or to claim the possibility that they can become other than what the Holocaust has made them.[5]

Kindertransport memoirs chart the lasting effects of their losses even if parents managed to escape or survive. Those parents who made it to England were mostly kept apart from their children by government policy and economic straits. Mothers had to accept jobs as maids or cooks and, if they were lucky, fathers could find positions on the same premises as chauffeur, gardener, or handyman. Most employer-families did not permit the presence of servants' children and few parents earned enough money to afford lodgings outside their employers' homes. And, even if they could, parents' work was often in parts of the country far away from their children's placements. Visits were rare due to wartime travel restrictions and cost and neither government policy nor employers showed much sympathy for parents' and children's need for emotional connection. While parents would have preferred to assume the responsibility of caring for their children, they suffered from similar limitations and problems of adaptation that prevented them from doing so. In addition to their reduced capacity to learn a new language and the often baffling social habits, traditions, and bureaucracies of their host nation, they had been traumatized by their escalating persecution under the Nazis. With little emotional reserve and no economic capital, their capacities were reduced by being in a dependent and disoriented state. In the end, while parents struggled with their narrowed prospects, it was the children who, for the most part, were the most resilient and who built new relationships.

For the children, there were emotional losses even as they found refuge in family homes or youth hostels. The qualitative range of care and sensitivity among foster parents, teachers, and supervisors varied as much as the social and economic circumstances of their foster homes and institutions. A poor or wealthy family could just as easily be sensitive and nurturing as cruel and indifferent. From the perspective of foster families, one cannot forget that they had no training or even warning about the care and consideration of children who were anywhere from two to fourteen years old when they were torn from their parents' arms and who as a result could suffer from such symptoms as bedwetting, nightmares, emotional withdrawal, and aggression. In Karen Gershon's novel *The Fifth Generation*, these symptoms also symbolize the alienation of children who no longer feel that they possess a stable Jewish or even any other identity. Just as their lives are beyond their control, so are their bodies. And to compound these effects of the children's traumatic schism, the foster mothers who bore most of these responsibilities had to contend with food preferences that seemed as alien as the children's language, clothing, and behavior. The children themselves quickly recognized their alien habits and status, as Lore Segal attests in a comic epiphany. A lovingly packed sausage meant to keep hunger at bay on the transport becomes a lingering sign of the child's conflict between attachment to home and adaptation: 'I woke in a thumping panic from a dream that a crowd of people had discovered my sausage' (*Houses* 44).

Questions of Jewish identity were mostly ignored, but it could also provide a shock of recognition, especially as other Jewish children from various social, cultural, and economic backgrounds all over Europe were gathered together. Geoffrey Hartman recalls such an eye opener during his stay at Waddesdon Manor, the Rothschild estate used as a boy's refugee hostel. Faced 'with a motley, unwashed crew... from the East, *Ostjudgen*' with unintelligible talk and gestures moves the young Hartman to expose the Kinder's internalized and ironic cultural hierarchies: '*We* (the German refugees) [would] have nothing to do with *them*' (*Longest* 17, author's italics). If German cultural hegemony was part of the Kinder's baggage, in Britain, as Diane Samuels shows in *Kindertransport*, Jewish identity was superseded by Christian or secular good intentions. Devout Christian families would take their Jewish wards to church services and if the child's own family was primarily secular or assimilated, yearnings for belonging could easily encourage the Kinder's attraction to Christianity. At the same time, unless a child from an observant home was similarly placed, religious practices and identity could very well erode with time and distance. As they grew up, some children rediscovered their Jewish roots while for others those roots remained a nostalgic mist.

The Kinder had to negotiate their own burgeoning ambitions between memories of parental support and alien British expectations. Ninety percent of the children never saw their parents again, but even for the few who made it to England before the fateful declaration of war or for those parents who survived, reunions did not bridge the gulf between separation and adaptation. Instead, reunions were already fraught with the children's interim struggle to adapt and defend against the pain of separation. When reunions did occur, the children had to rediscover the desire to be attached to parents they might not remember or to parents who were now strangers as result of their Holocaust experiences and the passage of time. As Ute Benz reports, 'family reunions caused new separations from the social relations to which children had become attached' (87). Meetings were often disappointing or even tragic as many children had distanced themselves emotionally from parents whose loss they already felt and who they could not have been sure of ever seeing again. Collective autobiographies of the Kindertransport testify to the tense emotions produced by the news of surviving parents and the possibility of reunion:

> [M]y sister and I... were flabbergasted and horrified. No! We didn't want to go. We belong to you, Aunt and Uncle! (Gershon, *We Came as Children* 114)

> I saw my mother after the war when I was seventeen, in Holland. The situation was highly charged emotionally – Mother wanting to protect me and make up for the long absence and I wanting to be independent. I found it difficult to establish a relationship; I felt guilty about this but couldn't do much about it. After all I had found a mother-substitute during my formative years. (Gershon, *We Came as Children* 114)

> I remember rushing down to meet them. I knew they were my parents, but it wasn't the same parents I'd left. They were much older and they were worn-out, and, obviously, we weren't the same children that they'd sent off. Suddenly I realized I couldn't say anything except their names, 'Mutti' and 'Papa', or I couldn't speak to them because I'd forgotten all my German, and they hadn't learned much English.
> We just stood there looking at each other. It was such a traumatic moment. It was wonderful, and yet it was terrible. (Harris and Oppenheimer 229)

If reunions were traumatic for the Kinder, they were equally so for parents. Renate Buchthal recalls that her younger sister became so attached to her foster parents that she 'became theirs', never to bond with her own parents again despite their having found work close by (Leverton and Lowensohn 50). As a result,

> Meetings were painful for everybody. It was hard for our parents to see us as someone else's children and I found each parting agonizing, expressing this by more sullen and resentful behavior to my long suffering foster parents. (Leverton and Lowensohn 50)

These children experienced a developmental rupture, in which their formative years were spent apart from the primary relationship through which we could expect them to have negotiated the adolescent transition from childhood to adulthood. Using Eric Erikson's model of childhood development to interpret autobiographical writing about World War II childhoods, Gillian Lathey notes children's wartime struggle with issues such as 'independence and freedom from parental constraint' in times of persistent crisis (48). The Kindertransport foreclosed such a struggle. Most children not only had no parents with whom to conflict, but they found themselves sheltered by foster parents whose notions of independence included binding expressions of gratitude and the acceptance of such social codes as constrained personal expression. Secrecy and silence were the hallmarks of adapting to such biological developments as menstruation. Ruth David reports that because 'the topic was unmentionable ... perhaps even dirty', there 'was a false modesty in operation' (112, 113). Equally suppressed but more traumatic in effect was the acceptable response to news of a parent's death. Instead of the ritual expression of grief in reciting the Jewish prayer for the dead, *Kaddish*, the matrons at Ruth David's Newcastle hostel preferred a silent if 'outward show', to wear 'the same grey frock for many weeks, if not months, an ever-present reminder of her [friend's] loss' (116).

Despite the radically different experiences they recount, Kindertransport and Holocaust memoirs share similar narrative structures to highlight the silences and absences that define them and the protagonists' attempts to fill them with knowledge. As James Young explains, the accretion of later knowledge reflects back on the method which introduces readers to the story's dire beginnings. Because the end is known, a question facing memoirists of both the Holocaust and the Kindertransport is how to design a plot line and characters when the very idea of gradual development based on a variety of settings and personal interactions is foreclosed by contextual issues: historical circumstances, our knowledge of the historical trajectory of the Holocaust, and what has become of the writer. Lore Segal addresses this narrative problem:

> I experience the calamities of my life as a palpable relief from the perennial expectation of calamity ... what I write will not be suspenseful ... It took me six years to write *Other People's Houses*. I was at pains to draw no facile conclusions – and all conclusions seemed and seem, facile. I want not to be able to trace the origin and processes by which the past produces the present. The novelist's mode suits me – I post myself as protagonist in the autobiographical action. ('Bough' 245)

The writer's position as 'protagonist' in the hybrid memoir/novel has important implications for readers as well. Our knowledge that the writer survived leaves us with little suspense except the fate of family and friends left behind and whether and how the experience of rescue and adaptation was more or less difficult. Neither suspense nor the thrill of the chase can drive the plot of their stories or our responses. In turn, despite the Kinder's relatively safe circumstances, we are constantly reminded that we are so experientially and emotionally distant from them, we cannot identify with them or their close calls with danger. Their losses undercut the possibility of *frisson*. Instead, the graphic detail of these conflicted and grieving narratives offer readers a cumulative sense of a complex and painful collective experience that is sufficiently far reaching to be considered one of the war's normative events. In fact, as Andrea Hammel reminds us, Kindertransport memoirs reflect not just an individual account 'but a shared experience [that] shaped their impetus to write and the form of their narratives' (64). Because each of the narrators governs our attention with different encounters with a variety of losses, friendships, and enmities (especially since so many of the Kinder lived in several foster homes and hostels), and with different rhetorical strategies, the apertures of their stories widen to allow us a vision of responses and consciousnesses other than that of the writer. While this vision is clearly mediated by the memoirists, they guide us to see through those devices that dramatize or disguise the authoritative or even self-doubting voice of the narrator. Because memoirs by their very nature preclude an omniscient narrator, they are all the more explicit in representing the child's consciousness; the writer must show the child's limited knowledge and ability to know what lies beyond her immediate vision. At the same time, as we follow the child's odyssey into knowledge, adaptation, and obstacles, we are invited to share the adult writer's perspective as well. Very often, the adult narrator provides historical contexts that apprise us of the dangers the rescued child and her narrative avoid.

As with other Holocaust experiences and life writing, Kindertransport memoirs not only continue to proliferate, but their forms are equally varied and multifaceted. My study of memoirs does not attempt any kind of sociological or historical survey; nor do I read them as historical discourse. Instead, I focus on the forms and voices of women who raise issues closely aligned with those of Anglo-Jewish women writing other forms of Holocaust literature. Because, as so many Holocaust writers attest, the ordinary language of our everyday rarely even approximates their extreme circumstances and suffering, many forms of irony become favored devices of women's writing to express the lexical and emotional distance. Several Kindertransport memoirs and fictions ironically juxtapose personal narratives with allusions to fairy tales in order to depict the often inchoate feelings of dispossession and disorientation as responses are complicated by the displacement of childhood with the onset of adolescence. Defending against such complication, fairy tales enable the expression of 'concerns, beliefs and desires in brilliant seductive images [that] utter harsh truths, to say what you dare' even as they 'disregard logic' (Warner xvii).

So often the internal narrative logic of fairy tales expresses the trauma of not knowing what happened to their families, an emotional void that led to feelings of isolation and 'obsessional nostalgia', as Rita Altman testifies

(Jewish Women in London Group 121). Memoirists Lore Segal and Karen Gershon show how their losses could often only be expressed as silences or shadows that are filled with ghosts or ominous figures from Central European fairy tales. For them and others, the Holocaust conjures up people and places that are so radically gone, they are beyond the negation perpetrated upon them. Their lost loved ones have no being. Instead, they are *unbeings* who disrupt the idea of a realistic representation.[6] With little or no family, these writers recreate their younger selves as imagining comforting fantasies of intimate love and attachment and violent ones of rejection and abjection. In combination, these fantasies indirectly express the loss of emotional ligatures that threatens to stall, distort, and create unstable relations to domestic, maternal, and other intimate relationships. While in some cases, these fantasies are narrated as the girl's ruminations, they often employ motifs from children's folk literature and fairy tales that, in effect, destabilize the traditional models of women's developmental journeys their refugee lives cannot accommodate. As Lore Segal testifies, 'My own exodus gave a strength that exacted a price. Cut yourself off, at ten years old, from feelings that can't otherwise be mastered and it takes decades to become reattached' ('Bough' 246).[7]

While this description of a gendered thematics probably seems too easy and even stereotypical, there are also extenuating social circumstances that may help to explain it. As many men have testified in the collective Kindertransport autobiographies, boys were pressured to find work even while in residence at refugee hostels or foster homes, and often at a younger age than girls; others were interned or they enlisted in the armed forces to activate their need to save their families, to fight the enemy which had orchestrated their fates, and to become independent. Separated once again from family life, men report that fulfilling external obligations saved them from interpersonal conflict and tensions about social and economic expectations. In accord with gendered expectations of the time, boys had more access to higher education than girls through government grants and scholarships, and in some cases from families that could afford the fees and for whom a boy's continuing education was the norm.[8] It was the exceptional girl who was afforded the same consideration. Even at a Jewish hostel run by Viennese refugee women, Ruth David was punished for choosing to attend a secondary school rather than find work, and, in this case, her school fees were being paid by a sponsor solicited by a supportive teacher. By contrast, Lisa Jura found that the support of friends and the supervisor at the Willesden Lane hostel and that of teachers at the London Royal Academy and governing staff at Bloomsbury House nurtured her musical talents and allowed her to pursue training and a career as concert pianist. Despite family expectations from early childhood that education would always be a priority, the girls' impoverished and most often orphaned refugee status only guaranteed pressures to find paid work as soon as the law permitted them to leave school at fourteen years old.

Another displacement that aggravated the Kinder's traumatic isolation from parents was the tradition of boarding school to which many middle-class and most upper-class Britons subscribed. So many foster families assumed that 'it was completely normal for children to grow up from an early age away from parents' (Gopfert 23). This assumption would lead their refugee foster children to cope not only with separation, anxiety, and grief but with the silence that accompanied a long-accepted tradition. As Lore Segal and Karen Gershon would discover, instead of companionable guidance, they were thrown back on their meager linguistic, social, and emotional resources to decipher what was not said but expected nonetheless. At the same time, for those Kinder who were placed in youth hostels or boarding schools, the other children could provide the companionship and solace that caring but reticent or inadequate foster parents could not.

In Kindertransport representation, social and emotional silences conspire with linguistic challenges to beg the following question. What kinds of narrative language and genres could convey the emotional conflicts infusing departures, receptions, and, ultimately, the development of a sense of self as a woman and identity as a Jew? This combination of personal loss and social disorientation about acceptance and attachment would have deep and lasting effects on the development of the children's sense of self, their personal and cultural identities, and the formation of attachments. In the women's Kindertransport memoirs, we find these effects expressed in many forms, of course, but particularly in different narrative choices about perspective and point of view. Lathey observes that the following forms reflect the 'creation of an identity in narrative': 'first or third person narrative; retrospective commentary by the adult writer; narration from the child's point of view; or the creation of a second self with a new name in some fictionalized accounts' (78).

Rather than remain discrete, however, in some women's memoirs, one point of view will be combined or alternate with another, as with Karen Gershon's Inge and her narrator or the child and adult Lore and Lore Segal. The narrative effect of this interchange can reflect different ways of interpreting 'the shifting nature of personal identity': the sense of one's varying personal and cultural choices over a lifetime or how the writing self constructs that of the child subject (Lathey 79). When point of view shifts without gesturing explicitly to these options, it may also represent both the uncertain effort to construct a stable point of view or the very action of disorientation. The focalizing character in a memoir who is looking outward for signs that would help her understand what is happening to her and her family as well as inward to fathom her emotional turbulence may also be destabilized by the vertigo produced by this double vision. In turn, in order to present a coherent story complete with necessary historical contexts, the adult narrator speaks to readers in counterpoint with the narrative's primary consciousness, the naïve and unknowing child. Any of these latter options raises several questions. Since the story of exile and loss and the process of adaptation represent emotional and experiential gaps and dissonances, we must ask whether and how the adult narrator can speak for the child. This question begs another: whether the construction of identity through autobiographical writing can be an 'act of fixing or stabilizing past and present selves in a narrative [that] is both therapeutic and affirmative' (Lathey 78). There may very well be a 'need to write for that wounded child within, to recreate that "small person far away" as part of a healing process' (Lathey 86). But of course that very process may reopen old wounds that refuse to heal and remain cankerous, as we will see with Diane Samuels's Evelyn and Julia Pascal's Sophia.[9] The recognition of such recalcitrant wounds can be found in recent interviews with Kindertransport members who 'link their failures as adults causally with their early childhood experiences…as a kind of inescapable fate' (Hammel 69–70).

Lathey reads memoirs of wartime childhoods as responding to an 'autobiographical impulse' that 'increases in urgency with advancing age' as childhood memory reawakens 'the need to conduct a dialogue with the past and to channel pain or retrospective guilt' (52). An important component of this guilt is that it is rarely felt in childhood or then revived (59). Instead, the guilt develops as the search for knowledge and reflection about the past moves adult writers to consider the psychological implications of their escaping an event that trapped so many. The process of fulfilling this knowledge-seeking 'autobiographical impulse' includes returning to particular moments, encounters, or events through attempts to remember or to invent, both of which offer possibilities for the writer to contain memory and trauma by shaping and reshaping it. As regards trauma, Lathey designs her discussion of memoirs and fictions of the war to show how the self-imposed pressure to write is often moderated by the tension between believing that this story is 'untellable' and discovering an appropriate narrative form. Various women's Kindertransport memoirs invite us to view their narrative forms as working to resolve this tension while expressing its irresolution as well. In effect, these narrative forms admit that 'adaptation to changing social perspectives' contains but does not eradicate the trauma it records (Lathey 87).

Most women's Kindertransport memoirs begin with scenes from the writers' prewar lives that portray their conventional middle-class habits and concerns as cultural, social, and domestic norms. Between a fair share of economic prosperity and the intensity of extended family and community life, even signs of antisemitism are woven into the norm. Thus even when Hitler consolidated his power, it was easy to disregard portentous signs of Nazi brutality and instead view them as either temporary and exceptional or as a magnified pogrom. Yet despite the memoirists' insistence on stability and continuity of family and community life, tensions emerge in their depictions of childhood. Like the workings of partial memory, most women memoirists portray childhood as singular moments strung together in a design that calls attention to the fragmented nature of both childhood experience and adult memory. As though reflecting the excruciating effort to create coherence from snippets of disconnected memories, the narrative design is often fractured and atomized. Regardless of religious observance or economic status, whether home is Stuttgart, Prague, or Vienna, bits and pieces of birthday parties, school days, summer picnics, and visits with extended families combine to express a yearning for memories of wholeness and connectedness. Paradoxically, these snippets also show how memories into which the material and emotional realities of home have dissolved, are piecemeal and punctured. To express the effort of recalling her departure from home, Karen Gershon creates a narrator who registers mostly doubt. Trying to fill in the gaps, the narrator expresses Kate's fears of loss that then merge with displaced memories to produce a coping strategy of ambivalence:

> Perhaps she was incapable of thinking of the moment because all her faculties were required to cope with it, she found living so difficult...Though she loved the town as much as it was in her nature to love a place – and that was passionately – it had ... failed to reciprocate her love.... She had not loved her home, had not been aware of loving it while she had it. She did know that it was the only home she had and that whatever home the future would provide her with would be no more than a substitute, a second best. (*Lesser Child* 195)

The emphasis here on 'home' forms a mnemonic pattern that accords with other women's Kindertransport memoirs to show the domesticated, family oriented nature of their lessons and doubts about belonging. For example, from a retrospective point of view, these writers will often project onto the past what they learned about the duplicity of neighbors who did not hesitate to betray the children's families. While such lessons unsettle more nostalgic memories, they can as well be juxtaposed with hopes for the future. In combination, these contradictory feelings reflect the discontinuities that define the woman memoirist's later experiences and represent the continuity produced by discontinuous lives – of insatiable desire for a sense of inclusion and stable home and identity, both of which have been lost. Written in retrospect, however, such desire often mirrors the equally potent sense that a coherent and cohesive past may be misremembered or illusory. We find both the desire for belonging and its elusiveness imparted through folklore that demonstrates the family's position in Central European culture. Growing up in Celakovice, a predominantly Christian Czech village, Vera Gissing recalls that her teacher 'inject[ed] us with her patriotism...A wonderful story-teller, she made our culture, heritage and history into one long, always fascinating fairy tale, and like all fairy tales, it had a happy ending' (23). The narrative forms developed by women memoirists struggle to negotiate the distance between the celebration of a national culture they were taught to claim as a safely contained home and their retrospective knowledge of a future marked by exile, estrangement from their own European Jewish culture, and the murder of 90 percent of their parents.

Many women's memoirs begin with attempts to persuade us of the family's comfortably domesticated integration before the Hitler era. A joyful and 'relaxed mood' sets the tone for 'the delights of picking strawberries, or cherries or redcurrents' (Zürndorfer 4), for the tree placed on a rooftop to celebrate the building of a new house (Drucker 2), or for the 'magical memory' of the 'fairy tale look of the brilliantly white, thickly wooded [Czech] countryside' (Gissing 26). If parents are represented 'as heroic figures who could do no wrong', Jewish childhood is often remembered in pastoral language and conventions as an idyllically safe Christian landscape.[10] Hannele Zürndorfer recalls when 'winter, lovely white, Christmassy, lamplit winter had begun!' (27). Because the families of many memoirists were highly assimilated or intermarried and decorated their homes with Christmas trees and Easter eggs while celebrating Chanukah and Passover, the idea of cultural difference or separatism is registered as largely absent. The Christian landscape is not only familiar and friendly, but integrated into the cultural lore of these Jewish families. Images of 'Hansel and Gretel' commingle with those of Saint Nicholas to reinforce a seamless German-Jewish identity in which the Christian fatherly figure presides over bringing the Jewish children to safety (Roth 22). 'Hansel and Gretel' and other childhood tales also serve to express barely understood responses to exile and adaptation in England. According to Ruth David, despite resonances of lost babes, recollections of 'Hansel and Gretel' and 'Little Red Ridinghood' could also endow 'an unaccustomed feeling of freedom' and friendliness to the otherwise alien English forests. The idiom of inclusion as an extension of assimilation is often inflected through the comfort zones of German nursery rhymes, folktales, or 'folksongs and songs by Schubert', recalled many years after the war by Martha Blend as 'some of the greatest treasures I took away with me from Austria' (17). Like a parable of resistance against ostracism and forced exile, Blend's statement insists that the totemic cultural artifacts that helped form her identity cannot be taken from her. Here, in the words of Oren Baruch Stier, 'memory takes the form of myth, understood as a sacred narrative that authorizes identity in the present, and of ritual, understood as sacred behavior that... authorizes one's connection to the past and... tradition' (2).

That the story of 'Hansel and Gretel' serves as a mnemonic image is not surprising, given the Kinder's escape from a devouring evil.[11] But the children's actual journey would also be a reminder that the beautiful woodlands that figured as an idealized domesticated homeland would ironically reflect the rhetorical devices that expressed Nazi ideology. On the one hand, pastoral conventions mark the Nazis' veneration of nature and therefore the natural superiority of German Aryan civilization; on the other, these same tropes could also be exploited to emphasize the degraded, barbaric nature of the Jews.[12] If we apply a similar strategy of inversion, we can see how memories of an idyllic childhood home and homeland are shattered by the translation of Nazi ideology into practice. And so the stories that convey childhood faith in an Arcadian myth are transformed into brutal realism when the woods of Central Europe become sites of mass killing and the protective father figure of Saint Nicholas morphs into a symbol of rejection and ejection from Christian Europe. Reflecting on this inversion when she visits Germany after twenty-five years, Karen Gershon writes:

> Yet not for a moment did I walk again in my childhood
> the wood did not echo a word all its magic had gone
> every path was for me a secret turning to Auschwitz
> there were traces of murder under every stone
> Nothing German remains that has not been desecrated
> beechwood* will now mean for ever a violent place
> nature is neutral my own culpable thoughts created
> a setting for tragedy where I might have seen peace

> (*The German for beechwood is *Buchenwald*; Gershon's note, 'In the Wood', *Collected Poems* 37)

Indeed, sharing the retrospective space of women memoirists, our historicized reading of Holocaust experience reverses the characterization of Saint Nicholas and the plot lines of 'Hansel and Gretel'. Instead of delivering benevolence, the Christian saint is a figure of paternal withdrawal for the Kinder; in effect, he becomes a monster – the father as tempter, like Samuels's Ratcatcher in her play *Kindertransport*. As regards the villainous witch in 'Hansel and Gretel', rather than achieving victory over her, the Kinder confront the triumph of her monstrousness as their experience revises the folktale. Memories of a safe home and nurturing mother translate into images of a prison and child devourer. Instead of force-fed children breaking free, shoving the witch into her oven, and reuniting joyously with their parents, most Kinder discovered that their parents had been starved and incinerated.[13] With this reversal of folklore into testimony, it's no wonder that Lore Segal quotes the concluding lines of the nursery rhyme and game, 'Ring around 'o rosies', to invoke the fate of her extended family: 'the baby, the cradle, the bough, the whole tree comes down, and the mommy and daddy, the grandparents, and all the aunts and cousins, they all fall down. Ashes! Ashes!' ('Bough' 231).

In light of the horrific fates of most families left behind, the nursery rhyme can be read as transforming idyllic childhood memories into the bitter ashes that represent the fates of so many parents and siblings. Segal's invocation of the rhyme reminds us of how the game and rhyme are typically repeated until the children fall down from exhaustive laughter. But of course the translation into Holocaust meaning is no laughing matter; rather the repetition is redolent with Nazis' inexhaustible machinery of extermination. The Nazi use of a mythical history to justify a science of mechanized death is the final step in a process that begins with the exploitation of the pastoral form. In this sense, we can see pastoral images mutating into a rhetoric of prescience: the invocation of nature as peaceful and fruitful transmutes into a lethal threat for the Jewish family and for Jewish regeneration. Our own reading strategies work with the familiarity of nursery rhymes and games and children's folktales to provide a multifaceted, overdetermined language of interpretation. In concert, reader and text dramatize a condensation of experience and response that contrasts with the more discursive and didactic language of realistic narrative. Both in their original forms and as we reinterpret them in light of Holocaust events, these tales and rhymes not only encapsulate a familiar homeliness but also have a complex tone that combines playful and bitter irony and affection and disinheritance. In short, many Kindertransport memoirs revise the folktale as they narrate the dissonance between a happy ending and the never ending memories of loss to demonstrate a generic extension of the pastoral. They become elegies, the narratives of mourning.

For example, 'Hansel and Gretel' is often read as a psychological allegory of children's separation anxiety and its happy resolution. But this anxiety ridden tale also offers a narrative opportunity to understand how the Kinder would never be able to resolve their own irreparable separation from home and parents or recover the sense of self that had derived from these and community relationships. As children watched their parents frantically acquiring identity papers and passage for them on the Kindertransports or, as in the case of Miriam Darvas, transport by members of the resistance, many were experiencing what they would only be able to understand years later. In turn, this belated understanding reflects back on the absent or partial memories for which childhood fairy tales could substitute and which could combine the pleasures and horrors of a lost identity and past while being denied the comfort of parental presence. In so many women's memoirs of child refugees, fairy tales fill the silent gaps of both understanding and communicating the terrors of inconceivably precarious fates. Barely coherent scenes and incidents are reimagined as graphically distilled scenarios whose images convey the child's mixture of emotion instead of the inadequacy of such single or generalized words as fear. Projecting a mixed brew of emotion into the frame of fairy tales allows it to develop into a narrative discourse whose logic of condensation and extremes mirrors both the workings of nightmares and fractured memory. It is from this retrospective and resonant view that Karen Gershon's novel, *The Bread of Exile*, introduces Inge and Dolph, brother and sister Kinder, with the mocking comment, 'How charming, Hansel and Gretel!' or more ominously, 'Oi Hansel and Gretel, what is to become of you!'(13, 19). The Jewish identity of which many Kinder were barely aware was simultaneously being imprinted on them and erased. When they became aware of their status as not belonging to the nation they had called home, all that was reflected back to them was their own strangeness, the recognition that they were suddenly unwanted outsiders. They were stamped, as Karen

Gershon notes, 'when I was coined a Jew / by all the mints of Germany' ('I Set Out for Jerusalem', *Collected Poems* 69). Regardless of their actual appearance, Jewish children were suddenly treated as though they were dwarfed versions of *Der Sturmer's* monstrous Jew – a distillation of the grotesque antisemitic cartoon. Not only were there no social correctives to this construction, but close family relationships could not help; they could only exacerbate the child's sense of alienation.

At the very moment of their departure to safety, the Kinder's need to put on brave faces was felt as a distorted self. To assuage their parents' anxieties about sending them away and their own fears about leaving alone, they mirrored the performances of parents who tried to protect their children from their own worst fears. Karen Gershon recounts this dynamic in her memoir, *A Lesser Child*, in the voice of a concerned adult narrator:

> Her parents did not tell her that they expected worse to come. They did not tell her, we are loath to let you go because of the possibility that we may never see each other again. On the contrary, to make the parting easier for the child they connived in pretending that it was not different in kind, that she was merely going further away.... This time she was going across the water and wasn't it an adventure? Of course the thought of it was, to Kate. (192)

The emotional effect of this charade is often expressed in women's Kindertransport memoirs as another transformation, as thinking of oneself, as Lore Segal recalls, 'for decades to come, of being a species of monster' ('Bough' 239). And when the Kinder arrived in Britain, this image was only reinforced, mirroring in kindness and good intentions their position as pariah in Europe. In effect, the misunderstandings that so often shaped their initial British experiences were reflected back to them as an image of a child monster – a changeling. As Edith Milton recalls, the journey to rescue made her feel like 'some monster hybrid halfway between an enemy alien and an English schoolgirl' (*Tiger* 14). When Milton appears in an English school production of *Midsummer Night's Dream* as Puck, she finds herself identifying with the 'Monsters and fairies: aliens. That was me' (*Tiger* 63). This sense of monstrousness does not erase the definitional line between human and animal. Animal is too positive a category of the living. Mirroring antisemitic perceptions, the image of monster here means an invasion of an indefinable alien being that threatens the integrity of the nativist body politic.

Forming a narrative pattern with other women's memoirs, such identification is stamped with expectations to look and act like happy campers at the site of British beneficence. And so Ruth David recalls visits by the Newcastle committee to the hostel it financed and how one of the Kinder called their parade of clean and smiling girls 'the *Affenschau*', meaning 'monkey parade' (77). As this image suggests, just as the metamorphoses, happy endings, and laughter of childhood games and fairy tales no longer obtained, neither did traditional children's tales. Odysseys of self-discovery and disillusionment that narrate the transition into adulthood and the world represented a reality that now was viewed as a wishful fantasy. Instead, the trope of monster suggests a different genre – the Gothic. As Judith Halberstam demonstrates, 'In the Jew, then, Gothic fiction finds a monster versatile enough to represent fears about race, nation, and sexuality, a monster who combines in one body fears of the foreign and the perverse' (14). The Gothic monster in women's memoirs is indeed a very serviceable trope. It expresses a response to having been identified as monstrous by the Nazis and alien by the British. Without a process of metamorphosis, the emergence of the monster can show how the Kinder internalize the antisemitic characterization and then use it to express their own sense of strangeness.

The abrupt transition to safe haven left the children in a liminal space, where they had to grasp that the rescuing nation was not offering them a home, but a temporary stay. Combined with the yearning for home and family, this precarious status would cast shadows on motivations to acculturate, to learn the new language and abide by a customary British restraint that seemed to conspire with traditional middle-class Central European decorum. Ruth David reports of her experience at the hostel where she was sent to live: 'We were not allowed to shout, or to laugh loudly. This was unseemly' (74). It was also, she adds wryly, 'A pity, as we so rarely felt like laughing' (74). As though symbolizing their liminal position, some Kinder adopted a combined language that could communicate only among themselves: ' "Immigranto" ' (David 76). It would take years, until the war ended, for them finally to understand that there was no return to a homeland, despite the trips to recover their families' final days and places and their own family identities. As Miriam Darvas recounts her return to her childhood home in Prague where her family fled from Berlin, the charming landscapes of Central Europe and baroque beauty of the city now evoke graveyards without graves. Every street and train is a reminder 'of death and despair':

> Black boots marched through my head and arms whipped my mother in unrelenting cadence. My mind shouted stop, stop. I wanted to pull the emergency brake and get off the train to flee. Where to? Flee from myself, from the images? There was no escape from the poisonous rage and pain.[14]

As so many have testified, the absence of that return journey to their childhood homes or its dearth of meaning left them with no heuristic narratives to guide them or in which to find their journeys into alien spaces and identities represented.

Looking back at their childhood selfhood as transient, between definitions and identities, women writers depict their instability by seeking models of childhood that run counter to traditional trajectories of development. Very often, according to Gillian Lathey, they 'redefine a stable view of the self [by] follow[ing] the process of questioning, redefining and seeking confirmation of an identity which had been called into question' (72). The Nazis, paradoxically, had confirmed their Jewish identities by marking the children for death. Having escaped to a safe uncertainty, Lore Segal and Karen Gershon choose narrative forms that dramatize the instability of selfhood by showing how that process of questioning and redefining is never ending. In ironic juxtaposition, despite saving the children's lives, England would offer them no experience that could confirm the identity they left behind. As a result, both Segal and Gershon left England to seek lives elsewhere, though Gershon returned after spending some years in Israel. She said that she preferred the certainty of never belonging to unfulfilled yearning. In most cases, with no parents against whom to test their burgeoning sense of selves, the children would enter adolescence with their challenging questions already silenced. In their search for narrative form to break the silence, as adult writers, they find that no archetypal stories of journeys to the climactic fall and awareness of sin can allegorize their own actual fates, those of most parents, and the mélange of awkward welcomes that awaited them. For the Kinder, bedtime stories of overcoming ogres and evil monsters had to be abandoned along with the cartography of a Central European character development. But along with abandoning childhood fantasies, any of which symbolize teleological hopes of home, the Kinder also left behind parents who were about to confront the reality of Nazi evil and the fantasy of possessing an authentic Central European character.

Although restrictions on Jewish movement, employment, and education had intensified once the Nazis took power in Germany and instituted the Nuremberg laws and then occupied Austria and Czechoslovakia, Kristallnacht is the watershed moment when Nazi brutality takes to the streets and cannot be explained away. This is when limitations on the Jews' freedom are condensed into a black hole of disappearance and death. On 9 November 1938, with the announcement that a Jew named Grunspan, incensed by the Nazis' brutality towards his parents, had assassinated a Nazi diplomat, a nationwide pogrom smashed Jewish homes and businesses and beat and arrested the Jews in their wake. In her poem 'A Jew's Calendar', Karen Gershon recounts the destruction of Jews and their culture:

> In the white hours of the night
> with lorry-loads of petrol cans
> they set the synagogue alight
> our right of way to German soil
> where roots of generations paused
> losing identity until

the weeding of the nation caused
this mutilation of its stones
(*Collected Poems* 25)

Bea Green confronted 'this mutilation' in the form of her 'father's bloody clothes' and face (Whiteman 134–5). In one of its first moves to disinherit Jewish children from 'German soil', Hitler's government evicted them from German schools. Having already been ordered to use 'a different door' to enter their segregated classrooms, Jewish children are now 'told to go home by the back roads' (Blend 28; Segal, *Houses* 22). Those like Olga Levy Drucker, who had never been inside a synagogue, were expelled from their secular schools and restricted to attending only Jewish schools where they enacted the comprehensive lessons of statelessness. In response to rejection, Olga's mother unearths a long-forgotten Hanukah menorah while seven-year-old Olga recounts the heroic story of the Maccabees and teaches her mother the holiday's celebratory songs.[15]

If the fate of the Jews demolishes the expressive utility of the pastoral and recalls the darker side of German fairy tales and Greek mythology, their hopes for protection find expression in ancient Jewish narratives. As Nazi screams of 'Schwein, Juden Schwein!' accompany beatings and pillage, Lisa Jura recalls her mother comparing Hitler to Haman, 'the evil advisor to King Ahasuerus' in the Purim story who 'wanted to kill all the Jews', but who was stopped by Queen Esther, who used the power of her marriage to Ahasuerus to 'save all the Jews' (Golabek and Cohen 20).[16] But if, according to this myth, Queen Esther's female Jewishness is no impediment to power or acceptance into another culture, political reality reaches back into history to answer the *what if* question, that is, what happens when the Jewish woman is not considered beautiful or a favorable political partner, and when no one else intervenes on the Jews' behalf? And so, in another memoir, Vera Gissing recalls her family being stripped of their Czech citizenship. As German tanks move into their town square and the family mourns the sudden recognition that 'our home was no longer ours', they cry and sing the national anthem 'Where Is My Home?' (28).

If one were to identify a myth that might capture the psychological experience of the Kinder's odyssey, it might be a version of Orpheus and Euridice. Those Kinder who lost their parents to the dark world of Nazi ferocity faced a different kind of labyrinth, composed of twisting doubts about their parents' fates and their own subjectivities and agency. As Martha Blend interprets the experience, 'I felt as though some force far stronger than myself was dragging me to an abyss and I had no power to prevent it' (32). The image of the abyss recalls Diane Samuels's Ratcatcher who leads the children away from their parents, suggesting the sense of abandonment that accompanied the tentative possibility of rescue. These texts convey the trauma of recognizing the futility of looking back to Europe for reassuring signs that parents are still alive and accessible. Their hopes only deepen these children's sense of powerlessness and guarantees that the adaptation to loss and the journey forward will be fraught with the pain of an amputated identity. The lost parents have become phantom limbs; the ache of absence is omnipresent and inconsolable. We see this narrative pattern in so many women's memoirs where scenes at the train station are drawn with the foreboding not only of separation but of grim loss. The wail of the train whistle accompanies the smoke-laden darkness of the platform to announce a journey to a radically alien elsewhere. And yet despite or perhaps because of this prologue to their journey into the unknown, many children were encouraged to feel that this was going to be an exciting adventure. Lore Segal recalls this mixture of adventure and anxiety as '*Walpurgisnacht*' ('My Knees Were Jumping'):

> I wanted to think that I was being brave, but even then I had my doubts. Many times since I've wondered whether not crying was such a good idea. The number I was playing on myself was to say, 'This is terrific, I'm going to England. What a lark! How exciting!' thereby cutting myself off from the disaster of leaving my parents – that was sent underground. (Harris and Oppenheimer 101)

Figuring as an overdetermined metaphor, 'underground' can be read as representing the child's denial and acceptance of separation and the labyrinthine fate to which most parents were going to be consigned. Despite their numbers and the efforts of the rescue organizations, the Kinder, like Orpheus, are left alone, with irreconcilable if well-intentioned instructions from their lost parents to adapt and yet not forget. The keepsake Lisa Jura's mother gives her at the moment of departure turns out to be her photo with the message, '"*Fon diene nicht fergesene mutter:*' So you will never forget your mother' (Golabek and Cohen 29). In the period of waiting for knowledge of their families' fates, anxieties that accompanied both efforts to remember and to forget produced a mourning process that began with separation and never ended. Like the songs Orpheus composes to mourn Euridice, Kindertransport memoirs become works of art that spring from tragedy and bring life to the lost. As though they transform the image of Orpheus torn apart by jealous gods, the women's nostalgic childhood memories become infused with the knowledge of the Nazi rage and atrocities suffered by lost families. The photo of the mother is all that remains of the possibility of finding a role model to emulate or against which to rebel.

The metaphoric use of fairy tale and myth to recount stories with no realistic antecedents produces a hybrid narrative that unevenly weaves together strands of a dimly remembered childhood and often traumatic transports and aftermaths. As though this structure is a trope for the Kinder's sense of themselves, we can read it as another kind of changeling. Precisely because the past cannot be grasped through a continuous chronological stream of concrete references, knowable people, places, and linear sequences of events, previous experience cannot produce understanding of the European past in relation to a British aftermath. Narrative acts of remembering take place in a liminal and anxious space between the injunction not to forget and the adaptations that overwhelm the past. As women's Kindertransport memoirs attest, the anxiety produced by the inability to stop the past from unfolding is compounded by the vagaries and mixed messages of a future in Britain. The writing that grows out of this fractured remembering and uncertain acculturation presents the progression of past to present as more of a caesura or a spasmodic series of fits and starts than as a unified journey.

> We cannot will ourselves a madeleine; nor can we rid ourselves of those memories which never cease their demands that we bear witness, that we write them into stories. (Segal, 'Memory' 65)

In counterpoint to the pressures of not losing the past, Kindertransport memoirs are replete with efforts to fathom the present. One of the first shocks occurred upon arrival in Britain when many of the children were taken from the port to Dovercourt, where, until foster homes became available, temporary shelter consisted of unheated and bare tourist cottages. Despite the best intentions of counselors and staff, the cottages besieged by the intensely cold winds coming off 'the flat black ocean' that winter of 1938–39 seemed to be signs of everything alien and forbidding (Segal, *Houses* 36). Once the selection process began, the Kinder had to confront a cacophony of visual and linguistic signs that made it impossible to identify potential foster parents as safe and therefore as representing a safe haven. As Miriam Darvas recalls,

> This then was England where my mother believed me to be safe, but I did not feel safe. I felt as if I were skimming across a thin sheet of crackling ice that was going to give way any moment and send me plunging into an abyss of darkness to drown. (89).

At twelve years old, having crossed the Tatra mountains from Czechoslovakia to Poland, having found the fishing boat that would transport her to Sweden and then by ship to England, Miriam finds herself on a railway platform in northern England from where she is taken to a country estate. Here she wanders 'aimlessly through echoing halls' and subject to well-intentioned attempts by her host, Miss Masters, at conversations that cannot be understood by the child who knows only German, Czech, and French (91). The feelings of insecurity such experiences produced were exacerbated by those where Kinder found themselves unwanted and perceived as unusual looking, unexpectedly too large or too thin, or too old. As weeks and months passed, anxieties about lost families intensified with fears of losing educational ground and hopes for the future professional lives which they had been raised to believe was their destiny. By March 1939, Dovercourt was abandoned as a refugee center and the remaining children were sent to hostels or group homes.

Lore Segal, whose acclaimed autobiographical novel, *Other People's Houses*, charts her Kindertransport odyssey, offers the double vision of the adult narrator representing and interpreting the anxious response of her ten-year-old protagonist to the British rescue whose uncertainty takes root at Dovercourt. Beginning with a Viennese childhood, the narrator traces Lore's development as her train journey sets in motion a series of displacements from one British foster home to another, to anxiety ridden reunion with her parents, a sojourn with family in the Dominican Republic, and her life as a wife, mother, writer, and teacher in New York and around the United States. The novel was first serialized in *The New Yorker* between 1961 and 1964, and its presentation and rhetorical effects could now be said to mirror the uneven, partial knowledge that kept the child Lore in a state of steady suspense about her fate. As the narrator reflects on the child's response to the jarring experience of being shunted from Dovercourt to a second camp, the place that 'was all wrong and strange' nurtures the 'mystification' that becomes Lore's 'habit of mind' (*Houses* 46, 64). As this 'mystification' leads to Lore's aphasic mirroring of British self-restraint, the narrator's voice affects her book's readers as being 'cool' or 'dry, cold, literal, even numb' (quoted in Lawson, 'Lore Segal' 307, 306).

Segal's narrator testifies to the match between the winter chill of the transport camp, the formidable presence of potential foster parents, and the child's numb response. And so Lore is given to remember that despite her eagerness to charm her way into adoption, she could only register fear when an 'enormous, prickly-looking fur coat rose sheer above me', from which emerged the face of an 'old woman' who 'looked at me with a sour expression from behind her glasses ... I had imagined that the family who would choose me would be very special, very beautiful people' (*Houses* 49). For the ten-year-old child, there is no negotiable imaginative space between the familiar and the foreign, between idealized acceptance and rejection. There is only a fearful apparition of maternal care, as though foster motherhood is not merely a poor substitute for the real thing but a monstrous transformation. With metaphorical flourish in a letter to her parents, the budding writer refers to the selection process as 'a slave market' (*Houses* 52). If the analogy cannot hold as a measure of accuracy, it nonetheless expresses a psychological reality. Childhood fantasies based on familiar and loving faces were suddenly overturned by an alien set of manners and morals that valued a stoic pragmatism which in turn left no room for empathetic and soothing lullabies. Despite the generous behavior of the Levines, Lore's foster family, the whispers and 'shut blind' doors of all English homes appear as material signs of an unfathomable system of communication and relating (*Houses* 64).

She discovers that even when she stands outside closed doors struggling to hear if she is welcome, she faces 'mystification' (*Houses* 64). When she tries to break the soundless barrier and introduce herself, she is too forward; when she retreats into her own reveries and silent tears or defensiveness against what she cannot understand, she is affectionately tolerated but considered withdrawn and unsociable.

Although it will occur again and again throughout her years in Britain, the emotional confusion created by this cultural impasse does not initiate Lore into the mysteries of British social culture. It does, however, offer her a position whose very vulnerability encourages her as a writer and shows that her narrative is as much about writing the Kindertransport as it is about the experience. Just as Lore must learn how to survive cultural 'mystification', so she must find the language and forms through which to learn to observe and represent this struggle. A recurring image that represents her anxieties is that of people with whom she identifies or for whom she fears 'spread-eagled high above the ground ... trussed up' and 'stuck on the telegraph pole wriggling helplessly between heaven and earth' (*Houses* 72, 74). As Phillip G. Cavanaugh observes, the image suggests an 'imagined crucifixion', but he does not note the irony that the foundational Christian story is about the killing of a Jew and that transforming Lore's victims into Christ figures converts the underlying Holocaust drama (n.p.). It is certainly persuasive that the image reflects Lore's emotional struggle to reckon with the powerlessness of parents who cannot restore her to her home.

But the image also suggests how fantasy expresses the child's vulnerable experience as well as the adult's anxiety about writing it: in short, how the adult narrator recounts how she views her childhood self as punishing her parents for victimizing her with their weakness. If her parents cannot find the mechanisms that will communicate their helplessness and stabilize their tenuous identities, then their adult daughter's writing task has intensified. She must create the narrative structures in which to portray a combination of childhood fears: that both parents and child are doomed to a stalemated fate, and that they are also fated to be wrenched apart even as the need for attachment intensifies. As cultural realities make demands on the child's anxieties, what Segal's account must achieve is a coherent narrative that conveys the connection between an epistemological and cultural problem. Parents and child will be trapped in a safe haven that has no pragmatic use for knowing them as they know themselves and therefore the Groszmann family finds itself positioned as unalterably foreign. Nowhere is this positioning made so linguistically transparent as when Segal deploys an ironic juxtaposition. When her parents finally arrive in Britain, their welcome consists of being labeled 'aliens of hostile origin' (*Houses* 109). When the Groszmanns find housing with other refugees, one of the cultural activities arranged for them is a lecture on 'What is Expected of the Alien in a Foreign Country' (*Houses* 120). The nice linkage of 'Alien' to 'Foreign Country' does not mean that

Britain identifies the Jews as compatible with its culture. Indeed, these similar words in the passive voice signal an enforced distancing that the alien should not expect to overcome.

Such cultural distancing finds its subjective correlative in Segal's narrative method and voice. At the same time that her use of graphic detail and narrative immediacy brings us very close to her experiences and responses, it also registers a strain that reminds us that what we share is a terrain where, like her, we can never really know. Although by the time Segal began to publish her memoir/novel in 1958, she had mastered English as a language and as a social culture, she uses her fluency in this work to represent the mastery of uncertain knowledge. In order to recount her experiences and responses as a refugee, she presents her material and social circumstances through a method and voice that dramatize the process of coming into knowledge, that is, the knowledge that she discovers as well as the dubious knowledge produced by her social disorientation at the time: 'I felt the blood pounding in my head – confused because [Mrs. Levine] was accusing me of thoughts I did not recognize, and not accusing me of thoughts for which I had long felt guilty' (*Houses* 69). The cognitive estrangement and dissonance expressed in this recollection are compounded by problems that beset the memoirist years after the events: forgetting, distortion, elision, opaqueness, and exaggeration. As Segal reflects:

> Recollection is a double experience like a double exposure, the time frame in which we remember superimposes itself on the remembered time and the two images fail to match perfectly at any point.
> The rememberer has changed, and so, in all probability, has the thing or the place remembered. ('Memory' 65)

Lore Segal's subject in *Other People's Houses* is the doubly exposed relationship between representing the developing consciousness of Lore's Kindertransport childhood and her adult memory and response to the child's anxiety and cultural disorientation. The adult artist's reflection is depicted both in the form of the past tense – 'I felt' – and in the parallel sentence design that indicates the mismatched accusations that beset Lore. Segal's artistic pattern manages to mediate but not obscure the drama of the girl's developing sense of self, which we see in Lore's learning to write narrative. Indeed, writing letters home becomes her saving grace; not only does Lore sustain connection with her own family but the act of doing so reinstates her as 'a good child' in the eyes of her foster mother who cannot understand Lore's silent rejection of British attempts at affection (*Houses* 51). At the same time, while affirming her presence as a writer, Lore's struggle for and against belonging must violate the constraints of a gendered girlhood goodness. Segal shows how this struggle relates to the pressures of religious identity in a portrait of another girl refugee whose emotional isolation drives her to vacillate frenetically between a fervent hold on her Jewish identity and an equally powerful wish to convert to Christianity. For such a girl, whose parents have been transported beyond reach, beyond the possibility of letter writing, there is comfort neither in a conventional female acquiescence nor in rebellion, only further alienation from a past to which one no longer belongs and a present that resists belonging. In despair, this girl cannot be made to believe in friendship or maternal guardianship and, in the displacement of trying to assimilate to alien expectations while clinging to a destabilized and vacillating sense of self, she kills herself.

While it includes manifold social and emotional displacements and misunderstandings, Segal's memoir/novel also registers an abiding awareness of the problems created by her good fortune. Unlike 90 percent of the Kinder, not only did her parents manage to escape the Nazi stranglehold, but they were admitted to Britain a year after she arrived. And while economic and political regulations prevented Lore from living with her parents and her father's weak health precluded his employment and adjustment, their combined presence and separation provided a safety valve for Lore's responses to Britain. Although parent–child reunions are a rarity in Kindertransport experience, the tensions of both having and not having parents lend an important perspective to Kindertransport experience, memory, and representation. As Alan Berger observes of Lore Segal, this tension produces guilt that is exacerbated by 'the absence of love for her father' (89). When the news breaks, just hearing of her parents' arrival lifts the burden of grief and guilt which, as Alan Berger notes, besets the child refugee. For the children, being sent away was equivalent to being abandoned and to abandoning their parents. Segal describes her relief 'as when the passing of nausea or the unknotting of a cramp leaves the body with a new awareness of itself' (*Houses* 73). If consciousness of the tangled knots of her relationship with her parents and with Britain comes with writing many years after the Kindertransport, then the choice of bodily metaphors is telling. Whether it is her throbbing blood or the figures wriggling helplessly on a telegraph pole, Segal refers us to images of the body because the adult writer can use them to express what childhood consciousness has not yet fathomed. The repetition of those helplessly writhing figures in concert with the involuntary responses of the girl's body suggests that Lore's identification with the defenselessness of others can also reflect an otherwise unarticulated ambivalence about her parents' presence. For, in addition to feeling 'relief' that they are alive, she finds herself burdened with their foreignness at the very moment she is trying so hard to assimilate to British culture: 'The manners I had learned from my parents no longer felt adequate or proper. These people seemed to me underbred' (*Houses* 162). Faced with a father in weak physical and emotional health and a mother in domestic service, Lore struggles emotionally and socially to decipher her relationship with them. Their altered gender roles, where her father has no capacity to take care of himself much less his family and her mother's many talents are compressed into domestic service, leave their daughter anxiety ridden about her responsibilities for their fates and her own. Years later, Segal the author finds the narrative forms through which to express this struggle.

We see this conflicted effort at the moment of the Grozsmann's reunion when Mrs. Levine asks Lore to 'Come on down and say good-by nicely', but instead, 'I sat on a step halfway up the stairs. I didn't know what to do with myself' (*Houses* 74). Graphically expressing her loss of emotional agency, Lore's body is caught between escaping from her parents' powerlessness and renewing their interdependent intimacy. Reinforcing this moment are the juxtaposed images of figures wriggling helplessly on telegraph poles and Lore's body entangled in an expression of acute ambivalence: twisting an arm around the banister, waving and wiggling her head (*Houses* 74). Only in the writer's ongoing and questioning memory and evaluation, expressed retrospectively in the present tense, do these images cohere into an epiphany: 'It seems to me that after my parents came to England life at the Levines' was less emotionally strenuous' (*Houses* 74). Despite her parents' frailties, their presence allows Lore to translate her frozen emotions from silent yearning to writing, as we see in the passage that follows the above quotation on the very next page and where she imagines herself as a character in

> a serial story, which I carried with me through the years, from one foster family to the next. New characters were added, but the protagonist remained a pale, tragic-eyed girl. Her hair was long and sad and she wept much. She suffered. She kept herself to herself.
>
> I regretted my daytime self, which was always wanting to be where everyone else was.
>
> Though I never did learn to come into a room without stopping outside to hear if they were talking about me, to gather myself together, invent some little local excuse, or think up some bright thing to say, as if it might look foolish for me to just open a door and walk in. (*Houses* 75)

As Philip Cavanaugh observes, these emotionally charged recollections signify 'the unrestrained intensity in the child's perception, desire, and response . . . which links the artist's perceptions to the child's' (7). As the above passage shows, however, it is only many years later and as an adult that Segal constructs the fictional nighttime self of the girl who can express the intense but silent suffering of her remembered 'daytime self'. The connection Segal creates between the two selves and past and present work as a microcosmic distillation of the memoir/novel's creative, psychological, and narrative structure. Using psychological models of *intrapsychic* dynamics where, regardless of external forces, one's own desires and fears create and enact conflict within ourselves, we can examine the story of 'daytime' and nighttime selves as an *intratext*. Here the interrelated psychological and social structures of her constantly interrupted development from girl to woman connect Lore the character to Lore Segal the writer who employs memory fragments to make her narrative cohere. The form of expression Segal chooses, moreover, in this passage and elsewhere as we have already seen, is that of body language that can convey feelings as yet untranslated into verbal articulations. Despite the emotional intensity expressed by these gestures, however, they question whether the girl's 'perception, desire, and response' can, as Cavanaugh claims, be viewed as 'unrestrained'. Even if it's true that such body movement expresses unconscious desires and fears, at every turn of her plotting Segal makes it clear that, in the context of her British setting, the girl learns that her feelings and forms of expression must conform to a model of female restraint. As one of Karen Gershon's Kinder recalls, 'she had lived for too long in England to act out her feelings'.[17] With its use of the narrative devices and tropes of fairy tales, Lore's tale can both express and restrain the abandonment and emotional isolation that characterize the suffering of her daytime and nighttime selves. Suspended from particular historical contexts, as in a fairy tale, the nighttime girl is portrayed archetypically. Like Rapunzel, 'Her hair was long and sad', bodily expressing the lack of relief to her isolation and stalled female development: 'she remained a pale, tragic-eyed girl'. But, unlike fairy tales, this story is integral to historical context, and so there can be no magical intervention. Instead, lacking both name and place in her tale, Lore represents the erasure of identity that began in Austria and continues in Britain, but which is reinscribed as she creates her own identity as a woman writer and continues her story.

Segal charts the development of Lore's identity as a journey in which Britain paradoxically provides a model for her rebellion against its cultural constraints. Positioning her young subject between British and Jewish institutions, Segal creates an emotional and vocal distance from both with her own ironic voice. In so doing, she replaces her tale of woe with a comedy of cultural clashes and social adjustments that reflects the often absurd conflicts about her British and Jewish identities:

> There had been a certain contest between the Jewish Committee, which saved me from Vienna, and the Church Refugee Committee, which had the care of my bodily needs in England. Each strove for my soul, without much passion. (*Houses* 147)

Maneuvering her way through the thicket of constantly shifting cultural expectations and disappointments, Lore creates an emotional safety valve through her persistent irony. Sometimes her ironic voice even targets her own excesses, as with her 'purist' efforts to observe Jewish dietary laws, her refusals to write 'thank-you letters' to her former foster families, or her rebellion against upper-class codes of decorum, by proclaiming her own status as a Jewish refugee and the domestic service of her parents (*Houses* 150, 151).

By the time she leaves foster family life for the University of London, she discovers that the road to self-determination is already paved with not only her history as a refugee but also the indelible influence of growing up British. She is now 'a temporary snob' and, despite six years in the Dominican Republic and building the rest of her life in New York, 'an Anglophile forever' (*Houses* 168).

Like so many other Kindertransport writers, Lore Segal constructs a critically affectionate relationship with Britain that breaks the silences and restraints of the mystifying society that rescued them. Giving voice and narrative form to the inchoate feelings of the rescued but alienated girl also fills the gaps between the fragilities of memory and the need to convey the story that argues for its place in the history of the Holocaust. The imaginative work of Segal's novel/memoir also addresses how memories of childhood and its imagined versions work together to create tensions between historical and fictional modes of narrating the Holocaust. As Sara Horowitz explains,

> In many works by survivors of the Nazi genocide, the liberties of fiction enable their authors to contemplate and express what could not be arrived at as well otherwise. It is not a matter of presenting the historian's work in a manner more emotionally or intellectually accessible to a broad reading public, but of representing one's own or another's experiences in a way that opens up complicated questions regarding atrocity, memory, history, and representation. (*Voicing* 13)

Precisely because the Kindertransport is not a story of genocidal atrocities, but of escape, rescue, and a different kind of survival, its memoirs raise new questions about flexing the boundaries of Holocaust representation.

2
Karen Gershon: Stranger from the Kindertransport

[T]he world's blood and my blood were cold
the exiled Jew in me was old
and thoughts of death appalled me less
than knowledge of my loneliness.

(Gershon, 'The Children's Exodus' [*Collected Poems* 22])

Like so many Kinder, Karen Gershon lost both her parents in the Holocaust and recounts the burdens of loss as the primary shaping force in her life and writing. As she comments in her video, *Stranger in a Strange Land*, 'I don't want to be reconciled, to put [the Holocaust past] aside. I want it with me.' Born Kaethe Loewenthal to a middle-class family in Bielefeld, Germany, on 29 August 1923, Gershon was the youngest of three daughters. A month after Kristallnacht, in December 1938, their parents sent Kaethe and her next older sister Lise on the Kindertransport. The oldest, Anne, who also came to England, died of anemia in 1943. In a gesture of assimilation to British culture, Kaethe changed her name to Karen but chose Gershon for her surname since its translation of her father's name into Hebrew reinforced her identification with Jewish tradition while its meaning, stranger in a strange land, noted the Jews' historical identity.

All of Gershon's published work, including translations, memoirs, novels, and poetry, is devoted to Jewish themes. Though she began writing poetry in German, her native language, and in the German romantic tradition, her 'subject matter was Jewish' ('Stranger' 10). According to Peter Lawson, her first volume of *Selected Poems* (1966) mines the Hebrew Bible 'to impose a stabilizing narrative on the disorienting Jewish experience under Nazism' ('Karen Gershon', *Holocaust Novelists* 107). She began to write in English upon her arrival on the Kindertransport, both to belong and 'in a revulsion against everything German' (Gershon, 'Stranger' 10). The effort, however, does not represent an unencumbered transition, as she reflects:

One cannot respond emotionally to words one did not know as a child, but as acquired consciously, with an effort; they never mean more than themselves, their quality cannot be felt with the senses. This makes my poetry very bare. On the other hand, when I began to write in English I had never read any English poetry and the experience was exhilarating, as if I were the first person ever to turn the language into poetry. Some of this excitement persists: the feeling that the meaning of a poem and the words to express it come from two different sources, the one unconscious and the other external; I am caught between them but in me they meet. It makes even the most personal poem seem more than my own: a discovery. ('Stranger' 10)

Invoking the master narrative of Jewish wandering from ancient times through the Holocaust, diaspora, and beyond, Gershon calls attention to her Zionist aspirations that she hoped would be realized when she emigrated to Israel in 1968 but which ended with her return to England in 1973.[1] In her author's note to the collective Kindertransport autobiography, *We Came as Children*, Gershon reflects on her odyssey:

When I came to this country I was on my way to what was then called Palestine. While working on this book, I realized that, for me, England would always remain a foster-home. I then continued my journey, together with the family I had made. Perhaps I had left it too late.

I feel more at home in Israel than I do in England, but I don't feel at home there either, and that is worse, because there I still expected to be able to feel at home. Here I am reconciled.

Having internalized and practiced wandering as integral to her identity, her characters, and even the forms of all her writing, she found creative expression in the productively liminal space she carved for herself in England. For it was in the Janus-faced welcome England extended to her that she could reconcile herself to her position as outsider. The different parts of her multi-hyphenated identity, German-Jewish and Anglo-Jewish, would remain in unresolved tension with each other, a product of her recognition that a synthesis of her identities was impossible, either in practical or psychological terms. Despite Gershon's desire to imagine a home in national identity, there would be no stable national or cultural foundation on which her writing could lean or with which it would identify. She remained in a state of productively ambivalent rootlessness, testifying in her video interview that she 'used English to write about an experience that's not English – the Holocaust'.

All of Gershon's writing is autobiographical, even when her protagonist is definitively transposed from a Jewish to gentile identity, as with Helen in *Burn Helen* (1980), or from female to male, as in *The Fifth Generation* (1987).[2] So intensely did she respond to the Kindertransport that at the time of its twenty-fifth anniversary, fearful that so many of its documents had been destroyed, and that the Kinder's memories were fading and so many were dying, she published a collective autobiography, *We Came as Children* to which 234 contributed. Her own published autobiography, *A Lesser Child* (1994), ends at the beginning of the Kindertransport, while the second, unpublished volume traces the decades following. Her autobiographical novel, *The Bread of Exile* (1985), charts a German childhood, transport and adaptation to Britain, and her protagonist's marriage to another of the Kinder. Each of Gershon's three published novels is distinguished by experiments with narrative form, subject, and voice and each provides a different critical perspective on the transport experience and its disorienting legacies. *The Bread of Exile* ranks with Lore Segal's *Other People's Houses* as an outstanding literary work in addition to its stature as autobiographically imagined Holocaust testimony. Unlike Segal's first-person narrator who reflects on her experiences from an adult perspective, Gershon uses a third-person narrator who appears to accompany her protagonists on their Kindertransport to displacement and adaptation.

Yet in its detachment from the immediacy of a first-person contemporaneous account, that third-person, seemingly conventional, narration integrates and reveals a voice and consciousness that also displaces any stable focalization or linear sense of character development. Andrea Reiter addresses this narrative issue in the fiction of children and the Holocaust. By emulating the child's situation, the adult narrator tries to overcome this predicament. 'In literary theory this limited insight of the child is known as a "void" in the text, which ... trigger[s] the productive imagination in the reader' (*Narrating* 232). Filled with a combination of self-doubt and both canny and misguided assertiveness, the character of Inge (who represents Gershon's experience) challenges the narrator and the reader about the possibility of representing a coherent Kindertransport character and cultural position. And so a major theme emerging from the novel is a question: what kind of narrative form can represent the confluence of a normative adolescent emotional turbulence and the destabilization of adolescent Kinder? Unlike a child character who, as Sue Vice notes, represents 'lost or impossible knowledge', Gershon's adolescent, like Segal's, may have access to knowledge of the childhood past but the emotional vicissitudes of adolescence create a distorting lens (*Children* 48). Choosing fiction over memoir or autobiography, Gershon suggests an imaginative response at the very beginning, when her narrator confides, 'Being refugees, they were both discovering, was turning them into liars' (*Bread* 29). Being liars, of course, presumes knowledge of the truth. In the experience of her refugee characters, however, the historical realities that might constitute what is true for them remain inaccessible until it is too late to perform a sense of being true to themselves or to others. Unlike so many refugee and Kindertransport memoirs and testimony, where truth lies in frustrated attempts to achieve historical accuracy and transparent descriptions of places and sequences of events, for Gershon the truth lies in the traces of relationships barely understood at the time but that become an integral part of forming the refugees' tremulous sense of self.

The novel's table of contents accords with the Kinder's constantly shifting forms of exile and identities in 'other people's houses'. For Gershon, because families are left behind, regardless of the Kinder's efforts and those of host families and institutions, home as a psychological and social space is gone. To replace it, as we see interspersed among the novel's hosts and foster families, are the characters' entangled relations: between Inge, her brother Dolph, and the two men she loves, Sebastian, the RAF flyer and son of one of her foster families, and Rudi, a Kind who becomes emotionally involved with both Inge and Dolph. The timeline of the novel covers the years from the Kinder's arrival at Dovercourt in December 1938 when Inge is thirteen until February 1942 when she decides to settle for 'more than she had the right to expect' (*Bread* 184). Forming the novel's conclusion, this retrospective self-doubt expresses a questioning relationship between the anxiety of the refugees' displacement and the voice of modern fiction. It reminds us that the Holocaust is not only a defining feature of modernity but that its expressive forms should be factored into our definitions of modern fiction. In its persistent self-reflexivity and meditations on the many paradoxical meanings of rescue, this fiction about rescue depicts rescue as a fiction.

> The experience of growing up in Nazi Germany has made me very distrustful of living in a Gentile society. (Gershon, 'Growing Disquiet' 61)

Among the dislocations *Bread of Exile* dramatizes is the underlying feeling, as Gershon presents it in her video, that 'the rescue was racist. We were exiled because we were Jews and rescued because we were Jews. No one cared who I was as an individual' (*Stranger*). Juxtaposing individuality with Jewish identity earmarks another identity category that is pivotal but disorienting for Gershon's characters: gender identity. From beginning to end, *Bread of Exile* dramatizes this identity dislocation, as we see in the characters' name changes that represent intertwined anxieties – not knowing if it is possible to rectify the dangers of having a Jewish identity and the gendered disorientation of losing it. In a self-reflexive move, the novel questions how this condition will affect the narration of selfhood. Even the narrator expresses doubt about her own ability to witness what she recounts. We see this combined anxiety in Gershon's portrait of Inge's brother Dolph. Wracked with guilt for not trying harder to rescue his parents, Dolph is motivated to apply for service as a British agent provocateur, ferreting out fifth columnists while assuming a false identity. The idea of false identity is multifaceted for him, reflecting not only whether he can pass as a non-Jew and be authenticated as a British Jew but also the question of what it means to be a Jewish man and a refugee.

Of course the irony that cuts through these questions registers for the reader but exhibits the character's naïveté. Like so many Kinder of his age, despite his desire to help the British defeat Germany, Dolph is interned as a potential enemy. As a Jewish man, he is considered an alien not a hero and as a German he is marked as an enemy, a threat; as a German Jewish man, he is dangerous three times over. The novel's structure foregrounds all of these dangers and ironies by opening with links between the origins of Dolph's name as Adolf, with Nazi terror, and also with medieval English pogroms. Prodded by Dolph, his father asks a German passport agent if the boy's name can be changed because 'it's not an English name' (*Bread* 9–10). In response, the agent mocks the possibility of the boy integrating into English society: ' "Don't worry, son, your passport will make it plain for all to see that you're a Yid." The English knew how to deal with the Jews, he told him, they had burned Jews and synagogues long before there was a German Reich' (*Bread* 10). Despite the suspicion with which we might react to the self-serving mockery of the British by a German, the reference satirizes any sentimental notion that the rescue of the Kinder represents an inherently benevolent English opposition to German antisemitism. Instead, Britain's bravura celebration of its political and moral distinctions from Europe does not resolve its wartime ambivalences that positioned Jewish identity as a problem for Jewish refugees. Quite the contrary. These ambivalences call attention not only to the antisemitic history Britain shared with the continent but also to British abhorrence of antisemitic activation.

The convergence of dangers emanating from Britain's past and Germany's present serves as a portentous warning the Kinder cannot escape even in the relative safety of the British Isles. Despite their own sense and performances of a destabilized identity, the Kinder are marked indelibly as Jews. We see, however, how this nightmarish vision is transformed into creatively critical expression when it reemerges in the form of an essay Inge writes in her English school. In response to the assigned topic, 'An Easter I shall not forget', Inge creates a story about Daphne, who is imprisoned for the holiday by her foster parents in a room with barred windows (*Bread* 47). Though Inge leaves Daphne's crime unspecified, the only one the budding author can imagine is hiding one's Jewish identity. This secret plus the victim's name link this tale to Dolph's request to serve as a spy, for Inge chooses the name Daphne because of its resemblance to her brother's name. Reinforcing the sense of gendered danger Inge inscribes, the novel interweaves internal, historical, and other gendered allusions with the presumed guilt and assured punishment of the Jews. Inge's interpretation of 'An Easter I shall not forget' resonates with historical memories of the medieval European pogroms inspired by the holiday; it also connects with the German passport agent's reference to England. In combination, the assignment and Inge's essay parallel the novel's retrospective and proleptic suturing of the Jews' perilous past, anxious present, and imminent future. Although the title of Inge's assignment is clearly intended as homage to Britain as a Christian nation, it also forecasts a theme and mantra that would continue to shape Jewish consciousness and identity long after the Holocaust – *Never Forget.*

The assignment reminds us that Easter was indeed an unforgettable time for Jews in medieval England and from then onwards in Eastern Europe. Coinciding with Passover, the Easter celebration of Christ's resurrection also resurrected antisemitic myths about the Jews. Akin to a ritual performance, commemorating the crucifixion and resurrection of Christ included the activation of hatred for the Jews who were blamed for the arrest, torture, and murder of the Christian savior, not to mention the use of Christian children's blood to make Passover matzos – the blood libel.[3] As Inge's imaginative response suggests, this was a Christian moment that spotlighted the precarious visibility of Jewish identity, for Jews were historically easy to identify by their closely knit living quarters, distinctive dress, dietary habits, and particular occupations. Circumcision was tantamount to being the mark of Cain. As living symbols of the rejection of Christianity, the Jews remained an affront to Christian European culture, inspiring the fusion of religious belief and antisemitic myth that translated into pogroms, the recurring frenzied and murderous attacks on Jews, their homes, workplaces, and synagogues.

Addressed to Christians, Gershon's poem 'Easter' is a reminder that Christ was a Jew whose message is distorted by those who use his resurrection to inspire hatred:

The Christian world commemorates
the crucifixion of a Jew
that old barbarity which grew
to stand for love by means of hate. (*Collected Poems* 18)

Instead of celebrating the Spring season as a time of rebirth, Easter revives 'pagan' blood rituals that not only poison Christ's message of love, but when 'the cross was turned into the sword of Christianity', this 'set the world upon a course / on which the sacred multitude/must save itself through suffering' (*Collected Poems* 19). The trajectory suggested by the iconic event of the crucifixion rotates backwards toward the appropriation of pre-Christian blood sacrifice, moves toward the medieval blood libels and retaliation against the Jews, and shows how Christ's suffering continues to be exploited, not memorialized. We see this exploitation reverberating in the twentieth century as Nazism synthesizes ancient and medieval myths of blood purity and blood sacrifice to perpetrate its 'revenge of race on the Jews' (*Collected Poems* 19). With bitter irony, Gershon's poem leads us to see that Christ's suffering can only be understood as Jewish and, in its continuation, unChristian.[4]

The poem 'Songs in Exile' powerfully condenses the history of this antisemitic violence by evoking the oppositional meanings of the fairy-tale scenes cited in so many Kindertransport memoirs as mnemonic pathways to Central European childhoods and the Holocaust. Gershon's poem depicts her ambivalent response to visiting her German birthplace by alluding to the 'mixed forest' whose 'legend quickens / to the captive child' (*Collected Poems* 9). In combination with finding 'symbols of anger' that 'are poised to impose / the mould of disaster', the legendary childhood landscape must now be seen in the light of the following lines:

> the primitive rages
> converge on the Jew
> the purge of the ages ...
> and barbarities advance
> on human indifference
> fainter and fainter echoes call
> have compassion on us all. (*Collected Poems* 11)

Of course in *Bread of Exile*, at the time Inge writes her essay, knowledge of the Holocaust lies in the future and she is never in danger but, doubly planted into the narrative, the room with barred windows speaks of fear and peril extending backwards and forward in time. This Janus-faced perspective establishes a pattern wherein Inge's unselfconscious expressions of displacement and alienation become opportunities for the narrator to provide a critical guide for readers. Inge's story bridges a history that has been read as distinctly separate from that of Britain's rescue mission – the fate of the Jews who could not escape and would not be rescued. Providing both historical and psychological linkages, the narrator uses Inge's apprehensive translation of an assignment that celebrates Christian British culture to inscribe the unforeseeable dangers faced by the contemporary Jews of Europe. The narrator's proleptic strategy memorializes the Jews' fates and inserts their story into the British narrative. Invoking the causal links between Easter and the pogroms also recalls the Jews' divided historical consciousness as they tried to fathom the causes and effects of the accretion of Nazi brutalities. For those who could not escape, enforcement of the Nuremberg laws, Kristallnacht, and deportations could be viewed either as comprising yet another if more lethal pogrom or as portending something incomparable. As Inge cannot know but her essay and Gershon's poem relay, the pogrom of the past, with its spasmodic violence, would be superseded by the Holocaust's meticulous planning and ritualized enforcement. In effect, the totalizing reach of the Holocaust could be said to constitute a universalizing religion of death.

Whatever good fortune the Kinder discover in Britain will be questioned by the meanings imposed on the rescue experience by the historical design of personal memories. A legacy bridging the divide between German persecution and British rescue is Inge's memory of being taunted by Hitler Youth. At that time 'she would have been happy to stop being who she was to be like the others; she thought that in England she would be able to do it; believed that she was already half-way there by wearing school uniform' (*Bread* 43). But, as it turns out, changing one's Jewish name signifies both guilt and wishful thinking on the part of the subject and of the British.[5] For the Kinder, changing one's name would mean disavowal of their imperial families and heritage while activating a desire to adapt to the host culture. Regardless of the authenticity or strength of the subject's desire or act, however, the novel calls attention to the probability of failure. As so much Kindertransport writing reports, fears run rampant with the children's attempts to integrate into British culture. Resonant with efforts to conceal one's Jewish identity under Nazi domination, assimilation into British culture is always threatened with exposure, as though it were a fictional performance incorporating a desire to deceive. Like false identity papers, changing one's name is scorned by the dominant polity as possessing no more integrity than a criminal lie against the nation.

And yet despite the doubts and double messages Britain expressed to its refugees, it never faltered in its steadfast invitation to them to perform the role of British subject. In her essay, Inge internalizes and expresses these fears, doubts, double messages, and their implied threats by conflating Nazi persecution with a developing sense 'that the English were hypocrites' (*Bread* 48). And so, in Inge's fraught imagination, the island haven becomes a prison where her invented character Daphne is left to subsist on moldy bread and use a bucket 'to piss and shit in – Inge spelled it peas and shite' (*Bread* 47). If Inge cannot free her sense of self from Britain's double messages, she can retaliate by maligning the abuser in culturally significant terms. In addition to using words that would be considered an affront to English decorum, especially for a young woman, she misspells the language she is being taught to respect and emulate. The latter malefaction is an affront twice over, for 'shite' transliterates and therefore privileges the German pronunciation. While serving as a form of retaliation, this linguistic gesture also expresses the gap created by not being understood either in German or English. The combination of gleeful and despairing voice with which Inge endows the narrator of Daphne's story is therefore an antidote to those occasions when 'she screamed, wordlessly', when not only language but also sound failed her (*Bread* 39).

More graphically, Inge's description of Daphne's plight suggests that if the fictional character is helpless, the writer is not; Inge can deploy her character's bodily waste to launch an aggressively defiant linguistic missile. In a metonymic function, Inge's hostile discharge of the adolescent's waste also implies a critique of the system that punishes her for embodying the need for rescue. With no acceptable outlets to express the anger and grief of mourning the traumatic losses of parents and culture, Inge's response will be 'misinterpreted as naughtiness or even as class-specific deficits' (Benz 86).[6] The effect is telling. In horrified response to the louche language and plot of the essay, the headmistress suggests that Inge's name be changed to Jane, 'a good old English name' (*Bread* 48). Though we can easily see the choice as archetypically British, privileging a no-frills ordinariness, a combination of factors suggests the play of additional signifiers. When Inge's foster mother objects to renaming her ward as a generic 'Plain Jane', literary history intervenes to create a commentary (*Bread* 48). The appellation recalls another outcast and rebellious 'Plain Jane' who also lacks parental protection and who is similarly constrained – Jane Eyre. We can't help but be reminded of Jane Eyre's ostracism to a claustrophobic red room and then her physical and emotional starvation in a British school; we are reminded of the oppression Jane Eyre must escape (*Bread* 48). Because of this childhood oppression, it is no surprise that Jane Eyre is invoked by other Kindertransport writers, such as Lois Keith, who, as a child in 1937 Austria, 'can feel the chill . . . and the torment Jane suffered with no loving family to guide her or keep her safe' (*Out of Place* 57). Karen Gershon reinforces and complicates this literary association with another – Jane's *doppelganger* – Bertha Mason. Bertha's physical and psychological confinement is even more closely aligned with Daphne than Jane Eyre and, in its Gothic expressionism, suggests the extremes of Inge's reaction to her island of rescue. Though Inge is never interned like her brother Dolph, and though the kind treatment of the Sparrows, her first foster family, contrasts sharply with Rochester's cruelty towards Bertha, her fantasy signals the angry pain of emotional and cultural deprivation. The benign forgetfulness and accepting pragmatism of Inge's British foster family make it a convenient foil for the Jewish girl's defensive responses. And so it becomes an easy target onto which Inge displaces the emotional and cultural turbulence wrought by parental loss, the transport, and adaptation to a foreign culture.

Gershon explicitly draws our attention to connections between these responses and Jane Eyre's story when Inge receives a copy of Brontë's novel from Dolph and, later, one of Daphne du Maurier's, *Rebecca*, from Sebastian, the son of one of Inge's foster families. Inge's Daphne and Daphne du Maurier certainly share Gothic plots. Clearly inspired by *Jane Eyre*, *Rebecca* teems with Gothic romance, betrayals, secrets, threats, and self-doubt. The timing of the first gift is no coincidence, either. It occurs at the very moment Inge realizes that the Sparrows have forgotten her birthday and learns that, because of the bombing, she will be evicted from their home. She will be evacuated to yet another unknown destination, in the charge of the austere and sanctimonious teacher, Miss Pym, who calls for Jesus to 'have mercy on this miserable Jew' (*Bread* 66):

> Instead of crying herself to sleep over it, Inge could not leave off reading *Jane Eyre* and blessed her for coming to her just when she needed her most, and decided that in future she would love only people in books, who could not fail her. (*Bread* 63–4)

But as her Kindertransport friend and compatriot Rudi reminds Inge, instead of bringing comfort, the stories she favors allow her to indulge her anxieties. There is neither mercy nor blessing in casting Miss Pym as 'the witch in the gingerbread house' or identifying with Jane Eyre 'who had been unable to escape being sent to Lowood or to get away from it for years and years' (*Bread* 77). (Miss Pym reads like a central casting candidate for a job at Lowood, Jane Eyre's infamously abusive school.) Like Lore Segal's 'serial story' of 'a pale tragic-eyed girl', Gershon's rendering of Daphne and 'Plain Jane' affectionately mocks the adolescent girl's self-pity. But both Segal and Gershon also provide recognition that if wartime conditions constrain the reticence of British self-expression to an extreme, they also camouflage a nexus of extant social codes that inhibit an adolescent refugee girl's dreams of self-determination. In both cases, as the girls' tersely encoded language and reception show, they are tantamount to silence. For Gershon, only a non-realistic, symbolic or fantasied form of representation would dramatize the tensions that constitute Inge's developing consciousness and sense of self.

As Gershon's novel implies, *Jane Eyre* provides the language to dramatize tensions between social realism and psychological desire and fantasy, a language of social and psychological displacement, and projection. Indeed, it is only fitting to recall that one of the major achievements of *Jane Eyre* is its narrative rebellion against British middle-class codes of emotional repression and sublimation. Given the emotional intensity of Inge's Kindertransport experience, we can understand her fantasy of the body working as a psychologically satisfying weapon to express the girl's frustrated desire for an unencumbered, ordinary passage into adulthood. Within and around its own fairy tale and Gothic elements, Brontë's *Jane Eyre* develops this plot of psychological and social oppression into one of restrained self-rescue and self-determination. It is because of its narrative emphasis on restraint that Brontë's novel can be seen as a reference point for the social and cultural codes that would shape the story of twentieth-century adolescent refugees in England.[7]

Gershon's reference and allusions to *Jane Eyre* should also activate our observations about the place of *The Bread of Exile*, not only as testimony to the agonies and occasional absurdities of Kindertransport experience but also as to how its fictional and testimonial forms relate to developments in modern literature. If we agree, as so many have argued, that the Holocaust is central to any definitions of what we might mean by twentieth-century modernity, then we can conclude that Holocaust writing becomes crucial to our understanding of what we call late modernism or, indeed, its demise. For the high modernists of the 1920s and 1930s, the catastrophes and human costs of World War I, the Great Depression, and the rise of fascism formed the launching pad for many of their political and aesthetic concerns and forms. While debates persist about the temporal boundaries of late modernism, we can see how experimental narrative forms that we now take for granted as integral to high and late modernism prevail even in today's narratives.[8] The rhetorical, political, and aesthetic nature of these forms is also transformed once artists acknowledge the atrocities of the Holocaust as central to modernity and respond by questioning and complicating the literary strategies of modernism. Tracing a particular form of non-realist narrative from the *fin de siècle* provides evidence for this trajectory. As we see in so many canonical and popular modernist texts, literary efforts to chart the psychological disorientations of war and technological and social change resulted in turns to such symbolic, non-realistic forms as the Gothic. Gothic terror, as embodied by the *fin de siècle* figures of Count Dracula, Dr. Jekyll and Mr. Hyde, and Dorian Gray, became a mainstay of British modernism in its graphic suggestions of a modernity infected with depraved, decayed, and savage instincts, and then, most horrifically, transformed by the death machinery of modern wars into a monstrously threatening pandemic.[9] In addition to externally ominous forces, the constitution of the self became a focus of moral concern, especially as such models of human psychology as psychoanalysis were emerging to challenge notions of individual rationality and responsibility. As Andrew Smith and Jeff Wallace point out, Gothic forms could express the 'fascination [of British modernists] with the potential erosion of moral value, and with the forms that amorality can take' (3).

The most graphic and malleable Gothic symbol of moral regression and psychological response was the body. Smith and Wallace note:

> In both modernist and popular discourses, the body can seem to promise authentic personal identity, yet is ghosted by a sense of something potentially alien and strange. Anxieties about the physical health of the collective body – human species, race, nation-state, culture – become anxieties about the idea of the self. (3)

Karen Gershon's invocation of *Jane Eyre* shows us how the female Gothic elements of Brontë's novel serve her narrative of being haunted by the Holocaust even at a peripheral site, Britain. In addition to atmospheric elements, such as the mysterious attic and Bertha's fires, the character of Bertha herself embodies a personal and cultural history that offers additional connections between gendered features of Gothic narratives, those endemic to modernism, and stories of the Kindertransport. Like Bertha, Inge is a foreign woman and both suffer the erasure of their names for one that's more culturally acceptable. Inge's home was in Central Europe, a place associated with anti-rational myths and where she would be identified racially, even in her homeland, with a demonic otherness. Tracing such an emanation to nineteenth-century fears of degeneracy, Andrew Smith shows how British anxieties about national decline and fears of the Other erupt in that iconic Gothic figure, Dracula. Making his parasitic way from the dark mountains of Translyvania, the murky heart of Central Europe, the figure of Dracula easily conjures up 'a perceived "alien invasion" of Jews from the East who, in the view of many alarmists were "feeding off" and "poisoning" the blood of the Londoner' (Smith and Wallace 154). The shadow of the Wandering Jew is particularly disturbing when we consider that this antisemitic specter from the Middle Ages haunts both Nazi ideology and British racial history.[10] This relationship reminds us not only of the German origins of the dark Grimm Brothers' fairy tales, but of their intimate links to the Gothic idiom.[11] That the Wandering Jew is conflated as both boys and girls in Gershon's novel shows how Nazi ideology and British racial history would not assume the innocence of the Jewish young. The fusion of these narrative forms dramatizes how the racialized constructions of Jewish children would haunt their odyssey from the past to the present and from State terror to the rescuing nation. In defining the Gothic, Victor Sage and Allan Lloyd Smith note the transmission of terror over time:

> Evidently the Gothic is not merely a literary convention or a set of motifs: it is a language, often an anti-historicizing language, which provides writers with the critical means of transferring an idea of otherness of the past into the present. (3)

Though both Bertha Mason and Inge are transported to Britain against their wills and live under rules of surveillance and restricted movement, they are perceived as threats to the dominant culture and to themselves. Bertha Mason's devolution into a sub-human form suggests that she has lost the capacity for rationality, an assumption that coincides with lingering cultural constructions of women's normal mental capacities. Brontë's novel depicts the logical consequences of such a gendered construction in that Bertha's madness demonstrates to her guardians that she has sunk below the boundaries of what constitutes a human self. Particularly as her nocturnal wanderings defy the chains and locks designed to constrain her, her very body seems to vaporize into a poisonous viscous form. With this image and Bertha's ominous movement from the Caribbean to England in mind, the portrayal of Inge's transport assumes an admonitory cast. We can thus see the story of Daphne's containment as Inge's internalized warning to see herself as the threateningly amorphous Wandering Jew. The origins of this warning lie in the response of Inge's British hosts to the misperceptions, silences, and outbursts that, like Lore Segal's, are often seen as defying girlhood normalcy. And just as Antoinette Cosway must become Bertha Mason to symbolize a defense against fears of the alien, so Inge's name is changed to Jill. Like some kind of magical gesture that would both symbolize and gain control over the fearful object, the name change not only denies any relation between a stable identity and sense of self but also mitigates against the cultural danger this instability and her escape would represent. For the writing subject, however, danger is offset by liberating possibilities. As we can see in the expressive metaphorical structures of Lore Segal's depiction of Lore's emotionally paralyzed body and Inge's story of Daphne's bodily rebellion against cultural disorientation and confinement, storytelling becomes a magical opportunity for the Kinder. Storytelling here is a self-assertive act; it represents and defends against the self being erased in mistranslation. As Inge notes, ' – *wildfremde*: there is no equivalent word for it in English, perhaps the English never feel wildly estranged' (*Bread* 68). Feeling 'wildly estranged' from any stable sense of self or Jewish or female identity, the child refugee invents a story of being buried alive, where the self feels and sees itself as entwined with the other in a monstrous synthesis of questionable being.[12]

The wish for a stabilized self expressed in Inge's storytelling becomes even more fragmented as it must contend with the realities of dislocations from Germany and within England. In turn, the combination of these dislocations creates strange misperceptions and self-doubts in Inge that serve as both support for and a countervoice to her fantasy of aggressive bodily expression. Her linguistic difficulties may be typical of refugee experience but they also represent how her disorientation about herself combined with her ambivalent attitudes drive her to misread others' motives. This combination is apparent in Inge's reaction to letters from her parents and from Dolph. In order to protect her parents from worrying about her and herself from worrying about them, she tells them lies and then absorbs the resulting guilt by assuming they lie to her. When Dolph compliments her linguistic ability by telling her that he relies on her letters to learn English, 'she thought he meant that if her English had not been better than his he would not have valued her letters to him at all' (*Bread* 50). The tensions operative in this dual expression of self-doubt are not confined solely to Inge's character. Rather as David Brauner notes, the tension is a fundamental one 'between self-assertion and self-denial' in British Jewish literature (*Post-war* 29). Examining the representation of Inge's character, we can see that this tension and the Kindertransport experience intersect. For Gershon, the characterization of Inge's emotional, gendered, and cultural displacements becomes a narrative opportunity to explore issues that tether more 'parochial concerns' of Jewish communities to those about relations between the Kinder and the British culture they confronted (Brauner, *Post-war* 29). For example, Inge misreads her own motivations and effects on others as well as the motives of others in relation to her. This individualized characterization begs the question of where narrative authenticity lies or what combination of narrative voices can authorize the integrity of this characterization. While these questions are also endemic to modernist fiction, the parameters of Kindertransport representation as testimony lend a significant historical overlay to be factored into the narrative workings and analyses of the text.[13]

The limits of Inge's ability to decode British social culture are like those of so many Kinder that relate to questions about writing and reading the Kindertransport. At every turn of Inge's story, she and the narrator remind us that the story they tell consists not only of gaps in information and memory but also distortions caused by emotional uncertainties and extremes. What is being narrated, then, is a story about the difficulties of writing and reading a Kindertransport story. We can never be sure about what Inge feels other than unresolved conflicts, tensions, ambivalences, and projections. Though we can trace these to the trauma of separation and adaptation, this kind of generalization or abstraction does not help us to discover or identify corre-lations between events, other characters, and Inge's responses. Because of this uncertainty, we can never be sure that what Inge sees, feels, or does coheres with the feelings or actions of other characters, including the nar-rator. While the narrator does report the characters' actions and reactions, because, more often than not, they respond to each other at cross-purposes, the effect is a guide to an epistemological state of doubt for the characters and readers alike. The doubt, moreover, only intensifies as the three Kinder protagonists make assumptions about the English and struggle to contain and even reshape their reactions in order to be accepted. Again and again we see the Kinder negotiating between their partial or inchoate understanding of the responses expected of them and fading memories of who and how they were in their original homes and homelands. Coaching each other to appear and sound British, they rely on 'hearsay knowledge' and having 'soldiered through the lies' (*Bread* 56). The result is the realization 'that being a refugee was like being in Looking-Glass Country', where misunderstood and even inverted or reversed expectations become the reality with which the Kinder must contend (*Bread* 79).[14]

The Bread of Exile intertwines both 'hearsay knowledge' and 'lies' in its depiction of the enmeshed relations of Inge, Dolph, and their friend Rudi. Telling lies becomes part of the shifting performances of the Kinder's 'hearsay knowledge' of what it means to be the selves they remember being and how to become and yet resist becoming British. As each of them learns to adapt an often conflicted developing sense of Jewish and gendered self to the ambigu-ities of cultural integration, their misperceptions of each other and of British culture commingle with their responses to their own and each other's losses, mutating identities, and developing desires and sexuality. While the plot takes us into the well-charted territory of the Kinder's constantly changing habitats, it offers a perspective on dislocation that is atypical of Kinder-transport narratives. The escalating intensity of the characters' intertwined desires for each other runs parallel to and presents a critical gloss on the pressures of assimilation and resistance. And just as this intensity and pres-sure grow, so the perceived boundaries between the characters' objects of desire almost dissolve. Ultimately, each of them projects or sees qualities of one in the other, all of whom reflect back on the perceiving self. In the novel's extended metaphorical import, each of the three Kinder is linked in the consciousness of the others with the loss of home and the failure of Britain to compensate. Thus, Inge desires both Rudi and Sebastian, 'half expecting Rudi to be like Sebastian, since she longed for him just as much, not real-izing that he mattered to her chiefly because he stood for continuity, was a link with her brother and through him with home' (*Bread* 104). Though the linkage between Dolph, Rudi, Inge, and their lost identities is an obvious one, the inclusion of Sebastian complicates any cultural oppositions we might apply to interpreting the Kinder's British experience. The sentimental or at least conventional linkage between the displaced and needy Kinder and between them and withholding Britons becomes erotically charged through the narrative of Inge's desires for Rudi and Sebastian.

As outsiders, Inge, Dolph, and Rudi cling to but also compete for each other to affirm feelings and gender identities nothing in their immediate British contexts can verify or explain. Rudi's bisexuality can thus be seen as a sexual expression of uncommitted adaptation to a culture that remains highly ambivalent about the objects of its rescue. Introducing Sebastian into the mix calls attention not only to the turbulence of an already destabilized or stalled adolescent male sexuality but also to his position as a British man in relation to the Kinder's gendered refugee Jewishness. Despite the fact that being an RAF bomber pilot endows Sebastian with the status of Britain's finest – a knight of the air fulfilling the myth of the few – his despair at bombing German civilians also establishes him as a critic of his nation's strategies to defeat the very enemy that also threatens the Jews.[15] As an outsider to the deeply held myth of British wartime and intrepid national unity, Sebastian is thus aligned with the Kinder. Even as his own home remains physically safe from German bombs, its associations with 'continuity' are blitzed by his alienation from the comforts of middle-class codes it is supposed to represent. The apparent stability of his home becomes the mocking mirror image of his participation in destroying the enemy's families and homes. We see this estrangement in his silences and sudden outbursts. Like Inge and reminiscent of Lore Segal, his response to the war's losses puts him at odds with not only the substance but also the stalwart expressive style that is coded British heroism. When his parents insist on his marriage to Inge, even as he lies dying from his wounds, the gesture is not one of acceptance or reconciliation, but a function of a desperate desire to restore the idea of the heroic soldier to his rightful place as saving and regenerating the threatened nation. In turn, this would resuscitate faith in the myth of the middle class as haven for the best of British values. In this novel, however, the nation's agency depends not on romantic masculinist myths, but on the resisting and anti-nationalist acts of its outsiders: Dolph becomes a commando to rescue European Jews and Rudi joins the British army to escape his family's censure of his homosexual behavior. Regardless of motive, however, as each assumes a role saving Britain and Europe from Nazi domination, it becomes clear that the steadfastness of Britain's myth of national unity is upheld only by the opposing reality of the nation's multiformity.

Beseiged by the threats of Nazi conquest as well as British pressures for a homogeneous and heterosexual national character, all the male protagonists are constructed as vulnerable. They cannot assume the role of savior, either of the nation or of the endangered heroine. As Sebastian's despair ignites into the air crash that burns him to death, the novel's allusions to *Jane Eyre* shadow the event's significance. The fusion of Bertha Mason's desperate leap from the fiery roof and Rochester's debilitating wounds and loss of his ancestral seat of power point to the vulnerability of the myth of British forbearance. Helene Meyers's analysis of the Gothic tradition in the twentieth century lends insight into the effects of war myths on gender roles and relations: 'the passively feminine woman who expects a man to save her is, most likely, a goner and hence functions as a monitory figure. Relatedly, the heroic capabilities of men are undercut or altogether destroyed' (23). In her revision of such expectations, Gershon rejects any romantic rescue plot for either her characters or the Nazi-besieged Britain. Sebastian's despair and death undercut the development of a romance plot not only between him and Inge but also between Britain and the integration of its refugees. While Dolph's return to Europe can easily be viewed as a heroic gesture, his disappearance from the narrative forecloses the possibility of a successful adventure. The result of these stalled plot turns is that Inge's Gothic- and Brontë-inspired fantasy of the hapless Daphne takes a realist turn. The young writer is left alone, without rescue, to make her own way through the cultural labyrinth of adapting to Britain.

In *The Bread of Exile*, just as the Kindertransport experience occupies a liminal space in the Holocaust narrative, so do the characters' sexual identities, sexuality, and sexual relations. And while sexual themes are important if not necessary to a narrative of adolescent development, in this novel they also shed light on the novel's focuses on cultural identity, adaptation, and its failure. As a commentary on Nazi antisemitism and its construction of the Jewish man and woman as sexually perverted, the novel offers a complex interweave of sexual identities and relationships. We see this connection in Inge's use of Dolph as a sexual model. At a time of displacement, her memory of Dolph as the role model for such experiences as starting school and celebrating birthdays coordinates with the desire to view childhood as meaning continuity and stability. Such desire seems to lead inexorably to Inge relying on Dolph for a lesson about human sexuality, complete with his demonstration of an erect circumcised penis. Though Gershon's narrator treats this scene and its protagonists with affectionate humor, and, if I dare say, deflates its erotic possibilities, the incestuous suggestiveness assumes a critical role.[16] At the level of characterization, the intimacy of brother and sister melds their identity anxieties and sexual exploration. Intimacy also demonstrates the novel's exposition of connections between the disorientations of refugee experience and the tremulous formation of the Kinder's gender identities. Though the oldest of the three, sixteen-year-old Rudi, is identified by the book jacket as a homosexual, Peter Lawson's note that the character is bisexual seems more accurate ('Karen Gershon', in *Holocaust Novelists* 109). More accurate because less precise and therefore in keeping with the characters' persistently ambiguous responses and the novel's insistence on correlations between cultural and sexual alienation. Such ambiguity also serves as a critical response to the antisemitic charge that Jewishness is shorthand for homosexuality.

The focus on this engagement begins in the camp at Dovercourt with cross dressing as the first sign of what will become the triadic sexual and gendered relationship of Inge, Rudi, and Dolph. In her need not to be separated from Dolph, contrary to camp policy, Inge dresses in his clothes. The point is not whether she succeeds in passing, but in her desire and Rudi's response: ' "You make as charming a boy as your brother", and put his hand under her chin so that he could look at her; it was such a caring gesture that she fell in love with him' (*Bread* 24). So begins a sexualized entanglement of the Kinder's gender development with that of adapting to British culture while searching for the meaning of their Jewish identity. While Dolph's heterosexuality is never in doubt, Rudi's desire for him and Inge's doubly transgressive emotional conflation of love objects suggest deeply interdependent, overlapping, liminal, and in-between sexual and cultural identities. In narrative effect, the emotional intensity of these relationships challenges the discretionary bonds of British social and familial codes of relating.

These cultural and sexual challenges are related as well to the past that carries its own ambiguous and unfulfilled affiliations. On several occasions, Inge sneaks Rudi or Dolph into her room to spend the night, but as their often oblique references and half-finished sentences suggest, the intimacy established between host and guest is complicated by shadowy references to desire for or by the absent one. In all of Gershon's writing, including her published and unpublished novels, poetry, and autobiography, the absent one denotes profound personal losses – of her sister Anne, who died in 1943, and of her parents who perished in Auschwitz. Absence also means a loss of selfhood attached to the past comprised of a lost homeland, language, and culture that, in concert, ultimately betrayed her. The yearning expressed in her writing for attachment, identification, acceptance, and unconditional love materializes again and again in the form of parents, brothers, sisters, lovers, husbands, and children on whom she projects self-doubts about deserving fulfillment. That these relationships should be sexualized testifies to intense desire for a connection that will imaginatively fuse her characters with their loved ones. In effect, neither mind nor body can become independent agents or instruments of resistance since they too are merged. If the German language represents a perfidious past and English an uncertain present and future, sexual communication becomes the vehicle of expression. For her sexually ignorant female characters, inexperience presents invitations to embark on adventures of illicit or incestuous sexual experimentation to achieve any sense of orientation with the selves that are otherwise dislocated and incoherent. Feeling themselves to be strangers everywhere, including, more often than not in their marriages, even in their own bodies, her women find only momentary delight as their bodies respond sexually. In the end, this delight cannot last because the past and its incumbent losses and doubts intervene. The lovers of her female protagonists are exposed as temporary respites or as poor substitutes for those who reside in fading and distorted memories as the women continue to feel abandoned by lost loved ones and feel their own abandonment of them.

Among the published Kindertransport memoirs and fiction, Gershon's is the most candidly and graphically sexual. With broad implications, her depictions of sexual feeling lend powerful insights into Holocaust representations of the lingering effects of family losses, including desires to reconstitute family intimacy. After decades of adaptation to English restraint and sexual submissiveness, the widowed and aging transportee in Gershon's unpublished novel 'Manna to the Hungry', recognizes, 'It astonished her to discover that what for years had felt to her like indifference should turn out to have been buried grief' (77). As Peter Lawson points out, the title of another unpublished novel suggests that sexuality is 'The Last Freedom'. For both author and characters, sexuality and sexual relations provide sites of rebellion against social and cultural constraints. In Gershon's personal and cultural history, such rebellion is a reminder of the Nazi policy of *Rassenschande* that marked Jews as sexually poisonous predators and justified prohibition of Jewish-Aryan sexual relations. Gershon's translation of *Obscene: The History of an Indignation* (1965) by the German Jewish social philosopher Ludwig Marcuse details how 'National-Socialistic anti-Semitism was imbued with sexuality' so that persecution of the Jews was as well (qtd. in Lawson, *Anglo-Jewish Poetry* 154). Gershon was also influenced by Marcuse's critique of the 'damaging metaphysics of Christian-German-Idealistic dogma' that found sexuality sinful; in contrast, he praised the Hebrew Bible's 'unrepressed sexuality' (Lawson, *Anglo-Jewish Poetry* 155). As Lawson shows, in her poetry and several unpublished novels, Gershon returns to stories from the Hebrew Bible to represent uninhibited sexual desire. Her novels of the Kindertransport and its aftermath can thus be seen as challenging the social constraints of British emotional expression as well. Nonetheless, as a reality check, her representation of sexual desire as both a healthy instinctual development of mind and body and an imaginatively emotional embrace of self and the lost other remains more a function of desire than of fulfillment.

Just as sexual desire remains unfulfilled in *Bread of Exile* so does Inge's need to rescue herself from belonging to the past. In the suggestively incestuous scene between Dolph and Inge, these contradictory desires are enflamed, fused, and defused as Dolph holds her hand on his penis while telling her of his plan to try to save their parents. The darkened room where they cannot see each other is no pleasure site, however, as it becomes a portentous sign of their parents' fate and the impossibility of confronting it or of escaping its impact. Sexual desire in Gershon's writing erupts spontaneously, often without provocation or stimulation but always in response to a man who reminds her female protagonists of a lost brother or of the lost opportunity to have sustained the German part of her self that cannot be separated from her Jewish identity. The latter case forms the plot of her unpublished novel 'The Last Freedom' where Eva, the sixty-year-old widow, briefly becomes involved with a German who after forty years of silence comes to England to confess how, by killing her brother, he saved him from Dr Mendele's sadistic experiments. Despite her deep sexual and emotional attraction to Bruno, his revelation kills her desire to build a relationship with him and she escapes from him and from Germany to England once again. Here at least, she had grappled with her family losses by becoming indifferent to and even disdainful of her own self-doubting feelings. In the emotional logic of Gershon's narratives, if intense sexual desire expresses 'buried grief', it must also be deflated in order for mourning to occur. Despite the union it may promise, the new love cannot replace primary family ties. Instead of satisfying and sustaining a fantasy for reunion with lost loved ones, sexual intimacy must be dislodged in order for memories and the buried realities of the past to be given emotional space in the woman's consciousness.

In *Bread of Exile*, the development of Inge's sexual desire and recognition of her buried grief is narrated through her relations with Dolph, Rudi, and Sebastian. Of the three, her relationship with Sebastian demonstrates most clearly connections between Inge's lost family and identity and the failure of sexual feeling to soothe or cloak grieving for the impossibility of reunion. Because Sebastian is English and bears no relation to Inge's family, the possibility emerges that he could represent a pathway to a future free of the Holocaust past. Conversely, her alien identity could free him from the constraints of conforming to British family and cultural expectations while giving him cause to identify with his role in the war. As their barely tentative relationship and deathbed marriage show, however, the war's tragedies keep each of them locked into identities that will betray and sustain the unresolved tensions between Britain's heroic gesture in the Kindertransport and the integration of the Kinder. Such tension is apparent in Gershon's unpublished novel, 'Manna to the Hungry', which concerns a woman whose struggle to feel safe and to belong in the nation that rescued her has driven her to convert to Christianity and marry a gentile. On a pilgrimage to her brother's grave in Israel to discover how he died, she recognizes that she can be at home nowhere: she 'felt that she had no right to have come although they had invited her. Just so she had felt on her arrival in England, which had offered to have her but received her as if she had not been meant to accept' ('Manna' 90). The self-doubt with which this and so much of Gershon's writing is stamped may, in classically psychological terms, stem from the early childhood experience in which she began to dub herself *A Lesser Child*. But even as she pursues this identity through personal and narrative choices, she reminds us that for the exiled Kinder, as for any survivor related to the Holocaust, there is no sustaining or abiding place or identity, only an abiding longing, and one that becomes a self-sustaining value in itself.[17] Gershon thus confirms Nicola King's psychoanalytic point about another Holocaust narrative, George Perec's *W or the Memory of Childhood*, that 'the process of identity formation is hesitant, provisional and incomplete, and . . . heavily invested with fantasy' (128). Another novel by Gershon uses fantasy as a method of exploring the effects of history on identity formation.

Gershon pursues the question of liminal Jewish Holocaust identity and identification in her 1987 novel, *The Fifth Generation*. A speculative fiction about a boy who may have been fathered by Hitler, the novel investigates post-Holocaust identity as a struggle to negotiate a sense of self while tethered to an ambiguous relationship with an indelible but elusive past whose origins and events cannot be remembered. Beginning with a quotation from Exodus 20:5, 'visiting the iniquity of the fathers upon the children unto the third and fourth generation', Gershon postulates a Holocaust theory of ontology. She imagines a fifth generation after the Holocaust composed of a character who, in his turbulent vacillations about Jewish or German identity, loyalty, and family ties, represents an unending series of questions about connections between the guilty Nazi past and the effects of Holocaust history on Jewish identity. This idea of the fifth generation is clearly important to Gershon's attitudes toward Germany today. In a review of a book recounting the recent experience of a British Rabbi teaching at a German Christian college, she reflects:

> I know from my own journeys back to Germany that it is a healing experience for someone with our background ... to sit down, now that the time has come for it, with young Germans and together confront the past ... One wants them to know about the Holocaust; but one cannot possibly want this to be *all* they know of the Jews. ('Journey' 72, Gershon's italics)

In *The Fifth Generation*, the torments of a past constructed by the Third Reich cannot be overcome despite the possibility of healing in a nurturing and empathetic English home. A glaring sign or scar of this indelible and ongoing past is a tattoo etched onto the buttocks of Peter Sanger. Peter is one of the few children who survived the Nazi plan to decorate and fashion young Jewish skin into lampshades. In her Author's note, Gershon tells us that although she invented the lampshade factory in her novel, the Nuremberg Military Tribunal of 1947–49 documented the manufacture of 'lampshades and other ornamental household articles' by SS functionaries from the corpses of tattooed prisoners (*Fifth* np). Gershon's choice of a historical fragment suggests the fragmented history and selfhood that beset Peter from the beginning of the novel to the end. Whether he can emerge from a history of being made into an object, a Nazi artifact marked with 'the devil's footprint', remains open (*Fifth* 49). In this sense Gershon has created a survivor, who is not only one of the 1.5 generation of Jewish children caught by the Holocaust, but the number also assumes symbolic value: 1.5 signifies one who survived Nazi atrocities but whose wholeness as a self-recognized person remains questioned. Peter's traumatized memory is on perpetual overload as it contains both too much and too little of the experiential past. He is also a version of a hidden child who has been saved at the cost of an irretrievable identity. When we are introduced to him, his life has been saved because of the Nazis' defeat and retreat from their death-slated orphanage. Psychologically, Peter is then saved by the loving care of two staff members at the British hostel harboring the surviving boys, nicknamed the *Ueberfleishel* or 'offcuts' (*Fifth* 17). Barbara, a Kindertransport refugee, identifies with the unadaptable, unadoptable bedwetting boy, finding him both irresistible and repellent.[18] With the support of her colleague Luke, a Welsh schoolteacher whom she marries, Barbara adopts Peter. Peter in turn, is drawn to identify deeply with Barbara who has also lost her family to the Nazis. Like other Gershon characters, Peter's childhood attachment and desire for lost family intimacy develops into a heterosexual but incestuous lust. Like the risks he incurs in his search for his origins, this lust approximates transgressive temptation.

Ten years after the war's end, when Peter is sixteen, his yearnings are lacerated by a return of the Nazi past. He receives a letter from a neo-Nazi leader asking if he is the German boy with the 'PS' tattoo, a question that highlights his position as a significant Post-Script to a war whose defeat and erasure of Nazism are now called into question. The letter also explodes the fragile equilibrium of Peter's Jewish identity and sense of England as his home as well as Barbara's efforts to assimilate. Once the problem of Peter's identity arises, between Barbara's horror at the invasion of her home by a possible Nazi presence and Luke's intervention on the boy's behalf, the idea of family as a site of healing and wholeness is questioned as a sentimental myth. Peter must now realize that like so many who endured the Nazi Holocaust and who lost the parents on whom their identities and sense of selves depend, wherever he resides or searches for his identity, he is a stranger to himself.[19] This sense of his own strangeness is mirrored in the neo-Nazis' perception of him; insisting that he resembles the Führer, they mandate his character and fate in the postwar, post-defeat present as 'A sort of frog prince who must be restored to his inheritance. Until that moment, he had not quite realized that in exchange for repossessing who he had once been he would have to relinquish who he was' (*Fifth* 47). Like much Kindertransport writing, this novel inverts the magical solutions of fairy tales to suggest an indestructible terror. Just as the combined image of the frog prince enfolds one into the other, so there will be no rescue from tethering a fragile Jewish identity to one that threatens it by promising transformation: 'loathsome as he had become to himself, the son of a Nazi was acceptable to a Nazi – it felt to him as if he were growing monstrous features, fangs and hairy claws' (*Fifth* 51). To become a fellow traveler among Nazis would translate his tattoo into 'the mark of

Cain ... cursed to seek refuge and flee again and find a home nowhere, penalized for trying to strike roots' (*Fifth* 48, 80). With breakneck plotting (the novel is only 160 pages long), Peter embarks on a voyage of discovery and self-construction that ends by affirming only an ambiguous, uncertain, two-faced identity and the need to perform both his Jewishness and Germanness. The novel performs Peter's unstable identity and yearning for family connection by creating a narrator who shares his uncertainty with an empathy that precludes knowledge on which readers can rely. At every narrative moment, even as it suggests a linear chronological trajectory, the narrator expresses doubt that registers a character's uncertain memory or inability to fathom what is happening to him or her and whether an incident or encounter is revelatory or deceptive. In tandem with Peter's focalizing consciousness, the novel thus creates a family whose tenuous relationships mirror the fragile certainty of the postwar hope for European reconciliation and Jewish regeneration and concerns about Britain's relationship to a new Europe.

This fragile certainty is revealed through Peter's travels to Europe to investigate his parentage. What his trip reveals is that the past has been overwhelmed by the unfulfilled and fractured needs of all survivors of the war, regardless of the roles they played. Any real historic space or story, he discovers, is shaped by distorted, partial, and selective memory and unstable evidence. The novel represents this epiphany as the shattered expectations of discovering some holistic and unequivocal truth about the relationship of a survivor to the Holocaust and through the discovery, a pathway to healing. Beginning once again with 'something remembered out of some fairy tale', the epiphany ends with an inversion (*Fifth* 133). Instead of fulfilling the desire to 'come home [...] he felt as if a swarm of bees had got inside him and the great keeper had trapped them there by blocking up his orifices' (*Fifth* 134). How can there be healing from the Holocaust, this fantasy asks, if the pain inflicted on the survivor has been internalized to the point where there is simply no access to its source or outlet for its expression? If the sign of this gaping wound is Peter's tattoo, it leads us to see that the part of the self that has been damaged beyond repair is his identity as a knowable self and knowable Jew. It is therefore unclear whether his tattoo represents Peter's real name or whether he is one of two boys listed as Peter Wedekind. In fact, Luke teaches Peter to make fun of his tattoo by playing word games with the initials PS. In the light of conflicting and unstable evidence and testimony, it remains an open question whether in the shadow of Europe's wartime past it is possible to construct a post-Holocaust survivor identity or memory or if the search for post-Holocaust justice will be determining. Peter's antithetical, dual identity is made even more uncertain because he has no memory or stories of his past; connections between past and present that would be comprised of family moments have been severed by a family that is missing or dead or fabricated. Because he has no stories or photos that would record his family's existence, his memory is empty.

Unlike the Second Generation who, as Marianne Hirsch has studied, suffers from traumatic memory transmitted across generations, Peter's 1.5 generation suffers the lack of transmitted memory from his own traumatic past to his empty memory. He only has fleeting images or fantasies of himself with a twin sister whose reality neither he nor anyone can confirm. Indeed, given the intensity of Peter's yearning for wholeness and for reconciliation with his lost family, both of which affirm his liminal subjectivity, it is also possible that his ongoing trauma of dislocation and disorientation has projected an imagined memory and self in the form of a twin sister who was killed by the Nazis. Such a recurring image, especially as its reality cannot be tested, can, according to Marianne Hirsch, 'be seen as *figures* for memory and forgetting' that are part of the reparative work described by Robert Jay Lifton whom she quotes:

> In the case of severe trauma we can say that there has been an important break in the lifeline that can leave one permanently engaged in either repair or the acquisition of new twine. And here we come to the survivor's overall task, that of formulation, evolving new inner forms that include the traumatic event. ('Surviving Images' 222, Hirsch's italics)

Peter's journey to Germany may be an attempt to patch the lifeline broken by Holocaust atrocity, but, as Gershon's narrative insists, it remains a sore reminder of a lost wholeness, like an incision for which suturing twine cannot be found and that leaves a gaping wound that will not heal.

Despite Peter's dogged search for his origins, meeting with one woman who may be his grandmother and another who may be his half-sister only confirms that in post-Holocaust Europe identities must be fabricated to assuage the guilt of complicity or indifference to the fate of the Jews. Just as Peter's surname remains an uncertain or even fluid signifier, so the identity of the Europeans he meets is contingent on the changing necessity of political affiliation. Therefore, to claim familial relationship with Peter requires a decision to sympathize or identify with the fate of the Jews or of the Nazis. For example, Bertha Priludsky, who may or may not be his maternal grandmother, cannot turn Peter away because even as she sees him as a Jew and therefore not her daughter's son, she thinks, 'let this be my own private bit of *Wiedergutmachung* (reparation)' (*Fifth* 113, italics in text). But just as Peter discovers family lies instead of family romance, so the idea of reparation becomes a legal fiction – how can mass extermination be repaired or repaid? If reparations to Jewish survivors of the Holocaust became a legal fictional reality, financial compensation for their plundered property and murdered families could ameliorate neither their loss of family nor their endless nightmares or grieving. And so all the family stories told to Peter by Bertha and others cannot cohere or materialize into anything more than fragments of testimony to survival strategies that could not embrace the victims. Bertha's affectionate and comforting gestures are accompanied by revisionary and partial stories designed to give Peter a story of his own, but only 'close enough to the truth to allow her afterwards to remember what she had said, and in enough detail to give her time in between to decide what to leave out' (*Fifth* 118). Veering between unfathomable and shifting stories, Bertha replicates the silence and disorientation that separate Peter from the traumatic history he embodies and creates a shield that protects her from confronting it.

Peter testifies to the inadequacy of reparative family stories in an act of violence against the family photographs Bertha displays on her sideboard. Looking for evidence of his genealogy, 'He had the knack of making his eyes as selective as his mind' (*Fifth* 117). But instead of offering a trace of the boy's presence in the family, the photos reveal only faces of those who were always lost to him, of people who have died from their war wounds or have moved on; Peter's fantasies of family are buried by a visual tale of disconnection, dislocation, and decay: 'All dead and dung' (*Fifth* 117). This reference to T. S. Eliot's 'East Coker' from his World War II epic poem, *Four Quartets*, 'Dung and death', suggests interesting cultural connections about disconnection ('East Coker' 183). As an 'off-cut', Peter is cut off from his personal and historic past; his character cannot participate in the epic vision of history Eliot invokes. Moreover, since the history mythicized, demythicized, and remythicized in Eliot's epic poem is about *olde* England and newly besieged Britain, we are reminded of Peter's very modern and very troubled place in any saga of British/English continuity. It doesn't matter whether or not Eliot is yearning for a conciliatory relationship to the past or one that's more on edge, more discomforted, because the poet's relationship to England/Britain is one that Peter can never claim. Part of what is so interesting about Gershon's invocation of Eliot is that he fit comfortably in his conversion not only to Anglo-Catholicism but also to the family of Englishness, whereas Peter will never have the pleasure.[20]

Neither will Peter be able to reclaim a German identity. This latter disorientation is confirmed by Bertha's confession that she told her daughter Heidi that her son was dead rather than have him committed to the Führer as homage to the Nazi cause. Of course the subjects of Bertha's family photos are not of dead Jews, but rather of Germans whose roles as bystanders or perpetrators cannot be verified because they are now as buried as the past they represent and thus remain beyond judgment. The realities represented by these photos are several times removed from Peter's and can neither bear traces of his history nor serve as a 'memory cue' to connect 'image and referent', as Marianne Hirsch describes the use of Holocaust photographs ('Surviving Images' 223). It is in the very lack of such traces, however, that Bertha's photographs constitute Peter's reality. The referent is the absence of Peter, the fact that, as a viewer, he is a witness to Germany's *Jewless* story of its past:

> He brought the legs of the chair down on the sideboard, among the photographs. Now he understood what Barbara had meant, when he had asked

her why she had not held on to anything which she had brought away with her from home, and she had answered that it was indecent to cherish things in a world where people made lampshades out of human skin. It was indecent of his Oma to cherish Heidi's photograph after coming between her and himself.

As he pulled the chair back it drew with it some of the photographs, swept them on to the carpet; they landed on top of each other, breaking some of the glass. He stamped on them, as one stamps out the first sparks; putting a hand out to steady himself he shook the sideboard ... knock[ing] down a Dürer etching from the wall. Seeing his inner chaos manifesting itself about him, to get away from it he fled from the house. (*Fifth* 118–19)

Hirsch finds that photographic traces 'underscore the material connection between past and present' that is confirmed 'by the witness who recognizes it' ('Surviving Images' 224). Peter's rage, however, expresses the opposite: where the witness recognizes the material *disconnection* between past and present ('Surviving Images' 224). When the Dürer etching falls, like Peter, we are reminded of Barbara's observation: how the Third Reich travestied Germany's cultural heritage by mutilating the Jews and despoiling their cultural contributions by transforming them into Nazi degenerate artifacts. That the Dürer etching falls also suggests the subversion of the artist's acutely critical work by those who would rather hide from the ghastly truths of the Reich.

Though the narrative gestures towards merging the two identities Holocaust survivors would find antithetical, Gershon is not appealing to an idea of reconciling or restoring German Jewish identity. Instead, her novel questions whether a unified and valid German Jewish identity was ever anything but an illusion. As all of Gershon's exiled characters learn, in its destruction of their families, Germany is where homelessness and wandering became their identity and an unending yearning for family reunion became their character. Assuming a shaping reality of their own, the experience and identification with severed feelings and destroyed lives acknowledges an irrevocable break in Jewish generation, where access to European Jewish culture has been lost along with its agents and actors. For so many of Gershon's characters, these losses lead to fantasies of union that without family continuity become transgressive, not only sexually as in her other fictions, but historically and affiliatively. As Peter searches for his identity, veering between Jewish or German identity, his desire to belong overwhelms their historical distinctions. His is the only lens through which we can view those he encounters and make any judgments about their real or imagined relations. Though the neo-Nazi agents who contact Peter are convinced he is Hitler's son and a pure Aryan heir who can restore the Reich, the novel's ending leaves us uncertain. For one thing, Dr. Buchholtz and a man called Morry, two of the German men who have been tending Peter, suddenly claim to be Mossad agents (Israeli Intelligence). As it is superimposed on the question of Peter's identity, this plot move and the role of agent intensify the novel's concerns with relationships between identity and agency. Though Buchholtz and Morry mock Peter's insistence on his Jewish identity and counter any evidence he draws from his odyssey to Germany, their oblique language and sardonic tone – 'Let's say that it suits us to believe that you are who we say you are' – magnifies the ambiguity of the boy's identity, leaving Peter and the reader in unresolved suspense (*Fifth* 155). That these men have been acting as both German and Israeli agents multiplies the overdetermined meanings of *double agent*. Added to the conventional meanings of spies or secret agents who have switched allegiances or who work undercover is the punning and question of *agency*, a combination we often see in the actions and dual identities of the agent who operates as a tool or weapon in a struggle for justice and/or power. The two men who take Peter to join their mission at the end exploit his great desire to be Jewish so that he will agree to be a decoy or another double agent in the capture of Adolf Eichmann. Whether Peter is actually Jewish or German, his desire to be Jewish and his role in capturing Eichmann deflate both neo-Nazi ideology and its projected consequences. Either way, he would be assisting the Israeli cause to use Eichmann to assert the Jewishness of the Nazis' crime against humanity. But just as there is no knowledge of his origins available to Peter or to the reader, so the open ending defies the construction of a solution. As readers are positioned to consider the narrative logic and viability of each identity, not just German and Jewish, but Nazi and Jewish, and thus engage in acts of balancing and assessing the viability of each one, we violate the value systems of both perpetrator and victim. For the Nazis, such equal opportunities would be tantamount to negating the supremacy of Aryan identity, producing, in effect, a kind of interpretive miscegenation. For Jews, endowing both identities with equal weight erases the guilt of the Germans and innocence of victims.

Whether Peter is German or Jewish remains an open question at the end. Peter's agreement to serve the Israeli mission marks his identification with Jews while he goes along as a Nazi. As imaginatively posited poetic justice, this performance would suggest that the Nazis' defensive creation of the slippery figure of the Jew has come back to haunt its creator. In the logic of Nazi antisemitism, the poisonous often unidentifiable Wandering Jew had to be classified and indelibly marked in order to be controlled and eliminated. If Peter is Jewish, then his disguise as the Führer's son and his role in capturing a captain of the Nazi death industry confirms the Jew's dangerously amorphous character. If he is German, then his induction into the Jewish cause is a betrayal of the Fatherland but confirmation of another antisemitic myth: the protocol to take over the world in the name of Zion. Of course this latter myth is a mirror of Hitler's plan for world conquest and domination. What these shifting alternatives confirm for Gershon's novel is its representation of a different kind of Jewish slipperiness and its defeat of the intractable ideology of the Third Reich. The combination of the novel's open ending, its multivalent, and insoluble debate about Jewish identity in the face of the Holocaust parallels a paradoxically steadfast Jewish discourse. As Benjamin Harshav describes it, Jewish discourse is 'argumentative, adversary, contrarian' (48). It answers 'a question with a question or with an example, anecdote, or parable rather than with a direct, logical reply ... [I]t was not the overall story or the logical continuity of a text but the imaginary coherence of the represented universe as a whole that guided the discourse' (48).

3
Dramas of the Kindertransport and Its Aftermath

Diane Samuels relates that the fiftieth anniversary of the Kindertransport inspired many people who had ... remained silent about it all their lives ... to identify themselves, finally facing an event that represented a watershed moment, a time when many of them turned their backs on family, religion, and country for a chance to live. It was as if a dark national secret had come to light. (Quoted in Rob Pratt np)

Born in Liverpool in 1960 and educated in the city's Jewish schools, Diane Samuels found herself an outsider for the first time when she was at Cambridge University. Here she confronted 'an English context' that made her 'feel like a foreigner because the vocabulary of [her] world and culture [were] very different to the English one' (Lyndon, 'Speaking' 20). Her study of history shaped her playwriting career that has always examined social and historical issues. In her author's note for the Playbill of the Vaudeville Theatre's 1996 production of *Kindertransport*, she recalls three incidents that led her to write the play. The first was a confidence shared by a friend about the survivor guilt she felt she inherited from her father's experience of the Kindertransport. The second, by another friend, was her mother's revelation at the father's funeral that she had been a prisoner in a concentration camp. 'The third was the ashamed admission by a fifty-five year old woman on a documentary about the Kindertransport, that the feeling she felt most strongly towards her dead parents was rage at their abandonment of her' (Playbill np).

Samuels's *Kindertransport* links the anxieties produced by severed family ties to the accretion of internalized pressures to identify with Britain, the rescuing nation. Performed expressionistically, this linkage reveals itself as the moment of departure and rupture shares the stage with its traumatic effects twenty years later. On one side of the stage we see the adult refugee Evelyn and her daughter Faith enacting tensions forged by twenty years of suppressing the Holocaust past and Jewish identity. On the other side, we witness the child Eva and her mother Helga as they prepare for the child's departure that will never heal.[1] Enacting a tableau of traumatic loss and repression, the two pairs of figures embody and express the traces of lost family and cultural ties.The few boxes situated on a bare stage compress all that has been left behind in order to survive adaptation to a British identity and culture that perceives itself as normative and even redemptive.

In addition to portraying the psychological costs of these anxieties for its female characters, the play centers on their consequences for the place and meanings of Jewish identity and culture in Britain. Samuels translates this adaptation as a dilemma created by a complex of silences that drives her to ask, how can we narrate a past that is being repressed or even resisted? Choosing drama, that is, performing rather than telling, she enacts the idea expressed by playwright/editor/critic Sonja Lyndon that 'playwriting is a form of public speaking' and designed 'to sway a large group of people at one intense sitting' (Lyndon 20).[2] She reports, 'When people cried at *Kindertransport* I realized, "I'm not alone with these feelings" ... For me there is something about the private becoming collective, the intimate made epic' (Lyndon 21). The way the private becomes collective in this play is to focus on women's intergenerational relations where domestic life encompasses and engages a history of being dislodged from the originary mother–daughter relationship. Exercising the power of her historical perspective, in *Kindertransport*, Samuels stages the repercussions of both British and Jewish post-Holocaust memory and silence on one and two generations of women.

Kindertransport concerns three mother–daughter relationships and transports its female protagonist from the anxious foreshadowings of the Holocaust in Europe to the plucky ordinariness of middle-class English life that prevailed, even during the war, and was presided over by women. Whatever its class differences, the nation's intrepid resilience is identified as the gendered hallmark of ordinary life during the war that threatened Britain's independence and marked its Empire for extinction. Nine-year-old Eva Schlesinger is sent by her parents to the relative safety of Manchester, England, from Germany, where a legalized antisemitism foreclosed the Jews' ability to live an ordinary life anywhere. Unlike most of the actual children who never saw their parents again, Eva meets her mother after the war, replaying the trauma of separation to show the prolonged and internalized effects of the racism that underwrote the Holocaust.[3] As dramatized here, this trauma is gendered as a mother–daughter interdependence that is fractured by their racialized identities. Based on Samuels's research and interviews, Eva's adoptive mother, Lil, resembles many British women who took in Jewish children and their often baffling Jewishness, but in Samuels's interpretation, despite a caring nature, Lil also participates in the trauma of a racialized separation and its relation to the pressures of a dominant British culture on Jewish identity.[4]

As though in response to this overdetermined set of Jewish and British maternal relations, Evelyn's daughter Faith disinters her mother's buried European Jewish identity and cultural traces, and the playwright gives them a living presence by dramatizing them as an ongoing identity crisis for Britain and its Jews. That this crisis is relevant to British subjectivity today is shown as Eva, the anxious Jewish refugee girl, shares the stage with her adult, nervously assimilated British self. Even twenty years later, Evelyn is so haunted by her oppressive past that it seems as though victory over Nazi domination has not only been costly to Britain but also to the Jews whose security is won at the cost of open Jewish expression. If Samuels is writing at a time when women playwrights have increasing access to production, her characters perform a doubly internalized constraint – as women and as Jews. We see this living but uncertain legacy in Evelyn's emotional paralysis, which is acted and projected everywhere on stage. The hidden objects and persistent presence of Eva and her mother tell us that the volatile, not so reserved Jewish past presses urgently on possibilities for Jewish women's self-determination. In turn, the turbulent Jewish past is shown to exert pressure on reconciling Britain's masculinized memory of its heroic imperial power and women's domestic roles in the nation's heroic ability to nurture others.

Evelyn's effort to feel safe in her constructed English identity and family suppresses but expresses the trauma of escaping the Holocaust and of embracing Englishness.[5] Choosing to be adopted by her English foster mother marks a definitive step in acquiring English middle-class homeliness and denying her Jewishness. Most definitively, she breaks the chain of Jewish tradition by rejecting her Jewish birth mother who survives the Holocaust. As a convert, she cannot, according to Jewish law, be the matriarchal bearer of Jewish identity. But despite her total identification as an Englishwoman, despite her baptism and altered identity papers,[6] Evelyn's Jewish identity and forced exile are staged as inextricable reminders of an intractable vulnerability. The audience sees this vulnerability in Evelyn's chain smoking; even her clipped English speech and compulsive house cleaning register as tics, disclosing her obsessive efforts to erase the past and perfect the self she has manufactured but whose credulity she doubts. Reinventing herself does not integrate her into a British narrative of national continuity and identity; it does not recreate a pretraumatic subjectivity or effect a post-Holocaust healing; and it does not create a cultural hybridity. Unlike postmodern writers and critics, who feel that the self may be no more or less real than a convincing performance, this play will not privilege aesthetic imagination as solace. In fact, the idea that identity is a performance that can satisfy as an expression of aesthetic imagination is questioned by the anxiety with which Evelyn's gentile womanhood is performed. Regardless of how successful we may assume Evelyn's passing to be in her social and personal spheres, her desperate mimicry of an ordinary British housewife and mother marks her as teetering between assimilation and alienation. Her impersonation of Englishness never fails to remind us of her displacement, her history of rupture, and imminent, unmitigated violence.

If a significant departure of theatrical performance from literary texts is the living presence or embodiment of the imaginary, then *Kindertransport* enacts and exposes the emotional and cultural costs of imagining the danger that Jewish assimilation is always incomplete, unstable, and vulnerable. It is as though the anxieties that drive assimilation have backfired. Regardless of success, fears of yet another rejection by the dominant culture prevail as a displacement that cannot be ameliorated by historical change or political safety. No matter how nurturing Lil is, what Evelyn expresses are impoverished emotional resources that not only foreclose her own performance of motherhood but also threaten to implode and cause this assimilated refugee woman to disintegrate. Richard Hornby theorizes that the 'special, magical feeling that we experience in the theatre is the result of our awareness that there is so much that can go wrong, that a performance always teeters on the brink of disaster, yet at the same time seems so solid, so tangible' (99). Applying this proposition to *Kindertransport* encourages us to see and to feel that the very nature of theatrical performance, its potential for 'disaster', intensifies the sense of danger Evelyn feels. In turn, this reading of the character is complicated by the demand on the actress who plays her, for she must convey anxiety while restraining its expression to reflect the Jewish woman's acculturation to a British style of reserve.

Evelyn's passing as gentile can also be viewed as a successful defensive strategy because it destabilizes all those categories that have fixed Jews and Jewish identity so as to contain or control their slippery differences. As Linda Schlossberg notes, 'passing ... disrupts the logics and conceits around which identity categories are established and maintained'.[7] But in addition to their chameleon-like fluidity, Jews have also been accused of constituting an equally dangerous and essential core of difference that includes the gendering of Jewishness. Whereas Nazi ideology constructs the Jewish male as a depraved and diseased sexual predator, the Jewish woman is an overpowering and poisonous seductress. In traditional patriarchal societies, women's sexuality is concealed by modest dress and deportment, but, in Nazi antisemitism, the Jewish woman's sexuality is doubly venomous for both its concealment and imagined transparency. This combination of invisibility, visibility, and intractability would make disguise or passing even more insidious in the imagination of the resistant culture, conjuring up the specter of monstrousness once again. In effect, such demonizing may explain so many of the Nazis' bizarre efforts to determine Jewish identity.[8] The monster they had created had usurped their power to terrorize. It is this imagined perception of an essentially fiendish Jewishness, especially as it evolved into the experience of persecution and rejection, that challenges current theoretical claims about racial passing. However white and assimilated the Jews may appear, however docile the Jewish woman, their fearfulness and Nazi eugenics only reinforce 'the cultural logic that the physical body is the site of identic intelligibility'.[9]

Evelyn's nervously complete assimilation questions two related claims for the destabilization that passing effects: that 'the process and the discourse of passing interrogate the ontology of identity categories and their construction' and that this process and discourse challenge assumptions 'that some identity categories are inherent and unalterable essences' (Ginsberg 4). Nowhere is this questioning more apparent than in the play's performance, where the reality of an actress impersonating the fictional character of Evelyn who is passing suggests not fluidity but the historically unalterable ontology of Jewishness. In order to succeed, the actress must show Evelyn's doubts about the success of her passing as an ordinary English housewife and, by inference, her underlying Jewishness. As Ernst van Alphen suggests, acting may very well mock the 'obsession with authentic vision by having the events represented by acting, the quintessential art of feigning, faking, cheating, and pretending. It is as if art itself is suspect in the face of the cultural need for authenticity' ('Caught by Images' 99).

With a panoply of Jewish historical references that unsettle the play's debt to the more generic themes and tropes of modern and postmodern theater, Samuels also encourages the audience's doubts and anxieties about Anglo-Jewish assimilation. In turn, these doubts are reinforced by the play's associations of a modern tolerant Britain with Germany's past and present. Gently prodding Eva to leave Germany, Helga says of England: 'They don't mind Jews there. It's like it was here [Germany] when I was younger' (*Kindertransport* 9). This statement juxtaposes three time frames and two listeners: it offers a warning to the audience in the present about the reassurance offered to Eva in 1939 by referring to an earlier era. Like a palimpsest of Holocaust memory, in this juxtaposition the lukewarm 'don't mind' suggests ironically that an omnipresent antisemitism lurks in the background of all places where Jews seem to be welcome, places that at any time can turn into a lethal threat. Helga's reference to her own youth conjures up a specifically ambiguous German past that by the time of Eva's childhood has come to represent the condemned future of Jewish regeneration. But instead of a successful escape, Evelyn has recreated a version of this lethally layered past, and this repetition reinterprets it for modern audiences. By burying the few traces of her Jewish identity in a box in her store room, Evelyn creates a fetish as a memorial to her childhood. The knowledge that the objects are safe provides her with the evidence that she is too; that she will remain safe is guaranteed by not disturbing the box of mementos. Not viewing them also keeps the past at a safe distance. The present will not become infected with the shockwaves of the past; in their static, untouched state, the objects also represent a wish to be untouched by change. Evelyn's relationship to the mementos of her childhood is unlike that theorized and observed by D. W. Winnicott, the British psychoanalyst, as transitional objects. Where transitional objects serve to comfort the child into an acceptance of separation from the parent and engagement with the external world, Evelyn's 'objects of the last moment' represent a journey 'on the long way to encountering trauma', the trauma of permanent separation and loss (Korte 120). Evelyn is unlike the Kinder who invested change in the objects they could bring with them and that were used to remember the past. Whereas for them, 'the affect that is tied to the image or object...become aids to mourning', Evelyn not only represses the affect once invested in her mementos, but never mourns (Korte 112).

The distance Evelyn creates from her childhood can be viewed as an ironic metaphor for her emotional reconstruction of Jewish imprisonment. Burying the fragments of her past all together resonates with the Nazi imprisonment and mass burial of Jews. Her act also evokes an even more distant and English past – the medieval expulsions of Jews. But Evelyn stops short of performing a symbolic act of historical conflation or of purging or destruction. Because her papers materialize as only partially visible to the audience, they serve metonymically to suggest the absent presence of her Jewish identity and past. And while these props signify an entire 'dramatic world', marking its fictionality and relationships between 'actor/character and mise-en-scène', their historical referentiality draws attention to the fragmented world that Evelyn inhabits.[10] As though suspended in resistance, in this play, the Jewish past of persistent persecution may be buried alive, torn up, and discarded, but not so completely that questions and challenges about the possibility of Jewish recuperation and revival are foreclosed. In fact, these questions and challenges hang in the air of the stage, as though they are part of the set design.[11]

The play is designed so that the stage is often divided between scenes from Evelyn's past as Eva and her present, in effect uniting her character as mother and daughter. Such a set design performs and challenges Evelyn's dual mindset and identities with the presence of her historical past. Reflecting her inability to escape the past, this stage set also performs a combination of what Dominick LaCapra calls 'historical' and 'existential trauma' (*History and Memory* 47). In Kindertransport, historical trauma would refer to the children's transport while existential trauma would denote their human psychological development through stages of separation and individuation. Though LaCapra warns against critics conflating the two types of trauma, as Sue Vice argues, 'in Holocaust literature it is often precisely their overlap that constitutes [trauma's] most striking and destabilizing feature' (Vice, 'Trauma' 100). We can see this overlap in many Holocaust narratives that combine evocations of a historical incident with fantasy that conveys a psychological haunting.[12] For audiences of *Kindertransport*, the role playing of the actresses calls attention to the impact of historical and existential trauma on Evelyn as well as the cultural and psychological shaping of the performance of her character. The more convincing the actress's performance, the more we are able to see and understand Evelyn role playing herself as an assimilated British woman. At the opposite end of the stage is a performance that serves as an unsettling projection of the childhood self contained within her. Unlike role playing within a role, as in Hamlet's feigned madness, this split exposes the perils of performing an assimilated reserved English self while the assertively distinctive Jewish self insists on being represented. A victim of the traumatic effects of antisemitism, the Jewish self reflects how it is deflected by but contained within the assimilated self. In turn, the internalized antisemitism of Evelyn's assimilated selfhood reinforces the tremulous nature of Anglo-Jewish culture by positioning Eva as fearful Jewish Other. The rhetorical effect of performing this split is to keep the audience in a tense relationship with Eva and Evelyn. If we feel defensively estranged as a way of warding off their combined anxieties, and because we may or may not wish Evelyn to embrace her Jewish self, we also cannot feel 'secure as to who the character really is'.[13]

Instead of representing the possibility of a total schism, characters from the past and present intertwine, as we hear when Eva or Helga seems to respond to something Evelyn or Faith says. The reverse also occurs, with Evelyn or Faith seeming to respond to Eva or Helga. This temporal and spatial interweave is also made dramatically visible when, for example, Act Two begins with Evelyn sitting in the attic surrounded by Helga and Eva. These designs convey not only the self-questioning tensions of the plot but also Evelyn's repressions. Together, these designs produce a certainty that the story of Britain's wartime benevolence and Evelyn's invented persona are resisted by Eva's uncertainty. Such resistance begs another tense question: whether Britain's wartime narrative required Eva to become Evelyn. In response, this play insists that Evelyn cannot abandon that part of herself which is Eva. Just as the name Eve, with its Biblical resonance, is part of the name Evelyn, so it might seem that a generative Judaism, dependent on Jewish maternity, still survives. But as the question continues to haunt the answer, the past remains unresolved while it serves as an incitement to remember. As scenes from the past and present cut each other off, preventing closure, they suggest a persistent traumatic disorder that is sustained by Evelyn's frantic measures to maintain a clearly defined identity through amnesia. The result is a complex destabilization: of Evelyn's character, of a redemptive myth of British stability and safety, and of the women's narrative of a regenerative Jewish family life and culture. This destabilization becomes climactically evident halfway through the play when we learn that Helga survived and came to England to claim her daughter. Her efforts to reunite and thus restore the Jewish family and the culture it represents are futile, however, in the face of Eva/Evelyn's rejection. But if Helga is made to disappear from Eva's life and the play by this rejection, she remains present nonetheless. Her presence is felt in the play's continuing rehearsal of the traumatic separation of mother and child, including a scene where Eva must leave her adoptive mother, Lil, to be evacuated to the safer countryside. Lil's assumption of the maternal role and experience of separation cannot, of course, encapsulate the anxieties and sense of loss experienced by mothers of the Kinder. Though we intuit these feelings in the brief scenes featuring Helga, because the focalized consciousness remains that of Eva/Evelyn, the full range of those maternal feelings is mediated mostly through Evelyn's emotional turmoil. The play does not, for example, dramatize the kinds of letters most Kinder received until their parents were either able to emigrate or were sent to their deaths. As one Kinder, Ester Golan, reports about such letters from her own mother,

> The mother tries as best as is possible, in spite of the distance, to guide her growing up daughter, growing up in a strange world and among strangers, with words that were chosen with the utmost care. Did the daughter understand the deeper meaning written under such extreme circumstances? This is doubtful. For her capacities at her young age were not up to such strain. ('Power of Letters' 1)

In tandem with the play's shifting chronologies, its repetitions of mother–daughter loss suggest that Evelyn's self-constructed plot 'is a traumatized text whose narrative voice starts, affirms, lurches, breaks off', but whether it 'laments', as Carol Zemel notes of Roman Vishniac's photographs, remains an open question for Evelyn and for the audience ('Z'chor' 79). Diane Samuels formulates this question as follows: 'What is the cost of survival? What future grows out of a traumatized past?' (*Kindertransport* vii). The 'cost' of Evelyn's suppressions and of absorbing and normalizing the Holocaust is apparent in her daughter Faith's bursts of anger at being disinherited from her mother's past – 'the deeper meaning'. If these outbursts as well as the play's parallel and cross-temporal structure signal the recurring feeling that characterizes Holocaust trauma, then it may just be that Holocaust memory cannot be laid to rest or worked through. As we shall see in other texts, this unhealed wound is the legacy of the First to the Second Generation survivor. Constantly jarring our senses and consciousness, like short-circuited and jump-started memories of trauma, scenes from her past seem to ignite the story of Evelyn's struggle in the present. Ernst van Alphen, who has pondered the ethics of imagining the Holocaust, writes:

> Trauma is failed experience, and this failure makes it impossible to voluntarily remember the event. This is why traumatic reenactments take the form of drama, not narrative. Drama just presents itself, or so it seems; narrative as a mode implies some sort of mastery by the narrator, or the focaliser. ('Caught by Images' 102)

If, as many argue, the intrapsychic nature of trauma defies linear logic or external referents, Samuels's play dramatizes the effects of having internalized systematic dehumanization and its coordinate in this play – de-Judaization.

We can see these effects tracked from Eva's experience leaving her mother and traveling to an emotionally precarious safety – her arrival as the gentile Evelyn. The earlier experience is staged as disrupted bits of memory, traveling like Eva, and bouncing from one point of Evelyn's consciousness to another. As these affective and thematic resonances jostle each story, connecting and disconnecting them, the dramatic effect involves the audience as more than spectators or eavesdroppers. As we work to understand this narrative instability, the play insists that Evelyn's struggle to hide the past and her Jewish identity designates them, not solely as her very own trauma and not as a postmemory that has been transmitted to a Second Generation to become part of a public or collective Jewish or British commemoration. Instead, the play argues for a vexed combination, as an insistent challenge to Evelyn's self-consciously constructed Englishness and to audience response. For rather than assume the audience's quiescent absorption of knowledge, Samuels is asking us to ask ourselves how we should face an unresolved and unforgiving Holocaust past.[14]

In *Kindertransport*, the traumatic Jewish past is a very dangerous foreign country. It threatens not only the characters in the European past but the safety of England. Scenes on Eva's train to England remind us of those victims being sent to their deaths in the other direction; as in W. G. Sebald's novels *The Emigrants* and *Austerlitz*, the sunny English setting is swathed in shadow and smoke. The past is also a place where imagination conspires with history and traumatic memory to defamiliarize archetypally ominous characters and places and to make safe spaces threatening. Such an ominous figure looms large and everywhere in several manifestations in *Kindertransport*. Called the Ratcatcher, he originates as a character in a German children's book entitled *Der Rattenfanger*, the prototype for the Pied Piper of Hamelin.[15] Diane Samuels describes him as follows:

> My vision of him is of a dark, shape-shifting being, definitely a Shadow figure who personifies deep, unspoken fears but is also charismatic and rather compelling, someone as much to lead a child into new, forbidden, exciting places as to lead them astray or into an abyss. Because he plays many characters in the play, he tends to be costumed in basic clothes over which he can wear his different uniforms. The actor playing him in the Soho production was blonde with blue eyes whilst Eva and Evelyn and Faith were all dark. I purposely do not describe him in the script because I want those who put on the play to use their imaginations with him. He can be whatever you want.[16]

Embodying a threat that extends from his origins in medieval folklore through his rendering as a symbol of Nazism, worst of all, he is never defeated or even demystified. But instead of being confined to a fairy tale or representing some kind of ineffably monstrous or abstract evil, he offers a test of historical realities. His omnipresence and omniscience and the fact that he is also the only male presence in the play call attention to the absence of any fathers from the beginning to the end of this play. Unlike fairy tales, where fathers reappear or transmute from foolish to wise men, their total absence in this play underscores the drama's gendered historical analogue: the real power of the Nazis to brutalize Jewish men into powerlessness and helplessness, men who cannot prevent the loss of their children. In short, any suggestion of 'once upon a time' is challenged by the specific historic moment. Moreover, where many plays are performed in and as real time, in this Holocaust play, a medieval threat suggests that the progression of the present is only real as it also performs the past, not just as a coda, but as invading the present. It is in this sense of mutated history that the omnipresence of the Ratcatcher suggests that the modernity in which the Jews are caught is itself monstrous. Despite his fragmented and shadowy appearances, the overdetermined and uncanny specter of the Ratcatcher also offers a sense of historic continuity. As he goes from place to place with his duplicitous mission, he conjures up images of the pre- and anti-Enlightenment, archetypal, antisemitic version of the Wandering Jew, blurring distinctions between past and present and hovering always between terrors that can be identified and those that remain unknowable.

Linked as well to Evelyn's hidden story, the Ratcatcher also hovers over the entire play structurally, from start to finish, over all the action, dialogue, props, and spaces in which the characters move. The very first stage direction, before the characters speak, is the playing of 'Ratcatcher music', a device that gives the audience symbolic access to Evelyn's persistent but hidden fears by correlating external danger with atmospherically induced psychological effect (*Kindertransport* 1). The first words he speaks declare that however mythically the terrors of the past are depicted, its real dangers haunt the unwary present: 'I will search you out whoever wherever you are' (15). The tale's meanings are dramatized as overdetermined when Helga reads it to Eva at the same time that Faith discovers it in the attic storeroom and reads it to herself. After Helga read lines from the story, it is Faith's summary that reveals its meanings in her mother's and grandmother's history. Referring to it as ' "The Ratcatcher ever-ready in the shadows"', Faith recounts the story as a grim childhood lesson:

> All the parents say, 'If you're not good the Ratcatcher will come and get you'. But the children don't listen. And he comes out of the dark night with his spiky nails and razor eyes and tempts them with sweets. And they're so naughty that they follow him into the abyss. (29)

For ordinary times, this story can easily be read as an allegory of growing up, of the terror and thrill of separation, individuation, and facing the unknown. Samuels ascribes the play's global popularity to 'the universal dilemma and contradiction' of 'separation' when parents want to save their children from danger and children 'would say, no' ('Q & A Exclusive' np). But the play's historical frame incorporates the temptations of a different developmental odyssey, one that rescues the child from Jewish danger into a safe but problematic British identity. We see this in the reference to 'whoever' and 'wherever' which in combination suggests the omnipresent peril of passing or conversion.

The evidence for the dangers of being tempted into Britishness as a safe haven is consolidated in the character of the woman rescuer – Lil. These dangers coalesce when Evelyn accuses Lil of being a 'Child-stealer', a slur several times over that conflates the male Ratcatcher with an archetypal female figure (*Kindertransport* 62). First of all, the accusation highlights the association of the name Lil with the demonic Lilith, Adam's original mate who transgressed several times over: by uttering the ineffable name of God, by insisting on being sexually dominant, and, most tellingly, who caused other women to miscarry, who murdered children in their cribs, and never had children of her own.[17] Too close for comfortable coincidence in relation to the biblical Eve, the association of Lil with Lilith also suggests a competition for women's cultural primacy, with Lil and Lilith defying the relevance of Jewish identity and possibilities for continuity while Eva or Eve represents the matrilineal imperative of Jewish identity. In reference to the Ratcatcher, the opprobrium, 'Child-stealer', indicts the woman by association with the masculine fiend. For Lil's very acts of rescue and mothering encourage the Jewish child to leave her past behind. In a response that associates assimilation with trauma and resonates with all the conversions that did nothing to save German Jews, Eva succumbs to the temptation to assuage the painful memory of parental loss with the solace of forgetting her Jewish past and identity. But instead of being figured as self-nurturing, forgetting assumes an ominous cast, as the persistently shadowing presence of the Ratcatcher suggests. Leaving the mother behind to an unknown and precarious fate or being separated from parents by British refugee employment policies might very well produce the child's guilt, especially as the foster mother becomes predominant. We see such guilt emerge in a statement by one of Karen Gershon's witnesses in her collective autobiography, *We Came as Children*: 'Gradually, as my foster mother took over my affections – and I welcomed this – my own mother's visits were still an agony but now because of the guilt feelings they aroused in me' (56). When Eva buries her own origins, her Jewish character and Jewish mother disappear, not to be memorialized, but, like those children who follow the Pied Piper into 'the abyss', the gentile Evelyn inhabits – an abyss of discarded memory.

Whether alternative choices and destinies are viable for the Jewish child refugee is scripted as questions about Jewish continuity, in its specifically British setting, but also beyond. In its deeply enmeshed plotting and figuration, the play casts Eva's Jewish mother Helga as much of a 'Child-stealer' as Lil and of course in competition with Lil for the Jewish child. The combination illustrates the pain intensified by the conflicted temptations of assimilation and Jewish continuity. Helga's effort to lure Eva away from England questions the possibility of healing the trauma of their personal rupture as well as the collective trauma of Jewish dislocation. Combining both, the

play's parallel stories align Helga's urgent pleas with the Ratcatcher's temptations and vengeance and the double bind that replicates British rescue. The
Jewish mother has driven her daughter out of one abyss – a death camp –
into one that promised shelter but with expectations that threaten the recuperation of a distinct and visible Jewish culture and identity. Associating the
Jewish mother with the Ratcatcher casts her as an emotional blackmailer,
exacting the same payment from her child as the British: loyalty and indebtedness. Like the parents in the original fairy tale, Helga's refusal to recognize
her own indebtedness to the British defeat of the 'rats' is linked to the final
loss of her child. Most problematic in Samuels's linkages is that of Helga's
character with antisemitic perceptions that undergird suspicions of the Jews
as unassimilable. As a fiercely avenging angel, the Jewish refugee mother
recalls the portrayal of Jewish women and men in European plays at the fin
de siècle who represent Judaism as a religion of vengeance in contrast to
Christianity as a religion of forgiveness.[18]

Yet Helga's character also challenges these associations by representing a
consequence of their antisemitic history: the Jewish victim.[19] The image of
the rat embodied in the identity of the Ratcatcher reflects Nazi propaganda
that characterized the Jews as poisonous vermin and parasites. His transfor-
mations also recall the imputation of Jews as wanderers whose 'markings
of Jewishness are ambiguous and multiple', and dangerous to any nation
because 'even Jews cannot always identify each other as such' (Erdman 48).
While we could easily worry about this conflation of Jews as victims and
villains, it also indicts an unforeseen effect of Nazi antisemitism. This is to
expose the process by which the Nazis inadvertently create the Jew as a mirror image or projection of their own monstrousness. Perhaps more startling
and more horrifying because the setting is not Germany, the specter of the
Ratcatcher in England on an English stage reminds us that the myth of a
homogeneous culture emplots the fear of immigrants as a parasitic infesta-
tion and how such fear becomes a plague in itself, victimizing its objects
even as it welcomes them. Samuels dramatizes the violence such xenophobic fear and dubious safety engender as the Ratcatcher's music plays in the
background while the older woman and her childhood self engage in a duel
that reconnects them:

EVA. He's coming.
EVELYN. Stop.
EVA. His eyes are sharp as knives.
EVELYN. Be quiet.
EVA. He'll cut off my nose.
EVELYN. He's not coming.
EVA. He'll burn my fingers till they melt.
EVELYN. You've not done anything wrong.
EVA. He'll pull out my hair one piece at a time.

EVELYN. You're a good girl.
EVA. Don't let him come. Please!
EVELYN. He won't come.
EVA. He will.
EVELYN. I promise. I won't let him. I'll do everything I can to stop him.
You'll see. You're with me now. He can't touch me. Do you understand?
I'm here. You're being looked after. I won't go away. I'll make it all
disappear. I'll get rid of him. He won't take you anywhere ever again.
(45–6)

Looming behind this dialogue, the Ratcatcher inspires a fantasy that enacts
not only the threat of Nazi violence but a replay of fears about abandoning the Jewish self to promises of innocence, forgiveness, and protection.
Evelyn's anxiety-ridden promise of protection in the dialogue above encapsulates the trauma of her mother anticipating the horrors that would befall
the Jews of Europe. The dialogue suggests a violent suture, with Evelyn playing the role of mother to herself as child. As Evelyn's promises evoke the
dangers she actually escaped, she also resonates with the remembered voice
of Helga, her own mother, reassuring the child Eva. This incorporation of
the memory of her own mother implies that instead of having successfully
abandoned her mother and her Jewish self, what is being played out here is
the unwilled rescue of her mother as she is manifest in Evelyn. In its presentation as imagined by Evelyn, the play rescues the Jewish mother who
will not be denied. In turn, Eva's voice revives the urgent pressure of fears
that no performance of maternal nurture or self-transformation can assuage.
Notice that even when Evelyn behaves maternally, attempting to allay the
child's fear, her final statements are so insistent, they only call attention to
the futility, the powerlessness underlying the mythic form of her promises.[20]
With no irony, these promises evoke a kind of hysteria or panic about the
threat of the Ratcatcher reappearing even in the safety of a British present, so
far removed from medieval persecution or the Holocaust. Every warning and
promise is overshadowed by our knowledge and Evelyn's suspicion that Eva's
fears have materialized, not in having experienced the Holocaust but in the
'cost' of her escape and rescue. As in the children's tale, the piper will be paid.

Unlike the Jewish mother or Jewish identity, the Ratcatcher cannot be
denied or forgotten; he cannot be relegated to myth or fairy tale or even
to the past, because he is present, like the dybbuk in Julia Pascal's play, in the
body and consciousness of Evelyn. The combination of her emotional paralysis and hysteria suggests that the humanity of the Jewish woman refugee
has been displaced by the horror of never being settled, with the result that
the stability that defines the traditional role of Jewish mother is also displaced. As with so many fictional and autobiographical narratives of rescue,
the displaced condition of the Kinder signifies a kind of devolution from the
human to an incompletely constructed category of being, more creature or

golem than man or woman. It is in this sense that the Ratcatcher combines features of all the characters in *Kindertransport*, but never achieves the status of a whole human character.[21] As his sinister presence materializes on stage, in his shadowy and shifting forms, he also subverts the quest plot of many myths or fairy tales. Instead of instigating a heroic rite of passage into knowledge of adulthood and community responsibility, he leads his young charges towards the death of knowledge and community. His temptations don't mold a hero or save the community; instead of the protagonist's victory over 'an enemy ... associated with winter, darkness, confusion, [and] sterility', he leads the children who represent the life and future of the community to the ultimate disappearance of both.[22] In *Kindertransport*, conventionally psychologized explanations of the dark forests and secret attics of our childhood tales no longer obtain. Fears that have been deemed fundamental to our human development, and have been attributed to the meanings of fairy tales, such as abandonment and projections of one's own aggressive desires or undesirable legacies, do not express individual psychologies in this Holocaust drama.[23] Such fears, even as they suggest the universality of human frailties, resonate differently and distinctly when the subject is the Holocaust. In Holocaust imaginings, dark forests and secret attics become perilous realities. In most fairy tales, as Jeanne Walker notes, 'risks involved in status change are frequently represented in symbols of death and resurrection', but Samuels's version of the Ratcatcher transforms the symbolic along with the possibility of benefiting from taking 'risks' (Walker 112). With their distinctively, historically bound emanations, the play presents shadowy stalkers from whom there is no escape, much less 'resurrection'.

Despite the historical realities of its context, the Holocaust past in this play and in Pascal's *Holocaust Trilogy* is not presented in a traditionally realist style that runs parallel to and is balanced with a myth of an English quotidian onto which realism has been grafted. But neither do these playwrights represent the Holocaust past in extremis – as outside of history, as sacralized or as an event that remains mystifying. Instead, in their expressionist styles, the overtly fantastic elements in their plays – Pascal's dybbuk and Samuels's Ratcatcher – highlight the acute historical extremes of the events that comprise the Holocaust. Yet Holocaust history in these plays is not left uncompromised. For audiences, both British and wherever these plays are performed, the Holocaust past has already been mediated through decades of public venues, producing varied responses that are filtered through continuing reportage, different memoirs about distinctive Holocaust sites and experiences, as well as other artistic representations and ongoing debate and interpretation. Perhaps in response to this mediation, Samuels and Pascal dramatize 'the question of knowledge; rather than offer knowledge of the Holocaust'; they reject the notion that they could recapture a Holocaust story and impart its 'truth'.[24] Incorporating the process of mediating knowledge through the plays' intricately woven tableaux, Samuels and Pascal remind us that no matter how we differentiate or combine stories of the Holocaust, they can never deliver the explanatory power we might like them to. Instead, their plays' coherence derives in part from their presentation of the history and emotional responses to the Holocaust past as fragmented. Both playwrights' versions of this history and response are always disrupted and unsettled. Samuels and Pascal also disrupt our efforts to make sense of the continuous flow of new information and testimony. As Michael Rothberg observes, many Holocaust memoirs reject 'the imposition of closure and meaningful wholeness' and therefore refuse to offer comfort to readers (226–7). Those writers he describes as 'traumatic realists', and Samuels and Pascal would be among them, 'undermine the conventions of storytelling without entirely forgoing narrative or its ability to document history' (226–7). For example, despite their representation of traumatic memory, their plays question the possibility of using such explanatory models as trauma and psychoanalytic theories to provide the comfort of making the incomprehensible horrors of the Holocaust accessible to our own intellectual and emotional responses as well as to our powers of identification and moral sensibilities. Instead, Samuels and Pascal use their dramaturgy to create and sustain a cognitive and emotional chasm between their characters' responses and ours. As Samuels shows us through the interlaced but conflicted emotional experiences and performances of Eva/Evelyn and Evelyn's daughter Faith, nothing about the Holocaust can be translated transparently into our already formulated feeling and knowledge, and what we learn from the play's spatial design, images, and dialogue will still leave a gap between what we see and hear and what we can know and feel. Even as these plays call for intense attention to their stagecraft and design, the conflicts enacted by the characters in the past, in the present, and between past and present are transferred to the irresolution audiences are made to feel between modes of Holocaust representation and history and experience.

For example, the play prods us not to abandon the anxieties and disjunctions of the Kindertransport story to more accessible literary psychological themes which fit so well – for example, the mother–daughter plot or a character's duality. Certainly, elements of the female *Bildungsroman* are evident in Faith's struggle for self-determination against the tide of her mother's and grandmothers' intergenerational conflicts. But we must also recognize that the dual and dueling dramas at opposite ends of the stage and the characters' parallel violent outbursts are driven by their brutal historical legacy. In effect, the two narratives and the split characters of Eva/Evelyn remain in an unresolved explanatory tension between history and women's individual psychological development. The women's desires for trust, maternal nurture, and for the encouragement to individuate are destabilized by their historical status as culturally dislocated and then expressed by the projections of Evelyn's unresolved fears and fantasies. The emotional power of these projections derives from the particularity of their historical circumstances. If

Evelyn will not recognize the historical realities of Eva and Helga and Faith's struggle to understand her historical legacy, their presence on the stage with Evelyn demands that the audience does. It is with this recognition that the audience becomes more than spectators; it participates in the characters' empowerment. Whatever explanatory power we find and relatedness we feel in ascribing the conflicts of Eva and Helga's relationship to the pressures of individual psychology, they are driven by Jewish history and culture.

Repeatedly, we see historical forces interfering with the mother–daughter plot. As Eva resists her mother's sewing lessons, we may be reminded of Faith accepting Evelyn's offer of cutlery and crockery, but choosing her own patterns. And while both daughters resist their mothers' help to face the unknown of living apart, another form of resistance is taking place. The mother–daughter plot of attachment and separation, of facing the psychologically precarious odyssey towards individuation, as we know it from literature and psychology, is jarred by the transmission of the Holocaust story. Instead of allowing the audience to relate to or identify with a major theme in western literature, the play presses into unfamiliar textual and historical space. Part of the unfamiliarity derives from the association of the attic space with unexpressed or repressed fears and desires – in short, a commonly designated trope for the unconscious. At another level, the store room in which the play explores the stresses of a young girl enduring exile and confinement resonates with the familiar story of Anne Frank. If the Franks' annex home turns into a dead end or trap, the attic storeroom in *Kindertransport* designates a displacement so radical that it questions Evelyn's frantic efforts to make a home anywhere or, like Anne Frank, to find 'refuge in the attic' writing her life (Frank 217). Any refuge in Evelyn's attic has been reserved for the objects of her past. Unlike Anne Frank, who went 'to the attic almost every morning to get the stale air out of my lungs', the air in Evelyn's attic is stale with neglect (Frank 193). With all the action and characters, past and present, confined to Evelyn's attic, the very idea and space of home have been hidden from view, like the objects and identity papers hidden there. Even at the end, when Faith and Evelyn reconcile and Faith exits with a box of her toys, instead of romanticizing nostalgic beliefs in a stable home and mother–daughter relationship, the play undercuts them with its final stage direction: 'The shadow of the RATCATCHER covers the stage' (*Kindertransport* 88). Like the restored sections of Anne Frank's *Diary*, this ending subverts any uplifting message that would comfort us.

The traditional principle on which middle-class British identity rests in Samuels's interpretation – a woman's creation of homeliness – lies beyond the horizon of the play, always out of reach. We never see the main part of the house, which would be metonymic for a secure British identity. Its absence, however, is highly suggestive in associating women's domestic roles with the stability and continuity of the nation's identity. The play's fragmented representation of home suggests that, despite victory over Nazism, the scars of battle have seeped into the heart of the nation. In its dramatic evocation, the idea of homemaking and homecoming are undercut by the Ratcatcher's shadow. As a stand-in for the shadow of the Holocaust, the omnipresence of the Ratcatcher effects an estrangement from any idea that a British home or homeland for Jewish refugees can be won by assimilating to a nurturing British identity. None of the Jewish characters can assume that their ordinary British home is a site of self-discovery or belonging. By extension, it is as though the Holocaust itself is not only a fearful memory of imminent destruction in this play but also a force that constitutes destabilization no matter what the Jewish character's location might be.[25] Holocaust history and memory have not only called assumptions about home and homeland into question, they dislocate any sense of selfhood. In this play, as Una Chaudhuri says of other modern dramas, 'otherness inhabits the discourse of home' (Chaudhuri 45). Here, otherness becomes so extreme, it is virtually erased. Unlike the crowded annex where Anne Frank creates a coherent sense of her developing self by writing, Evelyn's storeroom represents suppression; it stores rather than expresses the story she will not tell. The storeroom may be where her daughter Faith discovers her mother's story and past self, but as we might recall from Ibsen's play, *The Wild Duck*, such a space also represents a wilderness where even substantial clues cannot pave the way to resolution or reconciliation between past and present. In fact, Evelyn's hidden story also resonates with Britain's hidden story of the parental transport it rejected, and so suggests that both Evelyn's self-definition and Britain's destabilize each other. What is left is not at home, at rest or even located, but always in transit and always claustrophobic, an extreme interior space that lets in nothing from elsewhere.

As represented by the mother–daughter relationships in *Kindertransport*, the Jewish self veers between an 'expressionistic quest for personal liberation' from the past and the recovery of the self in that past (Chaudhuri 64). But neither quest can ever come to rest anywhere. Whatever emotional pain feels familiar to contemporary audiences in the depiction of Faith's war with her mother does not help us understand or prepare us for the perils of Eva's relationship with Helga. Although radically discontinuous from most of us, Eva's perils must be absorbed by Faith and us if we are to begin to understand the characters' attachment and alienation. The reverse is even more dramatically evident. The Holocaust in this play may very well remain in the realm of its mother–daughter stories, as Samuels insists. Nonetheless, the mother–daughter story cannot be translated either into a model for understanding the Holocaust determinants of Eva's failed relationship with Helga or be co-opted into an analogy or metaphor that has universal application. Whatever individual, cultural, or social psychology drives Faith and Evelyn apart but also allows them to heal may be shaped by Holocaust memory, but it has no bearing on the history that determines the irreparable rupture between Eva and Helga. Despite its antisemitic vicissitudes, Englishness is the safe state into which Faith is born, and its borders exclude the crises of Jewish history that drive Eva and Helga apart forever. It is in this sense of exclusionary boundaries that we can also read Evelyn's storeroom as hiding not only her story but containing that of Britain's other wartime story. In its extreme insularity, the exclusivity of Britain's oft-told tale becomes not only a national folktale but claustrophobic, eliminating the possibility of letting in the light of its Jewish history.

Instead, as historical and psychological literary plots perform together, the mother–daughter plot assumes the pallid complexion of the more historically unresolved story of Jewish survival and identity in Britain. On the one hand, the perilous state of Jewish survival is presented as an ironic combination of historical mutations and an insistent Jewish identity. On the other, Jewish survival in Britain must confront a British identity that, despite its claims to current multiculturalism, is provisional. This hesitation may offer one reason why Jewishness is so hard to integrate into British culture, which defines itself as the stable bulwark against such historical contingency as invasion. In this reading, Britain is a solid rock island, metaphorically suggesting its stabilizing rules of behavior. When Eva and the other Kinder invade England, their identities do not fit into British categories of acceptable identities. Even if Britain claims that its national culture is pluralistic, Eva has to be either Jewish or British; she can't be both. Within Evelyn's hysterical hold on her British identity lies the Jews' placelessness, their wandering, their designation as a nowhere people. The result in this play is a construction of the modern history of Anglo-Jewry as irremediably unstable, veering between accommodation and assimilation in a state of understated suspension. Alternatively, we can see how the trajectory of Jewish acculturation in Britain would sustain tensions between British styles of reticence and reserve and Jewish anxieties about their continued otherness. Here in this drama, there is ongoing intrusion and retreat, and fragmentation, not integration.

It is in the competing relationship between the play's fragmented structure, the characters of the past, and the struggling subjectivity and identities of the present that the performances of Eva and Helga suggest an unsettling dynamic suspension. In their tenuous states of being denied and their desperate insistence on survival, the characters of the child Eva and adult Evelyn suggest self-questioning possibilities for the fate of Jewish identity and culture in Britain. Embodying each other's losses, the two individual but entwined characters are ghostly remnants of the other and their combined status constitutes that of outsiders. In Samuels's play, the pressure on Eva to abandon her Jewish identity is considered a sign of progressive British culture. Unlike Jews who 'hang...on to the past', Christian Britain, Lil tells Eva, follows a Jesus who 'said that we needn't keep to the old laws any more. They had their day years ago' (*Kindertransport* 34, 33). Despite Lil's affectionate tone here, such supercessionist belief impugns Jewish practices as atavistic, recalling the censorious mission of British imperialism. But unlike other colonial subjects and despite their acculturation, the Jews' hold on their past could not be transformed except by expropriation or erasure. As Theresa in Pascal's play is erased in Guernsey, Evelyn finds a new life in England by superseding Eva. In Samuels's play, the child Eva simply disappears, never to be seen again. The shadows cast by the spotlight that holds our final glimpse of Theresa and the dimming lights that mark Eva's disappearance form a critical gloss on the story of Britain's rescue of Jewish refugees. Taking center stage, functioning more like actors than props or metaphors, these shadows develop a drama of their own. Both radically separate from and yet interwoven with a competing British narrative, the disappearing characters become sites of interpreting the consequences of the Holocaust and Holocaust memory and commemoration for the production of modern British culture. Precisely because drama presents an illusion of reality, that which seems to be real but which is also doubtful, it is a genre that can confront audiences with a story that has been taken to be true but about which we must now be disillusioned.

Of the play's many strands of suspense and suspended judgments, what remains questioned even at the end is whether the threatened, abject Jewish identity that defines the Jew's Holocaust past remains alive in the Anglo-Jewish woman's survival as a non-Jew. If we decide that Jewish identity has not survived, we are then left with the troubling suggestion that Eva's survival as Evelyn comes all too close to replicating the Nazis' efforts to destroy Jews as people and Jewishness as culture and identity. But even if this is so, the urgency of the issue of Jewish survival remains, and so the play leaves open whether the restoration of a distinctive Jewish culture and identity in contemporary Britain is possible. In her total rejection of Jewish culture and history, including the lessons of the Passover *Haggadah*, which Helga narrates as the story of 'how we survived and this is how we survive', Evelyn's adoption of Englishness certainly looks as though Jewishness may not be allowed into the portals of English identity (*Kindertransport* 52). But as the play ends, with Faith and Evelyn reconciled to each other and the past both torn up and absorbed, with Faith taking both the *Rattenfanger* book and the *Haggadah*, we are left with not knowing.

The past that ordered Eva's destruction survives not only as Evelyn's buried memory and defensive habits but also as a legacy of Jewish culture that her daughter will claim. We see how the past will not let go as Faith is intrigued by its hidden life and is inspired to keep it for herself. Her wish is to revive it in order to know how she is who she is as constituted by her maternal past. Discovering her inherited maternal identity not only revives the Jewish past but also replays its specifically historical trauma of Holocaust loss and rejection when Evelyn refuses to acknowledge herself as a Jewish mother who was an endangered Jewish child. For example, one cultural context of Samuels's play is a grand theme of English literature, the odyssey of innocent but abused childhood into adult disillusionment and adaptation. In this play, however, the trajectory towards disillusionment and adaptation is derailed by the disappearance of the Jewish child and woman and replaced by the endgame of the Holocaust – an itinerary designed not to disillusion but to destroy an entire people. We confront this historical and thematic revision as the adult gentile Evelyn in Samuels's play produces and directs the disappearance of the Jewish child Eva. Unlike Jewish victims who were deceived and robbed of agency, Evelyn is able to assert hers with a doggedness that conveys the sense of full knowledge of context and consequence. From Evelyn's perspective, the desired effect is to replace the traumatic story of death and destruction with an eternally safe British homeliness. But this effect is destabilized by her daughter Faith's need to know herself by reviving, perhaps restoring faith in her mother's story, the performance of which constantly interrupts that of Britain as a timeless safe haven.

As Samuels tells us in her 'Author's Note', 'Past and present are wound around each other throughout the play. They are not distinct but inextricably connected. The re-running of what happened many years ago is not there to explain how things are now, but is a part of the inner life of the present' (n.p.). This is a Jewish past that despite the almost total destruction of European Jews and their culture, despite its manifest presence in this play as bits and pieces – a children's book, a letter, a certificate – is a dynamic if ephemeral force, a complex character in itself, and one that must be reckoned with, even as it suggests the repetition compulsions and amnesia of trauma. One consequence of the intrusion of the traumatic past onto the ordinary present is that it serves as a disruption to the British plot, questioning the shape and fate of British liberalism and the formation of British character and culture after the Holocaust.[26] And while we might expect this disruption and questioning in Evelyn's character, it also applies to her daughter Faith and to the quintessential ordinary Englishwoman, Lil. Insistently, even as it is presented as attenuated and estranged, the Holocaust past is an obstacle that prevents the characters from developing unless it is acknowledged and integrated into the present. The very nature and legitimacy of Evelyn's Englishness remains unfulfilled and untenable without its Jewish historical ingredient, without the integration of the Jewish Eva into the Englishwoman. And though this integration may not stabilize Evelyn's identity, and may even suggest that it must remain betwixt and between Britishness and Jewishness, this is not the end of the story. As Evelyn's daughter Faith insists, her own character development is stalled unless her identity, that is, the genealogy of contemporary Britishness, is traced to its involvement with the Jewish past and refugees. This quest for knowledge represents a possible revision of the tale of the Ratcatcher: an odyssey from the fantasy represented by Evelyn's willed amnesia to historical truth. The lesson imparted by this revision may very well be that without the historically constructed Jew, the middle-class ordinary Englishness that Evelyn has adopted from Lil and that she would pass on to her daughter remains a myth, timeless but unreal.

Is it indeed possible to forgive and yet still remember? (Eilenberg, *Lucky Ones*, n.p.)

Rupture and reconciliation could easily serve as the subtitle of Charlotte Eilenberg's 2002 play, *The Lucky Ones*. Like *Kindertransport*, *The Lucky Ones* explores the effects of exile and adaptation by focusing on the responses of middle-aged refugees and their children. Eilenberg's opening scene, set in1968, marks that year of student-led revolutions in Europe and in the United States, the year of Enoch Powell's radical call for immigration restrictions, and, in the play, a middle-aged Kind's revolution of his own. Eilenberg was inspired to write the play by a family trip to accompany her father, an eighty-three-year-old refugee from Nazi Germany, to Berlin, where he had been invited to participate in ceremonies offering reconciliation along with commemoration. 'The four of us spent much of our time perplexed: over half a century later, what were we to make of these gestures of reconciliation?' (Foreword). Eilenberg wonders about the effects of escape from Germany and adaptation to Britain: 'how far would the desire to be a good – in this case – British subject, breed a necessary stoicism, and how far a self in denial of the rage and terror of an earlier helplessness? . . . And what kind of pressures might be put on the children to become . . . acceptable when the parents were not?' (Foreword). The playwright's brief becomes an investigation into an overlapping guilt, 'of the parent desperate for their child to get it right, and the guilt of the child who can never succeed' (Foreword). This combined desperation and guilt involves its transmission over three generations. But rather than track this guilt as a development over time, Eilenberg's three generations are all adults, whose 'helplessness', 'rage', and forms of adaptation have already shaped their characters. As Beth Mosenthal, the adult daughter of the aging Kinder, Bruno and Anna, bemoans, 'But what about me, and all those others, still feeling guilty for something we never did?' (*Lucky Ones* 84). As though in response to this overriding guilt, the play compresses the relations between the Kinder and their children into scenes of alternating repression and rebellious expression.

What is being dramatized throughout the play is the outward expression and enactment of internalized conflicts and anxieties that are the byproducts of the rescue experience that began decades ago but persist in relationships with other Kinder, their children, and a second generation German. Unlike Samuels's play, which enacts stages in the development and adaptation to the anxieties of separation, Eilenberg embeds the process in the drama of her characters' relationships. Just as we must infer the complex nature of this compressed process and the human relationships that respond to it, so we are left to interpret the play's expressive absences. For example, Eilenberg insists that the play is not so much 'about Jews and Jewishness than one about refugees' (Foreword). This assertion of absence is too enticing to take at face value, and so leads my investigation into questions about the place of Jews and of Holocaust memory in *The Lucky Ones*.

The play revolves around four middle-aged Kinder, now two married couples, who are embroiled in a debate about the sale of a country cottage they have co-owned for many years but which they have not used for a while. Hardly a birthright, in the hands of the refugees, the cottage in the New Forest becomes an ironically heuristic presence, charting the construction, progress, and stasis of historical memory. As Michael Billington notes, Eilenberg may have been influenced by Chekhov in using 'property as a source of tension' (np). While its setting evokes romantic images of English continuity and tradition, the refugees' use of the cottage as a vacation getaway calls attention to a borrowed identity and transience. Indeed, the mythical valences of the New Forest, evoking that foundational narrative of Englishness – the adventures of King Arthur – only draw our attention to the chronic dislocations of the Jewish refugees: 'Britisher[s] with a funny accent' who can neither 'go home' again nor make England a 'dream location' (*Lucky Ones* 40, 21). They can neither make a mark on English culture nor claim the cottage as establishing a place for themselves in the national heritage or as part of a cultural legacy. At the same time, whether the mythic English past still has cultural capital after the Holocaust is left open, for embedded in the romanticism of the cottage setting are the rather darker resonances of another forest – the Black Forest of Germany as the site of Grimms' fairy tales, filled with indomitable fiends and not always ending with rescue. Despite its sunny location in golden English fields, the Kinder's country cottage is haunted by the unresolved European past, as we learn from Leo Black's son Daniel. This Second Generation survivor recalls an illuminating childhood foray sneaking into a *verboten* shed in the garden. Considered Leo's 'most sacred place', the shed is a workshop where he builds frames for fading photographs of family murdered by the Nazis (55). In their position as concealed objects, forming no direct connection to the present action, these photos are totemic traces of the European Jewish culture targeted for destruction by the Nazis. But their resting place in the English countryside is not one that honors Holocaust memory, but rather, as in *Kindertransport*, signals its suppression. The confrontation of these hidden photos by the interloping Daniel is haunted by the guilt of survivors for being unable to save the victims, a guilt that is now transmitted to the Second Generation, enacted in his trespass.

Whether Leo intended to frame or display the photos remains a question suspended in time, like the memories transmitted to the Second Generation without explanation. In a double troping, what is framed in Daniel's recollection is the position of memory traces as an interpolated tale within the larger narrative and the position of the Second Generation as objects of their parents' unresolved memories. Daniel is also framed, in the sense of being set up to be tempted by the mysteriously locked shed, and so is exposed and trapped as a trespasser on the precarious site of his father's fetishized memory.

As we learn of his troubled relationship with Leo and that at thirteen he still wets his bed, what becomes clear is that just as framing also keeps its object in place, defining its character, so Daniel suffers the confines and projections of his father's anxieties inherited from his own father, the survivor. Whereas Diane Samuels's play rehearses the Kindertransport legacy through the vexed role of maternal nurture, Daniel's and Leo's damaged relationship shows the effects of a dislocated cultural identity on the development of masculinity. The photos in the shed of an earlier generation suggest that the historical contingencies shaping Jewish generation are constant if unstable. The shed itself encapsulates Holocaust memories as a destabilizing fulcrum. Like the Holocaust past, it has no presence in the play's setting, but, in its haunting invisibility, it is a place that for Leo represents escape from the present and the past by containing them both as locked up. Yet instead of implying safety, the shed also recalls the terror-ridden huts of concentration-camp incarceration.

Like the Kinder characters' German-inflected English and their middle age, the spaces they occupy are all liminal, marking partial identities carved out of an insecure past and unfulfilling present. Their own foundational narrative, like the biblical story of the Exodus, is one of exile and escape, as well as of an uncertain future in a land more difficult to inhabit and claim as a homeland or haven than it appears. This liminality betrays another absent narrative space. Unlike Diane Samuels's play and so many Holocaust narratives and memoirs, the childhood experience of a terrifying separation and transport is nowhere to be found in this play. Instead, the past of ordinary European family life and problems of adaptation to British subjectivity are expressed through a midlife enactment of displaced passions. If Samuels's play portrays the terrors of the Holocaust in the spectral figure of the Ratcatcher, Eilenberg dramatizes traces of hopeless and hapless fathers in the characters of the two male protagonists, Leo Black and Bruno Mosenthal. Both men project their legacy of Jewish powerlessness onto their son and daughter, reproducing only angry frustration and despair. England, for these men, has not fulfilled its promise of safety and a new life, only a safe stage on which to replay old and superating injuries. Letting go of the cottage may therefore represent a recognition and reconciliation with loss and the rejection of such comforting myths as 'a dream location'.

Despite the fact that there is only one scene in the play set in the cottage, it is a determining, indeed overdetermined presence and space. As the plot turns, selling the cottage only reinstates its hauntingly anxious promises of belonging and withholding, safety and uncertainty. Compounding this omnipresent sense of uncertainty, the indelible imaginary of the cottage is redolent with the horrors evoked by Samuels's fairy-tale figure, the Ratcatcher, and such fairy tale figures in Kindertransport memoirs. In *The Lucky Ones*, the nostalgic memories conjured by the cottage for Anna Mosenthal of her childhood in the German countryside near Wannsee are singed with that site's dark history. For Wannsee is where the Final Solution was imagined, instituted, and planned with cool rationality. In Eilenberg's retrospective vision, Wannsee represents the gates that were closed on additional possibilities for child rescue and that foreclosed the possibility of feeling safe even and ever after rescue. Anna's associative memories of child refugees romping in the English countryside, safe from German bombs and death camps, cannot eliminate the refugees' perennial sense of being endangered outsiders. It is with this association that Daniel's memory of stealing into Leo's shed authenticates only a counterfeit relationship to Englishness and a displaced relationship to the Holocaust. The Kinder and their children are Outsiders not only in Britain but also to Holocaust experience. Their marginal British experience is a constant reminder that their rescue was a prelude to their families' entrapment. Bearing this knowledge as a guilty burden, Eilenberg's Kinder experience a chronic anxiety that, compared to the fears of victims abandoned to their deadly fates, may have no legitimacy.

Despite the fact that a crush of unwanted and imagined memories has led to the avoidance and sale of the cottage, it looms both symbolically and mnemonically over all the action, dialogue, and relationships. Even the play's primary setting, the terrace and garden of the Mosenthals's London home, is only a façade, concealing the Kinder's anxieties behind its association with the conventional setting of English comedies of manners, from Noel Coward to Alan Ayckborn. In its mimicry of such gentility, but subverting the genre's unthreatened and unthreatening laughter, Eilenberg's play refuses integration into the time-honored English tradition. Instead, as in Samuels's play, *The Lucky Ones* satirizes the confidence of an enduring middle-class gentility as woman defined. Eilenberg's inclusion of male protagonists also highlights the incapacitating condition of exile on their cultural roles. None of the men in *The Lucky Ones* is able to participate in the English habit of designing and transforming nature to reflect confidence in British self-determination.[27] Eilenberg's north London setting serves as a sharp reminder of the tenuous place of these German Jewish refugees in a middle-class England. The trappings of stability suggested by such a home are undermined by the impact of the cottage on their sense of place, identity, and destiny. Just as Eilenberg asserts that the play has less to do with Jews and Jewishness than with refugees, so the characters' sense of their Jewish identity is present only in their concerns with the meanings of Englishness. In an ironic interplay, their nostalgic sprinklings of German cultural references are reminders of the failure of assimilation in their European homelands. In this combined sense, it is startling when Bruno Mosenthal finds credence in Enoch Powell's question, 'why – the – hell should Britain allow in every Tom, Dick and Harry who wants to come here ...' (*Lucky Onces* 2). Spoken like a true nativist, Bruno of course is native nowhere. Even in Germany, where Leo's and Anna's parents 'had been baptized as children', believing 'that the only solution to the Jewish problem was to become good Germans', Jews discovered their Jewish heritage could not be made to disappear into a talent for making 'poppy-seed cake' (25, 18). The dramatic interplay of persistent conflicts between Jewish and German historical memory erupts when the buyer turns out to be a German woman, married to an Englishman. Like the German Jews, she is a refugee who has not experienced but cannot overcome the history of the Holocaust. She too is innocent, but, unlike them, guilt lurks in her background. Her father is a real estate developer who probably got his start exploiting the plight of evicted German Jews.[28] In an angry eruption that is as much of a shock to the other characters as it is to the audience, Leo Black assails the buyer, Lisa Schnee Pendry, for her father's profiteering 'from the blood of the Jewish people', and then as a condition for the sale, demands 'an apology for the silence and the complicity of the German people (36, 37). Lisa responds as many in the audience very well might, that to do so would be to admit guilt 'by association – and just because by an accident of birth a German. You want to foist upon me all the guilt and blame for what you and your father suffered?' (37). In the second act, set in the present day after Leo's funeral, we learn that following Leo's challenge to Lisa, the avenging Jew and Second Generation German became lovers and, years later, gesturing some kind of recompense, Lisa now wishes to return the cottage to the children of the Blacks and Mosenthals.[29]

That the transfer of property, enmity, and affections is linked there is no doubt, but this dramatic nexus also asks a great deal of its audience's suspension of disbelief. As in Pascal's *Dead Woman on Holiday*, we are being asked to accept the travails of romantic love and betrayal as a metaphoric guide to understanding the guilt of Holocaust survivors. Just as we are given almost no information about the childhood experiences of Eilenberg's four Kinder, so no moment or process is depicted through which we can understand the passionate affinity between Lisa and Leo. All we are left with is a revelation after the fact. The only time we see Leo and Lisa alone together is in a flashback scene set in the cottage. That this moment also closes the play endows it with implications and meanings carried forth from the unfolding, conflicted, and unraveling relationships we witnessed earlier. The cottage scene is fraught with the kinds of domestic concerns associated with conventional marriage relationships, leading us to conclude that Bruno's and Lisa's relationship has healed the rift not only between German and Jew but also between a masculinist Nazi German past and its feminizing dehumanization of Jewish men. There is only a brief reference to the passion that united Leo and Lisa. We have been led to believe that this is a passion we can understand as having been incited by Leo's original pent-up hostility and Lisa's defensively angry response, but that combustible combination seems to have been tamed and also sustained by their idyll in the gentle/gentile domesticated English countryside. Indeed, instead of bearing the flames of antithetical German and Jewish historical memories, their passion and German-Jewish tensions have become as cozy as a cottage fireside chat. It is as though a temperate British clime and its myths of tolerance have been the mediating and moderating factors that end and even heal the ongoing political and gendered tensions between Jew and German and nurture their mutual desire.

Viewed somewhat differently, the play locates a pervasive ambivalence about assimilation, the perception, and status of outsider and Jew in Britain. Focused on whether he is properly attired to attend his son's wedding, an event about which Leo is intensely conflicted, his discussion with Lisa assumes the 'mannered' language and tone they mock in recalling that 'very English' film, *Brief Encounter* (*Lucky Ones* 89). In turn, the story of thwarted lovers in that film of the immediate postwar era, bathed in the gray of austerity, would seem to mock the refugees' all-too-rosy love affair and its manifestation in the shadows of the Holocaust. In their escape from any debt to that past, it is therefore only fitting that these refugee-lovers take their stolen moments in an English countryside cottage. In its resonances of *olde* England, it as though they have been transformed by the New Forest setting, much like the characters in the forest of Shakespeare's *Midsummer's Night Dream*. In turn, the enchanted air redolent in the lovers' takeover of the cottage also suggests that the myth of England's green and gentle land is made possible by the Holocaust memories embodied by the lovers. But skulking between the lines of the lovers' repartee are reminders that in their hands the cottage also defies the idea of Englishness as a lasting legacy, that is, as an emblem of tradition and cultural heritage. A commodity to buy and sell rather than an inheritance signifying continuity, this piece of real estate chides Lisa's and Leo's efforts to become English as well as to reconcile historical antipathies and build or integrate themselves into the national or Jewish community. While for Lisa, the cottage nominally represents a bucolic getaway from her hectic London home base, a 'dream location', in its mnemonic association with Wannsee, it cannot be disconnected from the violently guilty German past (21). It cannot become a place of fantasy where German and Jew can retreat from inherited identities endowed with traumatic memory. The cottage becomes the fulcrum of a narrative memory they try to perform beyond the very history that brought them together. As Ernst van Alphen reflects,

> narrative memory is retrospective, it takes place after the event. A traumatic memory – or better, reenactment – does not know that distance from the event. The person who experiences a traumatic reenactment is still inside the event, present at it. This explains why these traumatic reenactments impose themselves as visual imprints. The original traumatic event has not yet been transformed into a mediated, distanced account. It reimposes itself in its visual and sensory directness. ('Caught by Images' 103)

As the alliterative association of their names suggests, Lisa and Leo are both inside and distanced from the Holocaust. Each partner's identity transforms the other 'into a mediated, distanced account' of his and her own inherited trauma. Loving a German may mean reconciliation with the past, but keeping their affair a guilty secret and rendering her 'invisible', as Lisa accuses Leo of doing, reveals an unsettling and unresolved relationship to that past (*Lucky Ones* 92). Although Leo's wife never learns of their affair, it nonetheless represents a rupture from the bond of Jewish refugee identity and experience, including imperatives to rebuild Jewish life, culture, and community. Nowhere is this rupture more apparent than in Leo's response to his son's imminent marriage to an Arab woman, a response that he mocks by associating her not only with the PLO but also with his own 'sleeping with the daughter of a Nazi!' (93).[30] Just as Leo's crime of sleeping with the enemy is replicated in his son's matrimonial choice, so his mocking response 'mimic[s]' his own father's voice (93). In both a psychoanalytic and narrative sense, this replication is overdetermined. As he looks in a mirror, pretending to be his father's mocking voice, Leo enacts a direct visual and sensory reimposition of the Kindertransport trauma: 'do you fancy you're an Englishman or something – ?' (93). If the affair with Lisa is an escape from the fantasy of becoming English, his father's voice reminds him and us that the escape itself only embeds the original flight from tyranny and death.

In a parallel structure, the German Jewish refugee's affair with the German Englishwoman performs a reconciliation that is fraught with another rupture. As in Julia Pascal's *Dead Woman on Holiday*, the fantasy of escape from trauma encourages a revitalizing passion, but the structures of these plays show that this passion is also ignited by historical memory of mass perfidy and personal guilt. Whatever tension we might imagine from the interplay of historical memory and fantasy of escape is synthesized and enacted as personal betrayal all too reminiscent of the traumatic past. Even if Leo's and Lisa's romance validates love as healing memories of ostracism, brutality, and victimization, the cost of marital betrayal may be too high. Moreover, despite the acute domesticity of the scene depicting their relationship, as well as the mutual appeal of Otherness, nowhere is there any indication either of the commitment or tense continuity of day-to-day adaptation to one another, to the past, or as signaling a more propitious future. As in *Dead Woman on Holiday*, the sporadic and spasmodic nature of the love affairs reflects desperate moments – attempts to reenact and yet also erase the personal and political betrayals that cannot be worked through either in a psychological or moral sense. But of course before the guilt of betrayal can be erased, it must be assumed and/or acknowledged. And so one can read the affair between Leo and Lisa as both assuming guilt and acknowledging it, and by this I mean not guilty pleasure, but pleasurable guilt in a relationship that transgresses and perhaps transcends the boundaries of selfhood and identities shaped by the Holocaust. In their isolation from the emotional baggage and historical route of the Kindertransport, these moments are constituted as radically distinct, even wrenched from the Holocaust past or a post-Holocaust future. In a text that would not exist without the Holocaust, however, the lovers' moments together cannot transgress or transcend the Holocaust memory to which the play is dedicated. Despite their status as outsiders not only in Britain but also to the Holocaust, Lisa and Leo suffer the traces of Britain's role in rescuing the Jews. At the end, Lisa's reparative gesture can only represent the offering of a fantasied escape the remaining Kinder have already rejected.

4
The Transgenerational Haunting of Anne Karpf and Lisa Appignanesi

> Memory is an emotional climate, a thick set of sights and smells and sounds and imprinted attitudes which can pollute as well as clarify. (Lisa Appignanesi, *Losing the Dead* 6)

Even as efforts to gather the testimony of aging survivors intensify, the next generations confirm that the story of the Holocaust does not end with their parents' and grandparents' memories. Meetings of worldwide Second Generation organizations and the proliferation of their writing demonstrate that not only will the lived history of the Holocaust not be forgotten but also that its wounds will filter through the storehouses of memory and be felt. In transmitting the story of the Holocaust to their children, survivors leave a crucial legacy that cannot be lost or denied because it continues to shape the lives and identities of their children and grandchildren as well as our collective historical consciousness of the Holocaust. Regardless of whether survivor parents told their stories or kept silent, their children report that their own sense of self developed as identified with their Holocaust heritage.[1] As Marita Grimwood posits, Second Generation writing 'does not *represent* the Holocaust so much as respond to its ongoing effects in the present' (3, Grimwood's italics). Instead of considering their own stories and those of the First Generation separately, Second Generation writers write about themselves as inextricably linked into an intergenerational relationship. This relationship does not, however, represent an open, fluid, or mutual emotional interchange. As Julia Epstein and Lori Lefkovitz show, 'The identity formation of those who inherit a legacy of trauma with their family name apparently extends a compromised sense of the boundaries within and between selves into the next generation' (8). This question of identity formation includes whether children of survivors represent themselves as survivors. Because children of survivors experience 'feelings of belatedness' and 'vicarious memory', or what Marianne Hirsch calls 'postmemory', their identities, consciousness, and writing raise the question of '[w]hat does it mean to know, and what does it mean to own an experience' (Epstein and Lefkovitz 5).

As the Second Generation memoirs and fiction of Anne Karpf and Lisa Appignanesi attest, the anxieties and the struggles to find coping strategies, as well as the silences and stories of their parents and grandparents, have remained indelibly imprinted on their personal and Jewish identities. Their identities have been shaped by the feeling that their lives in the present are also tethered to a past they can never completely grasp, a past that remains elusive even as they doggedly investigate it. Yet as Helen Epstein implies throughout her book, we must not yield to the view of these haunted children of survivors as victims of irrevocable trauma. This would fuse their identities with traumatized survivors to the point of eliding their different historical and psychological positions.[2] In their efforts to create their individuality, they attempt to trace their parents' Holocaust memories back in a time and place that is distinct from their own. Yet to locate historically documented origins is an impossible mission from the start and impossible to abandon. There is no coherent story to be gleaned from recording testimony or from seeking the sites of the past painstakingly. There are rarely any family heirlooms or photos, only partial, selective, and hazily remembered images. Karpf and Appignanesi translate this lack of coherence into odysseys about two generations of interrupted but intertwined lives. What they can document are the powerfully felt traces of lost places to which they cannot claim belonging and the sense that the fragmented past will remain part of the searcher's selfhood. The fragmented past will have interrupted her development into an identity that feels whole. In their representations of their odysseys into the Holocaust past, that is, their shape and substance, an intergenerational consciousness emerges from memories that do not resemble the nostalgic longing and images with which Holocaust and Kindertransport memoirs so often begin. Instead, as Karpf and Appignanesi demonstrate, the identity consciousness they have formed produces writing that is witness to ongoing suffering. Their survival and responses combine mourning with healing to challenge the notion of working through.

In her book *The War After: Living with the Holocaust*, the sociologist and journalist Anne Karpf adds testimony, political history, and psychological analysis to the story of the enmeshed relationship between the character and fate of her survivor parents and her own. Karpf offers a comprehensive diorama of the ongoing trauma of Holocaust experience as she narrates the psychological suffering that erupted on her body. Just as her book gives voice to her survivor parents' escape from the Final Solution, so Karpf's testimony breaks the silence surrounding the struggles of her own Second Generation. As though rescuing her own subjectivity from her parents' overwhelming experiences, Karpf shows us that the emotional tortures of the Holocaust live on not only in her parents' memories and nightmares. Lori

Lefkovitz describes the in-between position of the Second Generation from her own experience:

> 'The second generation' at once occupies a position of privilege, closer to some rupture and origin than those who cannot number their generations and, at the same time, ours is a position of relative mediocrity, emphatically not first. Like Noah's children born after the flood, we are sensitized to the privilege of being on this earth yet know we are here through no merit of our own. ('Inherited Memory' 222)

Even the will to live and to love beyond the Holocaust can carry forth its struggle and pain as the children of survivors inherit the psychological vestiges of their parents' suffering. But perhaps most significantly, as Karpf's book chronicles the cognitive and communicative processes by which survivor stories are transmitted, it validates the psychological bumpy road that makes the Holocaust the Second Generation's own story.

Karpf dramatizes a beloved but fraught relationship with her survivor parents through the book's structure; its three parts represent her interpretation of how her life was born of her parents' stories. Part 1 of *The War After* is Karpf's memoir of growing up with and suffering the effects of her parents' Holocaust legacy, and this is juxtaposed with each parent's testimonies of their prewar, wartime, and postwar experiences. Ann Karpf was born in London on 8 June 1950. Her mother, Natalia Weissman Karpf, was born in Krakow, Poland, and trained to become a concert pianist. She performed in Poland before the war and in England afterwards. Anne's father, Joseph Karpf, was born in Galicia on the border of the Russian part of Poland. He studied law in Vienna and then also attended art school. He joined his father's many business enterprises, which, after his father's death, he ran until he was deported to Russia when the war broke out.

Josef and Natalia narrate their stories in this section chronologically, beginning with his grandfather's success in a timber business he established in eastern Galicia, the family's escape to Vienna with the Russian siege in World War I, an aborted art career, and the recognition of Hitler's danger to the Jews. Like the refugee memoirs examined earlier, Natalia testifies to her family's cultured upper-middle-class life which, despite its economic security, was vulnerable to the antisemitic taunts of their native Krakow. Musically gifted from early childhood, her training and burgeoning career were interrupted by her mother's unexpected death and the necessity of caring for two younger siblings who continued to live with her during her first marriage. Despite recognition of their danger once Hitler was on the march in 1938, Natalia's first husband refused to leave Poland. Each parent's stories in this section are preludes to their Holocaust experiences and end with a plaint of what might have been. Like a countervoice to nostalgia, they assume that the ordinary vicissitudes of married and family life would inexorably have intertwined with the Jews' discontinuous European history to create a continuum of disorientation on which one could rely for predictability.

The fact that her parents' testimonies were transcribed and edited and the book was written thirteen years after Karpf first interviewed her parents, reveals the intense emotional drama of Holocaust transmission, absorption, and interpretation. Karpf's book could be written only when she had established her own professional and personal life and was able to come to terms with the relationship between her parents' cataclysmic shifts in moderating their stories and her own. She tells us:

> So the accounts we produced are a combination of what I was then ready and able to hear, and they were then ready and able to tell. What's more they've been edited and shaped by a later self, one with a different perspective and its own preoccupations. (*War After* 18)

How and in what forms this 'later self' emerges does not represent only the legacy of her parents' Holocaust experiences and responses, but Karpf's struggle to negotiate their interpretations of their stories with her own. Among the prevailing preoccupations that challenge what it means for this daughter of survivors to be 'ready and able to hear' is the question, 'How can I write all this?' and her impulsive response, 'It will surely kill' (40). Of what that 'It' is composed and what it means to 'kill' it becomes the work and subject of Karp's book. She articulates the reverberations of these questions in her analysis of her interlaced relationship with her parents, an embedded psychological approach that moves from direct though edited narration of her parents' stories and hers to the questions that prompt, and therefore shape, the focus of the three narratives.

A major question she addresses about halfway through her book is whether her difficult relationships with her parents and her suffering can be attributed to the Holocaust. After all, painful experiences of separation and individuation are commonplace in families. In effect, these questions reflect not only her desire for insight into her own development but also her need to understand the nature of her parents' emotional responses and adaptations and their relationship to her own and to their history. She thus asks her parents questions in which we can feel she has included herself. Of her mother, she asks: 'Would you have liked them to have bombed the camp?' (88). And her father: 'Weren't you terrified?' (58). 'Didn't you feel a sense of incredible anger?' (61). With no escape from the feeling of belonging in and to her parents' stories, and yet physically absent from them, Karpf constructs the Holocaust stories of Natalia and Josef Karpf as a narrative thread knotted with her own post-Holocaust stories. The rhetorical effect is to read Karp's self-conception as originating within her parents' Holocaust and not afterward. Readers are then left to sift through and sort out her narrative construction and interpretation of how the Second Generation has constructed the meanings of all their lives.

The book confronts the shift from her parents' stable prewar lives to the catastrophes of their Holocaust experiences by interpolating Karpf's narrative of suffering in between. Only after we learn of her excruciating ties to her parents and their home do her parents' testimonies continue, recounting her mother's frantic efforts to pass as an Aryan and hide in plain sight, her arrest and torture, her incarceration at Płaszow and transports to Auschwitz and Lichtewerden, and her father's tortuous experiences in a Soviet forced-labor camp. Employing the trope so prevalent in Kindertransport writing, Karpf begins her interpretation of her parents' testimonies and her reaction to them by telling us that 'The Holocaust was our fairy-tale' (94). Karpf reflects that whatever childhood frights were transferred onto tales of 'goblins, monsters, and wicked witches' and heroic escapes from 'castles and dungeons' found their objective correlatives in her parents' stories (94). In turn, as Lisa Appignanesi recounts, her parents' stories became her childhood fairytales: 'hideous trajectories, skillfully navigated towards some kind of happy ever after. No one bothered with Grimm' (*Losing the Dead* 22). As Kindertransport memoirs show us, the conventions of fairy tales provide a language and narrative forms that could identify, contain, and express the anxiety for which no ordinary lexicon of emotion or realistic narrative could suffice. In the case of the Second Generation, fairy tales could express the anxiety that resulted from the parents' narrative elisions of their anguish. With their plot trajectories of threat, danger, incarceration, and escape, fairy tales could fill the more apprehensive emotional void that was their legacy. With little or no memory of a childhood that seemed not to have happened, Karpf interprets these tales of loss and recovery as performing the reconstruction and construction of lost memory.

Once Karpf alternates her testimony with that of her parents, the plots and language of fairy tales are replaced by other narrative models to reflect her voice as adult narrator and focalizer. Though she enters psychological therapy only after painful attempts to leave her parents' home and build a separate life, all the portions of the book that comprise her narrative are infused with the language of professional psychological analysis: the search for the motivations that drive the emotional responses to the incidents and people that form the core of meaning for her reading of her life. This language and form, however, are different from other types of Holocaust testimony. Hers resemble neither the 'simple un-metaphorical language' of oral testimony nor the attempt 'to shape emotional responses' by making 'aesthetic choices [that] can distort' (Bigsby 197). Instead, we find a self-deprecating and even self-mocking irony that marks the historically inflected distance between her times of suffering, her parents' experiences and losses, her own fears of losing them and, later, fears of losing her child. Questions abound after devoting long sections to historical background and context. How is she connected to events of which she had no idea but which are central to the cultural identity into which she is born and which she must learn to claim even as she learns to unearth history from national myth?

What is particularly interesting for the narrative relationship between First and Second Generation here is the dramatization of that emotional void in her parents' narratives that Karpf transcribes. Like so many Holocaust testimonies, emotional reaction is expressed indirectly, projected onto and embedded in detailed descriptions of brutalized bodies and heroically desperate efforts to withstand and escape torrential beatings and the ravages of starvation. Lacking the transmission key to this encryption, Karpf translates her parents' suffering into her own embodied narrative. Thus while she offers their testimony in their voices, it is not as though they are unmediated, as Karpf's questions and editing indicate. One senses, however, the lengths to which she went to ensure the authenticity of their narrations in the absence of her commentary. Instead, to guarantee the integrity of her parents' narrations and her own, she keeps them separate. Immediately following her parents' narratives, Karpf offers her own to demonstrate their interconnections and distinctions. In an effort to bridge the gulf between the heroic myths she had taken to be her parents' experiences and their realities, she fills the emotional void that results by narrating her etiology of psychosomatic suffering. It is as though the eruption of her fears of separation and loss into extreme bouts of eczema tell the tale of the elided emotion.

Because a psychological perspective on Karpf's book runs the risk of interfering with the impact of her analysis, I focus on her narrative structure instead. I find that her descriptions of her suffering create a reparative parallel in the structure of her book. The cycles of eczemic eruptions, self-damaging attacks of scratching, and embarrassed retreats from being noticed are signs, as Karpf tells us, not only of an explosive rage against her parents' violent history in the Nazi vise but also of a response to a history of indifference to the violence as it was occurring and to its aftermath: Britain's willing ignorance of that violence as it was being perpetrated against the Jews. But instead of ascribing a causal relationship between her parents' horrific experiences and her own, the book juxtaposes them to suggest that even as they become fused, as if by a strike of lightning, the meanings of each must remain discrete to be honored. We see this in the way Karpf and her colleagues in their Second Generation organization discover how they have had to learn how to understand their emotional responses in light of their parents' ongoing reactions to their Holocaust experiences:

> In my group one day we talk about what weakness must have meant to our parents during the war, when strength as imperative and vulnerability may have been literally fatal. (Quite often survivors who are peerless in a crisis get angry in situations where others might feel frightened or sad.)

We also talk about how we, for whom weakness would have had no such consequences, learned to view it with similar disdain and fear. (251)

As Karpf's reflections, her narration of her suffering, and of her parents' worries about her confirm, this learning process takes place as a disorienting emotional dynamic. The collective realization expressed above in the present tense shows how children of survivors absorb and then translate their parents' responses to Holocaust experiences into their own responses to ordinary circumstances. Following a developmental pattern we would consider normative, these children become socialized by mirroring their parents' affective responses to them and to the world around them. But in the Holocaust survivor family, children must also absorb and mirror an amalgam of perceiving and misperceiving danger. In effect, the Second Generation conflates and replicates their parents' perceptions of real wartime and imagined postwar dangers. Regardless of obvious differences in their circumstances, the Second Generation carries forward and assesses the feelings they have absorbed according to their parents' wartime situations. As Karpf's present-tense narration suggests, in concert with their parents' reactions, it is as though the Holocaust governs the realities of the Second Generation by making itself felt in a continuous present. Such misapplied assessments also misgovern the Second Generation's adaptations to their own cultural, social, and political situations.

If through her reflections and the tripartite structure of her book, Karpf can figure out and therefore demythicize her 'coterminous', fused relationship with her parents, she can discover a pathway to developing a self interdependent with their past but developing a character of her own (102). Her plot line would then suggest arcs of her own making. To do this, her narrative must also demythicize her parents' monstrous experiences to the point of distinguishing her own suffering from theirs. Although hers was born of theirs, and 'it *did* feel as if my crisis was somehow about her [mother's] ability to survive', the boundaries of historical and relational difference had to be emotionally understood as a barbed wire enclosure she cannot enter and trespass (107, Karpf's italics). Signalling this pivotal move is her recognition that her 'mother's extraordinary resilience' is a sign neither of superhuman heroism nor omnipresent threats of danger and loss that still beset them both (96). What her investigation will discover is that resilience is the necessary strategy through which her own development can negotiate and revise the portentous models of either ghoulish or triumphalist fairy tales and fables with which her childhood imagination had been invested. She would need to outgrow the need to be a child 'in a playpen of misery' (126).

Karpf's confrontation with her parents' Holocaust experiences and memories includes their transition from war-torn Europe to Britain and her realization that her legacy of trauma stems 'more generally to being Jewish in Britain' (143). Her ongoing anxieties relate both to her parents' adjustments to survival itself and to their own indeterminate integration into British culture. In addition to the Holocaust, the selfhood of the Second Generation is thus also shaped by their parents' postwar adjustment to a new life in a new land, which includes the socialization of their children, Eve and Anne. Once again, Anne leads her mother into suggestive implications for her own relationship to past and present by asking: 'Wasn't that difficult for you ... [that] the world outside resumed, almost as if nothing had happened?' (150). When Natalia and Josef left Europe, 'the world outside' became Britain, which was recovering from the war's human and economic costs, not as though 'nothing had happened', but as though the nation's sense of its stalwart character had been affirmed by bearing up under the Blitz and V-2 rocket attacks. Karpf recalls that the chronic and infectious 'cold' that lingers from her parents' desperate Holocaust experience fits ironically with the British penchant for a physically discomforting norm (4). Signifying for the Karpfs an indifferent and 'dangerous outside', the cold 'fog' of England merges with stories about the war that 'seeped into our home' (4).

Like so many Jewish refugees, Natalia and Josef Karpf faced the odd coupling of British xenophobia and Anglo-Jewish ambivalence. Much to their surprise, they were never approached, much less offered help, by any Anglo-Jewish organization. Help and understanding came only from other Holocaust survivors. Though like most refugees, the Karpfs felt grateful to Britain for taking them in, the combined laissez faire attitudes of the British and British Jews left them in a condition of silence 'a second abandonment' (167). No one wanted to hear their stories. One could also speak here of a third abandonment since it is a condition of silence that Karpf inherits three times over, from her parents and from their British and Anglo-Jewish environments. These are relational and communicative gaps that, in their overdetermined meanings, are expressed by her symptoms. Perhaps not so coincidentally, therefore, her glaringly aggressive symptoms can be read as defiantly responding to these silences. Recalling Karen Gershon's character Inge, one can only imagine how this assertive expression of the self and her unacknowledged pain would represent both confirmation and a breach of British reticence and reserve. After all, in response to the shame of her painfully apparent skin eruptions, Karpf covers up most of her body and speaks to almost no one about her condition.

Karpf devotes three chapters to place this totalizing and interrelated experience in the vexed context of Britain and its Jews from the Middle Ages through the present. In her overview of the periods following the Enlightenment, Karpf focuses on the double bind represented by assumptions about assimilation as necessary to progressive societies. On the one hand, it was assumed that as the distinctively recognizable qualities of Jewishness disappeared with assimilation, antisemitism too would be erased. On the other hand, the very invisibility of the Jews would mark their sinister, amorphously insinuating omnipresence. This section of *The War After* offers a history of

British attitudes and policies towards the Jews, including literary and other cultural representations, and Anglo-Jewish responses to pressures to accultur-ate. Foremost is Karpf's survey of Britain's obstructionist immigration policies in response to Hitler's threats to the Jews. Not only did the Home and Foreign Offices reject the possibility of saving European Jews, but also, she argues, despite the relative success of the Kindertransport, Britain's policies and prac-tices marked the government as sharing the hostile indifference of other nations and suggesting the Nazis' drive to destroy Jewish life and culture. That the British government had no humanitarian refugee policy is telling, for its policies excluded those Jews who tried to enter ' "under the rubric" ' of ' "alien immigration" ' (175).

If British officialdom represents the transformation of social antisemitism into political policy, official British Jewry, in Karpf's view, did little to assert an effective counterattack. By the 1930s, Anglo-Jewry had consolidated their anxieties into self-effacement, a bitterly ironic mirror of the dominant British style of forbearance and reserve. Yet Karpf also shows that despite or perhaps because of the subtlety of British antisemitism, prevailing fears of unantici-pated antisemitic outbreaks were not unfounded. The British Board of Jewish Deputies worked primarily to forestall any acrimonious response that might threaten the stable if always tense relationship between Anglo-Jewry and their gentile neighbors. As a result, the Anglo-Jewish communities would only make appeals on behalf of imperiled European Jews through Christian clergymen. And rather than openly welcome the few Jewish refugees who managed to escape and gain admittance, as we have seen in other accounts, Jewish organizations demurred to cultural constraints and offered the equiv-alent of eighteenth-century chapbooks of polite manners and morals that would help the newcomers keep a low profile.

Karpf is openly bitter about this history, and, in part, holds the Anglo-Jewish communities culpable for an 'apologetic stance' that would guarantee and legitimize a governmental lack of attention to the plight of European Jewry and to Jewish refugees (174). Even after the war, as Jewish refugees like her parents sought a new life in Britain, the Anglo-Jewish community organizations did little or nothing to reach out to them. Karpf connects the ongoing, postwar rejectionist policies toward Jewish immigration and the refugees' strongly expressed Jewish identity to her parents' experience. She researches and discovers the political contexts that help explain their struggle to adjust economically and culturally as well as define the nature of the world she was born into. But despite her castigation of this Jewish indif-ference to other Jews, she includes herself when she warns us that 'it's too easy to judge British Jewry with hindsight' (187). What we know today about pos-sibilities for broader attempts at rescue must be tempered with understanding the mindsets of the Jewish communities at the time. The intertwined fears of British Jews and the tragic and suspended fates of European Jews produce a looking-glass effect for Karpf. The arrival of traumatized and needy survivors could only have awakened the Jewish community's 'sense of guilt' that was defensively transferred onto the survivors (199). At the receiving end, the refugees then 'had to be careful not to upset those who *hadn't* been through the experience: survivors had been transformed from actual sufferers of distress into potential creators of it' (199, Karpf's italics). Part of Karpf's brief is to show how the entanglements of British Jewry's anxiety and the neglect of refugees undermined the ability of survivors' testimony to make a lasting impact. This of course accounts in part for the survivors' continuing silence about their Holocaust histories. Corroboration of feeling silenced could also be found in popular cultural constructions of the Holocaust in the 1950s and 60s, such as the expurgated edition of *The Diary of Anne Frank*, while films and plays about the wartime period provided political and ethical messages that elided the horrors of Holocaust experience. As recently as the 1980s and 90s, the rhetoric of antisemitism and emphasis on a Christian British character informed media reporting while incidents of 'extreme violence (defined as potentially life threatening)' inspired growing attention to security for Jewish buildings (214).[3] With this combination of events, Karpf reports, survivors in Britain have found multivalent evidence to support their continuing fears and to undermine the evolution of feeling safe and secure.

Although Karpf's historical survey is thoroughly researched, its design extends beyond informing the scholars for whom this material is well known and even for the general readers who also comprise her audience. In addition to its contextual and rhetorical value, this historical narrative represents a national etiology of psychological deprivation that would infect the Second Generation. The book's emphasis on this complicated history represents a critically ironic commentary on the tensions between Natalia and Josef Karpf's prewar, wartime, and postwar lives as well as between the world of the Holocaust and that of the outside. Instead of offering a pathway to create a new sense of wholeness and continuity, this history and the silence that would accompany it created 'a complete disjuncture between the world outside the home...and the world within' (200). As a rhetorical trope for this disjuncture, Karpf's narrative not only describes but also performs it as her alternations of personal testimony and historical narrative are not only woven together but disrupt each other. It is as though the chain of signification represented by her accumulated knowledge both raises new questions and questions itself.

For example, as though asking for confirmation of her own emotional experience of the Holocaust legacy, Karpf muses: 'When we were little, there must have been a lot of sadness in the house' (156). The juxtapositions of parents recounting their personal testimony to their daughter, the European past and British present, Karpf's direction, and life writing represent an interpretive strategy that is designed to provide both a confrontation with the traumas with which she feels infused and her efforts to heal and define her own identity. The subject of the confrontation is her irrevocable identification and attachment to her parents and its desired outcome is an individuated relationship – lovingly close but with emotionally safe boundaries. The interplay of the memory work of parents and child in *The War After* can be seen, in Ernst van Alphen's terms, as taking place after the event as retrospective 'narrative memory', but as also merged with 'traumatic memory' that he characterizes as a 'reenactment [that] does not know that distance from the event' ('Caught by Images' 103). Interestingly, as Karpf's parents recount their memories, they seem much more distanced than Karpf herself, who resembles Van Alphen's traumatized subject who 'is still inside the event' ('Caught by Images' 103).

Her book can thus be read as a plot to parse her parents' memories so that she can learn where her own traumatic memories have been born and how they have been fused with those of her parents. Karpf's persistent symptoms are not just hers alone, but serve as both emotional links and heuristic bridges to her parents' stories. But as the book develops and shows that its stories of parents and child coalesce, it leads us to understand that the combined fusion of Holocaust memory and emotional dependency is simply too much for one person to carry. Rather than register a complaint, however, the book's densely crafted accretion of graphic details reveals the urge to create a pathway to healing and, in the effort, becomes an analytic artifact. The analysis proceeds by offering figurative diagnosis rather than medical language and representations, and it is this figuration that tethers Karpf's etiology to her parents' stories. In effect, the emotional weight of her parents' stories and Holocaust memories on her own metaphorically suggest a swelling that, because it cannot contain the traumas of three people, becomes infected and engorged. If her bodily symptoms are an expression of the psychic and cognitive disorientation this fusion brings, then it is no wonder that they take the form of eruptions perpetuated by obsession. But as Karpf prods her parents' memories for the realistic details of their entrapments and survival, so she uses them to recuperate her own defensive memory lapses and thus flesh out and develop a more historically tested model for her own life and identity.

A significant feature of Karpf's story of the psychological reality of the Holocaust is the history of the reception of the Holocaust by the psychological establishments and their theories of trauma. Concerned primarily with children, psychologists of the wartime and aftermath, like Anna Freud, John Bowlby, and D. W. Winnicott, were motivated by witnessing the effects of evacuation, bombing, and displacement on British children to develop theories of separation anxiety and the struggle for individuation. They then applied their studies to children who had survived Nazi occupation. When they turned their attention to adults, they modeled their diagnoses of both returning soldiers and war-weary civilians on the documentation of shell-shocked soldiers in World War I. No attention was paid to Holocaust survivors. In Part II of her book, Karpf connects the political contexts of

British policies toward postwar Jewish refugees to the influential psychoanalytic community in Britain, whose ideas were shaped so powerfully by the rescue of Sigmund Freud and his daughter Anna from Nazi-ridden Vienna. Despite the fact that so many psychoanalysts were Jewish refugees, their theories and practices ignored the reality of Holocaust trauma. Providing an analysis of psychoanalysts, Karpf sees this void as the result of their own psychological difficulties adapting to social pressures to become British while coping with their own traumas of losing homeland and family who could not escape the Nazis. In turn, this segment of medical history sheds light on the failure of psychologists to recognize the transmission of Holocaust trauma to survivors' children, such as Karpf herself.

Like many Holocaust critics, she feels the urgent need to countermand those who would represent survivors as embodying heroically uplifting messages which audiences find personally inspiring. Thus she objects to projects such as the Steven Spielberg produced documentary, *The Last Days*, about survivors of the 1944 Hungarian roundups because none of them suggests any problems with their postwar lives in the United States ('Return to the Death Camps' np). In short, what is missing for her is any sense of a disturbing war after. Karpf, however, does not consider that the processes of adjusting to the social cultures of Britain and the United States may have affected the survivors' tone, responses, and outlooks – that what is missing is a function of the silences with which survivors were greeted. In order to fit into their new environments, refugees complied with well-intentioned encouragements to build new lives by laying the past to rest. They were told that it would be counterproductive to speak of the horrors, that to do so would reignite the trauma. Though she ignores this cultural and psychological contingency, Karpf's odyssey attempts to deromanticize and historicize the psychodynamics of post-Holocaust experience. She admonishes those readers who comfort and distance themselves from both survivors' 'necessary autism' and degrading experiences by imposing sacralizing or uplifting interpretations onto Holocaust testimony (249). On behalf of the transmission of survivors' psychic pain, *The War After* repudiates those analyses of the problems of the Second Generation that would see them as intra-psychically derived. That is, to diagnose their problems according to psychoanalytic theories that identified the source of emotional suffering within unconscious conflicted drives and needs as well as emotional conflicts psychoanalysis had universalized as deriving from early childhood issues about separation and individuation. These analyses, she argues, imprison survivors once again, only now within their own damaged psyches. She therefore suggests an alternative psychological model, one that would be grounded in the specific material circumstances that formed the relationships of the Second Generation to their parents' logical and appropriate responses – to life-threatening realities and to continuing anxieties about safety. Karpf's commitment to this contextualized model was already apparent three years before the publication of *The War After* in a review of a book about mother–infant bonding. With clear parallels with her relationship to her own mother, Karpf showed her concerns about decontextualized psychoanalytic theories of attachment and the transmission of psychic pain. She fully agrees with the book, which criticized the faulty research that led to myths valorizing mothers who 'were superglued to their babies immediately after birth' ('Gum Disease' 47). Like the author, Karpf emphasizes the external psychological realities that form mother–child bonding and that also validate the malleability of mother and child.

Part III of Karpf's book synthesizes her psychological and political narratives into a chronicle of her own experiences of loss, birth, and reconciliation. After years of combined physical and emotional suffering through self-mutilation and unresolved ambivalences about her relationship with her parents and lover, she embraces commitment to her marriage, two children, and to a negotiated peace settlement with her parents. Juxtaposed with diary entries chronicling her father's final year, she reflects on how her mourning of him induced her to recognize changes in her approach to the sense of loss she had derived from her parents' Holocaust experiences. Melding intellectual understanding with emotional catharsis, these changes are catalyzed in a trip to Poland, where she establishes the material historical and political contexts for her self-knowledge while raising questions about the emotional effects of this odyssey on her mother and on her narrative.

The book's overall juxtaposition of her parents' testimony with her own has the effect of giving equal weight to the experiences of Holocaust survivors and the Second Generation.[4] Instead of achieving such balance, however, this structure expresses the emotional strains issuing from the effort to achieve it. While the anger with which Karpf infuses her historical summary of British policies and British Jewry lends credence to the book as personal testimony, its consistency with the often strained metaphors of her personal meditations and with her anxious questions to her parents recreates the psychological disturbance the book is meant to be resolving. This is apparent in the way her questions and reflections shape not only her book but also her parents' stories. As a result, her book veers toward recreating the very attachment to her parents she struggles to relieve. These narrative tensions show how the search for subjectivity in relation to her parents' history may require analysis not only of their irrevocable attachment, but of their historical separateness.

Karpf's awareness that whatever her own suffering, it cannot be compared to that of her parents, produces an overlay of new suffering. Only now, suffering takes the form of guilt for balancing her story with theirs. Nowhere is this more apparent than when she returns from Poland with cassettes of Yiddish songs. Breaking down into 'terrible shocked sadness' and sobbing as never before, Natalia Karpf's response provides her daughter with an experience that cannot be balanced with an inherited sense of loss. As a result, Anne is moved to examine her motives for the entire project of recuperating her parents' past; she finally recognizes a new resolve of her own to embrace the present and the future through the experience of becoming a mother for the second time. It is this embrace that allows her to see her parents' coping strategies as a positive life force and not merely as evidence of lives submerged in the forces of terror. While her own suffering is tied to her parents', a more explicit acknowledgement of the incomparable nature of their experiences and the separateness of their stories would grant her the subjectivity for which her book expresses such powerful craving.

Karpf's book has been reviewed as a significant contribution to literature of the Second Generation. Although her historical research is not the result of her own archival investigations, but a synthesis of others' work, it is clearly necessary to the process of discovering the roots of her own suffering.[5] Combining her parents' memories with the history not only of Britain's obstructionist policies but also their ideological sources in nineteenth-century antisemitism allows us to trace the anger she expresses on behalf of those refugees whose integration into British society has been encumbered by provisional welcome. If, as so many have attested, ambivalence reigns as the attitude that ultimately forms a connection between Jewish and non-Jewish British society, Karpf's book shows that this is not a simple opposition between wanting to belong and a still hesitant invitation. Instead, as she and so many First and Second Generation writers show, ambivalence has also been a productive critical and creative force. It has been aligned with a liminal insider–outsider position that offers critical perspective on both halves of their position: the ongoing desire of the Jews to retain their cultural and religious difference from a dominant Christian culture and a creative opportunity through which to express their survival as individuals and as Jews.

The journey of Lisa Borenstein Appignanesi, her brother Stanley Borenstein, and her parents, Hena and Aron Borenstein from Europe is not one of escape or rescue from the threat or midst of Nazi terror. Even as other Jews were fleeing the Nazis' siege of Poland, they chose to remain with Hena's aging parents. Having survived forced labor, the ghettoes, and hiding in plain sight, even after the war ended, they found that life in the Communist era represented yet another struggle to survive. After the death of Hena's mother, they finally escaped what felt like relentless European oppression. Like so many survivors, the Borensteins made new lives in their new homelands by employing talents that were nurtured and encouraged by the constant danger that characterized their lives under the Nazis and Communists. It had by now become a habit to move from town to city to farm and back again, to work as traders, peasants, and clerks, and to change identities from Jewish to various Polish personae. And so they settled into post-Holocaust living by remaining peripatetic and disguising their Jewish identity. After a postwar sojourn in Paris, once they arrived in Montreal, they continued to move about in and around the city, its suburbs, and to a small town sixty miles north, even after they achieved a modicum of material success and social stability. After a time in Paris and years in Canada, Hena and Aron ended their lives in England, where their daughter had moved and where her own odyssey of discovering the Holocaust past began. Strictly speaking, theirs is not a story of Jewish acculturation to British society. Lisa's experience there has been professionally and socially fruitful and, in tandem with her earlier years in Paris and Canada, has inspired her to write fiction that centers on peripatetic Jewish figures as well as those non-Jews for whom the wartime period is but one of many equally formative periods in long and complex lives and relationships.[6]

Like Anne Karpf's memoir, Appignanesi's *Losing the Dead* alternates her search for the past with a story of her own self-discovery and with her parents' stories. She is motivated to write her book as her mother is slipping into the total memory loss of Alzheimer's disease. The time is very short and urgent as Hena has already lost a great deal of the facts and her wartime imperative to distort or embroider or to lie outright has now become a pattern of presenting herself to others. By the time Lisa decides to investigate her parents' past, her father has been dead nearly twenty years, and aside from her brother who was born in 1940, there are no living family members to fill in gaps and confirm or question each other and their stories as well as those disruptions that connect them. Unlike Anne Karpf, Lisa Appignanesi cannot expect anything that sounds like a coherent narrative from her mother and so many questions remain unanswered amidst a defensively self-referential pattern of insisting that only she, Hena, can tell the truth. Whereas we learn of the Holocaust experiences of Karpf's parents from their self-assured and confirmed narratives, Appignanesi must fill in her mother's elisions with conjectures based on possibilities she has derived from her research and other survivors' stories. Like *The War After*, *Losing the Dead* provides historical contexts that explain the immigration policies that consigned Jews to a state of desperate passivity, awaiting torture and death in Europe. Yet the Borensteins' story of immigration and assimilation in Canada also exposes the desperate ingenuities that defied the passivity imposed on them. The Borensteins are driven at least as much by their continuing survival strategies of disguise and deflection as by new encounters with old forms of local xenophobia. Although Canada's rescue record is overwhelmingly blank – they took in a total of five thousand Jews into their vast and mostly empty nation – the Borensteins' chosen residence of mostly French Catholic Québec presents a different set of assimilation issues for Jewish refugees whose apartness also encouraged the formation of their own community.

The brief of *Losing the Dead* is to make sense of a cacophony of Holocaust stories both for Appignanensi's sake and her mother's. If Hena loses more pieces of her story with each passing day, her daughter finds that in part it is her own 'sanity' that is at stake in deciding to investigate the past (80). How difficult this will be is evident in the effort to grapple with fading memories comprised of 'imprinted attitudes which can pollute as well as clarify' (6). That these attitudes would affect survivors' memories and stories we would expect, but interestingly, with hints from her asides, we can tell that Appignanesi's attitudes shape her own story as well as her narration of her parents'. Because of Hena's limited capacities to recall and to narrate, not only does her daughter fill in but also offers interpretive frameworks to help her and readers find ways of picturing unfolding events and constantly shifting identities and relationships. We see the need for this help in Hena's seemingly random repetitions of 'scraps of unruly experience which refuse the consecutive shape of story' and in her daughter's search for 'order, even if the voyage into the past is always colored by invention' (7).

Like Anne Karpf, Lisa Appignanesi finds that psychological explanations of individual and family dynamics guide her to create understanding of her parents' constantly shifting responses and attitudes towards their tumultuous conditions. As she faces her parents' painful declines and her father's death, she connects her parents' attempts to retain mental stability and her own. Unlike Karpf, Appignanesi suffered no psychosomatic symptoms as she grew up but rather developed the need to create a memory of her parents' extraordinary wartime vitality before their states of decline became the overwhelming images. '[P]sychological tropes' also map her voyages through Poland as she draws on her parents' and grandparents' pasts to shed light on the origins of her identity and the formation of her own memory and attitudes (8). The very risk she takes in inserting her responses into a Holocaust story produces an empathy that is powerful enough to read but that also prods us into new understanding of the legacies of genocide that congeal in the memories of succeeding generations. Unlike the neurological scientists who populate her novel, *The Memory Man*, and who search for the work of memory in the physicality of electrical charges and synapses, Appignanesi discovers that 'Memory is an emotional climate' (Appignanesi 6). Her book shows us what it means for the survivor to have gained and for the Second Generation to inherit an identity firmly rooted in the need to splinter it. In the face of losing all that served as the basis of traditional identity – family, personal and cultural history, home, and language – identity becomes both an instrument and the result of developing survival instincts. In their constantly shifting solutions, these instincts paradoxically represent the only stability amidst the disorientations of ever changing Nazi threats. Then, as these instincts are affirmed by survival, they shape the memory of Holocaust experience and the formation of the Second Generation. Identity for the Second Generation is thus like the work of memory, prey to the perceived and felt reemergence of danger and responses to its myriad, unforeseen, and inexplicable forms:

> Memory, like history, is uncontrollable. It manifests itself in unruly ways. It cascades through the generations in a series of misplaced fears, mysterious wounds, odd habits. The child inhabits the texture of these fears and habits, without knowing they are memory. (*Losing the Dead* 8)

Appignanesi's constructions and interpretations of her parents' Holocaust memories are deeply intertwined with the constantly shifting terrains of wartime and postwar Jewish identity. Without any direct access to this history, it is always mediated through her mother's and brother's partial memories and her own investigations of the earlier histories of her maternal and paternal families. A mnemonic icon that aligns her with the Holocaust past is also an object of self-mockery as internalized from the long centuries of anti-semitism. Her 'Jewish' nose and dark hair, signs of a genetic legacy from her father, set her dramatically as well as historically apart from her pert-nosed mother. In the context of the Nazis' Aryan ideology, Hena's famed blond blue-eyed beauty gave her the opportunity to hide in plain sight. Though she does not say so explicitly, Lisa's reference to 'belong[ing] down there with the darkies' tells us that, like her father, she would not have been able to pass (37). Identifying with the racial slur, she confirms that, like the 'darkies', she would be a victim of collective racism. If the opportunity to pass as an Aryan could be a lifesaver among the Nazis, blondness also registers as a symbol of a millennium of Polish-Jewish relations. Although the Jews were a protected and prospering minority in Poland since 1264, and had become the largest Jewish community in the world, their required occupations as tax collectors made them objects of envy and hatred among the peasant classes in thrall to the landowners and aristocracy. In turn, to protect themselves from local suspicion and antipathy, the Jews kept themselves as separate even as they were interdependent with Poles. Once these tense but tolerant relations began to disintegrate from the eighteenth century onward, and Zionism took hold among many Jews as an alternative destiny, the separation of the two societies became increasingly solidified.[7] By the 1930s, right-wing and centrist periodicals were calling for the deportation of the Jews who by then represented about 10 percent of the population and occupied at least half of the nation's medical and legal positions. Prodded by the death of Poland's liberating leader, Josef Pilsudski, antisemitic and fascist groups imposed professional limits on the Jews and perpetrated pogroms against them.

Appignanesi's maternal grandfather, David Lipszyc, had served in the Polish army in World War I while maintaining his distinctively traditional dress, observances, and Yiddish language, and aligning himself with the *Misrahi*, an important Jewish political party. At a time of radical change, he also embraced a modern attitude that encouraged questions about defining Jewish identity and a decision to support his daughter's secular education and teacher training. Her maternal grandmother, Sara Lipszyc, was a traditional orthodox wife and mother who accepted her place as important but as a 'lesser being' (*Losing the Dead* 40). Appignanesi's analytical approach to her mother's storytelling will not, however, take this assessment at face value. Noting that Sara's portrait derives from her mother's reverential reading of David Lipszyc's perspective, Appignanesi sees through it to show how her grandmother's practical wisdom also carried ethical weight in the formation of her daughter's character.

In contrast to her mother's vibrantly heroic self-portrait, Lisa's father 'never emerged as a hero of mythical stature' (52). And yet, his history of fearfulness offered Lisa a dramatic glimpse into the circumstances that brought him face to face with the terrors of Nazi brutality. His angry outbursts towards his children's minor misdemeanors may have seemed to contradict his passivity, but his daughter's psychological family history traces their connection to 'the scar history had left him with' (54). Even before the Nazi era, Aron suffered antisemitic incidents that showed him that he would never be treated as 'other than an undesirable alien', treatment that encouraged his Zionist affiliations (54). Unlike her mother who could hide her Jewishness behind her blond femininity, Aron's Jewish masculinity was always visibly threatening. His 'maleness' became 'an object of terror' (54). The fortunes of Aron's family had always been subject to the historical vicissitudes that beset Polish Jewry, including World War I and false accusations of treason, but family personalities and culture played their part as well. Aron's mother Rosa was a successful businesswoman and his father an authoritarian patriarch who, despite his son's intellectual gifts, insisted that the boy leave school at fourteen and work in the family textile firm.

Appignanesi's family history is important not just as a thumbnail sketch of prewar Polish Jewish experience, but because it serves as a template through which she and we can understand her relation to the history of the Holocaust. The categories of 'blonde and dark, fearless and fearful' against and through which she defines herself are key elements of an identity that cannot escape the legacy of Nazi antisemitism and perpetration (57). These categories also become tropes for considering the formation of Hena's political outlook and Lisa's narrative analysis: power and powerlessness, proud certainty and abject shame are set in oppositions that the memoir's narrative thrust attempts to deconstruct and even to bridge. But the narrative discontinuity between their experiences may be too great to bridge. Because the memoir was both inspired by a daughter's need to understand her mother and by the mother's charismatic but contradictory and ultimately elusive character, the deconstructive urge must contend with the character of the daughter's narrative as it emerges through its analysis. A key element in Lisa's negotiation with her mother's character is focalization. As we have seen, her analysis of Hena's self and family portrait addresses the question, who is seeing whom or what and from what perspective or point of view?

Interestingly, Hena's belief in 'the evil eye' provides an opportune trope through which to read Lisa's view and analysis of her mother's narrative (57). As Lisa reads this belief, 'the evil eye' substitutes for the power of the State because the latter is an abstraction that lies outside Hena's political perceptions. Since in its own epistemological framework, 'the evil eye' was a function of Hena's paranoia and superstitions, it could not be identified in any specific terms. Like an indeterminate or dissociated anxiety, it floats free of concrete references but could be attached to any and all. The level of its danger, moreover, does not need specificity since it is always at red alert, as its appellation indicates – a demonic force. Despite its omnipresence and ability to strike 'without your seeing' it, 'the evil eye' is not omnipotent (58). It must contend with Hena's identification with power, an identification that allowed her to look danger in the eye – to return its threat with her own seductive gaze. The blondness which conceals her Jewishness grants her a boldness that contrasts with the darkness that marks Aron's and, later, Lisa's suspect appearance. As so many incidents reveal, including her winning appeal to a Gestapo officer to release Aron from prison, Hena took risks that depended as much on her blond appearance as they were on her belief that she had power over others. What would happen to this self-confidence with emigration to Canada and how it would affect the formation of her children's identities shapes the rest of Appignanesi's memoir.

Though the wartime performances of feigned identities were a resounding success for Hena, Aron, and their son, this survival strategy also produced grave doubts in the postwar period about the viability of a Jewish identity emerging proudly and uncontested in a freed world. In turn, such doubts reproduced wartime strategies for dealing with anything or anyone perceived as a danger, from the nuns at Lisa's convent school to Canadian and American borders and their guards. Like a self-fulfilling prophesy, the Borensteins' choice to locate in the province of Québec reconfirmed and kept the memory alive of the precarious place of Jews even in a world that had remained free of Nazism. Like Poland, Québec was overwhelmingly Catholic, anti-semitic, and similarly stratified socially and economically. For these Jewish refugees, living in the province became a ripe opportunity to replay their wartime anxieties, evasions, silences, and disguises of the family's Jewish identity. That the family thrived in this inhospitable environment was an ironic testament to constructing sameness out of difference – their ethnic and religious difference from their neighbors and a setting so far removed historically and experientially from Europe. For the Borensteins, the dramatic differences between past and present and between wartime Europe and postwar Canada were elided by the power of their joint will to survive by risking confrontation with real and imagined dangers.

Because these emotional responses, decisions, and behavior were normative in the family, they were rarely questioned. In response to his wife's contorted perceptions and distorted facts, Aron mostly remained silent, just as he had often left wartime crises to her to solve. For their children, however, having to form friendships with local children and negotiate Québecois schooling, manners, and morals on their own distinctive terms, reality became 'a double world' (35). The 'lying' that had become Hena's modus operandi created double messages that implied 'there is something to hide either out there or in here' (35). As exterior and interior life melded for the

Borensteins, its objective correlative was always the Holocaust past. Instead of their new lives emerging with plans to participate in building Canada's budding Jewish communities and healing the wounds of the past, new layers of secrecy and lies seemed to be demanded by Canada. Instead of concealing it, such strategies only made the past more dominant. The signature wound and secret shared by the family and that kept its social boundaries tightly guarded were 'tainted origins' (35). If 'Poland was a bad place, a shadowy region, not good enough to foster my [Lisa's] birth', nonetheless it could not be separated from the family's Jewish identity. And so instead of reconceiving their identity as part of their escape from persecution, instead of celebrating their liberation from racialized Jewish appearances, what remained for the family was that 'Jewishness too carried a shameful taint, one which had on too many occasions proved mortal' (35). That Jewishness as a cultural and racial identity became a death threat under the Nazis, there is no doubt, but Appignanesi's commentaries dramatize the extent to which the shame of Jewish identity was incorporated into the family memory and chronicle.

In a reflection generalizing on her family's perception and experience of 'Jewishness' as 'a shameful taint', she declares that its absence 'would have been surprising' because

> We all internalize the discourse of the master, the colonizer, the aggressor. Jews, blacks, immigrants – all carry within them that little nugget of self-hatred, the gift of the dominant culture to its 'lesser' mortals. At times the nugget is dusted off, polished into brilliance, transformed into pride, brandished on communal occasions. But it rarely altogether dissolves. And it retains a bitter aura of shame. (*Losing the Dead* 35)

The contrast here between the Holocaust's legacy of an ineradicable 'shame' and 'self-hatred' and a fleeting 'pride' is noteworthy. There is no narrative movement in this passage in which the plots encapsulated in the memory of oppression can change either by choice or with new and different life circumstances. Pride cannot overtake and diminish, much less, defeat the power of shame which was a byproduct of antisemitism and persecution. As Appignanesi's metonymic narrative suggests, shame persists because the memory of being a Jew in Poland has solidified into a core so hard and so dense, it cannot be penetrated or cracked. Like the family's survival strategies of disguised identity, the 'bitter aura of shame' is no mere cover-up, but has evolved into a reality of its own. In their overwhelming and searing influence, the memory and identity of twelve years of oppression suggest an emotional universe that has expanded into such totalizing proportions it has crowded out the possibility of what in conventional responses to trauma is referred to as *moving on*. In effect, for Appignanesi, the Holocaust experience has been internalized to the extent of becoming permanently fixed scar tissue – an unstable but static condition for which any attempt at healing will have only cosmetic results. Therefore any celebratory gestures towards an affirming Jewish identity can not only be considered merely transitory, but they function like a coat of polish that makes the core identity of shame glaringly clear. And so Holocaust experience and its indelible memory may very well seem to preclude a trajectory of transformative experience and response. This is not, however, the whole story. In its alternations between several layers and perspectives on the past and the journey into its reconstruction, *Losing the Dead* emerges as a story constructed from the absence of one, a narrative of interpretation and questioning. It not only interprets and fills in Aron's silences and Hena's evasions and distortions but also questions Appignanesi's interpretation of her family's intertwined relation with Holocaust memory. If Hena defied the Nazi threat with her deceptions, her daughter exercises a creative defiance in searching for the truth. When it comes to this subject, however, complexity cannot simply lead to or signify a transparent and certain truth. Instead, *Losing the Dead* shows the limits both of investigating Holocaust memory and of Appignanesi's own inventions. A major element governing those limits is her efforts 'to break free from [her parents'] stories, even if their traces were so deeply imprinted they would mark any others one could live' (67). And so, '[f]inding a name which was as distant as possible from all the permutations of my parents' was a manner of signaling the break' (67). Such a break, however, always turns out to reinforce the ties of the Second Generation to their survivor parents' past. The break works like the return of the suppressed. Unlike the repressed, consciousness of the desire for the break persists, creating doubts about a new identity. In W. G. Sebald's Kindertransport novel, *Austerlitz*, the aging protagonist reflects on this guilty doubt: 'At some time in the past, I thought, I must have made a mistake, and now I am living the wrong life' (212).

Like Jacques Austerlitz, Lisa Appignanesi journeys to the family's European past to discover the identity which has shaped her but about which she has been given too little to make sense of her feelings about it. Where Austerlitz's journey to his Jewish past is to the unknown, Appignanesi's circulates around a rebellion against a story of deeply felt ambivalence about Jewish identity. Solidified by the war years, this ambivalence insinuates itself into the family's future; Lisa's brother Staczek, now Stanley, rejects his Bar Mitzvah tutoring but, fulfilling his father's Zionist dreams, lives in Israel for three years, and marries a Sabra before returning to Montreal. Lisa's commitment to exploring her family's history and her retention of her non-Jewish divorced husband's name declares her choice to straddle two worlds and to meld them into her identity.

Four years after the publication of *Losing the Dead*, in a novel entitled *The Memory Man*, Appignanesi explores a journey to the Polish Holocaust past as a test of choosing who one is as a survivor in the long afterward. Transposing bits of her family's characters and experiences onto Jewish and non-Jewish characters, the novel explores an enmeshed Holocaust history of

Polish-Jewish relations and their intergenerational Holocaust stories. When Bruno Lind, an eminent scientist specializing in the neurological mechanisms of memory, returns to his birthplace for a professional conference, instead of the intellectual challenges posed by colleagues, he confronts the emotional pitfalls of resurrecting Holocaust memory. Now in his seventies and a widower, he discovers that despite professional success and a loving relationship with his grown adopted African-American daughter, his golden years are not his to define or determine. Instead, whatever number and quality of years lie ahead for him, their meaning is tethered to the events and people that comprised his youth during the Holocaust. That he has repressed their memory has never been the subject of either personal introspection or his scientific study.

On the contrary, his personal and professional choices have been, albeit only partially consciously, determined by his need to bury his losses. His happy marriage to a non-Jew and their adoption of an African-American child complement his cross-cultural wanderings from Europe to Canada and the United States. Although his daughter has adopted Judaism, Bruno is not shown to pay any attention to his Jewish identity and the novel evinces little narrative attention of its own to the subject of Jewish identity after the Holocaust. Nonetheless, the subject is dramatically present in the novel as it plants a sporadic but relentless invasion into Bruno's dreams and reflections of splintered images from the Holocaust that seem to have a defiant will of their own and that resist his grasp:

> Images from the dream that had plagued him this last while leaped before him with the grainy effect of a battered old film on a loop. Figures kept falling: one after another, larger and smaller. Their faces were turned away from him. They refused recognition. The ground opened beneath them making a short fall into a terrifying drop. Deeper and deeper they fell, against razor-sharp granite walls, so that he had to open his eyes to stop the plunge and the barrage of German voices that accompanied it, like the deafening incomprehensible rumble of gunfire. (*Memory Man* 5)

If these dream figures refuse recognition, the novel implies, it is because they are not just a function of Bruno's unconscious. They have a life of their own. They demand a reciprocal relationship whereby Bruno would yield to the pressures of the past to be remembered and faced as his reality. As long as he resists their embrace, the figures will elude but haunt him, not only in his dreams but also as the plot unfolds, they will exact their revenge by challenging the primacy of his scientific thinking and by governing his movements. As Appignanesi demonstrates in *Losing the Dead*, emotions deriving from the Holocaust do not let go. Thus Bruno will discover that even when acknowledged, these emotions are so often translated into behavior that replicates wartime responses. And so he finds his body moving in the direction dictated by memory. On his first day in Vienna, without knowing how or why, he drifts into a strangely familiar neighborhood, looking up at the windows of a building and uttering the words 'Mami. Mamusia' (*Memory Man* 11). The scene resembles one in Sebald's *Austerlitz*, where, on Jacques's return to Pilsen, the scene of his 1939 Kindertransport, he is overtaken with 'the idea, ridiculous in itself, that this cast-iron column . . . seemed almost to approach the nature of a living being, might remember me and was . . . a witness to what I could no longer recollect for myself' (*Austerlitz* 221). Assuming the viability of such recognition, Bruno is filled with 'happy anticipation', but reality intervenes and he is knocked over by a skateboarder and collapses, thinking all the while that he is being beaten by an antisemitic assailant and it is 1938 (Appignanesi, *Memory Man* 11). There is, of course, no logical or scientific explanation for this uncanny coincidence that fuses nostalgic images from his early childhood home with nightmarish figures from the Holocaust past. Instead, the incident recalls Vienna as Freud's city and his idea of *Unheimlich*, where psychic forces are at play to defamiliarize the familiar by the latter's unexpected reappearance. As we shall see in the next chapter, the plotting here resembles Elaine Feinstein's examination of the mutually exclusive claims of emotional and empirical epistemologies. Appignanesi's plotting shows the crippling limitations of relying on only one by challenging each with the other. What has happened is that Bruno has reacted to a memory fragment while a real event happens in the present. If his science does not allow the meanings of dreams and of the unconscious a place in his search for definitive knowledge of the past, his return visit to Europe will demonstrate that however we accept or deny the idea of repressed memory, like his visit, its historical reality will return with a vengeance.

The novel is then structured by Bruno's search for his Holocaust past and the trajectory of his escape and losses, including various disguised identities and the slaughter of his mother and sister. As he moves backward in time and space and the narrative alternates between the present and the Holocaust past, that past becomes as embedded as his Jewish identity and one becomes an image of the other. This odyssey is also informed more by his attempts to translate his fragmented dreams and memories into a historical record than to perform a historical test of their emotional realities. The obstacles he faces, consisting of his and others' selective, partial, defensive, and fabricated memories and decimated, lost, and transformed places recall the indeterminate journey of Karen Gershon's Peter Sanger. Like Peter and like the author herself, Bruno will not discover who he is from the detritus and survivors of the Holocaust but that he must accept what history and the legacy of Holocaust identity dictate. Whether that history and legacy are gleaned from fearful images, a mother's story, or an image remembered and refracted through the media's representations and those of documentary research, they become the self's reality. The midnight knock on the door, the disappearance of fathers, and a life barely lived on the run constitute the plot of Bruno's past. Even the certain defeat of Nazi Germany has produced only uncertainty about the survivor's sense of self and identity:

> History wasn't bunk. It was a long trail of flashbulb memories... [S]imply because it was these our synapses registered over and over again, learned, until the emotion which had made them memorable in the first instance became trite, third-hand, voided. And then entire sequences disappeared into oblivion until they were discovered afresh. (*Memory Man* 39–40)

That this discovery is prompted by Bruno's daughter Amelia establishes the novel's relationship between the First and Second Generations and between their intertwined understanding of the past. We see this as mediated by flashbacks to Bruno's wartime experiences in which he and the narrator share the burden of interpretation. Having joined her father in Austria, Amelia tells him that they must go to Poland because she is entitled to discover along with him, the story that explains the 'mystery' and history she has felt as his child and its relation to the Jewish identity she has adopted (125).

Through a parallel intergenerational relationship, *The Memory Man* further explores Appignanesi's deep concern for Polish-Jewish relations. Irena Davies is also the daughter of a survivor, Marta Kanikowa, a non-Jewish Polish survivor who, like Appignanesi's mother, is sinking into the total memory loss of Alzheimer's disease. Unaware that she too is owed a story, Irena doesn't connect her identification with her mother's frequent agitations to the Holocaust until Bruno comes into their lives. Through his compassionate ministrations, Bruno deciphers Marta's seemingly incoherent gesticulations and obsessively repeated narrative fragments. In turn, as Bruno encourages Marta to reveal what lies hidden in her diseased memory functions, his empathy and her responses support the emergence of his own lost memories. The phrase that triggers her memory and his also joins them in both the present and the past: 'The murmur of, "Little Cousin"' (234). Repeated several times as the novel moves towards closure, this address registers the forgotten relationship between Bruno and Marta as well as the novel's political yearnings, its interlaced ties of love and politics. As Bruno pieces together and recounts his memory of their story, we and his listeners learn that in 1944 Marta rescued him after he was shot and abandoned and that they became lovers. Though he ultimately had to leave her to rejoin the partisans, she never gave up hope that she might see her 'Little Cousin' again.

In addition to its affectionate timbre, 'Little Cousin' expresses a desire to bridge the historical chasm of misunderstanding between Poles and Jews. Bruno's suspenseful journey of discovery builds toward establishing a loving relationship between the Pole and the Jew that will transcend their Holocaust history and provide a critical commentary on a dominant narrative: Polish complicity in the deportations and destruction of their Jewish neighbors.

To invent a Polish character who is a rescuer accords with the historical record. Yet we are also aware that this rescue and Bruno's and Marta's relationship develops in a forest isolated from and therefore unspoiled by the cities, shtetls, and camps that became the sites of Jewish destruction. Moreover, as we witness the scenes of tender love developing between Bruno and Marta, a narrative momentum is created that draws us in with its familiar and comforting conventions of a love story threatened by outside forces. Like the lovers, we are now in an illusory safe place, physically and emotionally far away from the relentless brutality outside their idyll. Once this love story develops, Bruno's narrative narrows the emotional and historical distance that Holocaust stories typically create between text and reader by asking us to focus on the primacy of their love, not just to blot out the killing, but to see this love between Jew and Pole as an alternative to it. As if to clinch this possibility, the novel provides the startling but perhaps not entirely unanticipated coincidence, that Bruno and Marta had a child and she is Irena. The combination of this fruitful if forgotten relationship and the lasting love for 'Little Cousin' suggests a yearning that is more provocative and even controversial than the love story – a yearning for a mutually nurturing relationship between Jews and Poles that can be read into the historical past and that represents a hopeful future.

Even as the narrative moves in this interpretive direction, it also undercuts it, however. 'Little Cousin' does not return until too late. Even if at some deeply submerged level of consciousness Marta recognizes a reunion of the family she and Bruno created, for all intents and purposes she cannot participate in their emotional bonding. This new knowledge, acceptance, and affection cannot lead to reinventing or hybridizing Polish and Jewish identities and relationships. Despite a move towards creating mutual Jewish and Polish responsibility for each other, to have Bruno see a Polish partisan as 'his double', and to entwine their fates, the novel ends by injecting a healthy dose of literary and historical realism into this emotional and historical fantasy of an extended Polish-Jewish family (*Memory Man* 251). Through Bruno's self-critical reflections, the narrative stops short of 'chasing the will o' the wisp' ending that would be 'more like one of Shakespeare's comedies than a recovered wartime story' (252). Instead of creating a mythopoetic synthesis of mutual understanding and reconciliation that transcends the mutually fraught collective memories of both the Poles and the Jews, Appignanesi takes Bruno to Mauthausen, the camp where his father probably perished and where, instead of reconciliation, there are only 'the childhood tears, never shed', that must remain as 'some kind of small memorial' (256).

Appignanesi imagines a Second Generation beyond the parameters of Jewish identity and history. Her children of Holocaust survivors are African American and Polish daughters who inherit different burdens of historical memory. Instead of the certain, almost absolute and essential identity claimed for those who are called the Second Generation, these daughters are born into and claim indeterminate Holocaust identities. Irena decides against a DNA test to determine if Bruno is really her father and Amelia is on her way to solidifying a love relationship with the son of the Polish partisan who shot Bruno and for whose fate Bruno may be responsible. Although Amelia has adopted Judaism, the fact of her African American identity and heritage adds the dimension and perspective of slavery to the inherited burden of uniquely extreme Holocaust suffering. In both cases, the burden of Holocaust memory and its stories must now be borne by those whose relation to the event extends beyond biological belonging and identification. As Bruno faces his irreparable past and Marta fades into hers, the novel leaves us with characters who will carry forward their parents' stories by showing how, regardless of our own historical legacies, all of us are related to the Holocaust and must hear all its stories.

5
Elaine Feinstein's Holocaust Imagination

Elaine Feinstein, acclaimed poet, novelist, biographer, radio and television playwright, and translator, connects English literary traditions to the dislocations of immigrant experience and to the consciousness of enforced or chosen exile.[1] While the Holocaust is not the featured plot line in her writing, its memory often appears as a subliminal pressure underlying dramatically embedded debates about the possibilities of choosing the course of one's life. Ultimately, her writing asserts that no post-Holocaust life is possible without acknowledging the unremitting presence of the past. Feinstein explains the connections she feels between Jewish history and the Holocaust:

> I have had no direct experience of the European horrors of the last century [because] my family . . . came from Russia too early to experience any of the trauma that I talk about in my novels. But that is only a part of it. The Jewish history is a complicated one and it feeds into my life quite deeply. I think that there is no question but that in a sense all those stories are all our stories. We are all survivors of that disaster and everything we think is, in a way, shaped by the knowledge of what would have happened, might have happened to us if we had continued to live in Europe. (Paul Farkash interview 20 April 2005, 1)

Feinstein first learned of the Holocaust at the age of nine but what she saw in films of the death camps and her father's hint 'at something quite evil going on in Germany, something we could not help' became pivotal to her artistic consciousness: 'I can't seem to shake that completely away' ('Inner Voice' n.p.). Despite this powerful influence, Feinstein insists that she could never write about concentration camp experience because except for exploring 'the situation of the survivor . . . one should not use such horror for fictional purposes' ('Dark Inheritance' 65).

Like Diane Samuel's use of the Ratcatcher and Karen Gershon's Gothic references, Feinstein often draws landscapes and architectural spaces that harbor but cannot contain the ghostly emanations of the darker side of

Jewish history. Whether this history predates or coincides with a medieval setting, presages or recalls the Holocaust, its European presence seems to be responsible for the mystifying or Gothic aura of so many of Feinstein's settings.[2] As memory of the Holocaust past is both desired and feared, it assumes characteristics we associate with Freud's concept of the uncanny, *Unheimlich*, where the familiar is defamiliarized and transformed into an ominous presence or specter. The memory of those who inhabited the past and who disappeared unaccountably produces anxiety about whether those who reappear in memory or dream are really the people who disappeared. The persistence of uncanny Holocaust memory is true not only for her Jewish but also non-Jewish characters; the latter may reject and ignore the Holocaust past as having any relevance in their lives decades later, but their struggles to do so only indicate its gnawing power. Like Gershon's and Pascal's Gothic and fairy tale or folkloric references, Feinstein's writing shapes Holocaust memory so that its expression gains a mythic power that expresses its historical certainty and complexity as well as a kind of covenant with those who were lost.

This artistic construction could be seen as responding to Roland Barthes's theory of myth by reversing it. Barthes defines myth as follows:

> In passing from history to nature, myth acts economically: it abolishes the complexity of human acts, it gives them the simplicity of essences, it does away with all dialectics, with any going back beyond what is immediately visible, it organizes a world which is open without contradictions because it is without depth, a world wide open and wallowing in the evident, it establishes a blissful clarity: things appear to mean something by themselves. (Barthes 143)

The mythic structures created by Elaine Feinstein and other writers studied in this book depict 'the complexity of human acts' by creating a three-way dialectic: between characters and the pre-Holocaust or Holocaust pasts, between these and the narrator's role and consciousness, and the interweave of these with narrative structures and tropes. If it weren't for this complex weave, each element would follow Barthes's description. For example, as we have seen with Kindertransport memoirs, the European past of childhood is often represented with idyllic 'simplicity'. Such 'blissful clarity' suggests a memory whose comforting outlines are supported by references to nurturing figures in fairy and folktale. Even Diane Samuels's critical and opaque use of a more sinister fairy-tale figure, the Ratcatcher, presents him as a mythic icon forming the nexus of an unambiguous threat. Feinstein, too, as we shall see, offers iconic ominous images and tales from the Holocaust past that to her characters represent the not-so-'blissful' 'clarity' of the Holocaust tale of innocence versus evil.

A compelling tension that emerges in Feinstein's three-way dialectic addresses the post-Holocaust Jewish obsession with unearthing its historical details and evidence by simultaneously showing how her characters turn to mythic structures to explain the inexplicable. In turn, her characters discover that these mythic tales defamiliarize and dissolve contemporary reliance on the rational and empirical as pathways to understanding Holocaust atrocities, resistances, and individual experience. Contradictions and ambiguity abound in Feinstein's dialectical novels and stories as the Jewish past, which is experienced or felt as 'the simplicity of essences', invades consciousness as a kind of blocked palimpsest: the partial, irretrievable knowledge of a stifling, disabling world whose tortuous depths of atrocity can never be fully 'evident'. At the same time, however, as they work in tandem in Feinstein's writing, myth, folklore, the history of Jewish exile, and the search for the Holocaust past provide an epistemology for the struggles of her contemporary Jewish characters to find a core of meaning in their Jewish identities. Many of Feinstein's novels engage and dramatize three epistemologies – science, poetics, and political or critical theory – that draw our attention to the relationship between the role of the reader, her characters' private obsessions, and Feinstein's ongoing concern with inquiries into Jewish history and continuity in light of the Holocaust. In turn, these ways of knowing are enacted by the characters as emotional, indeed erotic conflicts that embed debates about the power of knowledge.

Like her writing, Feinstein's literary identity is shaped by unsettling travels in time and space. Rather than blending her Leicester childhood, Cambridge education, and Russian Jewish heritage, she expresses their tense relations through her characters' sense of exile and ambivalence about belonging anywhere.[3] Whether her characters choose to be dislodged from their places of origin or Jewish identity or find that there is no such place as home, her writing is infused with memories of a profoundly affecting discontinuous historical identity. This discontinuity is mirrored in her own lack of personal connection to the event and her ongoing concern with the Holocaust. Regardless of whether her characters bear any relation to the event, it is the shadow of the Holocaust that often destabilizes the selfhood they represent. We see this in the recounted memories that materialize as imagined odysseys to medieval Europe or real ones to escape the Holocaust, to revisit Holocaust sites, war-torn or revolutionary Europe, or to a tumultuous Middle East.

For Feinstein, the granddaughter of Russian Jews who escaped the pogroms, the contemporary scene begins with exile 'in the mist of invisible English power'; it then stalls at the history of European antisemitism and the Holocaust, encircled by haunting memories and questions about being a Jew in a postmodern age.[4] Feinstein's women embody these displacements, and much of her fiction focuses on their struggles to distinguish themselves as women residing in a collective and patriarchal historical consciousness. As their Jewish past emerges to become a determining pressure, whatever identity they claim must be relocated, and this mutation redefines their sense of being a woman. Feinstein's writing raises questions about the burdens of Jewish identity for Jewish women. Since women are prescribed by Jewish law to be the bearers of Jewish identity, they also, in Feinstein's writing, embody Jewish history and endure the burdens of Jewish continuity, neither of which inscribes a story of Jewish women's self-determination. In Feinstein's 1992 novel, *Loving Brecht*, the German-born, assimilated Frieda Bloom is shaped by her 'almost earliest memory' of an English nanny identifying her as other – 'Like an animal or an African' (3). Later, when Frieda's Jewishness becomes a dangerous identity, she links her abuse to 'the two parts of myself' – Jew and woman (37). Like so many mutant figures in Gothic literature, she is neither completely human nor inhuman, but rather like Dr. Frankenstein's monster, constructed of ill-fitting pieces chafing against each other. In the context of the Holocaust, she is perceived by those who declare themselves the Master Race as both primitive and savage, but also decadent and passive, perhaps passive-aggressive. In this sense, her womanhood is corrupted by her Jewishness. Among those contemporary writers redefining Englishness and Britishness, Feinstein offers the perspective of those writers whose historical identity resides in the tension between choosing and resisting marginalization from both sides of their Anglo-Jewish identities.

A pivotal example is a short story that appeared early in Feinstein's career, 'The Grateful Dead'. Anna, the protagonist, who is enjoying her first pregnancy, barely acknowledges her Jewish identity, but discovers that the open-ended future embodied in her unborn child is frighteningly determined by the omnipresence of the tragic Jewish past. Her husband Michael would like her to accept the fact of her Jewishness. 'But the history frightened her. She wanted to be free of all that knowledge of what people could do to people' (113). And in the light of that Holocaust knowledge, the story encourages us to imagine that unborn child as Nazi racial science would have constructed her – as the regeneration of Jewish monstrousness. As Feinstein reports, this image has influenced both her own Jewish identity and the construction of her characters: 'And I'm very conscious that I am one of those people whom it was once possible to abuse in this way, and I will always identify with those people' ('Inner Voice' np). As Feinstein constructs her, Anna embodies a challenging tension between the English realist tradition of individual self-discovery and her collective historic identity. This tension suggests a historical reality and memories of its monstrousness which non-realist conventions can barely suggest and from which realist conventions offer no escape. Michael, by contrast, finds refuge from the pall of Jewish history by identifying with his father's books: 'as secret and silent as the tombstones of their two dead fathers lying in the same Jewish cemetery' ('Grateful Dead' 113). Throughout Feinstein's writing, and as we shall see in her novel *Children of the Rose*, such books contrast with the experience of her female characters. Figured as both the tomes and tombs of a patriarchal legacy of Jewish identity and destiny, these learned texts seek unified explanations for the cycles of persecution and destruction that mark Jewish identity and history, but their opposing methods deconstruct them all. As Anna's embodied knowledge demonstrates, the separation of rationalist from mystical wisdom proves to be as much of an illusion as the hope that disaster can be predicted or explained by the past. The usefulness of these books lies in a different epistemology. As the commentaries they contain testify, Jewish learning is never meant to represent the comforts of myth's cohesive clarity, but rather ongoing, often discordant, and inconclusive debates that register a necessarily unfulfilled passion for seeking coherence.

In Feinstein's fiction and poetry, rationalist and mystical or imaginative discourses undercut each other's truth claims. The title 'The Grateful Dead' refers to a form of knowledge that derives as much from history as it does from myth. Anna's Polish refugee maid narrates her husband's experiences of World War II as both the history of the Holocaust and its folk wisdom; she produces archetypes that challenge both Anna's individuality and her collective Jewish identity. The focus of the story is that Mrs. Kowalska's husband found and reburied an old Jewish merchant who had hanged himself in fear of the Nazis. The legend of 'the Grateful Dead is that he wanders between two worlds, responsible for any good that comes to his rescuer but claiming half': 'Not to take. If you offer half, he is satisfied and can rest' ('Grateful Dead' 117). The scoring of 'half' in concert with Jewish wandering combines two perspectives on the formation of Jewish character: the economic determinism of situating Jews in money-related occupations and the mythic evocation of Jewish dispersion since antiquity. Of course both perspectives were deployed by Nazi ideology to demonstrate Jewish avarice and inscrutability. This combination of myth and history presses the story forward to show how, even in their constitutive absences, historic Jews can be reduced to the simplicity of an essential evil. Despite the Jew's satisfaction and the Kowalskas' move to England, Mrs. Kowalska reports that her husband went mad waiting for the Jew's return. The story transforms Anna. Upon hearing it, she finds 'a voice she did not know she could muster . . . you shall not have my son. Your dead will do nothing to me, nothing. And I'll tell you why. They are my dead. You didn't recognize that, did you? Harm? They would rise in their millions to defend me' (118). Anna collapses from her impassioned identification with those millions of Jewish dead, but this does not portend tragedy. Instead, despite or because of her invocation of an aggressive spectral force, she gives birth prematurely to a healthy girl. When Michael tells her that Mrs. Kowalska has disappeared, Anna sees the birth of her daughter as a victory over both myth and history. In an aggressive act of Jewish regeneration and vengeance against the antisemitic vision of the poisonous Jew, Anna affirms the Jewish body as natural and healthy. In the story's narrative logic, the healthy materiality of the Jewish woman's body cures the world of Mrs. Kowalska's Polish antisemitism by dematerializing it.

Part of the story's achievement is its palpable expression of Anna's fear. Resonating with mythic and historic forces that are beyond rational understanding and therefore uncontrollable, her fear challenges Anna's sense of victory. Anna's response signals an ambiguous and therefore elusive and uncanny designation of the origins of her fear, identifying the threatening nature of both the Kowalskas and the dead Jew. As bearer of the tale of Jewish victimization and omnipresence, the Polish woman becomes both tortured and torturer. But, as Feinstein has asserted elsewhere, because she believes that 'Jewish faith has to stand up to Jewish experience, and ... [what] is strong about it is an obstinate denial of superstition', her interpretation of Jewish experience would exclude the possibility of a mythical or mystical presence in favor of an insistently historical construction ('Way Out' 67). In this light, the tale and the teller in 'The Grateful Dead' intertwine the legendary and historic relationship between Poles and Jews that, after a thousand years of uneasy symbiosis, ended in the death camps Hitler had built in Poland. For Anna, a marginally identified Jew, the Holocaust invades her individually defined selfhood and pulls her into the collective Jewish past which she can no longer resist. On the one hand, this sense of Jewishness is made fearful by being revived in the wake of the dead; on the other hand, giving birth to a new generation of Jewish womanhood offers the possibility of a revisionary triumph.[5] Anna's imaginative identification with Mrs. Kowalska's tale conflates material, mystical, mythical, and historic testaments to reality, and thus adds a new genre of commentary to the tomes of the patriarchs, one that only a woman has constructed.

It is not only through women's experience and transformation of anti-semitic myth that Feinstein offers a revisionary commentary on Jewish identity and continuity. Her narrative relationship between folktale and realist story questions and revises readers' expectations that history is truth. For as the folktale reveals, history as forensic narrative is fraught with emotional structures that remain with us and may overwhelm the facts we have absorbed. Coincident with conventions of dream logic, the folktale gives expression to fantasy, desire, and fear, and thus becomes, for Feinstein, the appropriate genre to suggest the collective psychological costs of Jewish history and identity through Anna's individual and spontaneous transformation. The story's realist elements are subordinated to the folktale's explanatory power, suggesting that Jewish history and identity cannot be explained solely by external material realities or protocols of empirical logic. Whatever characters may learn from recounting and analyzing historical events remains vexed by the need and fear of finding the narrative of Jewish history predictive. Although distanced by time, in this story, the Holocaust remains a haunting presence in the folktale, both for its teller and for Anna. Just as the Jewish merchant will not stay buried, so the event that caused his death will not be laid to rest. The memory of the Holocaust converges with fears of its repetition which cannot be allayed by the daylight safety of assimilated British Jews like Michael and Anna. And yet Feinstein does not completely subsume the rationalist element of the story. By insisting that a dark and terrible event must be kept alive as incontestable fact, the story embeds historical and social realities and prevents its folk wisdom from becoming Gothicized or romanticized, and therefore suspect as truth.

Feinstein's first novel established women's consciousness as the translator of social, psychological, and historic realities. Its title, *The Circle*, reflects 'the circle of [a woman's] own thought, listening' to her inner life and connecting it to irreconcilable tensions in her marriage (10). So, too the woman narrator of Feinstein's poem 'Marriage' observes that 'We have taken our shape from the / damage we do one another' (37). All Feinstein's writing negotiates an abyss between the desires of men and women which is never bridged. At best, beginning with *The Circle* and continuing into her later writing, a bemused if resigned understanding of their differences allows them to live with and without each other in a state of tense coexistence that later mirrors the relationship of her Jewish characters in a gentile world.

For example, in a compendium of three plays she wrote for radio, *Foreign Girls*, two couples and their daughters' love relationships remain suspended in their negotiations with each other and with being Jewish. One couple, their daughter, and the man she marries and then divorces are Hungarian refugees from the 1956 revolution who consider themselves victims more of communism than of antisemitism and have little feeling for their Jewish identities. Although mother and daughter have become successful artists, the plays show how their refugee experience in England is marred by the continuation of European and English antisemitism. At the plays' end, vandalized gravestones in the Jewish cemetery where their father has chosen to be buried parallel anti-Jewish incidents in contemporary Hungary. Rather than expressing such concerns about European and English antisemitism through Jewish characters, they are visible in Feinstein's early novels as certain narrative pressures she would later articulate as explicitly Jewish. Even when an Oedipal plot foregrounds a family romance, its structure extends to suggest tribal relations, enacting a sense of internalized, understood if unarticulated rules of allegiance to an identity outside individual family relations. It is as though the pressures of continuity and family ties signal a powerfully determining plot based on the nagging consciousness of a collective identity.

By revealing the Jewish past through women's consciousness, impossible but irrevocable marriages, and indeterminate endings, Feinstein invokes her own narrative of Jewish history to challenge its status as a received and determining text. A test case for my interpretation is Feinstein's 1976 (1975) novel, *Children of the Rose*, in which the Holocaust and its unmarked graves unsettle notions of Jewish continuity. This novel was inspired by Feinstein's journey in 1973 to Poland where she discovered 'a completely different cultural inheritance, which was mine, and which England didn't have' ('Dark Inheritance' 64). It was one of Poland's Jewish cemeteries which conjured up haunting images of Eastern European Jewish persecution. In its dramatization of such an experience, the novel expresses the feeling that neither actual journeys nor ritualized returns to the ancient Jewish past can serve as forensic possibilities for understanding the present. The protagonists of *Children of the Rose* are Jewish refugees whose attempts to build English lives are foiled by haunting memories of the Holocaust. This elaboration of the intractable marital impasse explored in such early novels as *The Circle* and *The Crystal Garden* clearly identifies the centrality of the Jewish past as pivotal.[6] Though their ill-matched desires for selfhood drove Alex and Lalka Mendez to divorce, they remain incomplete without each other and without the stories of their individual but entwined Jewish past. Linking personal desire to historical necessity, the novel charts the dissolution of the couple's relationship and their re-union as an unfinished process of historical discovery. As the past, the present, and the characters' historical consciousnesses become reflexive texts, the emotional locus of the novel becomes the painful recognition that Jewishness is not one moment or event, but continuity. The very first step we witness in the process of historical discovery appears to be a false one. Alex Mendez buys a dilapidated chateau in southern France whose original medieval history is totally irrelevant to him except that in renovating it lies the possibility of remaking the past in his own image; conversely, he will remake his image in rehabbing the chateau. We don't have to wait very long to discover the futility of wishful or magical thinking in this effort since Mendez knows it and the narrator announces it from the outset. The first paragraph of the novel tells us that the chateau is located in a deserted village, surrounded by 'a skeleton ridge of eroded stone', hallmark of a 'brutal landscape' (*Children of the Rose* 7). Such Gothic touches turn out to evoke more of the facts of history than the symbols of fairy tales and so mock Mendez's wish for transformation. As we learn, despite its secret spaces and murky history, the chateau casts a sinister shadow only as its history becomes clear.

The next faulty steps Mendez takes consist of rescuing the daughter of the chateau's former owner from prison and believing that he has impregnated her and finally has an heir on the way. A refugee from a romantic fling with hippie-style rebellion, Lee is sufficiently deficient in her capacity for commitment to satisfy and yet frustrate Mendez's Pygmalion fantasies of male nurture and regeneration. It is predictable from the start that their one night of sex is a dead end from which the only exit is to have no expectations. What is not predictable are the histories Feinstein constructs that link the characters to the Holocaust and its memories. In turn, these histories transform Mendez's chateau from an empty relic to a repository of memories of wartime heroism and betrayal. If the medieval history of the chateau is inconsequential, its modern history of Nazi occupation reverberates not only in Lalka's story and Mendez's but turns out to be a shaping force of Lee's character and of questions about Jewish regeneration. When Mendez takes Lee on a tour of his restoration work, we discover not only that he has converted the ballroom into a library of Jewish books but also that this is the room where, in 1943, Lee's mother had entertained the Gestapo in order to distract them from noticing that she was hiding Jews. Later, we learn that it was the three-year-old Lee who betrayed the hidden Jews and, in so doing, her mother as well. With no remorse but much resentment, Lee tells Mendez that she hated the Jews then and does so still: 'God, why are they so ugly, refugees? So ugly and smelly and so pathetically without dignity? Grateful. For anything – water, bits of bread ... I don't *care* what happened to them' (84, 85, italics in text). In light of this revelation of hateful indifference, the restoration of Jewish learning that materializes as Mendez's library may be another exercise in futility. What does the continuity of Jewish culture mean when it is haunted not by the specters of fairy tales or Gothic bogeymen but by the 'ghosts' of historically persecuted Jews? (83): 'Crouched in the old cupboards ... Old men with lice in their beards. And shit-stained children. Women as old as witches' (83). The meaning may lie in Mendez's response: 'Then why are you haunted?' (85).

Of course Mendez might just as well be speaking about himself, for his character and Lalka's are nothing more or less than ghostly embodiments of a Holocaust past that will not permit escape or reconstitution. What kind of progeny, his questions implies, can he possibly father, what kind of future does he represent if his 'haunted child' lover 'probably already smelt in his own flesh the sick pallor of the people she had feared and resented' (86). Clearly the idea of having a child with Lee for the sake of Jewish regeneration is a disaster, least of all because, as a non-Jew, she cannot bear a Jewish child. More damaging to Mendez's fantasy are the antisemitic references manifest in her description of the victims. While we might consider such remarks extraordinary thirty years after the Holocaust ended, the novel presents them as coterminous with questions about Jewish survival and regeneration in Europe.[7] According to another character, one who represents a French everyman, post-Holocaust Europe still takes its rejection of the Jews for granted. This 'true Provençal *bourgeois*' does not question the linkages to be made between his celebration of France as 'the health of Europe' and his continuing acceptance of those Pétainesque laws 'against foreigners' that stopped 'moral decadence' (36, 37). Participating in the Jewish tradition of ongoing and unsettled critical commentary, Mendez seeks answers to his tremulous place in European history and culture. He reads and talks back to his library of Jewish lore, but the only wisdom he discovers in the seers' appeals to God constitutes 'A macabre evasion', another form of silence (86). Feinstein does not present the problem of Jewish identity, history, and continuity as a dichotomy of self and other or victim and external forces of oppression. Instead, she situates part of the novel's reflexive structure in the Jews' construction of their history, as figured in the books Mendez inherited from his father. Both in their material reality and elusive meanings, these books are testaments to the endlessly contested sites and significances of Jewish continuity. The books take on a life of their own as they seem to absorb and inscribe the ambiguities of events that transpired in the chateau's ballroom.

That so many of these tomes date from the medieval period metaphorically creates a continuum of Jewish suffering that cannot be explained either through rational investigation or mythic allusions, as we saw in the story 'The Grateful Dead'. This Jewish history is, as the character Inge Wendler notes in Feinstein's 1984 novel, *The Border*, 'like an apocalypse' (73). In Feinstein's 1976 time-travel novel *The Ecstasy of Dr. Miriam Garner* an old Jewish family from Toledo, Spain, represents not only the continuity of Jewish culture and learning but also the history of 'an unhappy persistent people. Such a centuries-enduring memory' in this novel as in her 1978 novel *The Shadow Master* permeates Jewish history in relation to both Christianity and Islam (*Ecstasy* 126). In Elaine Feinstein's oeuvre, this vexed multicultural combination is what gives rise to the interminable and reflexive questioning that shapes Jewish learning and writing about the nature and continuity of Jewish identity. So we see when the drug-induced consciousness of Miriam Garner is transported to medieval Toledo, for hiding her mother's Jewish identity replays a pivotal chapter in the dispersion of Jewish identity: the Spanish history of Jewish persecution and the turn to Marrano or concealed Jewish identity. The result, according to Lilian, the astrologer character in *The Shadow Master*, is that like the Marranos, those Jews who have disguised their beliefs by so many layers they no longer know who they are. The accretion in Feinstein's writing of such obfuscating layers of disguised and assimilated identities, the experiences of chosen or enforced exile, and the narrative transports and characters' dreams and fantasies over time and space evoke a cumulative image of both the Wandering Jew and the Jew as rootless cosmopolitan. As an organizing principle of Feinstein's fiction, this image suggests that the search for Jewish continuity over time and in Europe and elsewhere is always disrupted by expulsion, Jewish ambivalences about Jewish identity, and destruction. Paradoxically, these disruptions form the story of Jewish continuity. To read Feinstein's fiction is to follow an epic of Jewish dispersion from Spain to Turkey and back to Europe where, despite its patterns of relentless repetitions, the oppressive past can never be preparation for the crimes and complicity committed by Nazi-occupied Europe. But even in the aftermath of such destruction, the concealment and disguise that characterize an ongoing history of disrupted Jewish identity and culture continues.

In *Children of the Rose* the search for Jewish continuity and meaningful linkages between the Jewish past, present, and future is foreclosed by the Holocaust. In this novel, typical of Feinstein's oeuvre, there is no esoteric ancient knowledge or theology that can bridge the epistemological chasm created by unimaginable brutality. As so many Holocaust writers have attested, the attempt to find answers or explanations leads only to irony. For example, it would be bitterly ironic to accept the ancient axiom that 'The meek inherit the earth' since the European earth is a compost pile of the bones, ashes, and detritus that represents the legacy of the continent's 'spiritual values' (88, 37).[8] Mendez's desire for a child to represent some kind of 'victory' over the hatred for the Jews and the hatred felt in return cannot, on the basis of a European heritage, work out (88). When Lee disappears with her boyfriend at the end, and takes the child with her, the loss is as ambiguous as the Jewish future, for not only isn't Lee Jewish but it is never clear who is the father. Furthering the novel's ironic juxtapositions between myth and history, Lee's choice of itinerancy over rootedness only leads to her entrapment in a story she would reject. Despite her disavowal of Jewish suffering, Lee's decision to leave the haunted chateau is no escape from it as her continued migrancy only recapitulates the ghostly figure of the Wandering Jew. A mythical figure signifying both a sympathetic view of interminable exile and an antisemitic rendering of the eternally insidious outsider, the Wandering Jew ironically binds the non-Jewish Lee to the Jewish Lalka. Though they never meet, their alliterative names suggest mirror images of insider/outsider and the search for and escape from the Holocaust past and its Jewish ghosts. On the one hand, Lee's disappearance poisons her meaning to Mendez as an elixir of youth and subverts his escape from the past by taking away the child who represents his new start. On the other hand, Lalka's reappearance at the end endows his chateau with meanings of stability and rootedness. Whatever magical thinking drove Mendez to transform the chateau into a site of personal restoration is glossed by the interpolation of a Polish myth about the Jewish presence in the town of Kasimiersh. Lalka's tour guide, Tadeusz, recounts its story: 'It was built by the King Casimir, because he fell in love with a Jewish girl, and made her his mistress. So he built a haven for her people' (122). This sunny tale is shadowed by juxtapositions with the novel's darker themes. Even at the level of a romance tale, because there is no indication of mutual love, the Jewish girl's position as the king's mistress points not only to her subordination but also to that of the Jews whose lives were dominated by edicts of the Polish monarchy. The disappearance of the Jews in the Holocaust also encourages a reading of the folktale as a defensive Polish gesture, especially in light of the novel's critical associations with Mendez's chateau as a 'haven' in which its hidden Jews were betrayed. Finally, just as the Jewish people disappear from Poland and France in the Holocaust, so the attempted destruction of Jewish culture destabilizes European Jewish identity, as the disappearing, ambiguously Jewish child of Lee confirms.

The destabilizing stroke that reduces Lalka to a state of childlike dependency requires a 'haven' that combines sanctuary and nurture and an acute awareness of the determination of the past. Having suffered a stroke while visiting Poland, Lalka now embodies the need to recover not only from the atrocity-filled Nazi past but also from her own bitter memory of escape that could be interpreted as a perverse and 'bloody victory' for 'the murderers. To leave the rest of us glad just to be left to live' (75). Though Lalka's bitter proclamation is the reverse of Mendez's view of 'victory' as a triumph over the hatred that infested the past, the novel asks us to reject them both. As in 'The Grateful Dead' and like the figure of the Wandering Jew, 'victory' is a disturbingly unstable signifier, deploying a universalized moral certainty to gloss over the anxieties that inhere in ambivalence toward its object. How, the novel asks us, can we acknowledge the ongoing traumatic effects of the Holocaust past if we gloss over them with the moral certainty that can either justify or deny hatred and its consequences? Where in the moral boundaries between villain and victim does hatred lie? As the Polish tour guide, Tadeusz, reflects: 'Lalka, if people want to hate, they will hate the poor Jews because they are dirty; and the beautiful because they are rich' (129). Like the paradoxically reified figure of the Wandering Jew, the moral certainty of victory is a dangerous myth, untouched by historical realities.

Lalka's journey back to Poland uncovers a paralyzing ambivalence about identifying herself with a landscape that conjures up a chronicle of remembered, confronted, and imagined images veering between nostalgia and dread, myth and history: 'droskies and push-carts, a child, holding someone's soft hand' melt into a crowded train, the vehicle of escape from the fate that awaited her – an unmarked grave where 'the bushes growing out of the soil looked sinister . . . There was blood in the grass. The weeds, the grass, and the rose all grew from that blood' (101).[9] If the antisemitism that underwrote the Holocaust constructed and destroyed the Jews as a malignant mass, it also denied the possibility of Jewish individuality. Lalka's journey becomes a struggle to find her individuality against this history but her struggle is not only with political history but as a gendered history. If love is conventionally opposed to hate, the novel shows both emotions to be equally paralyzing and subsuming when individuality is not protected and the object is submerged into the subject. Living apart from Mendez and now so far away from home, seeking her own story, Lalka is nonetheless irrevocably tied to him. On her return to Europe, she discovers that she is still considered Mendez's wife and, though she chafes against this identity and 'had defended her core from Alex', we learn that her life since their separation lacks purpose except for the home she maintains and which she had designed for his comfort (154).[10] Lalka represents questions that permeate so many of Feinstein's female characters in relation to dominant men: 'why do women behave like this, why do they let themselves be used, why do they accept so little, why do they not leave behind them these unhappy relationships? And the answer is, of course, because female masochism is a very real force' ('Dark Inheritance' 63). That this force derives from a history of women's historical and social positions is confirmed by Mendez's dependence on Lalka and by all of Feinstein's fictions.

Mendez too cannot find direction without Lalka despite his need to escape her 'desire to be his creature' (*Children of the Rose* 155). This mutual projection/misunderstanding is not, however, the stuff of romantic melodrama or a critique of modern marriage. Instead, this is a critique of mutually absorptive and conflicted fantasies that express the process through which a woman survivor replicates the threat to her life in the Holocaust. She sacrifices her sense of self afterward to her protector. In turn, such a configuration calls attention to what we mean by Holocaust survivor and the pressure on survivors to tell their stories. It turns out that what Mendez wanted from Lalka and that she withheld from him was her Holocaust story, the meaning of which drives her aborted journey to Poland. Despite their shared history of the imminent threat of destruction, their Holocaust experiences were very different. But when he brings her to his chateau, it is as though he carries the burden of Jewish history. And if Lalka has resisted Mendez's questions about her story, it is because not only does she wish to preserve the integrity of the form she gives it for herself but also, by not telling it, she secures the meaning it has for her – the knowledge that 'there was nothing there but death. And silence' (155). And if, at the end, she is committed entirely to Mendez's care and, indeed, is now in a position to be 'His only child', he will never hear her story because the stroke which may or may not have silenced her forever also enables her to withstand the pressures of his desire for her story (171).

Despite her dependency on him, her silence is a form of retreat from and resistance to his demanding/commanding presence. She and her story will remain separate from Mendez and his story. Free now of their incompatibility, their relationship teaches the reverse of his rationale for desiring to have a child. Instead, the novel reveals the Jewish past not only as continuous but also as fusing both its dead and its heirs. Though her body, like her mind, is now impaired, they perform her story and its message that she was never before able to confront and express. This is the message uttered by her sister who, more melodramatically than Lalka's fate, illustrates the ongoing psychic suffering wrought by the Holocaust. Besieged by an abusive marriage and poverty, Clara has developed an identity and purpose by accepting the Holocaust's damaging legacy: 'None of us really escaped, she said' (170). There is a rescue, however, that lies beyond this statement of despair and the sacrificial 'peace' Lalka may achieve in Mendez's care (171). The separately embedded narrations by Lalka and Mendez of their Holocaust stories grant each one its integrity while joining each other to form a multifaceted chronicle of suffering, resistance, escape, and no escape. If no survivor can escape the searing memories of Holocaust suffering, their stories can remain intact as their authors at least retain control over their forms of expression. If in their childlessness we see the scars of the Holocaust in whatever Mendez and Lalka make of their lives, and if their stories have no regenerative power, they do generate consciousness of the struggle to give expressive form to memory.

Feinstein's 1982 novel, *The Survivors*, explores women's agency and its relation to retaining memories of the past as a problem central to the destabilizing effects of two European Jewish families acculturating to England. While the pressures of Jewish continuity shape both Feinstein's men and women, she shows that women pay more for choosing to save themselves through transformation. Feinstein designs their assigned roles as Jewish Angels of the Hearth to mediate between the costs and benefits of a history of marginalization. To leave the hearth and minister unto others, like one woman in the novel who becomes a nurse during World War I, denies continuity with the European experience, especially as she will reject its ritual observances which mark the Jewish choice to remain a distinct people. Feinstein thus links both becoming English and women's agency to Jewish codes of self-determination. To be a Jew inscribes an identity that remains separate even as it crosses boundaries of individuality, time, and space. When World War I breaks out and the German sphere becomes the enemy, Jewish identity becomes inexorably problematic: 'We are Europe... perhaps the whole Jewish people, riven and divided by this war like no one else. We *are* Europe, eating and destroying itself' (86, Feinstein's italics). The price Jewish women pay for choosing their own separateness is to be 'riven and divided' within and between themselves and the world of the English. Hence, the character of Diana, like Feinstein herself, the first woman in her family to attend Cambridge, found she could not fit in between: she clung 'to bits and pieces of Yiddish... The question of loyalty was poignant... So many had died in mud and fire for being Jewish. To give up seemed a gross betrayal' (287).

The generative power of memory to recreate and reshape the Jewish past and its betrayals is the subject of Feinstein's 1984 novel, *The Border*. This novel returns to a European scene to dramatize the question of loyalty to Jewish history and continuity against the backdrop of the coming of World War II. Divided into different characters' narratives, the novel itself is riven by different perspectives, and so foregrounds the textuality of Jewish history, 'the content of the form'.[11] Because its time frame and plot skip over the years of the Holocaust and focus on its preludes and aftermath, the novel questions rather than dramatizes the possibility of imagining the story of its cataclysmic events. Like *Children of the Rose*, this novel is about discontinuous Jewish identity, a journey, and exile, but here the journey is to escape the escalating injunctions against the Jews that constitute the pre-Holocaust present and, later, to discover the past that made escape both possible and impossible. The novel begins and ends with the present as a frame – a visit in 1983 to Inge Wendler by her American grandson, Saul, a student of history at Oxford. The setting of the visit is Sydney, Australia, where Inge, a scientist, found refuge from Nazi-occupied Vienna. Inge's husband Hans, a poet and dramatist, was mysteriously killed on the last leg of their escape, in Port Bou. So, many years later, she is now called upon by her grandson to piece together and make sense of her memories of escaping Europe in 1938.

Instead of satisfying the historian's search for 'facts', the diaries and letters she offers Saul add up to 'stories [that] can be told many different ways' (83). Inge, who serves as archivist and repository of historical memory, connects the political and the personal, but her perspective cannot be universalized, questioning, as it does, any totalizing view of Jewish survival in the Holocaust. Feinstein creates Inge as a scientist whose analysis of the historic roots of the Nazi threat turns out to be no more explanatory than the ahistorical, deeply personalized sense of persecution felt by her poet-husband, Hans. Moreover, because we never learn how the historian uses this material, we can assume that, like him, we will construct our own interpretations, the central issue of which will be loyalty, since interpretation requires fidelity to a text. This meaning of loyalty also reflects that of a particular history: of a people identified with their book. The interactive process of characters' memories in Feinstein's earlier novels is elided here to privilege the reader instead of the narrator. Feinstein's emphasis on textuality and rhetorical strategy challenges us to struggle with the questions formerly given to her characters and thus transfers to readers the moral responsibility for bearing witness to the Jewish history that identifies Feinstein's writing.

Such responsibility, however, contains its own difficulties, for the rewards of reading private diaries and letters, with its suggestion of voyeurism, complicates any moral lesson. We are, after all, being offered history as a very personal story of obsessive passion and attachment, self-pitying narcissism, and private despair. As the novel progresses and as the characters respond to the intensifying crisis of Nazi conquest and Jewish persecution, they alternate with and intertwine the others' responses. With each step of their hesitations and decision to escape, as they must adapt to the different conditions of becoming increasingly isolated in Vienna, of being refugees in Paris, and on the run to Marseilles and southward, they find themselves unselfconsciously assuming the way of knowing they had previously rejected as too rational or too fanciful. As the novel unfolds through Hans's diary, the letters of Hans's lover Hilde Dorf, Inge's diary, and, finally, Inge's narration of their story to her grandson, it creates reflexive ways of discovering the past as a pathway to understand the shaping and nature of the present and the always failed quest to combine them as prophesy.

Nowhere is this reflexivity more apparent than in the way the story of the Wendlers parallels and references those of Walter Benjamin. We see this in the failed escape of Benjamin, who committed suicide in Port Bou, and in the efforts those others who were hounded and who tried to escape over the Pyrenees to unoccupied Spain and on to Lisbon where some could get plane or ship passage to safe harbors.[12] Although Hans's murder in Port Bou is depicted as ambiguous, with only a suspected murderer and motivation, it registers with the aborted escapes of so many as well as the ambiguity many critics have attached to Benjamin's motivation for committing suicide. Inge surmises that the killer could very well have been a former student turned Nazi nemesis, but, because Hans's face is shattered, she can't even be entirely sure the body is his. Thus she is doubly haunted, by the failure of his escape and by lack of certainty about his death. As the novel charts the Wendlers' ambivalent indecision, choices, uncertain journey, and Hans's ambiguous end, it suggests that the odyssey of escape, like that of actual Holocaust experience and the vicissitudes of Jewish identity, has neither resolution nor closure. In fact, although Inge is safely ensconced in Sydney throughout and after the war, her emotional experience remains in transit, as though her journey will never end. Like other writers considered in this book, Feinstein's inquiry into unfulfilled ways of knowing the Holocaust also evokes the trope of the Wandering Jew. Instead of providing understanding or critical frameworks to the characters' epistemologies and to the search for Holocaust knowledge, *The Border's* references to psychoanalysis and Walter Benjamin confirm the fleeting and ultimately questionable reliability and stability of new forms and sources of knowledge. As we have seen in *Children of the Rose* and other Feinstein writing, this would also involve older theories, wisdom, and reflections.

When Hans meets Benjamin and is taken with the latter's critical theories, his response is not an amalgam of critical questioning and imagination, but enchantment with a vision he romanticizes:

> – Magical. A Marxist who is not a materialist. He has come to grips with all the horrors of our time. Even the horrors of Nazism. And he has a whole library of which I know nothing to help him. Imagine. He uses the Kabbalah. The work of an old theologian like Abulafia. He laughed at me when I drew back from my own Jewishness. I didn't even know there was a Jewish mystical tradition. (*Border* 57–8)

Considering the extent and persistence of Hans's doubts about Inge's scientific logic and empiricism, his unquestioning acceptance of Benjamin's knowledge gathering might give us pause. While Hans's unabashed enthusiasm could strike us as prescient in relation to Benjamin's critical acclaim today, the poet's ignorant indifference to 'Jewishness' and Jewish traditions casts suspicious light on his critical acumen.[13] At the very least, the novel leads us to an ironic view of Hans's philosophical assessments by its historical distance which is established by the novel's frame and by our own retrospective knowledge of that moment in October 1938. Hans's infatuations with both Benjamin's 'mystical' Marxism and Hilde, his Communist lover, foreclose the possibility that he will establish the critical distance to question ideological and political relationships between the two systems. The lack of such distance, however, recalls the entangled philosophical attempts of many Marxist intellectuals at the time and even much later to distinguish their political philosophy from the practices of Communism.

To have created distinctions then would have required the acknowledgement and perhaps protest of Stalin's 1936–38 purge trials, the victims of which were mostly Jews, as well as the August 1938 Nazi-Soviet pact, which dissolved only with Germany's invasion of the Soviet Union in 1941. While it was intact, the agreement cast both ideologies and political systems in the shadows of despotism without exonerating Marxism as a separate critical theory. That the novel acknowledges the necessity of analyzing Marxism in relation to Communism is clear in its representation of Hilde's letters from the Soviet Union in which she depicts moving from 'a fairy tale' forest cottage to the political realities of Moscow (77). Despite offering sanctuary to Jews and publishing Yiddish writers, this is a place where people disappear without reason and 'silence' pervades the atmosphere, recalling for us the histories of Nazi-occupied Poland and France in *Children of the Rose* (80). While we don't know if circumstances ever dampened Hilde's enthusiasm, we learn from Inge that she was silenced – arrested on spy charges, sentenced to fifteen years' forced labor, and survived. We never learn how or in what frame of mind. Never a communist herself, Inge offers the perspective of those who were victimized by any complicity with the Nazis' drive for global power: 'I had no problems with the Nazi-Soviet pact. It was no more appalling to me than the English and French betrayal at Munich' (*Border* 83).

That Hans is happy to join Benjamin in rejecting a materialist Marxism could of course be considered consistent with a repudiation of the Nazis' materialist socialism: the Reich's industrialized and objectifying dehumanization and extermination process. But it also suggests that there is something misguided in Hans's certainty about Benjamin's having 'come to grips with all the horrors of our time', including 'Nazi horrors'. How could anyone except the perpetrators have full knowledge of the material realities of the deportations, torture, and killing of those deemed *Untermenschen* when so much was still unclear and unimaginable in 1938? Even Kristallnacht, the outsized pogrom that burned and pillaged synagogues and murdered thousands of Jews in Germany and Austria, is a month away from Hans's meeting with Benjamin. To have predicted these events would have required an epistemological system that was indeed 'Magical'. And yet by 1938 certain horrors were clear: the enforcement of the 1934–35 Nuremberg Laws that not only stripped Jews of their citizenship and economic livelihoods, but, as Hans's and Inge's escape reminds us, endangered Jewish lives and culture. In relation to Feinstein's concerns about Jewish culture and continuity, Hans's withdrawal from his Jewish identity reveals lack of knowledge not only about his cultural heritage but also about the Nazis' policy for its destruction. Between its 1983 frame and 1938 narratives, *The Border* juxtaposes the fate of Jews caught in the vortex of Nazi deception, philosophical self-deception, and the necessarily unfulfilling search to understand how victims and survivors negotiated their possibilities for survival.

This is not to say that there can be no avenue to gaining knowledge of the Holocaust, but rather that knowledge must remain incomplete and we must not confuse knowledge with understanding. As Elie Wiesel cautions us, instead of assuming we can understand the Holocaust, we can only ask questions:

It is against the answers that I protest . . . Answers: I say there are none. Each [theory] contains perhaps a fraction of truth, but their sum still remains beneath and outside what, in that night, was truth. The events obeyed no law and no law can be derived from them.

The subject matter to be studied is made up of death and mystery, it slips away between our fingers, it runs faster than our perception: it is everywhere and nowhere. Answers only intensify the question: ideas and words must finally come up against a wall higher than the sky, a wall of human bodies extending to infinity. (142)

We see the futility in looking for answers not only in Saul's quest as a historian but also in the way both Inge's scientific knowledge and Hans's poetic intuitions call attention to the partialities and unreliability of each perspective. One could argue of course that both Hans and Inge are too close, indeed trapped inside the volatility of their historical identities, including radical assimilation and even conversion, as well as their current circumstances, to have acquired critical distance. But even at the end, nearly four decades after the end of the war in Europe, on the other side of the world, neither temporal nor spatial nor investigative distance provides a perspective that might help explain all that remains incoherent and inconclusive about the past.

The novel plays out this illusory distance through questions that link the painfully symbiotic relationship of Inge and Hans to the 'death and mystery' of the Holocaust. As Wiesel cautions, none of us will find answers – neither we nor her characters nor their author. Estranged emotionally and intellectually, Hans and Inge also cannot live without each other. In another variation of the marital and family tensions so many of Feinstein's fictions depict, instead of introducing mutual respect and interesting complexity into their relationship, the different world views of husband and wife only result in clashes between their empirical and poetic temperaments.[14] While Hans complains that Inge's 'logic is relentless' and views her science as 'arcane, incomprehensible work in particle physics', Inge finds his passion for 'the modern' worthy of scorn: 'as if this whole century has not delighted in exhuming prehistory. It is almost a deliberate regression, isn't it. To childhood'(18, 19, 70). Instead of either character progressing by developing insight into the other's way of knowing and learning from it, once they are forced to leave Vienna and are cut adrift from their cultural bearings, terror overwhelms both empirical logic and poetic insight. Cultural exile also questions the characters' gendered stereotypes of how men and women should and do think. As terror destroys the capacity to formulate imaginative or critical questions or answers, Inge's scientific outlook gives way to emotionalism – a self-effacing dependency on her mercurial and exploitative husband that now feminizes her in his eyes. In tandem, Hans's poetic intuitions transform into pragmatism – a self-affirming independence he had previously denounced as Inge's masculine quality. As we witness each way of knowing subsume the other in both characters alternatively, it becomes clear that the separation of poetics from empiricism exacerbates the gendered gaps and the partiality and unreliability of the knowledge they seek. The novel provides several interrelated angles from which to view this cognitive and epistemological dissonance. Though Inge, Hans, and Hilde speak in their own voices, in their diaries and letters, not only are they self-deceptive and prey to the limitations of their singular modes of cognition but also, combined with their misgivings, suspicions, and misrepresentations of other forms, this plethora of false knowledge makes them unreliable narrators in triplicate. As we see with Hans's first diary entry, despite his analyst's advice to substitute writing for his 'stammering terror', the novel challenges the conventional wisdom that writing is a pathway to knowledge of self and others (17).

Instead, Hans's diary only confirms a narcissism that becomes a trope for the deluded self-interest that led so many to rationalize Hitler's power as a doomed anomaly in a nation whose democratic instincts and philosophical wisdom would prevail. While it has become commonplace to ascribe such a skewed vision to German followers of Hitler, to levy this criticism at Hitler's Jewish victims is startling, if not problematic. Instead, as so many have attested, between their citizenship and assimilation, German Jews were encouraged to feel confident that their position was secure. In conflating German and German Jewish responses to Hitler, Feinstein takes a creative and ethical risk that we might see as interchangeably compromised. I would argue, however, that Feinstein brilliantly tethers Hans's epistemological evasions to the moral evasion of a nation. This is pinpointed in one of his diary entries where he describes passing a figure who looks familiar, but whose abject poverty and look of madness disguise his identity. When Hans realizes that this was his 'old analyst' and that 'something terrible had certainly happened to him', he confesses, 'I did not risk finding out what it was' (41). The self-knowledge and empathy that might have been gained in work with his psychoanalyst have been trumped, not by the political necessity of self-defense, but by rationalization. Not so coincidentally, rationalization is the defense mechanism described by Anna Freud, the daughter of the father of psychoanalysis, whose escape from Vienna in 1939 shares the spotlight with this incident. In the setting of Hans's encounter with his analyst in February 1938, nine months before Kristallnacht, the confrontation between a Jew who has already been brutalized and one who still has options for escape reflects and expresses the psychic choice to withdraw from both individual and political responsibility. In denying the other man's subjectivity and the value of psychological introspection, Hans's defensiveness destroys an epistemological bridge connecting art and science to the moral imagination. Refusal to acknowledge the presence and desperation of the analyst thus casts a shadow over the writer's moral imagination and incites the reader's suspicion about the value of his writing and the values it espouses. In its most lethal emanation, Hans's rejection of the analyst's obvious need for help colludes with Nazi antisemitism in two intertwined ways: Nazi ideology considered Jews a craven, degenerate race and psychoanalysis a sign of Jewish degeneration.

In his inability to recognize the integrity and needs of another, Hans is not alone. In fact the novel's multivocal and reflexive structure points an interpretive finger not only at his philosophical and psychological politics and that of Inge and Hilde, the other protagonists, but at the society in which they live. The insidious design of the Third Reich isolates individuals so as to form a nation motivated by fear, distrust, and loathing of the other. That Hans does not even consider himself a Jew only testifies to an effect of radical assimilation that the Nazis would deploy against the Jews: the power of internalizing hatred of the other to produce self-hatred.[15] Though the characters are isolated by their rejections of each other's ways of knowing, the novel juxtaposes these responses so that each narrative provides critical perspective on the others that reflects back on itself. This method not only grants each narrative individual voice but also, in effect, demonstrates their personal interdependence and that with the State. Thus as a chain of signification, the novel's depiction of Hans's narcissistic relations can be read on several overdetermined levels. His emotional entanglements with Inge, Hilde, and his own creativity are both supported and contested by Inge's self-professed devotion to him. Combined, however, with her empirical logic, her selfless passion is viewed by him not as the stuff of romantic love but of claustrophobic desire and fuel for his self-absorption and rejection of her and her political insights. In turn, Inge's blinkered adoration of her emotionally manipulative husband blunts her political acuity. Adding another challenging narrative ingredient to her German-Jewish political critique, Feinstein joins these two characters in a mirroring relation to German society. Though both Hans and Inge are Jews according to Nazi decree, and about to be victimized accordingly, their relationship offers a lens through which to view those Germans who yielded their empirical logic and their self-determination to the man who declared himself their Führer. Working as a brief but intense chronicle of responses to the tightening Nazi vise, the novel illustrates the interweave of epistemological, psychological, and narrative strands that could have inspired critical wisdom, but were experienced as a triple cognitive bind. As we know from historical and personal accounts, this bind proved to be a very effective rationalization. Too many Germans paradoxically chose political and psychological paralysis and foreclosed the possibility of resistance. For some Jews, the bind stalled plans for escape while, for others, it propelled plans to escape even if most were unsuccessful. As the novel's multifaceted title suggests, if all too many national borders signified the entrapment of European Jews in the Final Solution, the meanings of the word border today are more porous. As we negotiate the distance between questions and answers, factual knowledge and philosophical understanding, in the voice of the poet, *The Border* asks of itself 'How to make you imagine' when 'only ghosts remain / to know that we exist' (111).

At the end of the novel which also concludes Inge's narrative, coinciding with the end of Yom Kippur, the Jewish Day of Atonement, she proposes a toast 'To the forgiveness of all our infidelities' (108). Her fleeting reunion with her grandson reconciles the 'unequal duel' between rationalist and imaginative visions, and between hope for Jewish survival and continuity and the history and visions of Jewish destruction (107).[16] Asking forgiveness on this day constitutes a ritual act that, replicated over historical time and across individual purpose, performs a stabilizing function that unites individual and collective consciousness.[17] Thus Inge's toast also reconciles her with Hans's vision, which he articulates immediately afterward in the poem that closes the novel. As though in response, he invokes a 'mission' to perpetuate his history as both indelible and ephemeral. The decentered content here is stabilized by the form. The imaginative and historic textuality of his poem resonates with the rituals of 'sing[ing] old prayers... at whatever cost' (112, 113).

Feinstein's 1988 novel, *Mother's Girl*, explores the 'whole' but 'riven and divided' modern Jew as a confrontation with the ghosts of the Holocaust past. Two half-sisters who meet after the death of their father Leo discover that their inability to locate and identify a stable sense of self derives from the gap between their experience of him and his hidden story of a Holocaust escape. Halina, the older sister, raised in Hungary primarily by her father, shares his European heritage, while Lucy is his American daughter doubly separated from him, for she lacks both the European experience and a Jewish mother. A dominant force in both their lives, Leo also controls access to the story of Halina's mother, Tilde, who disappeared at the end of World War II. Instead of deconstructing a golden age of Jewish identity as she does in *The Ecstasy of Dr. Miriam Garner*, Feinstein here constructs a dark age to question the viability and positioning of Jewish identity. The novel's replay of Electra's rivalry for the father's affections does not foreground a single family; instead the divided family represents individuality subsumed within a collective Jewish struggle for survival. Thus Halina and Lucy compete for individual and collective claims to suffering and oppression. When Lucy argues that her hospitalization for mental illness is an experience equal to the concentration camps, and Halina rejects the comparison, Lucy reminds her that 'You don't have any more claim on all that than I do' (*Mother's Girl* 125).

Ironically, the primacy of collective Jewish history is affirmed by the particular story of Halina's mother. It begins with Halina's memory of Tilde's self-centered career as a singer, but is transformed into the collective by reports of her work with Jewish socialists hiding Jews. Its enigmatic ending with her disappearance into the Soviet Union after the war, combined with Leo's silence about her, suggests the story of the Holocaust and its problem of representability. Feinstein genders this problem and links it to that of Jewish continuity by giving Halina the responsibility of rescuing her mother's story from oblivion. The story's emergence, as in other Feinstein novels, raises questions about the burdens of Jewish identity and history for

Jewish women. Just as Tilde sent Halina to England to save her from the Nazis, so Halina ponders the legacy of their story for her son: 'I mustn't give you my pain to carry ... it will damage you ... perhaps that damage is part of the human inheritance and the only terrible burden is to have no inheritance at all' (158). By revealing the Jewish past through women's consciousness and indeterminate endings, Feinstein invokes Jewish history to challenge its status as a received and determining text.

A key sign of this challenge appears in the character of Leo. To Halina, he 'was not only an enchanter; he was part of every fairy tale I read. He was the handsome prince, the hero, the one who could take on all the dangers of the world and defeat them' (12). The references here to the fairy tale/mythic persona call attention to his charisma, but also his unreliability both as a narrator and as a father. That his reality is far more fragile than his image is revealed by 'the terrible silence' between Leo and Halina's mother Tilde, a silence that, like Lalka's in *Children of the Rose*, diminishes her mother's presence as it hid not only her own suffering but also her own heroic fortitude (*Mother's Girl* 16). Like Hans in *The Border*, Leo considers himself a romantic and cosmopolitan figure of European culture, a citizen poet and one who resists his Jewish identity until Nazi persecution mocks his choice.[18] Though Lucy and Halina engage in a psychological attempt to understand their not-so-romantic family relationships, they discover that its driving force was historically circumstantial and, as in *The Border*, shows the questionable status of context-free psychoanalytic knowledge. Using *The Border*'s same pivotal moment, 1938, and resembling the political acuity of Inge, Tilde's behavior is motivated less by her husband's unreliability than by reading the danger signs of Hitler's encroaching power over the Jews. It is only on his deathbed that Leo reveals that she also served with the resistance and helped save Jews, including himself. Thus the sisters in this novel complete the story of modern Jewish history by rediscovering the mother at its center. For these women, Jewish continuity means departing from a male-centered tradition and its domestic center of practice. By featuring the women's consciousness as a conduit to the Jewish past and by confronting it with the intransigence of its patriarchal texts, Feinstein reveals that the power men associate with Jewish continuity allows them to rationalize and dismiss the knowledge that women gain through their struggle against belief in a romanticized past. By revealing the Jewish past through women's narratives, she questions the extent to which patriarchal knowledge as inscribed in sacred Jewish texts constitutes the whole story. And because she leaves her women with indeterminate endings, Feinstein suggests that the discourse of Jewish history and continuity remains an ongoing process of revision and discovery. Feinstein addresses this process in her poem 'Song of Power' where the narrator/mother revises the taunts of her son's classmates who call her 'a witch' because of her 'wild hair' (*Collected Poems* 18). Deploying this antisemitic stereotype of Jewish women, the narrator calls out to those like herself 'to make their own coherence / a fire their children / may learn to bear at last / and not burn in' (*Collected Poems* 19). Women's historical knowledge will rebuild Jewish resolve to survive.

In *All You Need* (1989) and *Loving Brecht* (1992), women who hardly know they are Jewish journey back and forth between a history of persecution and the burden of continuity because they embody Jewish identity as mothers.[19] Amidst all the turbulence of modern Jewish history, this embodiment remains a constant, even as Feinstein's women learn to struggle against it. The recognition of this combined embodiment and historical consciousness forms the narrative voice of Feinstein's 1997 poem, 'Allegiance'. In its juxtaposed perspectives, 'Allegiance' shows how the Jewish narrator's pleasure in touring Jaffa with an English friend is overwhelmed by her identifying with the continuity of a terrifying Jewish history. While the conversation about 'the Roman exploitation of Caesarea two thousand years ago' proceeds neutrally, in an easygoing, leisurely fashion,

The scared, open faces of the soldiers
look like oppressors to her, while my inheritance
– Kovno, Odessa, packing and running away –
makes me fear for them, as if they were sons.
So I can't share the privilege of guilt. Nor could
she taste the Hebrew of Adam in the red earth here: the iron, salt and
blood. (162)

Looking into the confident blue eyes of her English friend, the Jewish narrator recognizes that her own history denies any association with imperial power. Instead, it has consisted mostly of being anxiously on the run from oppressors, even in the Jewish State. The privileges of Englishness invite a critical detachment from British imperial history but include a projection of imperial oppression onto the Israeli soldiers who, for Feinstein, protect the Jewish homeland.

The mirror image of this arrogance is that it allows an all-too-easy condemnation of those on whom it projects colonizing blame. Thus rather than assume any responsibility for British imperialism, the English friend sees Israeli soldiers as 'oppressors' (162). She has conveniently disregarded, perhaps selectively forgetting, Britain's own role in the contested narratives of Middle East politics. By contrast, the narrator's 'inheritance' includes a different kind of responsibility – maternal anxiety for the soldiers who she identifies as 'sons' (162). For the Jewish woman narrator, the continuity of Jewish history consists of brutally punctuated events that are strung together by fear. The past is therefore never neutral, but haunts the present with the fear that continuity is always threatened and this fear is devoid of feeling guilty. The narrator may be British, but it is Jewishness rather than Englishness that constructs her historical identity.

This continuity of fear extends as much over place as it does time in Feinstein's work. Her poem 'Hotel Maimonides' positions the Jewish woman narrator in the medieval Jewish quarter of Cordoba, between a modern hotel named after the Jewish philosopher-physician and the Jewish ghosts who are beloved in and probably because of their absent presence. This absent presence also guarantees the Jews' silence, so that, no matter how they are interpreted, they are denied a crucial part of their own tradition: critical commentary. In this sense, the name of the hotel travesties the meaning of Moses Maimonides' work. For his philosophical writings were not only commentaries on Jewish law and custom but also reflected the position of Jews in places where they were valued but endangered minorities. As Feinstein's narrator links the lingering Jewish past with her own identity, it becomes clear that neither Maimonides' philosophy nor health science could provide the wisdom or cure for Jewish history.

The narrator's confrontation with the Jews' perennial state of rejection and exile wrenches her consciousness back to Britain where her immediate ancestors are buried along with memories of the displaced past and the stability of her own British identity. It is only by conjuring up images of 'the fanatic Middle East' that she can confront the Jewish identity that Britishness obscures (205). For the search for 'a homeland' does not end in Britain, but shows how the temptations of assimilation only highlight an underlying identification that no exilic span can erase (205). As the poem ranges in historic time and space, it locates the origins of the story of the Jews' expulsion from Spain in the original dispersion from their ancient 'homeland', that endangered 'coastal strip' that is so impossible for the rest of the world to assimilate into their political consciousness (205). For this narrator, the denial of Israel's legitimacy is tantamount to expulsion of the Jews from their own historical narrative and identity. Between these expulsions lies the story of the Holocaust where expulsion was translated into extermination. In this sense, the beloved ghostly absent presence of the Jews is no cause for celebration but, as the hotel name indicates, a travesty and exploitation of the Jewish past and present.

Feinstein's novels struggle with connections between ancient, medieval, and modern Jewish history to find crevices in which women can find the artistic and scholarly learning as well as the social and political skills with which to insinuate themselves.[20] This historical and cultural sweep is the setting of Feinstein's 1994 novel, *Dreamers*. A saga of Jewish life in Vienna from the revolutionary year of 1848 through the realization of some stability in 1864, it portends the continuity only of Jewish dislocation. And once again, it is a woman who embodies this condition.[21] Wandering into Vienna, the figure of the orphaned Jewish girl, Clara, unsettles Vienna's multicultural and multiclass panorama. Born into a Jewish family that had converted to Christianity, of a mother whose search for self-expression drives her to rebel, Clara represents the anxious history of Jewish assimilation and rejection. She is destined to live on the margins of both Jewish and Christian society. In servitude first to a prostitute and then to a Jewish banking family, raped first by a Viennese aristocrat and then by a Jew, Clara registers the inability of political and cultural Europe to integrate the revolutionary presence of a woman into its life.

A voracious reader of anything available to her, Clara becomes a student of European history and culture and a sign of its failures to all Others, including women. For although this woman is clearly gifted intellectually, she is constrained by the Cinderella plot, a European favorite that teaches the lesson of women's desire for subjugation. For the fairy tale insists that women find fulfillment only when they are rescued by a man who represents civilized virtues. In turn, these virtues serve as a guide for the infantilized, primitive woman – associated of course with the hearth's ashes – to make herself socially acceptable. That she requires a man's tutelage but evolves only as the object of his desire reflects back on her primordial primitive state. Feinstein, however, makes sure that we can't ignore the primitive state of men's desires. The prevalence of rape in this novel testifies to how the virtues of the male are more rhetorical than real. Like the masked balls of which Vienna is so fond and around which the story of Cinderella swirls, these virtues provide a disguise that conceals the violence underwriting but shaping so many of the myths and fantasies of Central Europe's self-image.

But instead of yielding to Vienna's frothy fairy tales, Clara resists the male-dominated romance that would merely rescue her into passive domestication. Instead of being confined to glass slippers, she becomes a writer. When she is advised to publish under a man's name, a common nineteenth-century practice, she refuses, and for a reason that connects women's traditional plights to that of European Jews: 'I don't like the idea of pretending [...] Would you pretend, in my place? Would you pretend not to be a Jew?'(*Dreamers* 254–5). Clara's rejection of a male pseudo-identity includes the romances men create to captivate women and assign them the role of victim. Thus her writing makes 'no mention of love, no thoughts of men; she was writing about the women of the streets and what they could hope for.... What she hated most...was the acceptance of being helpless' (290–1). The connection here between the violation of women's bodies and their identities reflects back on the position of the European Jew. Feminized and demonized by nineteenth-century race science, Jewish men were depicted in cartoons and their accompanying texts as devious, craven, and manipulative, all signs of a paradoxically powerful weakness that proves their incapacity for civilized relationships – in short, an unmanly character. As Sander Gilman (*Jew's Body*) has shown of nineteenth-century German culture, both Jewish men and women were victims of a stereotypical double bind in which men were viewed as both sexually voracious and cravenly unctuous and weak, while women were cast as sexual aggressors who embodied the dangers of their decayed civilization. Both Jewish men and women were accused of being diseased, the symptoms of which were evident in their dark skins and hunched over postures. That this darkness was really a sign of poverty and being denied hygienic living quarters was of course never considered.

When the novel asks, how can we 'put our faith in the liberalism of German culture', the answer is suggested by Clara's resistance, to her subjugation both as a woman and a Jew (*Dreamers* 80). Clara's resistance writing is the only action that keeps its critical distance from the lure of what the novel determines is 'idolatry', a false god – the worship of high German culture, expressed in the languages of its music, philosophy, and literature (80, 242). Clara is portrayed in opposition to Joseph, the character of the Jewish prodigy violinist, who builds a successful career out of becoming a German cultural icon. The novel only allows him to discover his love for Clara when he realizes that this celebrity is a false note, that he is the plaything of Viennese patrons, not an integral member of their society. He discovers, not a moment too soon, that though he is invited to play for the likes of Cosima Wagner, Jews can't possibly 'make any contribution to the German language' since they have 'no mother tongue' (246). Although the novel pays a great deal of attention to the trials and successes of Joseph's career, and so he may seem to be its protagonist, it is Clara's presence and the fact of her revolutionary writing that inscribes a 'mother tongue' to challenge accusations that the Jews are parasites, subsisting on the bounty of Europe. If the novel seems to embrace a fairy tale ending with the marriage of Clara and Joseph, the thread of this Jewish woman's rebelliousness is what ties its romance to social reality. The 'mother tongue' she constructs disrupts the revolutionary moment and its reactionary aftermath. So even as Clara may seem to disappear into domesticity and we have no way of knowing if she continues her writing, her critical impact has already altered the narrative of European cultural supremacism.

For so many of Elaine Feinstein's women characters, Jewish continuity means departing from a male-centered tradition and its domestic center of practice and to develop a critical relation to the Jewish past. By confronting that past with the intransigence of its patriarchal texts and tales, Feinstein reveals that the power Europe associates with Jewish continuity allows it to ignore Jewish women's struggle against the culture that has entrapped them in the guise of its own sacredness. Furthermore, by revealing the Jewish past through women's consciousness, Feinstein questions the extent to which patriarchal knowledge as inscribed in sacred Jewish texts constitutes the whole Jewish story. And because she leaves her women with indeterminate endings, Feinstein suggests that the discourse of Jewish history and continuity remains an ongoing process of revision and discovery. Thus even the female narrators of the poems I discuss earlier represent this process.

Perhaps most importantly for today's literary and geopolitical concerns is Elaine Feinstein's persistent linkage of women's consciousness as representing the fate of Europe's Jews to the fate of Europe itself. For as this most recent novel, *Dreamers*, takes us back into history, it also projects us forward, to ask the question: what does Europe's historical attitudes towards its Jewish presence tell us about Europe's fate as its face becomes increasingly multicultural? For as the poem 'Hotel Maimonides' shows, this multifaceted face may be just rhetorical, while Europe's Others remain ghosts on its margins. Even as global politics may allow us to diminish the importance of this question, to make it seem merely a domestic matter, the persistently questioning voice of the British Jewish woman writer dramatizes the inescapability of Jewish history as other. Elaine Feinstein insists on the presence of the past in the present, as she takes us not only across the English channel but also across continental divides, to dramatize how it is not just the figure of the Jew who is haunted by the past but Britain and Europe that should be.

6
Displaced Witnesses: Julia Pascal's and Sue Frumin's Holocaust Dramas

What is Jewish culture? What is it to be a Jew? Why does one go on making culture in the face of death? (Julia Pascal, in Bolchover, 'Between Two Plays' 17)

I wrote my play *Theresa* under the compulsion of an unassuaged anger engendered by the apathetic amnesia almost universally encountered among British people in regard to the adoption into a British territory's legal system during the Second World War of the Nuremberg Race Laws, with their inevitable consequence of stark horror for those to whom they applied. (Julia Pascal, 'Guernsey and the Holocaust')

Playwright Julia Pascal has no personal connection to the Holocaust; she lost no family to the Third Reich and was born long after and far away from the atrocities. Yet even in her plays that focus on other events and political and cultural tensions, the shadows of the Holocaust permeate the atmosphere. Raised in 1960s Manchester, Julia Pascal was introduced to a multicultural world tinged with racism: 'At primary school a blonde girl with straight hair yelled at me: "You killed Jesus"...I am glad that I was not protected and learned the savagery of racism so young. Although I was born here my parents always spoke about "the English" and so I always wondered who I was' ('Parallel Lives'). With Holocaust history never far from her creative and critical instincts, Pascal reminds us that racialist discourse 'is the language of the Third Reich' ('Parallel Lives'). The precise location Pascal ascribes to this deadly language would appear to mark the culture of the Third Reich as distinctively exclusionary and antisemitic and to bear no relation to the antisemitism of modern British culture. And yet because of her own antisemitic experience and perception that Jews still struggle to be welcomed into British society, all of Pascal's writing addresses the tenuous place of Jewishness in Englishness.

Much of Pascal's work as actor, director, producer of her own theater company, and as playwright, is concerned with intersections between Jewish responses to becoming British and British reception of a Jewish population and cultural presence. Despite what seems to so many British Jews as their secure place in British society, with government support and promotion of a Holocaust day, fears remain, in her view, 'of being seen as "too" Jewish' ('Millennial' 11). The result of efforts to allay such anxiety is, she reports, a lack of Jewish philanthropy in support of Jewish cultural projects. Pascal's interest in British-Jewish relations has inspired plays whose themes are both cultural and political and whose voice is most often polemical. Even when her subject is a positive moment in British Jewish history, it serves as a protest against darker moments. She was thus recently inspired by 'the hole in Jewish culture caused by England being *judenrein* for over three centuries', and so wrote a play about Cromwell and the Jews and the readmission of the Jews in 1656 ('Millenial' 11). Despite this reparative effort, however, she feels 'a teasing question remains: "Are we officially here?"' ('Millenial' 10). This question resounds from an earlier work, the first play of Pascal's 1995 *Holocaust Trilogy* (published 2000), *Theresa*, about a twentieth-century expulsion of Jews from British soil.

   Theresa was inspired by a belated and stunning World War II news break. As Pascal reflects, 'Brought up with the myth that the British would never collaborate' if the Nazis invaded, it was therefore shocking to Britons to learn the truth of what happened on the Channel Islands, which were occupied by the Nazis (4). In 1989, a key moment in Britain's Holocaust remembrance, after Kindertransport survivors reunited, *The Observer* revealed that not only was it a British policeman who handed over three Jewish women to the Gestapo, but that he 'forcibly kept' one of them 'on the island even *before* the Nazis arrived... Theresia Steiner was murdered in Auschwitz in 1942' (*Theresa* 4, Pascal's italics). When Pascal traveled to Guernsey to research the play, she discovered 'that it was not only this police inspector who was guilty of events leading to Theresa's murder but the whole of the island government, with one exception' (*Theresa* 4–5).[1] Pascal's play has been banned in Guernsey ever since but, because airwaves can't be blocked, her 1996 radio version, *The Road to Paradise*, found its way there.[2] *Theresa*, which Pascal describes as 'pure documentary', dramatizes her interpretation of Guernsey's wartime history: 'a secret history full of shame, guilt and cover-up' about British complicity with Jewish deportation from the Channel Islands (quoted in Montague, *Theresa* 4). By emphasizing this segment of British Jewish history as a dirty secret, Pascal's play questions Britain's stalwart island identity and sense of benign imperial power with implied linkages to Europe's complicit role in the Holocaust. The word complicity, moreover, is equally challenged by a combination of pressures and choices. As Pascal discovered, the government in Guernsey was not threatened by the Germans to yield its Jewish residents but chose to do so.[3] But, because the playwright also insists that '[t]he betrayal of Jews [occurred] on British soil', she links the island's complicity with that of Britain. In fact, the Channel Islands are independent of

Britain, yet answerable to the Crown – a situation devolved from Norman times. Pascal reports that Britain's connection to the Nazi occupation of the Channel Islands 'is a subject no one's got round to teaching us at school'; therefore she will do 'her utmost to prevent her audience from wallowing in ignorance. "I relate to the history of Jewish women troublemakers"', she says, ' "and I'm going to do my best to be one"' (Corner n.p.).[4] Pascal's representation of Theresa's fate makes trouble by raising significant questions about relations not only between the imperial antagonists and the Jews trapped in the middle, but between a vexed wartime history and the play's role in ongoing debates about the Nazi occupation of the Channel Islands.

The historical debates are very important to any consideration of the play. At the time Pascal was writing and producing, the Guernsey archives were still closed and she did not have wide access to letters, diaries, and Channel Island survivors of the occupation. Since the archives opened, historians have been adding complexity as well as uncertainty to the story, not only of the occupation itself but also to the question of collaboration, and the deportation of the Jews. What is generally agreed upon is that with the advice of Channel Island authorities, most Jewish residents left and sold their businesses. In March 1941, the remaining five Jews on Guernsey and twelve on Jersey, mostly single women Austrian and German Jewish refugees, had their identity cards conspicuously marked with a red 'J'. After three years on Guernsey working as a nurse, Theresa Steiner was twenty-six when she was deported to Drancy and on 20 July 1942, she, Marianne Grunfeld, and Auguste Spitz joined 824 people who were sent to their deaths in Auschwitz three days later (Bunting 110). The question of official culpability in the fate of the three Jewish women refugees remains contested. Most recently, Hazel Smith has sought to add complexity with additional interviews, diaries, letters, and archival documentation. She argues that, despite discriminatory immigration policies, 'there can be little doubt about the Island administrators' general Utilitarian approach to the problems of the Occupation. To achieve what amounted to the greatest good for the greatest number of Islanders... they did not intervene as much as they might have done to protect their Jewish citizens', but, like the general populace, they 'did not know what the enemy was up to, or at what cost to the rest of the population would be any refusal to follow Orders' (147). This position counters Madeleine Bunting's conclusion that 'The truth is that no official in either Guernsey or Jersey considered the welfare of a handful of Jews sufficiently important to jeopardize good relations with the Germans' (Bunting 113).

Smith's investigations reveal 'little evidence of any ill feeling towards Jews in the Channel Islands' and she buttresses this conclusion with comparisons with the 'virulent Anti-Semitic material' circulating in Europe and, in particular, the ruthless anti-Jewish policies of the French (150). Smith's extended research leads her to a multifaceted portrait of a Holocaust tragedy in which Channel Islanders played an unintended and circumstantial role. From her perspective, wartime conditions forced people to create as much normalcy as possible, and cooperation with the Germans was designed to do that. It is not complicity but rather the Islanders' failure to notice the presence of any Jews after the initial evacuation that enables the passage of anti-Jewish legislation. To Smith's credit, her book provides counterexamples and arguments for each issue she raises about collective and individual collaboration. Altogether, however, the accretion of evidence, selected interviews, and arguments adds up to representational and historical questions. As we learned from Hayden White, history writing employs narrative strategies and tropes that may seem to simulate historical reality or what actually happened, but is always an act of interpretation. Does Smith's evidential and analytical balance support her book's concluding defense of the Islanders's ordinary, quotidian responses to fears manufactured by enemy occupation? Or do this balance and conclusion belie Smith's desire for a conclusion within the moral norms of ordinary times and thus obfuscate issues arising specifically about the Holocaust? I maintain that the book's quest for moral normalcy implicates itself in the Islanders' desires for normalcy and so compromises its claims for objectivity. The desire for normalcy is not equivalent to the norms from which one makes moral judgments – normalcy explains but does not absolve. Moreover, to position the Islanders as bystanders reduces them to being witnesses, not actors. In her challenge to the British nation as a whole, Julia Pascal insists on the moral agency of the Islanders and challenges their actions and inaction.

In extremis, Pascal imagines the consequences of the Islanders' failure to take risks on behalf of its Jewish citizens and refugees. In addition to challenging the myth of Britain's stalwart resistance to Nazi conquest, Pascal's story of Theresa also questions the island nation's claims to indomitable democratic instincts. Because it is a work designed to serve as testimony, Pascal's play replicates dialogue from her Guernsey interviews. Though Pascal herself is not a character in the play, she is nonetheless present as absent interviewer and this raises critical questions embedded in the play's design as testimony. As a work combining investigative reportage, polemic, and creative structure, how is it imagining the relation between British Holocaust history and fiction? Given extant concerns about the historicity and authenticity of Holocaust representation, how do we assess Pascal's polemical imagination and use of historical evidence, especially since, at the time the play was first produced, Guernsey's archives were not fully accessible? This absence is filled not by the search for historical objectivity, but by Pascal's politically critical response to those who were there at the time and 'are resisting the slur on their past' (Anon., 'This Banned Play' n.p.). In her introduction to the published text of her Holocaust trilogy, Pascal reports that Richard Heaume, director of the Guernsey Occupation Museum, gave her access to 'official documents', including 'the obsequious letters from the Bailiff to the *Feldkommandatur* detailing all elements of Jewish life on Guernsey' (*Theresa* 5).

The composition and production of *Theresa* relates to debates about referentiality, realism, and imaginative writing about the Holocaust. As regards retrospective imaginative writing by survivors, there has been general acceptance of their fictional frames and forms of self-representation as well as the conscious and unconscious shaping of memory as significant contributions to Holocaust understanding because they are assumed to provide historical, ethical, and emotional insight. Thus although critics debate whether Elie Wiesel's *Night* is fiction or memoir or whether its various language editions and alterations affect its authenticity, the work is universally lauded as a hallmark of Holocaust representation. In the case of retrospective imaginative constructions or reconstructions by non-survivors, the historicist stakes are raised. Novels such as Anne Michaels's *Fugitive Pieces* and Sherri Szeman's *The Kommandant's Mistress* remain controversial because their narrative experiments and interpretations of sexual and other intimate relations appear to some readers as presumptuous and even transgressive about what did and could have happened in the Holocaust. *Theresa* raises an additional category of concern. Because it is based on an actual historical event which casts a critical shadow on both the Guernsey and British islanders, do its experimental form and emotional power 'entice the viewer to accept the belief that he or she has now seen the object [the event itself]'? (Wolff 158). As I shall demonstrate, the play cautions us not to position ourselves as a traditional audience and suspend disbelief and just sit back and enjoy the show. Instead, as we shall see, the play asks us to factor its fictionality into debates surrounding the Channel Islands' wartime history.

Pascal's theater notes guide us to view her political critique as throwing down the gauntlet and joining the polemical British theatrical traditions of Shaw's biting social satire, Osborne's angry outcries, and Pinter's theater of menace. And so she uses the response of Theresa's wartime Guernsey friend to a question about Theresa's character: She 'was very pretty except for her big Jewish nose' (*Theresa* 5). Pascal's wry comment betrays her angry belief in the ongoing vexed position of Jews in Britain: 'This was 1990: anti-Semitism certainly has not disappeared from the island' (*Theresa* 5). Unlike Hazel Smith, Pascal does not normalize British antisemitism by comparing it to any other. Instead, like other writers discussed in this book, Julia Pascal constructs a British identity that in its encounters with antisemitism and endangered Jews, challenges its traditionally progressive and enlightened self-image. These writers insist that the Holocaust cannot be reified as the horrific past but must be recognized as integral to the racism that upheld imperial domination.[5] *Theresa* interprets Britain's self-defense in World War II as failing to renounce the antisemitism that was integral to its imperial racism. By the end of the play, as Theresa flees the antisemitism of one empire for another, she is not only colonized but trapped by both.

Like Samuels's play, *Kindertransport*, discussed in Chapter 3, *Theresa* begins in 1938 at the moment of Kristallnacht, but in Vienna, where the 'sweetness' of 'The Blue Danube Waltz' and of Black Forest cake mark the end of nostalgia for one empire, the Austro-Hungarian, and the fearful aggression of another (*Theresa* 18). With no props or set, starkly suggesting that nostalgia is an illusory luxury the Jews can't afford, Theresa dominates the stage, at first, as she dances a symbolic rendering of her jagged history and memory, and then as she describes the crystal-glassed café that she cannot afford to enter.[6] Pascal's focus on a woman, which coincides with Sue Frumin's play *The Housetrample*, discussed later in this chapter, expresses the desire to dramatize 'a story of differences and of surviving in an alien culture' (Frumin 107). But since this play also raises bitter questions about the Jews' efforts to find safety in Britain, the repeated references to 'highly polished glass' prod us to view this scene as a window into Britain's responses (*Theresa* 16). Pascal has written that her view of London in the late 1930s is shaped by imaging Theresa's perspective but, as she wrote:

> [With] the final part of the play where [Theresa] spends two years under Nazi occupation being banned from going to the cinema, skating rinks, public parks and cafes because she was a Jew, I began to imagine all of Britain under Nazi rule. If the Channel Islanders could betray the Jews and betray one another by settling old scores, then what difference on mainland Britain? ('On Creativity and Anger' 39).[7]

Eschewing the ambiguity and irresolution that shape Diane Samuels's play *Kindertransport* or Hazel Smith's attempt at historical objectivity, Pascal's verdict about Britain's role in the deportation of the Jews from the Channel Islands is bitterly certain. Guernsey may be geographically and even to some extent culturally separate from mainland Britain, but for Pascal its behavior under Nazi occupation reflects attitudes that are too close for Britain's comfort to those of wartime Europe. Like Britain itself, Guernsey is an island, but its independence is always questioned by the possibility of European invasion and its failure or inability to resist. However beneficent the Kindertransport proved Britain to be, *Theresa* provokes an unsettling question, one that is unanswerable historically but that now haunts the story of British resistance. How would mainland Britain have responded to Nazi occupation?[8] Would the image of Britain purveyed in wartime propaganda, World War II films, and as perennial narrative, as humanitarian nation and benign or even nurturing empire prevail?[9] As we see in *Kindertransport*'s shadows of the past, and in the staging of *Theresa*, those emanations predict a dark future. Indeed, much of the time the actors perform in darkness or shadow, with spotlights or torches highlighting Theresa's isolation or captivity by those on whom she depends for safety. Pascal's stage direction to have the same actors play various British, Jewish, and German roles produces the effect of transfusing Nazi malevolence into British officials and civilians, with Jews situated at their conjoined lack of mercy.

Within its unequivocal performance of indicting British collaboration, *Theresa* questions the position of British Jews throughout the United Kingdom. Where Diane Samuels worries about the pressures of assimilation, Pascal asks if the Guernsey betrayal represents a rejection of Jewish cultural production in Britain. Given the positive reviews of the play, however, there is clearly an audience that is quite ready to hear its polemical interpretation.[10] Dramatizing Pascal's concern, the play presents Theresa as a professor of music whose talents, mirroring the historical record, are rejected in favor of her performing domestic service.[11] Regardless of whether Britain could actually have found employment for a refugee music teacher, Pascal connects its rejection of Theresa's talents to her dismissal from the Vienna Conservatory and the Nazi designation of Jewish culture as 'degenerate' (*Theresa* 20). In an essay, Pascal remarks that in addition to a lack of Jewish community center theaters, British Jews are still uneasy with the notion of producing a rich body of explicitly British-Jewish work: 'There is a climate in Britain which, rightly encourages black, Asian and Chinese arts, but does not give Jewish theatre the same funding possibilities... The very act of making Jewish theatre is a way of reconstructing what existed before Hitler. The Holocaust did not just destroy Jews, but also left a huge hole in Jewish – and indeed European – culture' ('Drama out of a Crisis' n.p.).

Theresa offers a critical reconstruction of the destruction of European Jewish culture, but on and about British soil. With their European identities, two of the actors serve as a cultural bridge between British and European history as well as embodying interpretations of whether that bridge is viable. In Freddie Rokem's terms, 'they become a kind of historian... who makes it possible for us... to recognize that the actor is "redoing" or "reappearing" as something/somebody that has actually existed in the past' (13). In the original productions, Pascal chose Ruth Posner, a survivor of the Warsaw Ghetto who had passed as a Polish Catholic, to play Theresa, and Thomas Kampe, whose father served in the German army, for all the male roles. These roles include Theresa's son Josef, a German refugee in London, the British police inspector, William Sculpher, and a Gestapo officer. Whereas the play *Kindertransport* dramatizes the adult character Evelyn and her childhood self Eva separately to symbolize and show the process of their psychological and cultural rupture, *Theresa* splits the performances of its actors to show the political pressures that explode into fusions of German and Guernsey characters. In a scene depicting 'The Occupation of France', Kampe morphs from a child merrily singing 'Frere Jacques' into a victim of Nazi brutality as his song drifts into the German version, 'Bruder Jakob'. The actress who plays a Guernsey woman seduced by a German soldier's smarmy promise of a silk blouse also plays the nurse who betrays Theresa. Pascal's direction notes that this double performance 'suggests she's the same character' (*Theresa* 48). Collaboration here leads not only to personal and political betrayal, but to a British isle sacrificing the Empire's persona of liberation and resistance to becoming the colonial agent of the Reich.

The production's international and multilingual character links not only Pascal's view of 'the occupation of sleepwalking France' and that of the Channel Islands but also of how the fate of European Jews and their culture was betrayed by the slippage of British authority into collaboration with the Nazis (*Theresa* 5). Not only does this assessment indict the British for their political collapse but it also questions how its imperial power would prevail on the battlefield if at the same time it suffered a moral collapse with a land invasion on its home front. In one scene, where Kampe turns around and around, transforming repeatedly from British policeman to Gestapo officer by simply changing hats, we are made to feel that, if only he could move fast enough, one figure would simply melt into the other. This fusion of political character and representation reflects the play's generalized indictment of British collaboration by questioning the Island officials' decisions regarding the Jewish refugees. Given the officials' legally empowered responsibility over all the Islanders, could they have refused to enact the legislation forced upon them by the German authorities and so have established themselves as a model in case the mainland was invaded?

The play individualizes the problem of complicity in its depiction of the two women whose plights mirror and shed critical light not only on each other but also on Anglo-Jewish women writers' concerns about women's wartime roles and representations. As Susanne Greenhalgh importantly notes, 'All Pascal's protagonists are female, characters whose situations are in part an autobiographical projection of the playwright's or actor's personal history as well as of self-identification with the victims of the past' ('Space' 31). In one deeply ironic juxtaposition, reflecting Pascal's passionate identification with the questions she raises, Lydia, Theresa's English domestic employer, reads her own outsider status as mirrored in Theresa's story. Despite Lydia's safe position as an upper-class British citizen, she has been displaced by social codes that have isolated her emotionally.

Read in tandem with the rules of conduct greeting Jewish refugees and with Evelyn's repressions in Samuels's play *Kindertransport*, Lydia's plight can be seen as the logical consequence of a culture whose pride in its distinctiveness translates into a state of acute separation anxiety for its women. As so many critics and writers have noted, despite the vast network of women war workers, with very few exceptions, this sense of British distinctiveness did not include women's participation in Britain's political culture outside the domestic sphere. Instead, for women as for the Jews, mainland Britain is represented as a gated society: if Lydia is entrapped within its exclusionary social codes, Theresa never has a chance to enter. As one of its important contributions to Holocaust studies in Britain and elsewhere, Pascal's play offers a chain of signification in which the interlaced figuration of woman and Jew sheds historical and cultural light each on the other. Under British rule, the play asks, how are Jewish and gender roles negotiated through each other? Studied together, all of the Holocaust writing considered in this book questions whether there is a place in British cultural themes for confronting and integrating a Jewish history and a gender history that unsettle the memories that continue to shape the nation's identity?[12]

If Lydia can tell her story only to Theresa, it is because the Jewish woman's undisguised expression of profound anxiety is, like Lydia's story, beyond the pale of that hallmark of British civil society – polite restraint. Based on this credo of politically implicated cultural distinction, Pascal's story of British collaboration with the Nazi occupation becomes even more startling. Rather than being asked to see Britain's intrepid isolation as heroic, we are confronted with its synthesis of internal and external dangers. Both the performance and written text of the play insist on this synthesis. In the opening scene, Theresa's English monologue is accompanied by a chorus of voices reciting her words in German, and when she reverts to her childhood Polish, the chorus speaks in English. In performance, these languages and voices are expressed simultaneously while in the text they are printed as twin columns, a way of approximating simultaneity but remaining necessarily separate. Though we can't possibly read the dual language presentation in concert, as our eyes dart from one column to another or even if we read or view (depending on our proficiency) one at a time, we too perform an interweave, but one that dramatizes the voices as more dissonant than harmonious. Unlike the performance, where the effect is both dissonant and harmonious, reading creates a critical gloss on the play's intended synchronicity. For whether we read or merely look at the languages we might not know, especially those without English translation, instead of mutual translation, the different languages effect a destabilizing stammer. Because this reading experience can only be disconcerting, it suggests Vivian Patraka's 'theatre of disturbance' (*Spectacular Suffering* 44).

If we consider translation as a metaphor, as Patraka does, then we see how Theresa's voices highlight 'the difficulty of representing the experience of the Holocaust', even for one in the thick of it (Patraka 10). Pascal herself has said that her method expresses the 'wall of silence' that, as she was growing up, was 'full of huge questions and terrifying imagery', and that, as she has met survivors and listened to their haunting stories, she has wanted to meet 'the challenge of how to tell Holocaust stories in a way that will affect audiences in a new way. Theater has to move non-naturalistically and it seems to be a good medium to explore the inexplicable' (email correspondence 20 August 2004). Combining physical theater with Theresa's voices produces a 'soundscape' which, in her discussion of Pascal's play, Susanne Greenhalgh describes as 'an interrogation from other sensory perspectives of the problematics of the visual, either to document or to imagine the past' ('Stages of Memory' 219). From the perspective of the voices themselves, the interjection of German and Polish alongside the English reminds us that Theresa cannot escape her foreignness, either to pass or to assimilate. All her performances are doomed to failure. The concurrence of the voices means that they hear, address, or understand each other, and the lingering effect is a fusion that both validates and erases them. In the context of the play's historical interpretation, the merger also reminds us that all of Theresa's voices are erased by a trajectory of Germany's invasion and occupation, from Austria and Poland and on to Guernsey, with the lack of British resistance simulcasting the deletion of Theresa's voices.[13]

While performing this political fusion and erasure, the voices' simultaneous translation conveys the play's convergence of individual and political history: Theresa's emotional and political isolation, the traumatic effects of terror on her as an individual character and as representative of the other two Jewish women deported from Guernsey. In its compression, Theresa's character intensifies their collective betrayal and suffering but it also points to a question raised by Vivien Patraka:

> What happens when the actor's body is signifying not an individual death, which presumably all of us can conceive of, but a mass death, which basically none of us can conceive of? It may be that representing genocide theatrically means the absence/presence of the body and the ruining of representation that the absent/present body causes. Are live bodies the basis of theatre in a way that we can't get beyond? (98)

Theresa and her fellow refugees may be present in both voices and affirm their relation to what Greenhalgh calls 'contemporary "cosmopolitanized" Holocaust memory, broadly European rather than specifically national' ('Stage' 220). The erasure of these characters' voices, however, also suggests not only a representation of the conditions which brutalize them but also of the effects of these conditions on the character's subjectivity. Erasing Theresa's voices leaves a silence that can be understood as her historical condition as well as the traumatic effect of muteness, where vocal expression takes the form of a silent scream. The combined meanings of silence here produce a performance that suggests a ghostly fusion of absence and presence, conveying a sense of Theresa's irretrievability.[14] Despite Theresa's presence on the stage and in the text, as we see, hear, and read her, we confront the meanings of *Forms of Gone*, the title of Yerra Sugarman's collection of Holocaust poems that signifies our relationship to Holocaust victims. We are haunted by the echoing versions of Theresa's story in her different languages, each of which leaves traces no matter where she goes. In this reading, the double columns inscribe an imperative to retell Theresa's story until it is heard. But given her forced exile from Poland to Vienna and then to England, Guernsey, and Auschwitz, given the cruel indifference and betrayal that await her, despite the fact that they accompany her, the echoing voices are ultimately cut off.

Unlike the refugees who managed to stay in England, Theresa is not even valued as a victim. Her work as a domestic servant keeps her in thrall to her employers, not quite a slave but, as she's not even considered an immigrant, more like a colonized subject. When Theresa is rejected by potential British employers, by the British policeman, and the Gestapo officer, her reasonable responses have no meaning: 'Subject closed', she is told on two different occasions (*Theresa* 26, 35). In its encoded form this response may help us see why Hazel Smith's interviewees could find no 'overt anti-Jewish feeling in the Channel Islands', the expression of which David Fraser found in 'the actions of the Bailiffs, Law Officers, local lawyers and bureaucrats', which he concludes 'were always informed by indigenous and widespread anti-Semitism' (Smith 147; Fraser quoted in Smith 142). The repetition of 'Subject closed' emphasizes the doubleness of Theresa's erasure: her murder and the deletion of her story. The word 'subject' reminds us that Theresa will be denied the protection awarded to British subjects and that her subjectivity and the intervention of her story will be denied by Guernsey's official narrative. Even Lydia's warm response to Theresa is suspect, as it reflects more of her own needs than those of her servant. After all, she endangers Theresa by not considering Guernsey's preoccupations except as they mirror her own. Reflecting an omnipresent danger for all audiences of Holocaust stories, we are being cautioned by Lydia's example that no matter how we sympathize with Theresa, we must sustain an emotional distance so that we don't overwhelm the integrity and urgency of her story by relating to it through our own needs.

So how will Theresa's story be validated? Since Theresa's fate is known from the start, we can only be belated and helpless witnesses to the dangers and crimes that befall her. Nonetheless, as the play proposes to shape our perceptions of her history, we are prodded into an active role. Richard Hornby argues, 'Since drama is always addressing itself to the ways in which society views reality, human perception is a latent theme of all drama' (121). If this is true within drama, Pascal carries this idea into the audience. In the context of Pascal's interpretation and ongoing debates about Guernsey's history, we can view the political valences of this play as expressing emotions so intense that the play projects an urgency that strains the emotional and historical boundaries between the events it portrays and the audience. As audiences watch the past and Theresa's present enacted in our own present, we are also being asked to see our present through the lens of Theresa's fate and, like the simultaneous translation of Theresa's monologue, this reflexive perception creates a critical interweave. The fact that the play is still banned in Guernsey and yet participates in public debates about the island's collaboration connects the rejection of Theresa's story in the past to the present. And so for audiences anywhere the play is performed, *Theresa* is mediated through the absent presence of this ongoing history. In addition to performing Theresa's story, the play performs the paradox of its own exiled status and integration into public discourse. Regardless of whether audiences are aware of this ongoing history, they are situated as participants in it.

Unlike Brecht's theater of alienation, where audiences are emotionally distanced from productions in order to activate their political consciousness, the presence of an audience at a performance of *Theresa* is already a political act. And, in its explosive affective forms, not a comforting one. When this play is produced, typically in a small theater, the enclosed space that enwraps players and audience creates an atmospheric overlay that may be experienced as claustrophobic or worse. At the time of its 1995 revival, Pascal reported that the play 'is often too much to bear. "People who lived it have walked out because they couldn't take it"' ('Corner' n.p.). *Theresa* is hard to take. Its 'nightmare expressionism' screams at us, impelling us to watch in concert with Theresa's increasing entrapment (*Theresa* 6). Like the plays of Sara Kane, it traps us with its spectacle of suffering; we see how Theresa is brutalized by past events; but despite the play's insistence on our presence, unlike Kane's plays, Holocaust history intervenes to disinvite us from sharing its ever escalating tragic trajectory. In the extreme, this liminal positioning of the audience suggests that if, at any point we feel the need to escape, our act would be tantamount to yet another desertion, not only of *Theresa* the play but also of the memory of Theresa the historical character. Intensifying our relationship to the play's performance is this confrontational method. Very often, when the sympathetic characters, Theresa, Lydia, and Josef, narrate their troubled lives, they face the audience no matter whom they address on stage. As they confront us with their stories, the play addresses questions of whether the foretold doom of a Holocaust plot can be open to interpretation by the audience. In other cases, the play's 'elements of absurdism' highlight historical and epistemological distances between characters and audience that make us even more aware that, whatever our responses, no matter how historically or politically informed, they are futile (*Theresa* 32). By contrast, when *Theresa* was performed in Germany, as Pascal reports, the mostly student audience recognized 'their own living German history' in the story about Guernsey and their fathers and grandfathers in the German actor playing the Gestapo officer ('On Creativity' 43). Pascal concludes from this experience, 'In Germany I learnt of the cathartic weapon of theatre and how such work can help bring together the children of former enemies' ('On Creativity' 43).

Whatever epiphany *Theresa* may inspire, unlike universalizing literary masterworks by Shakespeare or Joyce, the historical and ethical specificities of Holocaust representation create barriers to catharsis. The distances between Holocaust suffering and virtual spectatorship are absolute. The closest audiences, and most actors – survivors and survivor actor Ruth Posner are exceptions – may be able to come to the performance of Holocaust terror is the realization that there is neither restoration nor redress for the multiple betrayals of the endangered Jews in this play. Only the simulated replay of trauma. Dramatized by its circular structure and fleeting, momentary scenes, the play's dramaturgy of trauma begins with Theresa narrating her position as outcast in Nazi-occupied Vienna and ends with the escalating sound of a train drowning out her voice and transporting her back to Europe to a final expulsion. Her presence is transitory, offering only a partial, fragmented view of her equally disjointed but brutally imprisoning exile. In this reading and viewing, the double columns may reflect Theresa's need to recount her story, and its echoing versions in her own different languages validate that the story is the same no matter where she has been. In fact, when we first see her, she is peering into the Vienna café and, as her voice shifts to her childhood Polish, this reference to earlier times and two sites of activist antisemitism becomes multilayered in irony. An unaffordable Napoleon pastry in a Warsaw bakery reminds us not only of the emperor's imperialistic designs on the land that would become Poland but also of his code that liberated the Jews. In Pascal's play, disillusionment destroys faith in the story of an irrevocable divide between Britain's identity as the free world and the villainy of Hitler's Europe as Theresa's arrest in Guernsey is accompanied by the strains of 'The Blue Danube Waltz'.

By the time the scene ends, the crystal glass window of the Viennese café reflecting the equally unaffordable Black Forest cake confronts us with the shockwaves of another portentous moment – Kristallnacht – a performance in its own right of the Nazis' implementation of anti-Jewish laws. At this early point in the play, the history of Jewish liberation has already turned rancid as elderly Jewish workers are shown being beaten and defiled in the street by Hitler's henchmen. The scene extends the Black Forest metaphor as the brutality foreshadows the Nazis' mass murder of the Jews in the forests of Europe. And in another reflection prompted by the crystal clear glass, while 'the well-dressed men and women in the café continue sipping their chocolate and ordering another cake', we are being asked to confront the indifference that marks complicity with the Reich's oppression, including that of the people of Guernsey (*Theresa* 19). These different settings are as reflexive as the glass window. Whereas Austria welcomed annexation to the Reich and its legalized antisemitism, Britain's aim was to defeat the Axis empires before it too became a victim of a global racial conquest. The play argues that regardless of fears of reprisals and recriminations, by yielding the Jews under British protection, a major battle against the Reich is lost.

The play's many short scenes, shifting from one catastrophic setting to another, depict the political chronology of Theresa's story. By contrast, its expressionistic style and narrative discontinuities convey a political argument that is still struggling for validation as historical reality. Shifts between dance, song, and dialogue in different languages suggest a joyless ride through Pascal's destabilizing arguments, beginning with the play's Prologue, where Theresa begins to dance gracefully to 'The Blue Danube Waltz'. But as her movements splinter over several minutes, they are 'expressed jaggedly against the sweetness of the Strauss' (*Theresa* 15). Pascal's stage directions choreograph the dance as a microcosm of the play's ineluctable political and historical journey:

> Memories of a first ball in Vienna. Being in a concentration camp and observing horror. Reaching out to fellow camp inmates: it is a foretaste of the play itself. It also suggests the end of an empire. (*Theresa* 15)

Theresa's expressionist dance elucidates Vivian Patraka's insight that 'Because performance is so heavily grounded in the presence of live bodies, it is a particularly useful site for investigating our accountability to the unmanageable injury and injustice done to bodies in the Holocaust' (10). The juxtaposition of a Viennese ball and concentration camp, of the froth of one empire and the foulness of another, challenges any claim that any imperialism can be benign. Note that Pascal does not name the empire that needs to end. Instead, her generic empire connotes a legion of contenders. Not only is the Jew trapped in the middle of imperial succession – from the Austro-Hungarian to the Third Reich – but in the war between the British Empire and the Reich.

Pascal's retrospective expressionist history situates the Jewish woman refugee as an ethical litmus test of what kinds of conclusions we can draw from investigation and debates about the Guernsey occupation. In creating a Theresa Steiner who becomes a pawn in Guernsey's self-protective cooperation with the Nazis, Pascal destabilizes the exculpatory testimony on behalf of the Islanders. Her polemical dramaturgy interprets the Islanders' attitudes and behavior as determinate for themselves and as a lens through which to express concerns about Britain writ large: the British Empire's will and powers to protect its citizens and those in its care. Theresa's rejection by the Islanders and by both imperial polities telegraphs these concerns. If we accept Guernsey's position as a fearful bystander whose only agency was to crave normalcy, then Theresa disappears once again, for neither she as a Jewish person nor her condition falls within the purview of what the Islanders considered their norm. Contesting the Island's self-defensive position, Pascal's theater of resistance impels her audiences to recognize that normalcy as a satellite of the Reich meant accommodating to its antisemitic values. The playwright challenges her audiences to join her in remembering Theresa Steiner as a determinant of our judgment.

The title of the second play of Pascal's Holocaust Trilogy, *A Dead Woman on Holiday*, echoes with Primo Levi's sardonic notation of a Nazi guard who called a Jew in a concentration camp 'a dead man on holiday', and, in so doing, confronted the brutal fate of the Jews as inevitable. Yet unlike the three Jewish women deported to their deaths from Guernsey, there is no doomed fate for the protagonists in this play, only a disquieting open ending that connects the play's two subjects: the protagonists' adulterous love affair and the Nuremberg War Crimes Trials. Like Evelyn in Diane Samuels's play *Kindtertransport,* Pascal's female protagonist, Sophia Goldenberg, escapes the Nazis by coming to England and marrying an Englishman. Confronting, rather than suppressing the legacy of the Holocaust, Sophia chooses to return to Germany as a translator for the Nuremberg Trials where she meets a married American who becomes her lover. Unlike Evelyn, Sophia remains faithful to her Jewish identity, even insisting on using her family name rather than that of her non-Jewish husband; she also rejects British 'bourgeois, intellectual, liberal' culture by marrying an 'uneducated, working class' soldier and then challenging the British credo of fair play with her assertion of personal need (*Dead Woman* 60). These acts of defiance mark a transformative process whereby the refugee veers between claiming her own agency and assuming a crucial, even decisive role in translating the perpetrators' testimony for the purpose of rendering judgment. Whatever problems she creates for others and in revitalizing her own life, she becomes instrumental in the construction and performance of justice for the Nazis' crimes against humanity. Every time she translates the German into English, overtaking the 'I' of the accused with the intonations of her own voice, as well as choosing words and syntax, her voice assumes authority over the translation process and text even as she recoils, even as she interrupts the testimony when she is driven to vomit from its impact. At the same time, speaking the heinous testimony of perpetrators performs an act of ventriloquism that like a dybbuk's takeover of its host body and soul shows that whatever rescue the British enacted cannot transform the Jew's embattled state of being, even in the post-Holocaust world.

The play presents the Nuremberg Trials as a complex if impossible effort to translate the incomprehensibility of the crimes into universally accessible and acceptable judicial language, to work through the rage at perpetrators, and to satisfy desires for victors' and victims' revenge. Although the multivalent meanings of translation in this play are presented similarly to those in *Theresa,* the fictional project of *A Dead Woman on Holiday* offers yet another interpretation. Pascal's guide to this critical approach is contained in the very title that designates Sophia's and Paul's work of translation; it is the 'INTERPRETERS' who 'give the impression of multiple, simultaneous, and translucent translations' (*Dead Woman* 61). Pascal has said that for her, the interpreters are 'an allegory of her own generation, those who interpret what happened to their parents' (Email correspondence 20 June 2005). The play presents the Trials as overwhelmed by their own brief to delimit and broach cultural boundaries through simultaneous translation that honors but transforms the languages of individual testimony. Through the depiction of this mandate, the play enters a representational minefield in its presentation of perpetrator testimony. In one depiction, the play's only German woman character, a concentration camp guard, portrays herself as a victim of the Jews, defends the Nazi hierarchy unabashedly, and in addition to regretting that 'Hitler didn't live long enough to finish the job', calls for forgetting the whole thing (*Dead Woman* 82).[15] If allowing her testimony to be offered uninterruptedly endows it with integrity, the viciousness of her post-Holocaust antisemitism is its own undoing. Her hatred of the Jews is so unrelenting and unremorseful that with no German countervoice it gestures towards undifferentiated German guilt, and can only incite the audience to feel disgust towards her noxious self-defense.

Other scenes, performed in counterpoint with her testimony, show that however meticulously the Trials may have been designed to allow the accused and witnesses to present unencumbered testimony, the antagonists emerge as a cacophony of incongruous voices jostling between interpreters whose translations seem more in competition with each other than a cooperative effort at judicial understanding. Susanne Greenhalgh makes the salient point that 'Even the supposedly rational processes of justice and the impartial discourse of the law are made senseless by the testimonies of the trials' ('Space' 34). Although I disagree with the judgment of 'senseless', I do see Pascal's play working with the testimonies as disconnected dialogue. In dramatic effect, these testimonies are fragments of a whole that can only be imagined since the play rejects the idea that the post-Holocaust search for repair and reparation can ever be achieved.[16] Nonetheless, as Michael Marrus has definitively shown, though the perpetrators' disjointedly defensive testimonies challenged the tribunal's efforts to render justice, they did not impede the Trials' effectiveness in establishing guilt through constructions of categories commensurate with the extremes of Nazi brutality. In this play, there is no whole story or character, only lacerating confrontations and a tenuous conclusion. What the play in its entirety represents is not the defeat of the most malignant empire in human history and the beginning of a search for humane justice, but the uninterrupted continuity of fractured connections punctuated by brief moments of longing for what cannot be recovered. Whatever collective and complex truths, wisdom, and justice are written and enacted by the British, French, Soviet, and American judiciary and translated simultaneously into English, Russian, French, and German, are splintered not only by the play's dialogic forms but by the destabilizing construction of Sophia's individuality.

Pascal takes many risks with this play. In addition to implying universal German guilt, *A Dead Woman on Holiday* enters debates about Holocaust representation by juxtaposing and therefore relating what Freud called ordinary personal unhappiness to the incommensurable suffering and traumas of Holocaust victims and survivors. In turn, the setting of the love affair at the Nuremberg Trials presents the problems of judging the genocidal crimes against humanity by dramatizing those of personal betrayal. Expressed as a drive to live passionately after the Holocaust shattered normalcy and adaptation as conditions of life for Jews, the play's presentation of Sophia's willfully justified violation of marital fidelity runs the risk of marginalizing the very suffering to which she responds. On the one hand, Pascal 'was looking at the idea of whether someone damaged by the Holocaust can really love' while 'looking at domestic love (Paul and [his wife] Dee Dee) in opposition to a less conventional marriage of souls and exiles' (Email correspondence 20 June 2005). On the other hand, the play's context and text also suggest that the guilt of nations here is transposed to guilty love while the suffering of victims and survivors is both presented and enacted by someone who escaped. Although Sophia survived the war safely in England, in scenes of private moments and encounters, she speaks the language of the fiercely pent-up emotions we might typically associate with Holocaust survivors. In effect, whether she is speaking for Holocaust victims, avenging their fate or exploiting it, her quest for a passionate life marks a dislocation between Holocaust suffering and ordinary emotional frustration as well as between personal and collective guilt and responsibility. Her affair may serve as testimony to the question of what is right and wrong, but whether its assumptions of normative morality can provide analogical and interpretive connection to Holocaust trauma and victimization or to the crimes of perpetrators or even bystanders remains open to question.

And yet because complete knowledge and understanding of the Jews' collective suffering are just about impossible to grasp, the focus on Sophia's struggle reminds us that narratives of individual suffering humanize the victims whereas the discourse of statistics and numbers, the graphic images of a 'heap of shoes' and piles of corpses, only objectify their suffering once again (*Dead Woman* 61). Nonetheless, despite the human rendering of the Holocaust subject through Sophia's story, the context and subject of the Nuremberg Trials highlight the conventional valences of a tale of marital betrayal. Pascal, however, insists that this conventionality marks a more allegorical struggle, 'between wild love and the tamer one of a long marriage', representing 'the struggle between economic and emotional stability against the anarchic love which comes in the midst of terror and grief' (email 20 June 2005). The idea of anarchic love set within the context of another struggle, to construct rules of law out of the detritus of Nazi legalized atrocity, intersects with critical concerns about trivializing or creating allegorical or universalizing meanings from Holocaust suffering. Whereas 'wild' or 'anarchic love' is grist for a bodice-ripping romance, anxieties about 'economic and emotional stability' would have been a luxury in the midst or aftermath of the Holocaust. Instead of being mutually exclusive, however, the juxtaposition of the trials of love and the Nuremberg Trials creates the effect of a two-sided mirror. Like the translators' voices, Sophia's personal angst and the global implications of the Trials may seem to be situated in competition but turn out to serve as mutually critical commentaries. The Trials are more than backdrop to this tale; the idea of restoring rules of law and order and creating a systematic judicial procedure as a response to the Holocaust and as a universalizing precedent is tested by the tale of marital betrayal. If there is no legal or political precedent for the Trials, the conventions of the love story offer grounds on which emotional categories, that is, those informed by the responses and testimony of survivors, must be considered. The play translates the acute rationality of the Trials into affective evidence and language of expression as its scenes alternate with those of Sophia's hard-hitting demands for a life worth living.

Instead of privileging romantic emotionalism as a realistic or reliable criterion for judgment, however, a scene introducing Sophia and preparatory to her role as translator offers a critical framework in the title of her doctoral thesis, 'Against Romantic Love: A Discourse on the Princess of Cleves by Madame de Lafayette'. However we judge Sophia's angst and affair with Paul, this framework serves as an ironic commentary. Not only is her romance with Paul challenged by Sophia's professed disbelief in falling in love after Auschwitz, but her thesis interrogates love as a responsibility that raises doubts about her protestations. Moreover, the troika of female subjects and authors of the thesis creates a tension between the dispassionate methodology indicated by the thesis title and the emotional intensity invested in Sophia's search for subjectivity and agency, a reminder of the tension between historical and expressionistic renderings of Theresa Steiner's story. Set against the Nuremberg Trials, the trials of Sophia's dislocated discourses may ultimately be a test of the work of imaginative theater of the Holocaust. Pascal's translation/interpretation of the Nuremberg Trials into expressionistic theater is not intended to erase or supersede or distort the proceedings as they were performed in real history. Rather, her play shows the impact of the Trials in several spheres. Historically and judicially, the Trials continue to reverberate in the emergent nexus of ideas about how to institute and exercise judgment about war crimes and crimes against humanity. Pascal's expressionistic interpretation of the Trials' effects positions the audience and critic to see that, like Sophia, every way that is designed to live and create after the Holocaust world must do so within its shadows.

The third play of Pascal's *Holocaust Trilogy*, *The Dybbuk*, resituates and thus reinterprets the 1920 Hasidic folktale by S. Anski (Solomon Zainwil Rapaport) as well as Waszynski's widely celebrated 1937 Yiddish film version. While Anski's original, according to Yohanan Petrovsky-Shtern, should be read as a critical interpretation of Hasidic spirituality,[17] Pascal connects both versions to the Holocaust and to modern Anglo-Jewish identity and cultural production. As in other Anglo-Jewish plays discussed in this book, the past in Pascal's play is a vibrant presence, but what haunts the characters and is performed in *The Dybbuk* is not a repressed personal history. Instead, the play shows a cultural past intervening in the devastations of modern Jewish history. Beginning in the present, Pascal's play suddenly moves to an unnamed ghetto setting where five assimilated Jewish characters are trapped by the Nazi ideology that dictated their Jewish identity and fate. To while away the anxious and brief time left to them, the characters share stories from ancient and medieval Jewish lore, but the one that captivates their attention is that of 'The Dybbuk', which they decide to perform. As Susanne

Greenhalgh observes, this version is not only an improvisation but also incorporates the production history of the play, including its interpretation by the Israeli national theater, Habima, as a Zionist allegory of resistance to persecution and testament of self-determination ('Space' 36). Pascal's play invokes an additional production history, one that threatens to overwhelm the optimism of the Israeli adaptation: the historical epilogue to the 1937 film version. Waszynski's film celebrates the vitality of Yiddish culture, but its production date has led contemporary audiences to read the wasting and wasteful death of its young lovers as teleological signs of the coming Holocaust.

All versions of 'The Dybbuk' concern the takeover of a woman's body and soul by the man who loves her but who kills himself when her father rejects him as her husband. In Anski's original version, this is an equal opportunity, since the woman, Leah, becomes the embodiment of a new mystical male-female vision – a new gendered identity based on the woman's ability to give life. This vision promises reconciliation and transcendence in the form of rescue – a 'fusion' of biology and destiny. The young man, Hanan, takes refuge from her father's rejection and the loss of his beloved in Leah's body (*Dybbuk* 121). Instead of rescue or transcendence, however, a darker fate unfolds in Pascal's play when Leah becomes a victim, not only of her beloved's 'invasion' of her body but also of the Holocaust (*Dybbuk* 124). The very idea of transcendence is obliterated twice over. The end of the woman means the end of Jewish regeneration. There can be no reconciliation. Because of its wartime ghetto setting, the idea of taking over the body and soul to deny individuality, identity, agency, and ultimately life itself, resonates with the Nazi takeover and destruction of the Jews. In fact both the story and internal performance of *The Dybbuk* are threatened by the Final Solution each time a scene or dialogue is interrupted by associations with incidents on the ghetto streets or with Hitler himself, who becomes the focus of a debate about whether killing him would be a sin, either in Jewish or Christian terms – the admonition, 'Thou shalt not kill' or the plea to 'Turn the other cheek' (*Dybbuk* 117). In a play about the loss of Jewish subjectivity and continuity, where the search for coherence and unity produces only fragmentation, such moral choices cannot be performed.

The despoliation of Leah's subjectivity extends to all the characters of the ghetto, effecting a paradoxical combination of fission and fusion but with the woman as nexus. However differently they define themselves as half-Jews, non-religious Jews or Jewish by default, whatever contestations, even quarrels emerge from their interpretations of *The Dybbuk*, the characters/players are shackled to the same plot that fuses their fates. Any idea of Jewish individuality, Jewish regeneration through the woman, or Jewish cultural differences has been erased by Nazi ideology which has distilled them via propaganda and then circumstantially into a poisonous witches' brew. Even as the characters/ players insist on differentiating their plight from that of Leah and the dybbuk, the answer is the same: 'RACHEL: (*as Leah/Dybbuk*)... All the roads are closed to me... (*as herself*) England, America, Africa. But nowhere, nowhere is there a space for me' (*Dybbuk* 126). While this rejecting space obviously refers to the abandonment of the Jews that facilitated the Holocaust, it also serves as a stage direction for the structure of Pascal's play. First, it introduces the claustrophobic space of the characters' ghetto hiding place and how it restricts differentiation of the characters. This restriction then becomes analogous to the enclosure of Leah and the dybbuk into each other. In turn, as the actors each play more than one character in their ghetto version of *The Dybbuk*, the performative and critical space between the play's characters and between player and characters contracts until their confinement locks them into each other. This latter merger does not, however, constitute a community. Like the character of the dybbuk, whose raison d'être necessitates its invasion of another, instead of forming a metonymy of peoplehood, the constantly interrupted dialogue of the ghetto prisoners suggests rupture and dissolution: the terror of losing individuality and being alchemized into a monstrous collation of antisemitic racism. If the conventional structure of a play within a play rehearses self-reflexive fictionality, as Greenhalgh notes, the doubling of *The Dybbuk* introduces the critical perspective of historical reality to *The Dybbuk*'s status as folklore. In effect, just as they have no place to go, Jewish lives in Pascal's play are broken off from the continuity of a Jewish story. At the same time, Rachel's lament quoted above conjures up the question of any safe space for the Jews threatened by the Holocaust and allowable space for Jewish cultural production in Britain.

Pascal's play grew out of several trips to Germany which for her 'always seems like a country filled with the ghosts of those who died too early' (*Holocaust Trilogy* 7). She 'wanted to write a play about Jews who were so assimilated they knew almost nothing about their religion' (*Holocaust Trilogy* 7). Of course Germany was only one European nation of several where Jewish assimilation counted for nil. In comparison, to perform this play in England raises the issue of how British assimilative pressures affect the presence and expression of Jewish culture when historical memory takes the form of Holocaust commemoration. Pascal's warrant for the continuity of Jewish identity and culture is to

> remain Jews to honor those who died... I am not looking at Anski's play merely as a metaphor for loyalty and love, which it is, but as a means of showing how art can serve as weapon against oppression. It is in this area that I go on the offensive, trying to help a new generation of theatre-goers understand the nature of Jewish life and culture; that the sins of the fathers have not disappeared. (quoted in Sonin)

Like *Theresa*, this play begins with a monologue that questions the viability of Jewish life and culture in Europe and, by implication in Britain.

But instead of a proleptic bitter end, the contemporary German setting and imagery of *The Dybbuk*'s prologue resonate with the horrors of sixty years earlier. Trains that still run on time, burnings and injections, silence and denial all lead Judith, the modern British Jewish woman, to wonder whether 'Hitler won?' 'Where is my generation? Where are my cousins? Where is the dream of assimilation?' (*Dybbuk* 106). The answer finds her as she finds herself 'haunted by faces, different accents, different bodies, all the lost cousins and aunts and uncles who I want to have known' (106). In addition to these stated differences, this knowledge becomes interactive and reflexively critical through a fusion of women's voices. The actress who portrays Judith also plays Rachel, a prisoner of the ghetto, and Leah, the dybbuk's beloved, the combination of which responds to Judith and raises further questions. Transgressing the boundaries of annihilation, like the shadows in Diane Samuels's *Kindertransport* and in *Theresa*, these dybbuks take over Judith's character and the play, and become haunting revenants for the audience, of Hitler's plan to annihilate the Jewish people and their culture.While the play's expressionist forms – its music, dance, interchange of actors and roles, and audience confrontation – resemble those of *Theresa*, instead of a tragedy of collective betrayal, *The Dybbuk* is an elegy and restoration of the multifaceted Jewish culture that was born and burned in Europe. That this culture should haunt a modern British woman testifies to the resilience of both.

In an interview, Pascal articulated her personal connection to *The Dybbuk*'s themes:

> I want to use Anski to express what concerns me most...My questions with myself. Identity and assimilation. What is Jewish culture? What is it to be a Jew? Why does one go on making culture in the face of death?...Inside each contemporary Jew are the souls, the dybbuks of those who were destroyed. The play is an act of defiance against the silence. There has not been enough grief about the Holocaust. We will take it to Germany and to France. German kids will cry. We will make connections that have been broken...(Bolchover, 'Between Two Plays' 17)

As soon as Judith's monologue ends, the other four actors turn to face the audience. But any connection they make is already disrupted by our knowledge of the characters' doomed fate. The Holocaust icons they bear remind us that the characters are being led to their deaths even as their performance represents a protest. Dropping the suitcases that have become metonyms for the death camp transports, the four actors/characters expose the emblems of their doomed Jewishness – the yellow stars sewn into the fabric of their clothes and lives. This is a moment of several intertwined transitions between their grim fate and 'defiance against the silence'. The monologue's expressed anxiety of losing Jewish identity in the wake of the Holocaust ends as the restoration of Jewish culture begins with the characters of the ghetto debating what it means to be Jewish and then performing their version of *The Dybbuk*.[18] In turn, the absurdist tension produced by their exchanges communicates the futility of any of their questions and definitions in light of the essential Jewishness legislated by the Nazis.

But then, as though protesting the possibility of Hitler's victory, the continuity of Jewish identity asserts itself in the characters' adaptation of a Jewish cultural artifact. Instead of reflecting their certain death and silence, their version of *The Dybbuk* evolves over the course of the play to express the vibrancy of Jewish identity and culture. Like the Jews' adaptation to the different places of their diaspora, this interpretation of a Jewish cultural artifact suggests a combination of internal Jewish translation and dynamic achievement. The ending of the ghetto performance of *The Dybbuk* then works as a prelude to the protest enacted by the close of Pascal's play, which depicts both 'death and rebirth' with the stage direction, 'You can kill a people but you cannot kill their culture' (*Dybbuk* 127). The dybbuk's final refusal to leave Leah's body and the Nazis' takeover of the ghetto merge along with the combined protest of Leah/Dybbuk and the 'defiance' of the five ghetto characters as they carry each other to join the 'murder of six million' (*Dybbuk* 126, 127). Unable to finish enacting the play as they are seized, instead of suitcases and yellow stars of Jewish identity, the ghetto characters carry away the knowledge that could so easily disappear along with them. The play itself, however, protests this erasure by reconstituting and transmitting it as knowledge for the audience.

The construction of the Jew as dybbuk in Pascal's Holocaust play is consonant with the idea of monster in a dual sense as regards the Jews imperiled by the Nazis. On the one hand, Jews were constructed by Nazi ideology as monstrous others, sucking or poisoning the blood of the German people, as threatening to take over German civilization and life itself. On the other hand, this construction also reflects the monstrousness of Nazi policies. In many narratives of Holocaust rescue, including Kindertransport memoirs and novels, as we have seen, the idea and image of monster become the locus of refugees' fears that overwhelm the political and social distance they travel from Nazi-occupied Europe to England. In some cases, even in conditions of safety, monstrousness is internalized as Jewish self-hatred or projected onto the condition and circumstances of alienation or even onto the place of rescue itself. But the idea and image of monstrousness can also be disguised by a diffused range of responses to exile, from frustration to anxiety about whether rescue, integration or assimilation to British culture are realistic possibilities. Whether ordinary British circumstances and social responses are perceived as concealing messages of rejection or threatening expulsion, refugees are shown as expecting the worst. In their experience and perceptions, the nation of rescue assumes an ominous cast, often seeming to mirror the terror they escaped. So many characters in contemporary Anglo-Jewish Holocaust writing react to Britain not as a coherent place of stability but as a discordant elsewhere or worse, a nowhere or a void, where the language of reserve and circumlocution is more akin to silence than expression.

How, these characters ask, can one achieve a sense of personal and social development in a place that communicates its own sense of identity as static and withdrawn? Whether this sense of British identity and social code is a function of cultural myth, of national folklore, or an imposed stereotype is dramatized by Anglo-Jewish women writers as an unnatural leap from fore-stalled childhood to a continuous state of incomplete adulthood. Where Pascal's *The Dybbuk* protests the European rejection of Jewish culture, the incompletely integrated British Jew in so many other writings becomes analogous to another figure from Jewish mythology, the *golem*. A racialized figure of horror, the *golem* is incompletely human even as he is constructed by men to protect the Jews from harm. What the *golem* cannot do and becomes aligned with in representation is to develop beyond his monstrous state of wandering.

The Jews in Pascal's plays produce emotional responses appropriate to the imminence of always threatening danger. But as we have seen in other writing by and about refugees, even when wandering ceases and they find safe haven in Britain, the sense of being precariously integrated Others prevails. As the refugees negotiate their desire to belong with their perception of the British demand for reserve, they struggle to find forms and voices that tell their stories with restraint while breaking free. As though in support for this struggle, the expressionist style of Pascal's plays provides a venue for the anguished outbursts of both the rescued and victims. Recognizing this venue, reviewer Lyn Gardner assesses *The Dybbuk* as coming 'up with something distinctly and refreshingly un-British' (n.p.). Dramatized decades after the end of the war, as a belated commemoration and performance of persistent anxiety and trauma, the outbursts of Pascal's women also memorialize the dislocation of Holocaust Jewish culture from its origins in Europe to a problematically assimilative state in Britain. In so doing, she addresses Victor Seidler's concern about the postwar years when Holocaust refugees were trying to assimilate, a concern that the 'dominant English culture had not begun to come to terms with the ways the Holocaust challenges fundamental terms of modernity' and identity (Seidler 7). Overall, Pascal's plays should be viewed as giving voice and creating a form of cultural production that responds to the political, social, and psychological crises of Holocaust and rescue experiences. That audiences will assess Pascal's polemical interpretations according to their own concerns, there is no doubt. Indeed, her expressionistic style and spotlight on the emotional subjectivity of Jewish women are designed to move the audience towards recognition of Britain's roles in their fates.

Each of Pascal's *Holocaust Trilogy* plays is an act of remembrance that performs the severance of its characters from their moments of slaughter while imaginatively recreating the terror that accompanied the slaughter and the anxieties that are its legacy. That this memorial assumes expressionist form also assimilates these Holocaust plays to a contemporary British culture at the same time that it testifies to a long history of theatrical production. British theater has always stormed the barricades of reticence and reserve while rendering these qualities as grist for satire and stereotype. From Shakespeare's political and sexual fantasies through Wilde's satires and John Osborne's anger at bourgeois gentility, Pinter's ominous pauses, Caryl Churchill's searing satires, and Sarah Kane's eruptions of psychological violence, British theater has always authorized dramas that upset the apple cart of social and political decorum. It is within this cultural history that the troubled efforts of Jewish refugees to integrate and assimilate find their language of expression.

That selfhood could be bound to a missed Holocaust history is the subject of Sue Frumin's play, *The Housetrample*. *The Housetrample* dramatizes the anguish of placelessness through Frumin's own performance that represents her mother's Czech past and experiences as a new refugee. Written in 1984 when Frumin attended a theater arts course, she was inspired to focus on women because their stories were mostly 'not documented nor assumed to be a relevant part of women's history' (*Housetrample* 107). From the beginning of the play, the lack of documentation and the continuous condition of displacement become reflexive metaphors for each other. Like Pascal's concern with concealed or ignored historical documentation, Frumin's play focuses on what Gerhard Bach calls 'a shift from objectifying testimony to subjectified witness' in contemporary Holocaust writing (83).[19] Both Pascal and Frumin complicate this shift by showing how the historical reception of 'subjectified witness' has relegated it to another category – displaced testimony. In other words, the Holocaust plays of Pascal and Frumin perform the historical and cultural ideologies and processes that led to the elision of subjectified witness from Britain's historical consciousness and in so doing, the plays recreate subjective witness as embodied in their displaced female characters.

In Frumin's play, the female characters and their subjective testimony are doubly displaced. The word *Housetrample* means cleaner, but as Frumin writes it, despite their jobs caring for other people's places of work and home, the idea of house and home become trampled for the women refugees. Her focus on women characters reflects her desire to dramatize 'a story which not only had resonances for Jewish women, but for all women from immigrant backgrounds; a story of differences and of surviving in an alien culture' (Frumin 107). We see these differences in Frumin's decision to perform the story of a survivor and a victim as a friendship between two women, one who decides to 'Run', and one who decides to 'Fight' (106). In turn, their different stories corroborate not only the centrality of women's voices to Holocaust knowledge but also the integrity of their countering decisions.

The play opens in 1945, at a London train station, where Vera Brunner awaits the safe arrival of her childhood friend Lili. While Vera had escaped on the Kindertransport, Lili remained behind to serve as a partisan, only to disappear into the vise of Nazi terror. The futility of Vera's wait marks a story that is always in transit, between past and present, where even the safe harbor of Britain guarantees only displacement and irreconcilable difference. At the same time, Vera also awaits the train that will take her from Britain back to Europe where she was first endangered and where she will now work for the Americans as a censor. The destruction of a past that cannot be recaptured or repaired, whose reality is forever censored, is represented by her lost and seized war diaries and the bitter reality that she cannot rewrite them as she would like, as a film script. Even her memory and imagination must fail her. There will be no testimony of her experience facing the threat of Nazi conquest. Only a perpetually incomplete, unread, and unheard narrative. If the problems of survivor memory and testimony have become part of scholarly debate on Holocaust representation, Frumin intervenes with her play. In its own writing about writing, *The Housetrample* testifies to the difficulties of reimagining merely one segment of an event, the whole of which has been judged unimaginable but necessary to represent. Venturing into the empty spaces of loss and silence, Frumin intersperses the Czech experience of Nazi occupation with that of immigrating to Britain through the fates of Vera and Lili. In fact, from the first scene onwards, the play moves back and forth between past and present and between Czechoslovakia and Britain in such a way as to suggest that what can be represented is no more or less than a historical and experiential void.

In concert, the sealed and lost past and the play's reflexive structure suggest there is no closure or resolution to the European Jewish tragedy for those who escaped. At the end of the play, instead of resolution, amputation of the past becomes a strategy necessary to surviving the memory of the Holocaust. As Vera is about to get the train back to Germany, she announces to the audience: 'I'll just have to cut off the past and go forward. I've always been able to do that. I think that's what saved me' (*Housetrample* 106). As the play unfolds from the beginning, however, the past cannot be so easily discarded. Instead, the past is persistently mirrored in the play's present, where only questions and irresolution lie. One example of such mirroring is how Vera's experience in Britain is fraught with a malicious ignorance that resonates with the unwillingness of occupied Europe to consider the Jews civilized human beings. That Britain will not rectify the Jews' position as unassimilable is already established in Czechoslovakia when a Lady Diana Huntingdon-Smythe of the Society for Anglo-Czech Understanding instructs the would-be emigrants at the English Institute in Prague. As though parodying the written instructions for refugees on arrival in Britain, reprinted in my introduction, this role model for proper British deportment makes a mockery of welcome. She begins by insisting that her audience find 'the nearest English equivalent' for their 'unpronounceable names' and learn the appropriate forms of address according to social class, from the royal family to government officials and ending with the class they will be assigned to, 'the very common people at the bottom' (*Housetrample* 101). Lest we think that such disdain reflects merely the snobbery of the upper classes, Vera fares little better with middle- and working-class employers in Britain, all of whom are fully aware of the refugees' plight. Even her Jewish host, Mrs. Goldberg, can only complain about the evacuees' ineptitude and threaten to have them sent 'back to Germany or wherever it is you're from!' (*Housetrample* 104).

Though such figures are drawn with broad satiric strokes, each time Frumin returns to her portrait of Vera we are made aware of the deep hurt endured by the refugee who has no recourse except to slip in and out of the menial, thankless work offered by her host nation. Frumin, however, does not paint either of her female protagonists as passive victims of a heartless haven. Vera's response to her variously dismal jobs is to slip in and out of various voices that berate the powers that exiled her and those who perpetuate her displaced and disabling status. Implicating her British audience in her fate, Vera speaks in a voice that expresses her growing understanding and assimilation of irony as encoding British decorum: 'If I don't lose my temper I get lots of rationing points' (*Housetrample* 104). Then, as though she feels armed with the assurance that she has ingratiated herself with her British audience, she immediately translates her irony into a mocking response to her antagonists in the play. The target of her greatest contempt and wanton burlesque is the Führer himself, depicted by Vera as he is having trouble writing *Mein Kampf* and seeking distraction in being entertained by a racially pure but clumsy dancer performed, with biting irony, by the Jewish Vera:

> I am very bored, unt mein spellink is going wrong! Bring me a flower of German girlhood to dance for me. (*Housetrample* 98)

Despite Vera's limited choices and vocabulary of volition, the doubling effect of such mockery and commentary forms an active protest against a prevailing climate that connects Hitler's antisemitic racism to the xenophobic anger of Britons: 'Bloody foreigners coming over here and taking our jobs' (*Housetrample* 104). If the British outburst is at all embarrassing for a contemporary audience, its juxtaposition with the Jew's ridiculing of Hitler's language and sexist racism questions the comfort and complacency one might feel when the target is politically correct.

In effect, the play functions as an angry response to Britain's combined welcoming and withholding. The mockery of Hitler's spoken German and writer's block calls attention to the historic distance of the play and the audience from the actual political power of his prose. At the same time, this mockery expresses the anxiety embedded in Vera's precarious status at the time of her writing the sketch moments before the Nazi occupation of Czechoslovakia. As this anxious moment is projected onto an audience whose complicit laughter has been solicited by the Hitler sketch, the play distances itself from its own satiric thrusts with incidents involving Lili's increasingly threatened status in Nazi-occupied Prague. Working metaphorically, the play's distance asserts that even in the moments representing Vera's safety and savvy acculturation, Britain remains a distant and tenuous harbor. Indeed, it is that very position of alienation that enacts a subversive critical questioning of the besieged but, as she sees it, the sedentary culture that fosters her. Being neither here nor there, but a sojourner always vigilant for signs of discordance between herself and her hosts, this wandering Jew also takes risks that bespeak a rebelliously critical mindset. Though she is neither interned nor given any sign of being considered an enemy alien, Vera recognizes that none of her encounters even begins to suggest that integration into any British community is possible. Her friends are other refugees and the only affinity available to her is at the Czech Club.

One of the play's achievements is to link Vera's British experience with that of Czechoslovakia. With their obvious differences always before the audience as historical memory and fact, the play's linkages between its realism and political critique offer us the opportunity to understand the processes through which Vera recognizes her lack of belonging anywhere. Just as Britain is a constant reminder of her status as a foreigner, so the play keeps taking us back to Czechoslovakia, where we are shown the accretion of events and hostile reactions which propel Jews into the status of enemy aliens in their homelands and even in safe harbors. The play's movements between places also dramatize how Vera's memory works to connect past and present, as incidents in Britain and Czechoslovakia recall and shed some light on each other. Reflecting the difficulty of remembering the past at all or with any accuracy, Vera's efforts to recall her childhood are replete with the name changes of her home town from Czech to German and then its postwar renaming. Just as the experience and idea of home town or homeland are denied to the Jews, so Vera cannot reclaim the places of her past as her own. Even before the moment she is transported from her home and family, her condition is dramatized as one of exile. And then later, as she has difficulty recreating and writing her life before exile except as fragmented incidents, so it seems that her origins are only to be found in a state of estrangement. Similar to Pascal's *Theresa*, each of Frumin's flashback scenes dramatizes an incident fraught with estrangement from the social and cultural codes in which her family negotiates its place in a society rapidly devolving into fascist oppression. In turn, as these scenes alternate with those in Britain, they foreshadow the disorientation awaiting her. Beginning with her childhood, when she was only ten, what Vera recalls is that she 'was a compulsive liar', or taken to be one since her explanations of accidents and misdeeds are shaped more by the logic of fables than confessions of ordinary dereliction (*Housetrample* 96). As her mother comments, 'and the canary flew outside, and the cat tried to rescue it from the tree. Really, Vera, you do tell the most ridiculous lies!' (*Housetrample* 96). As though asserting her sense of a self already alienated from social conventions, all of Vera's stories rebel against narrative constraints of assigning agency and responsibility and of logical and linear progression. Moving immediately to another rebellious scene, Vera's friend Lili incites a 'girls' revolution' based on a story of women in 1500 Bohemia who 'emasculated the men' when they did not meet the women's demands (*Housetrample* 96). With these women as role models, Vera and Lili draw up a list of demands including 'No cooking', cleaning or sewing, and, perhaps most defiantly, 'To be allowed to read whatever we want' (*Housetrample* 96–7).

Conflating early modern gender constraints with a perilous modernity highlights a continuum of women's self-determining struggles to resist the role of passive victim. That the girls are apprehended and expelled from their school because of their manifesto follows the logic of middle-class European propriety, but also reflects a more lethal code. In its retrospective portrayal, the incident and its aftermath anticipate Nazi doctrine and practices. To insist on one's own reading choices will defy the Nazi prohibition of whatever it considered degenerate art and writing, an edict that began with book burning. That Vera's punishment should include attending a Catholic school mimics the Nazis' view of Jewish culture as degenerate. The school's cooking class also recalls Nazi gender policies, especially the insistence that women leave their work outside the home and return to *kirche*, *kinder*, and *kuche*. Presented as bitter satire, Vera's memory of the class includes the instruction to beat a carp to death, an action that targets Nazi gender policies as brutally coercive while overturning the values of tenderness and nurturing traditionally assigned to women.

The relationship between the shifting grounds of the past, the language through which it can only be suggested, and the instability of memory also simulate the very process of writing for Vera and perhaps for the playwright herself, especially as she not only writes but also plays the part. As the play dramatizes its own attempts to find coherence and structure, in its need to draw attention to its story, it exposes the urgency and anxiety of the Second Generation to commemorate and not betray the past even as the desire to cut loose from the horrific past is expressed again and again. One problem faced by Second Generation writers is how to construct and maintain a safe distance from the past that always threatens to engulf the present and therefore the writer's identity. A solution presented by *The Housetrample* is to atomize the past until the story of the Holocaust it produces is discontinuous and reflects a constant shift between past and present. This shifting movement, moreover, also becomes a performative metaphor for the erratic movements forced upon those who were trapped by the Nazis' locked borders and those who tried to escape. As Pascal and Frumin both show, even the transport to rescue is fraught with overwhelming anxieties at every train stop and confrontation with strangers. Both playwrights, Julia Pascal and Sue Frumin, can be described as strangers to the Holocaust. Pascal's only personal connection is her profound desire to confront audiences with Holocaust stories that have been erased or elided. As a Second Generation survivor, Frumin's access to Holocaust experience is her mother's stories and her research. For both playwrights, and as we have seen with Diane Samuels and Charlotte Eilenberg, writing the anxieties and terrors of survivors and victims engages their own anxieties as they make decisions about the language and forms through which to transmit and translate lost or neglected stories into their imaginative and investigative visions. Because these plays have no narrator, unlike other literary forms, their performances dramatize not only the story but also the results of the playwright's decision making. Without a narrator to mediate the distance between audiences and performers and, in Frumin's case, being both playwright and performer, there is no voice, presence, or narrative form to explain or justify either the style or interpretive substance of the play. This mediating absence, however, has a place on stage as it leaves the interpretive space for audiences to confront what Vivian Patraka calls 'the goneness of the Holocaust' that 'foregrounds the constructedness of representations of these events' (5).

Perhaps nowhere is this constructedness more visible than in the performance of the play as a shared experience. As audiences react to the combination of sets, music, and characters, they participate in the creation of the plays' connections and tensions between the Holocaust past and the present and between the interpretation proffered by the particular performance of a play and those of the audience. Especially as Pascal chooses a survivor to play a victim and Frumin performs her mother's story, the past is performed as a living presence or embodiment of memory that speaks to the audience. In turn, the audience's knowledge of the playwrights' and actors' personal or critical relation to a Holocaust story adds a connection to the past that becomes a critical bridge between the performance and the audience. This critical bridge performs another drama, one that breaks any mimetic illusion of reality or transparency. As Claude Schumacher notes,

> dealing with plays about the Shoah, the actor on stage clearly signifies the absence, from the here-and-now, of the character he is presenting. His being there proclaims the absence of the 'other' and the spectator must, in order to make sense of what is presented, reconstruct in his mind the missing reality and lend his own being, thoughts and emotions, to the character evoked by the actor. (5)

This absence or missing reality is confirmed not only by the bare stages in which Pascal's and Frumin's plays are set but also when the final curtain is lowered and actors, characters, and story are gone, leaving only their haunting traces in the memories of the audience. Patraka observes of this overdetermined absence: 'The Holocaust performative acknowledges that there is nothing to say to goneness and yet we continue to try and mark it, say it, identify it, memorialize the loss over and over' (Patraka 7). In allowing ourselves to witness the losses portrayed by Julia Pascal and Sue Frumin, in allowing ourselves to participate in their memorializing theater, we accept Frumin's injunction 'not to cut off the past' and instead follow Pascal's imperative to 'attempt to raise some of the questions which surround the Holocaust in the knowledge that there are no answers' (*Housetrample* 106).

Afterword

To study the writing of the 1.5 Kindertransport generation along with that of the Second Generation can easily be justified categorically because both groups consist of Jewish children who survived the Holocaust without having to endure its atrocities directly. Yet even though they were rescued, found safe harbor, and built productive lives, Kindertransport writers like Lore Segal and Karen Gershon endured the acute anxiety that came from separation, the fragmented knowledge their parents communicated from Europe, and, most often, the silences and then irremedial loss. Unlike the position of the Second Generation who, as Henri Raczymow notes, 'cannot even say that we were *almost* deported', the Kinder had a direct experience of their own – of being exported, but to safety ('Memory' 104, author's italics). Nonetheless, safety did not mitigate the separations and losses of families, losses that were exacerbated by ever fading and partial memories. Even in safety, adult, adolescent, and child refugees experienced the war as an effect of being catapulted from a known world to one that was as alien to them as they were to it. This alienation provides another link to the Second Generation because, as Anne Karpf and Lisa Appignanesi testify, while Holocaust memories and stories became second nature to them, like the Kinder, while growing up, the lack of Holocaust experience made them doubt who they are. In both cases, writing serves as an investigative and imaginative pathway to the knowledge that brings them a little closer to understanding their historical and emotional origins. Writing also reflects the hard-won psychological space in which to create an identity that is tethered to the past but never stops straining against it.

Because, however, this book also studies those writers who have no personal or community link to the Holocaust, it begs the question of how we identify and group them as Holocaust writers. Writers like Elaine Feinstein, Diane Samuels, and Julia Pascal neither experienced nor inherited family stories of the Holocaust; they are beset neither with its fragmented memories nor traumatic dreams. Instead, although their Holocaust writing relies on research and interviews, it is primarily imaginative, and, for this reason, continues to evoke concerns about the ethical and aesthetic limits of Holocaust representation. In light of these ongoing concerns, it is worthwhile to consider non-fiction writing about the Holocaust by historians, psychologists, and philosophers and how that is assessed differently. Even if these non-fiction writers are survivors or children or grandchildren of survivors, they are credited with the intellectual rigor of their disciplines, and, as far as I know, no questions have been raised about their being either too close to their subjects or too subjective. In fact, since Hayden White's interventions, it is now generally accepted that regardless of its scholarly documentation and forensic evidence and charts and graphs, historical, psychological, and philosophical writing is shaped not only by subjective identification and concerns but also by the narrative and tropic forms that we associate with imaginative writing.

I do not raise this qualification to denigrate non-literary Holocaust writing as an argument for the legitimacy of imaginative writing. Instead, I want to argue that it is the imaginative dimensions of both literary and non-literary post-Holocaust writing that reach out to us. It is the imaginative work of these writers that compels our attention and implores us to assume the resolve to learn what we can never really understand. It is also the subjectivity invested by these writers in their own pursuit of Holocaust knowledge that joins the testimony of survivors to become our legacy of Holocaust knowledge and insight. I think one way of establishing a connection between them and those writers who survived the Holocaust or inherited its memories would be to identify them also as a generation – the first generation of imaginative witnesses. Like others of this generation, the Anglo-Jewish women studied here feel compelled to write Holocaust stories, but to follow if not fulfill an imperative that derives from their own British identity and history. They want to insert the complicated history of Britain's responses to antisemitism, to the Holocaust, and to the rescue of Jewish children into the contemporary narrative of multicultural Britain. In their work of writing their stories of this history, they also interpret Anglo-Britain's collective relationship to the Holocaust. In addition to asking us to listen and to see, they want us to join them in seeing through the sustaining myths of British national culture and collective memory. Their writing represents a plea to join them in their imaginative odysseys to recapture the pain that accompanied heroic rescue and cowardly betrayals. In the words of Geoffrey Hartman, they are 'haunted interpreter[s]' (*Longest* 1).

Like testimonies that are given so long after the war, these widely diverse imagined stories remind us of the vast and complex scope of the Holocaust, and, in their various genres and narrative forms, they offer us guideposts to interpretation and meaning. They show us how they wish these stories to be continued to be transmitted. In their imaginative forms, these writings expand our definitions of Holocaust testimony and literature as well as different responsive and interpretive strategies. Filtered through their dramatic and narrative reconstructions and constructions, these writings transmit and emphasize the necessity of including the emotional and cultural effects of suffering and adaptation for audiences and readers who, like the writers, are so distant from the events. These writers remind me of W. G. Sebald's narrator and protagonist in his novel *Austerlitz* because they attempt, perhaps just as obsessively, to retrace the steps of the Holocaust past and 'to realize that there was no transition, only this dividing line, with ordinary life on one side and its unimaginable opposite on the other' (297). Having invoked Sebald in my introduction, as I end this book, I want to draw attention to the silences he broke by writing in Britain as a Second Generation German survivor of Nazi terror in dialogue with Jewish survivors.

As though responding to the question of how we can negotiate the distance between ourselves and Holocaust stories, the writers I discuss invert, reverse, and exploit such familiar narrative icons as fairy tales and figures to which we *can* relate. Now, however, these revisionary tales transfigure familiar bogey men into monstrous emanations of historical realities. Especially as these figures are incorporated as fragments of childhood memory and consciousness, they intensify the effect of a fractured past by coinciding with the narrated and acted shards of people, places, and incidents that originate in a long-distant past that may always remain beyond our grasp. In turn, these emanations and narrative bits and pieces make us shed the expectations of coherence, reconciliation, and happy resolutions that made these tales bearable to us when we were children. Instead, we are being asked to use these figures and tales as mind maps that link us imaginatively to the characters' and narrators' attempts to piece their memories together. Though the stories will not achieve anything resembling wholeness or equivalency to our own emotional storehouses, as Sara Horowitz shows us, they can 'cohere through empathic imagination and willingness to bear witness' – a willingness 'to engage wholly – intellectually, emotionally, imaginatively' (*Voicing* 224).

Given the emotional, intellectual, and imaginative intensity of their writing, we can see these writers creating a relationship to the Holocaust past that, despite or because of historical and experiential distance, can be seen as a form of filiation. Recalling Lisa Appignanesi's novel *The Memory Man*, we can see his African-American daughter Amelia in Geoffrey Hartman's terms, as one of 'those who have become witnesses by adoption (who have adopted themselves into the family of victims)' (*Longest* 8). As Susan Suleiman notes of writers who were children and adolescents during the Holocaust, while their

> works are highly individualized in literary style, [they] bear 'family resemblances' in tone, genre, and emotional or narrative content that place them in significant dialogue with each other. Themes of unstable identity and psychological splitting, a preoccupation with absence, emptiness, silence, a permanent sense of loneliness and loss, including the loss of memories relating to family and childhood, and, often an anguished

questioning about what it means to be Jewish after the Holocaust dominate many of these works. Equally compelling is their preoccupation, either explicitly stated or implied in their formal choices, with the question of *how* to tell the story. (*Crises* 184)

Avoiding the pitfalls of their own identifications with or relatedness to the atrocities, the imaginative writers I study here self-consciously explore the emotional and epistemological divide and conclude that, just as they have a responsibility to tell the stories that have been left untold, so we must listen.

Notes

Introduction

1. Most Holocaust critics begin by offering their interpretation of Adorno's warning about art after Auschwitz and 'appropriate' Holocaust representation, with some arguing that narrative experimentation or, in the extreme, even the use of figurative language effaces the historicity of a Holocaust story. Berel Lang shows that 'imaginative writing about the Holocaust...typically, eschews standard literary devices or figures in favor of historical ones – purporting to present factual narratives which are not factual at all, splicing actual juridical testimony into fictional frames, appealing to historical genres like the diary or letter or memoir but as imagined rather than historical means...and in...film disguising its virtuoso powers under the more severe constraints of the documentary' ('Second-Sight' 24). See as well Lang's *Holocaust Representation*. Recent contributors to debates on Holocaust representation include Michael Rothberg, who argues that 'the desire for realism and referentiality is one of the defining features of 'Holocaust study' (99). Janet Wolff argues that 'realist work...that presents a literal, illusionistic representation – performs a premature movement of closure, enticing the viewer to accept the belief that he or she has now seen the object (...the Holocaust itself). This seduction...forecloses for most viewers...the recognition that this is in the end only a story...a combination of false coherence or closure and refusal of dialogue between work and viewer' (158–9). Marianne Hirsch and Susan Suleiman note the persistent 'tension between referentiality and aestheticism' (in Hornstein and Jacobowitz [90]).

2. In addition to Judy Chicago's Holocaust Project, the New York Jewish Museum's Images of Evil exhibit inspired not only debate but also protests by survivors. Interestingly, although Binjamin Wilkomirski's *Fragments* has been exposed as a fraudulent Holocaust memoir, critics remain fascinated by it and have even rationalized its value as unconsciously driven fiction.

3. Hartman refers to President Ronald Reagan's appearance at a commemoration of the fortieth anniversary of Germany's freedom from Nazism that also included a memorial to SS and Wehrmacht officers. While the memorial was obviously deeply offensive to both the memory of their victims and to survivors, the President not only did not defend its inclusion but also implied that they were all victims.

4. Nowhere is this problem more apparent than in Poland, whose sense of its own suffering under the Nazis was challenged with the publication of Jan Gross's *Neighbors*, about the Polish slaughter of Jedwadne's Jews.

5. Sebald's fame in English came with his 1996 novel, *The Emigrants*, which consists of four stories, all interrelated, but, as Carole Angier points out, it 'is the opposite of a tricksy, self-conscious postmodern novel. It is exquisitely written; but it is modest and quiet, and does not draw attention to itself at all. And yet this book raises the question of its own status more vividly, more directly, than any frivolous literary game' ('Who Is W. G. Sebald?' 10).

6. Marita Grimwood notes that the reason why so many current Jewish family memoirists are women may very well be that Jewish identity is carried by the mother.

Studies of women and the Holocaust have proliferated in recent years and I am particularly indebted to such scholars as Sara Horowitz, Judith Baumel, Carol Rittner and John Roth, and Dalia Ofer and Lenore Weitzman, among so many who have made us aware of the gendered nature of Holocaust suffering that consisted of different horrors, same hell.

7. Cheryl Malcolm discusses Brookner's novel *Latecomers* as a Holocaust Kindertransport narrative about expressed and repressed memory. Malcolm's view that the novel 'can be regarded as a tale of recovery' makes this an exception to the writings I explore in this book (160). Lucy Ellmann objects to 'proprietorial attitudes towards the Holocaust' and responds to the criticism that the love story in her novel *Man or Mango?* 'cannot carry the weight of the Holocaust', by claiming that the representation of ordinary human cruelty and suffering in today's fiction must resonate with the Holocaust (Matthew Reisz 16). Sue Vice and Bryan Cheyette discuss the critical confluence of postmodern and historicist representations of Jews as reflecting a prevailing ambivalence toward them – always both strangers and familiar. But they both favor a historicist approach to avoid an essentialism within postmodern indeterminacy that 'historically, generated a semitic discourse in the first place' (Cheyette, *Constructions* 274–5). Among recent critical works on issues related to Holocaust narrative experiment and postmodernism by British scholars, see Robert Eaglestone (*Holocaust and the Postmodern*) and Ann Parry ('Lost in the Multiplicity of Impersonations' and 'Caesura of the Holocaust').

8. The Kindertransport was organized by the World Movement for the Care of Children and brought 9354 children to Britain, including 7482 who were Jewish. This figure represents only 10 percent of Jewish children who had to remain in Germany by 1939. Priority was given to orphans, children from single-parent homes, those whose parents were in concentration camps, and boys targeted for incarceration. Each child was permitted one suitcase and ten Reichsmarks. As in a scene in Samuels's play, valuables could be confiscated by guards who had learned to look for jewelry sewn into clothing or tacked into the soles and heels of shoes.

9. Denmark and Bulgaria were exceptions and saved their Jews. Records show that resistance to rescue includes North America, for after debates in Congress and in state legislatures, after complaints that refugee children would take over the jobs of American citizens, the USA decided against any such rescue. For all its vast emptiness, Canada took in a total of 5000 Jews. Tony Kushner notes that in 1938–39, 'more than 40% of the Jews who escaped the Nazis found refuge in Britain', albeit on temporary visas (*Holocaust and the Liberal Imagination* 51.) The history of British refugee policies begins with the Aliens Act of 1905 which, with further restrictions implemented before and after World War I, limited Jewish immigration from Eastern Europe. From 1933 to 1938, the British government tried to effect policies that would balance its desire to appear humane and self-interest. The result was to admit those who brought wealth or scientific, artistic, or technological talents, albeit against the protests of professional organizations. By 1938, visas were granted to those who were economically self-sufficient or had British guarantors. Jewish women were also admitted on domestic service visas. The Kindertransport was made possible by refugee agencies guaranteeing fifty pounds sterling for each child to be paid against their subsequent re-emigration. For details, see David Cesarani's introduction to Harris and Oppenheimer. British immigration policies regarding Jews through the end of the war are discussed in detail by Bernard Wasserstein and Louise London.

10. As Neil Levi and Michael Rothberg point out, psychoanalytic studies of trauma represent attempts to amend poststructuralist theories 'with urgent ethical concerns posed by catastrophes of the twentieth century' and their 'demand for referentiality in the face of suffering' (16). Although Cathy Caruth claims that the traumatized person suffers from the experience of historical savagery, as Sue Vice points out, Caruth's model is still a metaphorical use of trauma, and, for myself and other critics, this is a problematic usage. See Vice's essay 'Trauma, Postmodernism and Descent' for a critical analysis of trauma theories and their relation to postmodernism in current British Holocaust literary criticism. Debarati Sanyal is very critical of using Holocaust trauma in this way because it threatens to subsume the historical specificity of Holocaust experience and memory. In discussing autobiographical Kindertransport accounts, Andrea Hammel registers objection to postmodern celebrations of 'the fragmented self [that] deny the right to see the changes and ruptures in their lives as traumatic' (72).

11. The word abandon developed many meanings in Kindertransport experience. Anne L. Fox recalls the letters from her assimilated parents that indicated 'an abandonment to fate, an apprehension of what was to come, and a trust in God, a last hope that He, who had been driven away from their community…would care for all the poor uprooted people' (55).

12. Despite differences between 'populist and non-populist' definitions and perspectives on the attitudes of different classes and regions of Britain, British rhetoric of World War II (reinforced by American journalists in London) is only upheld by the fact that 'the British people did endure the Blitz without cracking' (Paul Smith, *Review* 28). In contrast, those British civilians who endured wartime suffering abroad were excluded from this narrative. Writing for *The Times* in 2005, Michael Evans reported that a British citizen imprisoned by the Japanese in World War II finally won a landmark case against the Ministry of Defence after it rejected her claim for government compensation on the grounds that because she was born in Hong Kong and her parents were from India and Iraq, 'she was "not quite British enough" to receive the ex-gratia award for her suffering' (29).

13. Colin Holmes attributes this difference to the fact that, in Britain, 'antisemitism never secured a major policy foothold within the political establishment and where the forces of a stable social-political system could be deployed against those who threatened to make antisemitism a major issue' (226). For further discussion, see David Cesarani, 'Reporting Antisemitism', and Jones, Kushner, and Pearce, *Cultures of Ambivalence*.

14. Even after the liberation of the Camps, some by British troops who witnessed massive piles of corpses and walking skeletons, even as the extermination and torture of European Jewry were being confirmed by the Nuremberg Trials and reportage, Britain remained stingy in its immigration policies. Instead of using the facts of the Holocaust as a lesson against antisemitism, the government continued to consider Jews as unassimilable. Only with the full economic support of Jewish organizations did the Home Office give permission to adopt one thousand Jewish orphans from the camps. Strict guidelines produced only 732 children, mostly from Auschwitz and Theresienstadt. See Anton Gill and Barry Turner.

15. The Colonial Office claimed that the colonies, including Kenya, Tanganyika, and Northern Rhodesia, couldn't 'make a serious contribution to the problem' (Sherman 103).

16. The literature on identity formation is growing even as I write this, but there seems to be a consensus based on the work of British cultural critic, Stuart Hall,

interpreted most recently by a study of Jewish identity by Laurence Silberstein where the latter argues that 'rather than viewing identities as eternally fixed in some stationary, recoverable past, critics increasingly see them as subject to the continuous "play" of history, culture, and power' (3).

17. Kushner also reminds us that, despite this difference, tolerance remained an obstacle to attacking the freedom of Jews to practice their religion. See *The Holocaust and the Liberal Imagination* for a trenchant analysis of relationships between liberal ideology, immigration policies, and concerns about British national identity. In response to arguments critiquing liberalism for its homogenizing impulses, Todd Endelman asserts that 'The real culprit is the ruthlessly genteel, monolithic and exclusive character of English culture or, more specifically, the culture of the propertied and educated strata of society who have always formed the reference groups for upwardly mobile Jews', but he adds, in their incapacity to accept alternative modes of Englishness, 'socialists and conservatives have been no different than liberals' ('New Anglo-Jewish History' 55). For the ongoing debate, see Cesarani, Feldman, Kushner, Mandler, Mazower, and Wasserstein, about 'England, Liberalism and the Jews: An Anglo-Jewish *Historikerstreit*'.

18. Of course population statistics belie the myth of homogeneity. A 2005 survey conducted by *The Guardian* showed that 'Between 1991 and 2001, when Britain's population increased by 2.2 million, to 58 million, more than half the increase was made up of people born in other countries' (cited by Alan Cowell np).

19. Holmes and Bolchover agree that, despite British differences, 'a tradition of antisemitism in Britain' was not 'insignificant' and to dismiss it as such would be 'a cruel deception' (Holmes 234). At the Conference on Antisemitism and English Culture held at Birkbeck College, University of London, July 2007, David Feldman made the point that abrupt English switches between philo- and antisemitism and vice versa depend on whether the figure of the Jew can be seen as a victim or not. As historian Anne Summers acutely noted, at the same conference, 'What is absent is the possibility of the Jew being an ordinary historical agent like anyone else. It's rather like the madonna/whore dichotomy in regard to women.'

20. In contrast to this attitude, that of the government's Refugee Children's Movement recommended children whose situations were urgent, including those in orphanages which were easy targets, children of arrested or deported parents, and teenage boys who were at risk for arrest (Curio 44). On the receiving end, problems for placement in foster homes arose out of suspicion of children who came from institutions, if children came from lower-class families or if their mothers were unmarried, while small children and girls were favored (Curio 50).

21. The German Jewish Aid Committee (12).

22. Gershon, *We Came as Children* 89. Unlike the individual Kindertransport memoirs discussed in this book, which use the form of the *Bildungsroman*, this excerpt from Karen Gershon's collective autobiography is, as Sue Vice notes, 'individualized' but 'not personal', and its 'choppy, multiple form' reflects the Kinder's experiences of dislocation (*Children* 41).

23. Although antisemitism assumed activist forms during the war, Tony Kushner shows that the British Union of Fascists and the English National Association attracted a pitifully low number of voters in wartime by-elections (*Persistence* 44).

24. By 11 June 1940, with the impetus of the fall of Dunkirk, military pressure succeeded in galvanizing public fears and '27,000 enemy aliens were interned, with over 7,000 sent overseas' (Kushner, *Persistance* 145). By December, over 9000

were released. One thousand older teenagers among the Kindertransport were also interned. Approximately 6000 were sent to Canada and Australia while hundreds of Italian transportees were killed when their ship, the *Arandora Star*, was torpedoed on 1 July 1940. See also, Maxine S. Seller.

25. Zygmunt Bauman has shaped current arguments about antisemitism and philosemitism by employing the term allosemitism, which casts 'Jews as the embodiment of ambivalence' whose identities and practices defy all extant categories, a threatening state of affairs despite the postmodern embrace of the 'variety and plurality of the forms of life'. Bauman notes two discourses shaping perceptions and representations of Jews: 'the *abstract* Jew, the Jew as a concept located in a different discourse from the "empirical Jews," and hence located at a secure distance from experience and immune to whatever information may be supplied by that experience and whatever emotions may be aroused by daily intercourse' (148, 155).

26. Supercilious as it may seem, even today, British politicians parry about an authentic British style. Newly installed Prime Minister Gordon Brown mused in public that it would be a good idea to celebrate Britishness as Americans do, by 'taking a bit more pride in their flag', a suggestion that was mocked by David Cameron, Tory leader: 'We are understated. We don't do flags on the front lawn' (Cowell n.p.). That Brown is a Scotsman and Cameron an old Etonian may be telling.

27. In her discussion of British post-Holocaust novels, Ann Parry shows how the status of refugee and victim collapses any notion of indeterminate identity for the Jew, effacing 'the capacity to move between different subject positions' and making 'Englishness more tenuous' (' "Lost" ' 8).

28. The emancipation process began with the abolition of the sacramental test for naturalization in 1825 and was finalized in 1871 when the entire panoply of oaths and declarations restricting Jews from political office was repealed. It was supposed to reflect Britain's liberal toleration, but during the debates that ensued Jews were criticized for their foreignness, their divided loyalties, and their craven materialism. How Jews internalized this criticism and its implied antisemitism is illustrated by an editorial in the *Jewish Chronicle* of New Year's Day 1937, asking the community to renounce 'the materialism which is rampant among some of our people' (cited in David Cesarani, 'Reporting Antisemitism' 268). Bolchover cites the debates about whether British non-Jewish society ever had any idea of an emancipation contract that dictated the actions of each side. Even if such dictates were never openly articulated, many historians think that the contract was implied in the contradictions of liberalism, where an ideology of tolerance could co-exist with the 1904 Aliens Act that restricted immigration of eastern European Jews. Bolchover concludes that British Jews conflated liberalism and antisemitism into an ambivalent emancipation contract that required them to be loyal and grateful to the nation that had accepted their presence while developing its own brand of antisemitism, albeit an antisemitism that British Jews saw as marginal, rarely involving physical or verbal attacks or discrimination, and understood as the result of 'poor education, economic rivalry, or one uncharacteristically bad experience with a Jew' (*British Jewry* 43). Shatzkes rejects the presence of such a contract, real or imagined.

29. Daniel Snowman's study of Jewish refugee artists, scientists, and intelligentsia to Britain shows that no matter how highly their contributions were valued, because of British ambivalence toward Europe, they were considered 'exotic and filtered through a prism of Englishness' (55).

30. Very few of these writers, such as Naomi Alderman, deal with the Holocaust but still address issues about Jewish identity in Britain. Bryan Cheyette's anthology *Contemporary Jewish Writing in Britain and Ireland* contextualizes the literary history of British Jewish writers by pointing out how the included selections can be seen as a multicultural Jewish presence in Britain. In a 1996 article, Cheyette coined the term 'extraterritoriality' to 'question the misconceived certainties embedded in both an English as well as a Jewish past', to distinguish British Jewish literature in 'that it neither universalizes Jewishness out of existence nor straitjackets it in preconceived images' ('Englishness and Extraterritoriality' 36, 37). In the Holocaust writing considered in this book, the Jewish past is tied to historical specificity that prevents preconceived or universalizing tendencies. In 2000, the multi-media organization YaD Arts held its first performance to celebrate contemporary Anglo-Jewish created music, art, and theater. Josephine Burton, YaD's creative director, notes that 'there are many more Jewish artists in Britain creating a dialogue with their Jewish identity than I had imagined a year ago' (Burton and Walton, 'Diaspora in Motion' 70). For a pungent discussion about being a Jewish woman writer in Britain, see Fainlight, Kahn, Pascal, Samuels, and Wandor.

31. Jill Swale observes that unlike the Jewish American literary tradition, 'Fear of antisemitism and pressure to merge into a monolithic English culture meant that recognizably Jewish novels appeared very infrequently until the 1960s when ethnicity became acceptable' and even now they can expect a small readership ('Feminism and the Jewish Novel' 47).

1. *Other People's Houses*: Remembering the Kindertransport

1. Debates about distinctions between autobiographical and memoir writing abound. Laura Marcus distinguishes between autobiography as evoking a life wholistically and memoir as a series of anecdotes. Kindertransport writing attempts to capture a whole life through partial memory and anecdotes. Sue Vice notes structural distinctions between memoirs and autobiography in that memoirs focus on the personal and historical past of the first person narrator and intersperse the author's stories with those of others ('Writing the Self' 191). Caroline Sharples points out that the largest number of memoirs by refugee groups has been produced by the Kinder but with little critical analysis (41).

2. Gillian Lathey reports that, before World War II, children's autobiographical writing was rarely published because it could only recount how little they understood the events that shaped their wartime experiences and could neither heroicize nor criticize policies that led to and prosecuted war (28).

3. In her Holocaust memoir, Ruth Kluger confronts her readers and reflects on their possible reactions and her responses to them about the barriers to their mutual understanding. She is especially critical of the kinds of reader responses that have been primed by platitudes and universalizing clichés.

4. See, for example, Turner's *And the Policeman Smiled* and Bentwich's *They Found Refuge*.

5. Perhaps because her mother survived and remained with her, Ruth Kluger traces her jagged personal development as marked not only by postwar treatment of survivors but also by her ongoing conflicted relationship with her mother, particularly as issues of mother–daughter dependency and responsibility are enacted as alternating roles.

6. I am grateful to Allan Hepburn whose trenchant dissection of allegories of death as violent nonbeing stimulated my own observation about Kindertransport memoirs.

7. Susan Suleiman's study of the 1.5 generation, the child survivors of the Holocaust, offers insights into the emotional plight of younger Kinder. Segal would be included in the group 'old enough to remember but too young to understand' as well as those 'old enough to understand but too young to be responsible' ('The 1.5 Generation' 283).

8. For surveys of men's and women's responses, see Karen Gershon, *We Came as Children*, Mark J. Harris and Deborah Oppenheimer (eds.), *Into the Arms of Strangers*, and Bertha Leverton and Shmuel Lowensohn (eds.), *I Came Alone: The Stories of the Kindertransport*.

9. Lathey uses Lacan's psychoanalytic theories to buttress her analysis but, as much as she extends his interpretations, they constrain her textual analyses by limiting them to his model. To use a term borrowed from object relations psychoanalysis, both the process of constructing a self and the shape of that self are often overdetermined, that is, incorporating unforeseen as well as oppositional meanings that challenge extant models of explanation. Also, while language is clearly crucial to the formation and deformation of identity, as Lacan insists, as many memoirs attest, even one's native language also becomes the vehicle to express the inability of language to express inchoate or painful feelings and the visual images they conjure.

10. Caroline Sharples notes that this heroicizing sentiment expresses the Kinder's gratitude for their rescue as well as serving to memorialize Hitler's victims (46). She also claims that 'The very act of writing has proved a cathartic process, providing a means for the working through of a traumatic past' (43). I find more ambivalence in these testimonies.

11. Beate Neumeier observes how 'the ambivalence implicit in fairy tales between reassurance and destabilization, epitomized in ... "Hansel and Gretel" ', is both frightening and shows the 'necessity to develop abilities to conquer obstacles, survive and succeed in life' (63). I would add that the tale would have different meanings before and after leaving home and parents.

12. I want to thank Donna Coffey for this observation in her paper, 'The Pastoral and Holocaust Poetry', read at the American Comparative Literature Association meeting, March 2006.

13. *The True Story of Hansel and Gretel*, by Louise Murphy, is a recent novel that transposes the outlines of the fairy tale to narrate the adventures of two Jewish children left by their desperate father and step-mother in the winter of 1943 to find their way to survival in the primeval and mysterious Bialowieza Forest. Renamed Hansel and Gretel, the children are rescued by a woman called Magda who is considered a witch by the nearby Polish villagers. Their ensuing adventures and traumas, woven into historically researched facts about the Nazi occupation of Poland and the Polish resistance, shape an inquiry into meanings of cultural and personal identity and memory. Elaine Feinstein has also written a short story, 'Hansel and Gretel', which reverses the classic tale by also making the old woman kind and sorrowful and because the children suspect her of being a witch, they push her into the fire. Though their cruelty is attributed to a wicked stepmother's coldness, and the children steal the old woman's trinkets to save their parents from their poverty, they are punished when a snowstorm blocks their way home.

14. Darvas 190. Unlike many memoirs that eschew personal reflection for densely packed narratives of events, Darvas's conveys emotional effects that lend candor and eloquence to her writing. One such response, unfortunately, is scarred by her problematic portrait of an Orthodox Jewish family who, during the Blitz, rent a room to Darvas and a friend. Though there is no reason to doubt the punitive behavior of the Rosenblums in response to their boarders' violations of *kashrut*, Darvas's disdain for the observance of Jewish dietary laws becomes offensive in her mockery of the family's Yiddish accents, especially as she depicts no other refugee's accent, including her own.
15. I use the writer's first name to designate the child character and her last name as the writer.
16. James E. Young discusses such references to ancient biblical stories as the destruction of Sodom and Gomorrah and modern pogroms as inadequate analogues to Holocaust experience that produces 'a self-reflexive questioning of the available archetypes to frame it' (*Writing* 95).
17. Like the troubled girl in Lore's school, Eva in Karen Gershon's unpublished novel, 'Manna to the Hungry', yields to the pressures exerted by English society, but neither conversion nor intermarriage makes the hope for integration an emotional or social reality. For discussion of Jewish integration and assimilation into British society, see Endelman, *Radical Assimilation*.

2. Karen Gershon: Stranger from the Kindertransport

1. In interviews conducted for the video *Stranger in a Strange Land*, Gershon's husband, Val, and her four children, three of whom stayed in Israel, express complicated feelings about Karen and Val's return to England. Her eldest son wishes his childhood had been in Israel, not England; Tony asserts that 'the Jews' only home is Israel', and Naomi reports that because her father never understood why she and her two brothers made Israel their home, they drew apart. Tony says that his father 'didn't take to Israel' and that since 'Karen didn't write while she was in Israel', returning to England 'wasn't so bad'. Stella returned to England with her parents. For other biographical and bibliographical references, see Lawson, 'Karen Gershon', in Kremer.
2. This is also attested by Gershon's unpublished novels where her sisters and even parts of herself are conflated into the character of a brother and where her own character is infused with parts of theirs. Sue Vice notes the novelistic structure of Gershon's childhood memoir, *A Lesser Child*, which also serves as 'a memorial, and a literary text' ('Writing the Self', 204).
3. The last blood libel trial took place in Tsarist Russia in 1913. The defendant, Menahem Beilis, was acquitted but still endangered and had to leave Russia.
4. Peter Lawson notes that whereas Christianity sees the New Testament as superseding the Old, Gershon reads the New 'as presaging the Holocaust' (*Anglo-Jewish Poetry* 148). Lawson also situates Gershon's treatment of Christian symbols in a twentieth-century poetic tradition that includes Siegfried Sassoon and Isaac Rosenberg.
5. In her discussion of her parents' refugee experiences, discussed in Chapter 4 below, Anne Karpf notes that the pressures to anglicize names in Britain is related to the lack of acceptance of hyphenated ethnic identities, such as Anglo-Jewish. She quotes Rosemary Friedman, an Anglo-Jewish novelist, who 'remarks that "I am

aware that the declaration of my name to a non-Jew is greeted with a frisson, signaling the fact that the "Jew" is encountered before any attempt is made to reach the person" ' (*War After* 216).

6. Ute Benz here summarizes Anna Freud's observations of how mourning by children evacuated to Britain was misinterpreted.

7. Helene Meyers points out, 'Gothic romance has been preoccupied with women's economic, psychological, and physical vulnerability' (18). As Gershon's novel shows, we should add political and racial vulnerability.

8. As essays in the journal *Modernism/Modernity* and papers at the Modernist Studies Association attest, modernism appears to have overtaken what we only recently have earmarked as late Victorian and postmodern fiction. Interest in both the origins and ends of modernism seems to have been subsumed by an all-inclusive modernist studies.

9. Judith Halberstam reminds us of the necessity of viewing the Gothic as always historicized around such issues as 'class and race, sexual and national relations' and 'the gothic monster is a combination of money, science, perversion, and imperialism' (21).

10. Carol Davison traces the figure of the Wandering Jew as an antisemitic icon from nineteenth-century British Gothic literature through Nazi propaganda films which 'fostered a new and terrifying stage in the development of the vampiric Wandering Jew: he blurred yet another boundary by purportedly wandering into "reality" where he was deliberately manipulated to intend harm. As the immediate audience reactions to these films and the establishment of the death camps attest, these nightmarish projections were hugely successful in their aims' (160).

11. Beate Neumeier insists that because it is 'problematic' to use elements of 'gothic fiction' to 'represent the unrepresentable, the utterly non-assimilable other', the Gothic must be 'defamiliarized' to foreground 'the trauma' of the Holocaust ('Kindertransport' 63). Andrea Reiter's discussion of 'Children of the Holocaust' is relevant to Kindertransport memoirs: 'The child's limited perspective is less guided by logic than by the magical world of the fairy tale' ('Kinds of Testimony' 3).

12. Halberstam makes this point about *Dracula* and *Dr. Jekyll and Mr. Hyde* and goes on to apply it to 'the Anti-Semite's Jew' in her chapter on *Dracula*, where she summarizes the specter of the Jew as it 'unites and therefore produces the threats of capital and revolution, criminality and impotence, sexual power and gender ambiguity, money and mind' (20, 95).

13. Debates about authenticity in Holocaust writing lend an interesting perspective to those concerned with modernist representations.

14. Peter Lawson notes many references to *Alice in Wonderland* and mirror images in Gershon's novels that suggest the disorientation of 'imagining one's reception in a new language and culture' wherever her protagonists go (*Anglo-Jewish Poetry* 153). While Lawson sees comfort in imagination for characters in other Gershon novels, in *Bread of Exile* and, as I shall discuss, in *The Fifth Generation*, imagination can offer frustrated desires and expectations.

15. Modris Eksteins's observation about World War I flying aces remains applicable to World War II: 'Flight has always possessed an enormous symbolism for man; during the war that symbolism was heightened. The air ace was the object of limitless envy among infantry, mired in mud and seeming helplessness. Soldiers looked up from their trenches and saw in the air a purity of combat that the

ground war had lost. The "knights of the sky" were still engaged in a conflict in which individual effort still counted, romantic notions of honor, glory, heroism and chivalry were still intact' (264–5).

16. The focus of Gershon's unpublished novel, 'Love Is Not Enough', is the eruption of a sexual relationship between a brother and sister who meet many years after he escaped to Palestine and she remained in England. The novel is not a success but its evocation of fusing desires for sexual gratification and reconstitution of family intimacy demands serious attention. I'm extremely grateful to Peter Lawson's generosity in sharing his prodigious research, including copies of Gershon's unpublished manuscripts.

17. I wish to thank Derek Rubin for this insight in his paper at the Conference on Postwar Jewish Writing in Ghent and Antwerp, November 2006.

18. Claudia Curio's research shows that many rescued children 'suffered serious emotional or mental problems in reactions to ... the pressure' from Nazi persecution 'and that continued in the new surroundings, albeit in a weakened form – they were told only inconspicuousness would protect them from hostility' (54–5).

19. Nicola King's psychoanalytically shaped discussion of George Perec's *W or The Memory of Childhood* invokes the idea of the absent presence of families lost in the Holocaust (127).

20. There are many points to be made about Gershon's poetic and cultural relationship to Eliot, but that is a subject to be pursued elsewhere. However, Gershon's poetic indictment of Christianity and antisemitism is pointedly relevant not only to Eliot's arguments for a Christian civilization that deny the place of the Jew but also to ongoing debates about Eliot's antisemitism.

3. Dramas of the Kindertransport and Its Aftermath

1. An interesting structural feature of the play is its parallel with the 'temporally split narration' of Holocaust memoirs and fiction written from a child's perspective as described by Sue Vice where past and present are narrated 'side by side', with each 'disrupting a teleological and backshadowing view of history' (*Children* 12). The split staging, naïveté of Samuels's child character, and repressions of the adult Evelyn are signs of such disruption.

2. Lyndon situates Samuels as a woman playwright in a British theater world that was still, in 1994, 'dominated' by 'a masculine way of thinking and of creating art', and claims that Samuels violates a traditional 'taboo about women speaking out', especially about deeply felt ideas that can change people (Lyndon 21, 20). While this claim about domination is debatable, given the popular and critical acclaim of such outspoken British women playwrights as Caryl Churchill and Sara Kane, Lyndon is considering them as exceptions.

3. Many children tried to stay in touch with parents, even as the Red Cross and other agencies were being rebuffed by the Nazis. But, even as late as 1944, Red Cross messages were being conveyed from Theresienstadt to the children. For the few parents who survived, reunion was very painful. The children had grown up into British culture and parents were ravaged by their horrific experiences.

4. Many children were taken to Jewish hostels, but though Jewish organizations tried to place others in compatible homes, the experience was mixed, from outright abuse to acceptance and even love. One transportee reports, 'On the day I arrived they gave me a hot drink and an hour later I did the ironing for the whole family

Jewish Museum [...] What frightened me most was the thought that I would be giving strangers absolute power over me' (Jewish Museum 54).

5. Claire Tylee notes that 'Evelyn and Faith are an integral part of contemporary British society', but my reading questions whether this integration was and still is possible ('Diane Samuels' 1084).

6. In the actual experience of the Kinder, conversion had many meanings. Where the foster home atmosphere was both supportive and churchgoing, conversion became the logical extension of finding a new identity. In other cases, developing affinities to Christianity was part of the identity of 'upper-middle-class, highly cultured families [...] it was part of Englishness, like poetry, music, and art' (Kleinman and Moshenska 40).

7. Schlossberg's analysis is also postmodern but her discussion of Jewish identity serves as a critique of ahistorical or transhistorical slippages ('Rites of Passing Introduction', Sanchez and Schlossberg 1). The seminal postmodern work to which Schlossberg is responding is that of Jean-François Lyotard.

8. Sander Gilman's research has provided the basis for continuing work on cultural and political responses to *The Jew's Body*.

9. Elaine K. Ginsberg (4). Though Ginsberg's study focuses on American culture, where Jews have expressed their identities very differently from the British experience, the British perspective complicates the meanings assigned to race and passing.

10. The certainty of Stanton B. Garner's presentation of theatrical props as ordering principles cannot be universalized, as Holocaust drama demonstrates (89).

11. Samuels questions the viability of publishing dramatic texts since they are 'rather difficult to read' and work as 'a guide [...] for the builders and enacters to follow in order to create that spatial and physical phenomenon, the performance' ('Jewish Theater' 77).

12. In 'Trauma, Postmodernism and Descent', Sue Vice reviews various theories of trauma emanating from the work of Cathy Caruth and Shoshana Felman and shows how current British Holocaust criticism moves these theories in new directions.

13. Richard Hornby delineates various strands of voluntary and involuntary role playing that have been usefully provocative for my analysis (74). His example of involuntary role playing as influenced by the realpolitik of Nazi Germany and the Soviet Union shows how characters are 'manipulated by an unseen, mysterious, powerful authority' (82). In *Kindertransport*, 'authority is associated not only with the threats of Nazism', but of a dominant British culture. His discussion of British 'character acting' adds a layer of interest to the acting roles of Eva and Evelyn insofar as it 'resembles involuntary, inwardly controlled, compulsive role playing' where the actor 'is not detached from the character; nor does he remain himself, exploring his own identity introspectively. Instead, he becomes a *new* self, is possessed and driven by it' (86).

14. Marianne Hirsch has coined the term postmemory to distinguish the actual memories of survivors from those they transmit to the following generations.

15. The story is based on an unspecified catastrophe that the town of Hamelin, Germany traces to 26 June 1284. The oldest remaining source, in Latin, has been dated from the mid fifteenth century. A rhyme inscribed on the *Rattenfängerhaus*, built in 1602/03 in Hamelin, has been translated as follows: 'In the year 1284, on John's and Paul's day was the 26th of June / By a piper, dressed in all kinds of colours, / 130 children born in Hamelin were deduced and lost at the "calvarie"

(place of execution) near the "koppen".' In 1816 the brothers Jacob and Wilhelm Grimm reworked the story from eleven sources, but its most famous version is Robert Browning's 1849 poem, later illustrated by Kate Greenaway. Some critics speculate that the fable originally represented the recruitment of settlers for new colonies in Eastern Europe, while others find evidence for references to a plague or a children's crusade (Jonas Kuhn, 'Pied Piper Homepage', <http://www.ims. unistuttgardt.de/~jonas/piedpier.html>). See also the Hamelin homepage. Beate Neumeier links the ambivalence of Samuels's Ratcatcher to historical reports of discontented youth leaving home to find more satisfying environments, 'reflected in an abundance of sociohistorical, political, mythological, and psychological explanations of the story' (67).

16. Personal email correspondence (11 May 2004). Samuels has also written that 'The written text [of a play] is in many ways a guide, an architectural blueprint of sorts' ('Jewish Theatre' 77).

17. See Jacob Lassner, who also points out that Lilith is a 'model of sexual independence; a rejection of biological imperatives that relegate women to roles of procreation and nurturing; and, more generally, a defiance of male authority' (4). The figure of Lilith originates in ancient near eastern mythology.

18. Harley Erdman traces this figure back to Shylock and through such plays as Forbes Heerman's *Down the Black Canon* (1890) and Charles Townsend's *The Jail Bird* (1893) which employ costumes and dialect that 'reflect and perpetuate certain anxieties about Jews in general, since Jews, unlike some other ethnic groups, cannot be so readily categorized and labeled by distinctive, consistent sets of physical traits [...] These villains therefore address gentile anxiety in much the same way as does Shylock's exotic paraphernalia' (Erdman 34).

19. In a conversation about tensions between antisemitic and philosemitic creations of Jewish characters, Samuels noted that Shakespeare's 'Shylock was a projection of Jewishness created by a non-Jew and that as a Jew he did not feel to me to represent very much in any depth about the nature of the Jewish psyche and experience as I knew it from my life and community [...] many of Harold Pinter's characters were far more profound and quintessential Jewish characters than Shylock [...] Pinter's genius was that he had managed to make Jews seem universal and so made his work widely acceptable and admired by the English. For this alone he deserves to be hailed as a real revolutionary' (email note 5 September 2003).

20. John Peter views Evelyn's maternal behavior as 'a determination to be calm at all costs. It is not a question of who wins and who loses, but of who can be made to see that the other is being totally reasonable' ('Rats in the Attic' n.p.).

21. Reviewer Jeremy Kingston notes that 'Eventually the child-destroying rat-catcher is identified, shockingly, as everyone who once felt they were acting as the child's savior' (n.p.).
    Beate Neumeier sees the Ratcatcher's multiple guises as indicating 'the persistence of the power of the past over the present as well as the continuity of the fears about the future' (Neumeier 67).

22. For a comprehensive analysis of this theme in children's literature, see Jeanne Murray Walker, 'High Fantasy, Rites of Passage, and Cultural Value'.

23. See Jack Zipes (*Fairy Tales*), who has studied the psychological and nationalistic implications of Grimm's fairy tales, but does not discuss Nazi nationalism. Maria Tatler reports that the Allied command at the end of the war banned the Grimms' fairy tales in Germany. Despite his demolished clinical reputation, Bruno

Bettelheim's psychoanalytic study of fairy tales is still useful in exploring how children's fantasy lives are reflected in the tales' violently depicted sexuality.

24. Vivian M. Patraka (62). Susanne Greenhalgh draws attention to the play's 'multilingualism' as an 'aural "memoryscape"' that marks 'an unstable, and destabilizing, terrain for identity in the post-Holocaust world' (' "A Space" ' 33).

25. Una Chaudhuri creates the term 'geopathic discorders', meaning 'the suffering caused by one's location', but Holocaust writing would have to be seen as trans-geopathic, given how its suffering is not confined to specific sites and, indeed, does not stop at borders (58).

26. Tony Kushner shows how 'the combination of exclusive nationalism and univer-salistic liberalism has made it hard for British society to confront the racisms of past and present at home and abroad which its particularistic minorities have had to face', and this includes 'the academic community'. As the critic James Agate said to an aspiring Jewish actor: 'What do you look like? Jewish? All right. Too Jewish? Not so good [...]' (Kushner, 'Remembering to Forget' (238).

27. A most recent play about the constructedness of English gardens and the evo-lution of their styles and meanings is Tom Stoppard's *Arcadia*, where academic research on the history of a country house garden is satirized as equally artificial and utterly romantic and self-serving.

28. Claire Tylee interprets the play as a protest to wartime and postwar propaganda images of the 'harsh, bullying *Vaterland* that dominates British stereotypes of German culture, the lost, succoring feminine culture that is eclipsed by war and propaganda' ('Community' 191). Nowhere does Tylee distinguish between the Third Reich and its Nazis and a pre-Nazi or post-Nazi Germany, marking the essay as ahistorical and therefore unreflective of the destructive masculinist Nazi German culture which should not be 'eclipsed' by literary criticism.

29. Reviewing the play for the *Daily Telegraph*, a review later reprinted in *Theatre Record*, Charles Spencer asks about the absence in the play of how Lisa learns Leo has just died and why she wants to give the cottage back to Leo's son Daniel and cousin Beth. While most reviewers were deeply moved by the play's subject and Leo's passion for some kind of justice, they also criticize the disjunction between past and present as divided between Acts I and II and express strongly divided preferences for either the first or second act.

30. This relationship recalls that of Martin Stone, a German Jewish refugee, and Karin, his East German lover, in Emanuel Litvinoff's novel, *The Lost Europeans*, which cannot be sustained because of his sense that his people were murdered by hers: 'They were taboo to each other [...] Love between them would be like an act of miscegenation' (88).

4. The Transgenerational Haunting of Anne Karpf and Lisa Appignanesi

1. Second Generation writing was propelled by Helen Epstein's 1979 *Children of the Holocaust: Conversations with Sons and Daughters of Survivors*. In recent years, scholars who are children of survivors have turned to Holocaust studies, starting with family memoirs and going on to analyze other Holocaust representations. See Hirsch, 'Surviving Images'.

2. Marita Grimwood concludes her study of Second Generation writers by stressing a combination of individual and collective 'relationship to history' (136). Karpf

worries about how this relationship leads to 'the notion of lessons to be learnt from the Holocaust' ('Memories' n.p.).

3. As I write this new Anglo-Jewish fears have arisen in response to a proposed boycott of Israeli academics and goods by various British trade unions and the continued castigation of Israeli policies regarding the Palestinians in language that sometimes recalls antisemitic stereotypes and myths. The fact that the British courts declared even the unions' debates illegal does not mitigate antisemitic fears.

4. Critics note that her journalistic talents allow Karpf to negotiate the difficult terrain of this project to produce a compelling narrative. Moorehead assesses Karpf's gifts for storytelling as inscribing enough detachment 'to describe a childhood not so much unhappy as singular' (Moorehead 36). Cheyette, in contrast, like Golding, finds an occasionally overheated and inflated rhetorical flourish, as when she 'speaks of making an "internal concentration camp of my own" ', communicating a sense of her continuing 'perplexity and unclarity about her place in her parents' experience, and in the world outside' (Cheyette, Review 45; Golding 238). As Esther Isaacs notes, however, the book makes a powerful contribution by working against the grain 'of the stereo-typified survivor family' (Isaacs 4).

5. See, for example, Bernard Wasserstein and Louise London.

6. A case in point is Appignanesi's 1992 epic novel, *Memory and Desire*, which covers European and American ground from the 1920s through the date of writing. Although the male protagonist, Jacob Jardine, has a Jewish father, and there is a long section devoted to wartime perils and resistance efforts to rescue Jews, issues concerning Jewish identity and continuity are not plotted. The trajectory of the plot revolves around characters' sexually obsessed and often abusive entanglements and the unsteady stream of consciousness about liberating oneself. The female protagonist, Sylvie Kowalska, is a Polish non-Jewish subject and object of sexual obsession, whose one moment of sanity is her heroic efforts to rescue Jews during the war.

7. Among the many histories of Polish-Jewish relations, see Anthony Polonsky. Eva Hoffman, also born in Poland after the war, who also emigrated with her family to Canada, has written eloquently of returning to Poland and then researching its history of relations with the Jews. Like Appignanesi, her writing expresses yearnings for mutual Polish-Jewish understanding and for a more mutually accepting history.

5. Elaine Feinstein's Holocaust Imagination

1. Bryan Cheyette assesses Feinstein's career as having 'led the way' in her creation of poetic novels that re-imagine a 'European past in terms of limitless "magical" wordplay as well as acknowledging the insurmountable ' "borders" of history' ('Moroseness' 24).

2. Peter Conradi notes that in the early 1970s Feinstein was influenced by 'the new gothic' of writers like Angela Carter, J. G. Ballard, and Emma Tennant, who replaced realist conventions that represent 'the consoling fantasy of a stable world' with 'the grotesque, science fiction, black farce, or gothic' to represent a destabilized world (296). The new Gothic 'provides a code or convention by which past time can bring its exotic revenges to the present' (296).

3. Broe and Ingram show the critical acumen women develop in voluntary and involuntary exile as conditions of race, gender, class, and culture. Feinstein's

women combine these categories and develop critical faculties both consciously and unconsciously. Yosef Hayim Yerushalmi shows how Jews from ancient to modern times respond to the biblical injunction to remember so as not to forget their historical past 'in which the great and critical moments of Israel's history were fulfilled. Far from attempting a flight from history, biblical religion [is] saturated by it and is inconceivable apart from it' (Yerulshalmi 9). Feinstein's fictions combine questions about this imperative with those in medieval Jewish chronicles which assimilate contemporary events to the idea that 'Persecution and suffering are, after all, the result of the condition of being in exile, and exile itself is the bitter fruit of ancient sins' (Yerulshalmi 36).

4. My use of the term *postmodern* is indebted to Hayden White's assertion that making meaning of history is necessary, but as its meaning is constructed in language history is inseparable from literature. The weight of the Holocaust's significance is borne out by ongoing debates about the moral issues concerning its representation, as noted in my introduction.

5. Jill Swale notes that Anglo-Jewish writer Gerda Charles considers Feinstein 'the most feminist of today's established Anglo-Jewish novelists', and that her novel *The Survivors* features a clear case of the tradition and rebellion against denigration of women's intellectual capacities (49).

6. Though Victoria Glendinning applauds the seriousness and intensity of *Children of the Rose*, she 'longs for' the relief of a 'few jokes at the gates of hell' and the presence of the 'hard and frivolous goy' characters ('Ghost Hunt' 489). Susannah Clapp observes the Mendezes' marital discord as related to their being 'in the grip of a flashback or nightmare' ('Ghost Hunt' 445).

7. This implication is particularly prescient in light of the resurgence of antisemitism in Europe at the same time that new Russian Jewish refugees from Russia and Israelis are immigrating to Germany along with Israelis who live in both places. See Morris and Zipes as well as Ignanski and Kosmin.

8. It should be noted that the 1975 publication of this novel coincides with the memory of Vichy which, as Susan Suleiman discusses, 'had become, since the early 1970s, a national obsession' (*Crises* 80).

9. Claire Tylee notes that Feinstein uses a poetic technique in this novel where a character's visionary experience reveals 'literal truth' and also sees 'love flourish' at the end of the novel, but I think Feinstein is problematizing romantic love ('Elaine Feinstein' 330).

10. Feinstein remains interested in oppressive marriages where women fear their husband's desire to probe the depths of their consciousness and to strip them of any private self. See her story 'Draught' and the 1976 novel, *The Ecstasy of Dr. Miriam Garner*, where the protagonist of the same name admits: 'I'm not a good woman, am I? It's because I don't like being eaten alive. Isn't that what goodness means in a woman?' (9). In a 16 July 2004 interview, using the example of *Mother's Girl*, Paul Farkash addresses the issue of dominant fathers, to which Feinstein answers: 'He's in some ways enchanting and in other ways very dangerous, and particularly for a daughter, I think. I think daughters are probably quite damaged if they have too strong an attachment to their fathers. On the other hand, you can't win. If you don't have such an attachment you'll probably never fall in love at all' (297).

11. Feinstein's fictions dramatize an uneasy tension that Hayden White describes as follows: 'the historical narrative, [measured] against the chronicle, reveals to us a world that is putatively finished, done with, over, and yet not dissolved,

not falling apart' (21). Her novels create historical narratives that are unfinished, dissolving boundaries between cause and effect; even the past is unfinished. She raises questions of how to represent sites of moral responsibility instead of answering 'the demand for closure in the historical story [which] is a demand [. . .] for moral meaning, a demand that sequences of real events be assessed as to their significance as elements of a moral drama' (21).

12. For a chronicle of this passage, see Lisa Fittko.

13. Bryan Cheyette sees the 'fissures' in Benjamin's character as reflecting the novel's structure, 'which reads an arbitrary version of its own story back from a contemporary perspective' ('Englishness and Extraterritoriality' 31). Of course the novel's competing narratives puncture any sense of arbitrariness. Tim Dooley sees Benjamin as offering 'hope of a marriage between the material and mystical' and between ' "insight" and the "world of cause and effect" ', but even if this is true of Benjamin's actual thought, Feinstein's focus on Hans's response and relationship to Inge undermines the possibility of such a marriage (Dooley 632). Feinstein's earlier novel, *The Shadow Master*, which embeds a version of the seventeenth-century Shabbatai Zevi epic in a modern tale, exposes faith in rationalism as a defense against anxieties about an apocalyptic end of Jewish culture and identity.

14. There may be a trace here of the rift in Feinsteins's own family, as she revealed to Belinda McKeon where she describes the influence of her intellectual paternal grandfather who preferred to read and think and leave the family business to his children; her maternal grandfather by contrast devoted himself to business success ('Inner Voice').

15. For a comprehensive account of this process see Sander Gilman's *Jewish Self-Hatred*.

16. James Lasdun found the novel perplexing because he feels it relies on the reader's 'share of historical consciousness to supply the hidden shapes beneath' (51). Stephen Bann finds that Feinstein 'has not constructed a mystery which lends itself to being solved' (18).

17. In his discussion of medieval Jewish historiography, Yosef Haim Yerushalmi avers that 'whatever memories were unleashed by the commemorative rituals and liturgies were surely not a matter of intellection, but of evocation and identification' (44). Though in most of Feinstein's fiction, women combine these, in *The Border* and in *Children of the Rose*, her male characters are shown struggling to do so.

18. Bryan Cheyette and Nadia Valman discuss how 'The figure of the Jewish cosmopolitan (both Hebrew and Semite) was [. . .] . . . always double-edged as they embodied the ideal of culture and, at the same time, threatened to exceed the only vehicle deemed suitable to institutionalize this ideal' ('Introduction' 9).

19. Feinstein's consciousness of Jewish identity and continuity is framed within the history and experiences of modern British Jewry and their experiences of social and economic pressures to assimilate. For recent discussions, see Todd M. Endelman and Geoffrey Alderman. Karen Alkalay-Gut notes that Feinstein's 'seeming reticence' about raising Jewish issues in her poetry is really 'subtlety' and that it 'is actually imbued with a Jewish approach to life, to others and to social issues' ('Beyond Borders' 68).

20. Gerda Charles notes that Feinstein strikes a balance by supporting a woman's right to personal happiness and, at the same time, poking fun at the excesses of feminist group theater (see Jill Swale 49).

21. Feinstein identifies herself as 'a pre-feminist writer' because she began writing in 1966 when no feminist's support network' existed ('Dark Inheritance' 61). She

206 Notes, pp. 152–61

emphasizes that, even with a Cambridge University degree, women were expected to be housewives and stay-at-home mothers.

6. Displaced Witnesses: Julia Pascal's and Sue Frumin's Holocaust Dramas

1. In 1995 during a production of *The Holocaust Trilogy* and the fiftieth anniversary of the Nuremberg Trials, a journalist noted that Anglo-Jews feared a resurgence of antisemitism from the Right and 'prefer[red] to keep a low profile' (Arditti 11). Pascal notes the brutal treatment of 'thousands of Eastern Europeans, including Jews and Germans [...] opposed to Nazi rule', brought to Alderney 'as slave labourers'; some were 'thrown into concrete and deliberately drowned at sea' (Neil Roland n.p.).

2. Pascal notes 'that her title for the radio play was inspired by the ironic use of the Nazi description of Auschwitz' (*Holocaust Trilogy* 6). The press and Pascal were told that the play was rejected because of its 'distasteful' language, while the theater, 'a converted church, was not equipped to stage the play' (Alan Montague n.p.). 'In actuality, the only language distasteful to Guernsey authorities was the naming of their Bailiff who was a Petainist. The production of the play is Suitcase Theater style and therefore, according to Pascal, there was no problem about staging it in a converted church' (email 20 June 2005). Mary Luckhurst examines the censorship of the play in historical context.

3. The Guernsey official has been identified as Bailiff Victor Gosselin Carey, who passed on a list of Guernsey's Jews to the Nazis, and who was knighted by the Queen Mother in 1945. Theresa's brother Karl, her only relative to survive, learned her fate in 1993 when the Guernsey Occupation archives were opened. He was welcomed by people willing to share their memories of Theresa and guilt about not hiding her. Other islanders claimed 'that no one had had any idea of what was happening to the Jews in Europe' (Bunting 113).

4. Pascal's professional history attests to her pride in making trouble for the British cultural scene. As an actress, she demanded a chance to direct and, as a result, became the first woman director at the National Theatre in 1978. She then published an exposé of the slim prospects for women directors and formed her own theater company that produced such controversial plays as Seamus Finnegan's *Soldiers*, about Northern Ireland (Arditti 10).

5. Todd Endelman notes that Britain's imperial power is seen in histories of the Jews as pivotal, from its influence in the Middle East and the Suez Canal, as well as its role in Palestine (*The Jews of Britain* 3).

6. Pascal chose Ruth Posner to play Theresa because she was a survivor and a professional dancer, and so she changed Theresa's age from 24 twenty-four to her fifties. For further discussion of the Nazi occupation of the Channel Islands, see Paul Sanders.

7. Interestingly, as fears were rising about the rise of fascism not only in Europe but in England in the 1930s, several dystopias imagining a fascist takeover in England were published. Among them, Storm Jameson's 1936 *In the Second Year* and Katharine Burdekin's 1937 *Swastika Night* are the most notable. For discussion of these and other interwar and wartime dystopias, see my *British Women Writers of World War II*.

8. Two British films postulate a Nazi invasion of Britain: Alberto Cavalcanti's 1942 speculative Ealing Studios anti-Nazi drama *Went the Day Well?* portrays 'an idyllic South of England village infiltrated by German soldiers who are, implausibly, fluent in English and English customs and courtesies as part of a "dry run" operation for a mass follow-on invasion' (Boxwell email 2 August 2007). Following suit with its plucky message, the film features a cheery postmistress bashing in the head of one of the baddies with a spade. Kevin Brownlow's 1966 independent film *It Happened Here* is a much darker film showing the gradual erosion of British resistance to the Nazi invasion and a growth of collaboration (My thanks to David Boxwell, for his generous and dauntless scholarship and pithy description, email correspondence 2 August 2007).

9. For discussion of this propaganda, see Angus Calder and Ian McLaine. Evelyn Waugh's 1943 novel, *Put Out More Flags*, punctures this myth by satirizing the class warfare that fractures the nation's hold on its unity. The Nazi occupation of the Channel Islands has now become grist for the pop culture mill, with disturbing effects. Although the plot of Elizabeth George's 2003 thriller, *A Place of Hiding*, turns on the Nazi occupation of Guernsey, although her murder victim had come to the island as a Jewish child refugee, and the novel's jacket blurb refers to 'the history haunted island', responsibility for and fate of other Jewish refugees remains a mystery. The 2004 BBC/PBS TV miniseries, *Island at War*, absolves the Islanders of responsibility by focusing on stock Nazi villains.

10. Most critics laud the play's fragmented and multi-media structure and focus on its portrayal of Theresa's European experience. Some do not mention its Guernsey scenes but those who do are either ready to be or are persuaded by its story of British betrayal. Denise Watson lauded the play for giving 'chilling insight into the terror the Jews felt under Hitler', Jeremy Kingston found the play 'poignant and bitter', and Alan Hulme notes that the subject of Channel Island residents' collaboration is still 'highly sensitive'. Clearly in agreement with the play's argument, Sophie Constanti adds her own polemical comment about British police being 'as confused as to whom they should be serving then as they are today' (n.p.).

11. Ironically, in relation to Britain's assimilative pressures, Vienna was the German-speaking city that most encouraged Jews to assimilate and advance professionally. Though illusory, assimilation for Viennese Jews 'represented the continuation of Jewish identity by other than religious means' (Anthony Grenville 16).

12. Endelman notes that one obstacle to including Jewish history in Britain's is the lack of ethnic or national diversity before World War II except for the Irish.

13. Because of this erasure I interpret Pascal's 'fractured universe of exile' as a darker vision than does Greenhalgh, who associates Pascal's 'self-affiliation with the European diaspora' with other British women's theater, and internationalizes their concern (Pascal, *Holocaust Trilogy* 5; Greenhalgh, 'A Space' 31–2).

14. For the most richly complex discussion of giving voice to the silences of the Holocaust, see Sara Horowitz, *Voicing*.

15. As I write this note, in the week of 17 September 2007, an album of photographs taken by a Nazi officer of Auschwitz guards has come to light. For the first time, we can see a group of men and women guards off duty, frolicking and laughing, and showing no concern or even awareness of the gassing and burning they are protecting. See the U.S. Holocaust Museum website for a full viewing: <www.ushmm.org>.

16. Pascal 'researched the Nuremberg Trials in the Imperial War Museum where the films are on old stock which is breaking up. Consequently I saw fragments and this led me to structure the Trials in fragmentary scenes. It wasn't just to imitate what I was looking at but rather to show the fragmentary nature of memory' (email 20 June 2005).

17. Written originally in Yiddish, Anski translated the play into Russian, but it was only first performed after his death. Petrovsky-Shtern shows how Anski hoped his research for the play would show 'Hasidism as a powerful counterbalance to the corrupted reality of European decadence. Only Hasidism was able to redeem Jewish culture from the evil spirit of relativism and cynicism. Influenced by Nietzschean symbolism, Ansky compared the Hasidic behavioral pattern to *elan vital*, to fire, outbursts of passion and self-sacrifice, in a word – to revolution', but in the end it only confirmed his 'perception of the decaying spiritual power of Hasidim' (17, 24).

18. 'The five Jews in the play don't remember anything about their religion yet they are about to die for being Jewish. This is the only piece of their culture they can remember' (Matthew Kalman).

19. Gerhard Bach argues that in their imaginative additions to 'the mental maps' readers create about the Holocaust, 'writers who were never "there" ' confront us with 'how to deal, in aesthetic terms, with the "nature of the offense"' (78).

Bibliography

Primary sources

Appignanesi, Lisa, *Losing the Dead* (New York: Vintage, 2000).
— *Memory and Desire* (New York: Dutton, 1992).
— *The Memory Man* (Toronto: McArthur, 2004).
Blend, Martha, *A Child Alone* (London: Valentine Mitchell, 1995).
Burdekin, Katharine, *Swastika Night* (London: Feminist Press, 1985).
Cooperman, Jeanette, Hannah Kanter, Judy Keiner, and Ruth Swirsky (eds.), *Generations of Memories: Voices of Jewish Women* (London: The Women's Press, 1989).
Darvas, Miriam, *Farewell to Prague* (San Fransisco: MacAdam/Cage, 2001).
David, Ruth, *A Child of Our Time* (London: I. B. Taurus, 2003).
Drucker, Olga Levy, *Kindertransport* (New York: Henry Holt, 1992).
Eilenberg, Charlotte, *The Lucky Ones* (London: Methuen, 2002).
Eliot, T. S., 'East Coker', *Collected Poems* (London: Faber, 1963).
Feinstein, Elaine, *All You Need* (New York: Viking, 1989).
— 'Allegiance', *Collected Poems and Translations*: 162.
— *The Border* (New York: St. Martin's, 1984).
— *Children of the Rose* (Harmondsworth: Penguin, 1976 [1975]).
— *The Circle* (Harmondsworth: Penguin, 1973).
— *Collected Poems and Translations* (Manchester: Carcanet, 2002).
— 'Dark Inheritance', interview with Paul Farkash, *London Magazine – A Review of Literature and the Arts* (February/March 2004): 58–68.
— 'Draught', *The Silent Areas*.
— *Dreamers* (London: Macmillan, 1994).
— *The Ecstasy of Dr. Miriam Garner* (London: Hutchinson, 1976).
— *Foreign Girls*, three performed but unpublished radio plays, 1993.
— 'The Grateful Dead', *The Silent Areas*.
— 'Hansel and Gretel', *The Silent Areas*.
— 'Hotel Maimonides', *Collected Poems and Translations*: 204–5.
— 'An Inner Voice that Sets Her Apart', interview with Belinda McKeon, *Irish Times* (10 May 2005): n.p.
— *Loving Brecht* (London: Hutchinson, 1992).
— 'Marriage', *Talking to the Dead* (Manchester: Carcanet, 2007).
— *Mother's Girl* (London: Hutchinson, 1988; London: Arena Books, 1989).
— *The Shadow Master* (New York: Simon and Schuster, 1978).
— *The Silent Areas* (London: Hutchinson, 1980).
— 'Song of Power', *Collected Poems and Translations*: 18–19.
— *The Survivors* (Harmondsworth: Penguin, 1991 [1982]).
— Unpublished interview with Paul Farkash (16 July 2004).
— Unpublished interview with Paul Farkash (20 April 2005).
— 'Way Out in the Centre', interview with Peter Lawson, *Jewish Quarterly* (Spring 2001): 65–9.
Fox, Anne L., *My Heart in a Suitcase* (London: Valentine Mitchell, 1997).
Frank, Anne, *The Diary of a Young Girl*, ed. Otto H. Frank and Mirjam Pressler (New York: Bantam, 1995).

Frumin, Sue, *The Housetrample*, Lesbian Plays: Two, selected and introduced by Jill Davis (London: Methuen, 1989): 93–109.

George, Elizabeth, *A Place of Hiding* (New York: Bantam Dell, 2003).

German Jewish Aid Committee in conjunction with the Jewish Board of Deputies, *While You Are in England: Helpful Information and Guidance for Every Refugee* (London: Woburn House, n.d.).

Gershon, Karen, *The Bread of Exile: A Novel* (London: Gollancz, 1985).

— *Collected Poems* (London: Papermac, 1990).

— *The Fifth Generation* (London: Gollancz, 1987).

— 'A Growing Disquiet', interview with Julia Neuberger, *Observer* (11 March 1990): 61.

— 'Journey to the Past', *Jewish Quarterly* 144 (1991–92): 71–2.

— 'The Last Freedom' (ms, 1986[?]).

— *A Lesser Child: An Autobiography* (London: Peter Owen, 1994).

— 'Manna to the Hungry' (ms, 1990–91).

— *Selected Poems* (New York: Harcourt Brace, 1966).

— *Stranger in a Strange Land*, DVD Video, John Pett (Producer and Director) (Plymouth, UK: South West Film and Television Archive, 2006).

— 'A Stranger in a Strange Land', *Jewish Quarterly* 7:1 (1959): 10–11.

Gershon, Karen (ed.), *We Came as Children: A Collective Autobiography* (London: Papermac, 1966).

Gissing, Vera, *Pearls of Childhood* (New York: St. Martin's Press, 1988).

Golabek, Mona, and Lee Cohen, *The Children of Willesden Lane: Beyond the Kindertransport: A Memoir of Music, Love, and Survival* (New York: Warner Books, 2002).

Golan, Ester, 'The Power of Letters: Letters Written from Berlin 1939–1942', Unpublished Reflection, quoted with permission of the author.

Harris, Mark J., and Deborah Oppenheimer (eds.), *Into the Arms of Strangers: Stories of the Kindertransport* (New York: Bloomsbury, 2000).

Island at War, John Rushton (Producer); Stephen Mallatrot (Writer); Peter Lyden (Director)(Granada TV, UK: 2004).

It Happened Here, dir. Kenneth Brownlow and Andrew Mollo (Lopert Pictures, UK, 1966).

Jameson, Storm, *In the Second Year* (New York: Macmillan, 1936).

Karpf, Anne, 'Gum Disease: Review of Diane E. Eyer, *Mother–Infant Bonding: A Scientific Fiction*', *New Statesman and Society* (5 February 1993): 47.

— 'Memories Aren't Made of This', *Guardian* (26 January 2001) <http://education.guardian.co.uk>.

— 'Return to the Death Camps' (ZA@Play: *Daily Mail* and *Guardian*) <www.mg.coza/mg/art/film/9911/991104-lastdays.html> (3April 2001).

— *The War After: Living with the Holocaust* (London: Heinemann, 1996).

Keith, Lois, *Out of Place* (Manchester, UK: Crocus Books, 2003).

Kluger, Ruth, *Still Alive: A Holocaust Childhood Remembered* (New York: Feminist Press, 2001).

Litvinoff, Emanuel, *The Lost Europeans* (London: Heinemann, 1960).

Michaels, Anne, *Fugitive Pieces* (New York: Knopf, 1997).

Milton, Edith, *The Tiger in the Attic* (Chicago: University of Chicago Press, 2005).

Murphy, Louise, *The True Story of Hansel and Gretel: A Novel of War and Survival* (New York: Penguin Books, 2003).

Pascal, Julia, 'Drama Out of a Crisis', *Jewish Chronicle* (n.d.): n.p.

— 'Guernsey and the Holocaust', *Review of the Guernsey Society* XLVII: 1 (n.d.): 4–5.

— *The Holocaust Trilogy: Theresa; A Dead Woman on Holiday; The Dybbuk* (London: Oberon Books, 2000).

— 'Millennial Longings', *Jewish Quarterly* (Winter 2005/6): 10–11.

— 'On Creativity and Anger', *Contemporary Theatre Review* 2:3 (1995): 39–48.

— 'Parallel Lives Will Only Feed Racism', *Guardian* (13 December 2001) (<http://www.guardian.co.uk/racism/Story/0,,617871,00html>).

Raczymow, Henri, 'Memory Shot Full of Holes', trans. Alan Astro, *Yale French Studies* 85 (1986): 98–105.

Roth, Milena, *Lifesaving Letters: A Child's Flight from the Holocaust* (Seattle: University of Washington Press, 2004).

Samuels, Diane, 'Jewish Theater Coming Out', *Jewish Quarterly* (Summer 1998): 77–9.

— *Kindertransport* (London: Nick Hern Books, 1995).

— '*Kindertransport* Writer Diane Samuels Q & A Exclusive' (30 November 2004) <http://www.octagonbolton.co.uk/KindertransportAddedExtra.htm>.

Schieber, Ava Kadishson, 'Labyrinth', unpublished poem (2005).

Sebald, W. G., *Austerlitz* (New York: Random House, 2001).

— *The Emigrants*, trans. Michael Hulse (New York: New Directions, 1997).

Segal, Lore, 'The Bough Breaks', in David Rosenberg (ed.), *Testimony: Contemporary Writers Make the Holocaust Personal* (New York: Random House, 1989): 231–48.

— 'Memory: The Problems of Imagining the Past', in Berel Lang (ed.), *Writing and the Holocaust* (New York: Holmes and Meier, 1988): 58–65.

— *Other People's Houses* (New York: Harcourt Brace, 1958).

Seller, Maxine S., *We Built up Our Lives: Education and Community among Jewish Refugees Interned by Britain in World War II* (Westport: Greenwood Press, 2001).

Sugarman, Yerra, *Forms of Gone: Poems* (Riverdale-on-Hudson, New York: Sheep Meadow Press, University Press of New England, 2002).

Szeman, Sherri, *The Kommandant's Mistress* (New York: Arcade, 1993).

Waugh, Evelyn, *Put out More Flags* (Boston: Little Brown, 1942).

Went the Day well?, dir. Alberto Cavalcanti (London: Ealing Studios, 1942).

Wiesel, Elie, 'A Plea for the Dead', in Lawrence Langer (ed.), *Art from the Ashes* (New York: Oxford University Press, 1995): 138–52.

Wilkomerski, Binjamin, *Fragments: Memories of a Wartime Childhood*, trans. Carol B. Janeway (New York: Schocken Books, 1996).

Zürndorfer, Hannele, *The Ninth of November* (London: Quartet, 1983).

Secondary sources

Alderman, Geoffrey, *Modern British Jewry* (Oxford: Clarendon Press, 1992).

Alkalay-Gut, Karen, 'Beyond Borders', review of Elaine Feinstein, *Selected Poems*, *Jewish Quarterly* (Summer 1995): 67–8.

Amis, Martin, Bryan Cheyette, Lucy Ellmann, and Joseph Skibell, 'Writing the Unwritable', *Jewish Quarterly* (Summer 1998): 12–15.

Angier, Carole, 'Who is W. G. Sebald?', *Jewish Quarterly* (Winter 1996/97): 10–14.

Anon., 'National Identity', *Daily Telegraph* (27 July 2005): 14.

Anon., 'This Banned Play Creates a Stir', *Telegraph Extra* (7 February 1992): n.p.

Arditti, Michael, 'There Are Still Stories to Tell', *Independent* (22 November 1995): 10–11.

Bach, Gerhard, 'Memory and Collective Identity', in Alan L. Berger and Gloria L. Cronin (eds.), *Jewish American and Holocaust Literature* (Albany: State University of New York Press, 2004): 77–92.

Bann, Stephen, review of *The Border*, *London Review of Books* (5 July 1984): 18.

Barthes, Roland, *Mythologies*, trans. Annette Lavers (New York: Hill and Wang, 1972).

Bauman, Zygmunt, 'Allosemitism: Premodern, Modern, Postmodern', in Cheyette and Marcus, *Modernity, Culture, and 'the Jew'*: 143–56.

Baumel, Judith Tydor, *Double Jeopardy: Gender and the Holocaust* (London: Valentine Mitchell, 1998).

Behlau, Ulrike, and Bernhard Reitz (eds.), *Jewish Women's Writing of the 1990s and beyond in Great Britain and the U.S.* (Trier, Germany: Wissenschaftlicher Verlag Trier, 2004).

Bentwich, Norman, *They Found Refuge: An Account of British Jewry's Work for Victims of Nazi Oppression* (London: Cresset Press, 1956).

Benz, Ute, 'Traumatization through Separation: Loss of Family and Home as Childhood Catastrophes', *Shofar* 23:1 (Fall 2004): 85–99.

Berger, Alan L., 'Jewish Identity and Jewish Destiny, the Holocaust in Refugee Writing: Lore Segal and Karen Gershon', *Studies in American Jewish Literature* 11 (1992): 83–95.

Bettelheim, Bruno, *The Uses of Enchantment: The Meaning and Importance of Fairy Tales* (New York: Random House, 1977).

Bigsby, Christopher, *Remembering and Imagining the Holocaust* (Cambridge: Cambridge University Press, 2006).

Billington, Michael, review of Charlotte Eilenberg's *The Lucky Ones*, *Theatre Record* (9–22 April 2002): 491.

Bolchover, Richard, 'Between Two Plays', *New Moon* (July 1992): 16–17.

— *British Jewry and the Holocaust* (Cambridge: Cambridge University Press, 1993).

Brauner, David, *Post-War Jewish Fiction: Ambivalence, Self-Explanation and Transatlantic Connections* (Basingstoke: Palgrave, now Palgrave Macmillan, 2001).

Broe, Mary Lynn, and Angela Ingram, *Women Writing in Exile* (Chapel Hill: University of North Carolina Press, 1989).

Bunting, Madeleine, *The Model Occupation: The Channel Islands under German Rule 1940–1945* (London: HarperCollins, 1995).

Burton, Josephine, and Jonathan Walton, 'Diaspora in Motion', *Jewish Quarterly* (Summer 2001): 69–72.

Calder, Angus, *The Myth of the Blitz* (London: Cape, 1991).

Caruth, Cathy (ed.), *Trauma: Explorations in Memory* (Baltimore: Johns Hopkins University Press, 1995).

Cavanaugh, Phillip G., 'The Present Is a Foreign Country: Lore Segal's Fiction', *Contemporary Literature* 34:3 (Fall 1993): 475–517.

Cesarani, David, 'Introduction', in Mark Jonathan Harris and Deborah Oppenheimer (eds.), *Into the Arms of Strangers: Stories of the Kindertransport* (London: Bloomsbury, 2000): 1–20.

— 'Reporting Antisemitism', in Sian Jones, Tony Kushner, and Sarah Pearce (eds.), *Cultures of Ambivalence and Contempt: Studies in Jewish-Non-Jewish Relations* (London: Valentine Mitchell, 1998): 247–82.

Cesarani, David, David Feldman, Tony Kushner, Peter Mandler, Mark Mazower, and Bernard Wasserstein, 'England, Liberalism and the Jews: An Anglo-Jewish Histerikerstreit', *Jewish Quarterly* (Autumn 1997): 33–8.

Chaudhuri, Una, *Staging Place: The Geography of Modern Drama* (Ann Arbor: University of Michigan Press, 1995).

Cheyette, Bryan, 'Englishness and Extraterritoriality: British-Jewish Writing and Diaspora Culture', *Studies in Contemporary Jewry* XII (1996): 21–39.

— 'Moroseness and Englishness: The Rise of British-Jewish Literature', *Jewish Quarterly* (Spring 1995): 22–6.

— Review, *The War After*, *New Statesman* (5 July 1996): 44–5.

Cheyette, Bryan (ed.), *Contemporary Jewish Writing in Britain and Ireland* (Lincoln: University of Nebraska Press, 1998).

Cheyette, Bryan, and Laura Marcus (eds.), *Modernity, Culture and 'the Jew'* (Cambridge: Polity Press, 1998).

Cheyette, Bryan, and Nadia Valman, 'Introduction', *The Image of the Jew in European Liberal Culture, 1789–1914, Jewish Culture and History* 6:1 (Summer 2003): 1–26.

Clapp, Susannah, 'Ghost Hunt', *Times Literary Supplement* (25 April 1975): 445.

Coffey, Donna, 'The Pastoral and Holocaust Poetry' (American Comparative Literature Association, March 2006).

Conradi, Peter, 'Elaine Feinstein', in Merritt Moseley (ed.), *Dictionary of Literary Biography*, Vol. 194 (Detroit: Gale Research, 1998): 292–7.

Constanti, Sophie, 'Theresa', *Guardian* (22 May 1990): n.p.

Corner, Lena, 'Truthsayer', *Big Issue* (13 November 1995): n.p.

Cowell, Alan, 'Under a Big Umbrella, but What Else Do They Share?', *New York Times* (1 February 2006): n.p.

Curio, Claudia, ' "Invisible" Children: The Selection and Integration Strategies of Relief Organizations', *Shoah* 23:1 (Fall 2004): 41–56.

Davison, Carol, *Anti-Semitism and British Gothic Literature* (New York: Palgrave, 2004).

De Jongh, Nicholas, Review: Charlotte Eilenberg's *The Lucky Ones, Theatre Record* (9–22 April 2002): 491.

Dooley, Tim, 'Mystical and Material', review of Elaine Feinstein's *The Border, Times Literary Supplement* (6 August 1984): 632.

Eaglestone, Robert, *The Holocaust and the Postmodern* (Oxford: Oxford University Press, 2004).

Eksteins, Modris, *Rites of Spring: The Great War and the Birth of the Modern Age* (New York: Anchor, 1990).

Endelman, Todd, *The Jews of Britain 1656 to 2000* (Berkeley: University of California Press, 2002).

— 'The New Anglo-Jewish History', *Jewish Quarterly* (Spring 1995): 53–5.

— *Radical Assimilation in English Jewish History: 1656–1945* (Bloomington: University of Indiana Press, 1990).

Epstein, Helen, *Children of the Holocaust: Conversations with Sons and Daughters of Survivors* (New York: Bantam, 1980 [1979]).

Epstein, Julia, and Lori Hope Lefkovitz, *Shaping Losses: Cultural Memory and the Holocaust* (Urbana, Illinois: University of Illinois Press, 2001).

Erdman, Harley, *Staging the Jew: The Performance of an American Ethnicity, 1860– 1920* (New Brunswick: Rutgers University Press, 1997).

Evans, Michael, ' "Not British Enough" POW Wins Compensation Ruling', *The Times* (8 July 2005): 29.

Fainlight, Ruth, Barbara Kahn, Julia Pascal, Diane Samuels, and Michelene Wandor, 'The Situation of British and American Jewish Women's Writing Today: A Panel Discussion', in Behlau and Reitz: 301–14.

Fittko, Lisa, *Escape through the Pyrenees* (Evanston: Northwestern University Press, 1991).

Gardner, Lyn, 'Julia Pascal's *The Dybbuk*', *Independent* (9 July 1992): n.p.

Garner, Stanton, Jr., *Bodied Spaces: Phenomenology and Performance in Contem- porary Drama* (Ithaca: Cornell University Press, 1994).

Gilbert, Ruth, 'Ever after: Postmemory, Fairy Tales and the Body in Second-Generation Memoirs by Jewish Women', *Holocaust Studies* 12:3 (Winter 2006): 23–39.

Gilman, Sander, *Jewish Self-Hatred: Anti-Semitism and the Hidden Language of the Jews* (Baltimore: Johns Hopkins University Press, 1986).

— *The Jew's Body* (New York: Routledge, 1991).

Ginsberg, Elaine K., *Passing and the Fictions of Identity* (Chapel Hill: Duke University Press, 1996).

Glendinning, Victoria, 'In the Swim', *New Statesman* (11 April 1975): 489.

Golabek, Mona, and Lee Cohen, *The Children of Willesden Lane* (New York: Warner Books, 2002).

Golding, Martin, Review, *The War After*, *British Journal of Psychotherapy* 14:2 (1997): 237–9.

Gopfert, Rebekka, 'Kindertransport: History and Memory', *Shofar* 23:1 (Fall 2004): 21–7.

Greenhalgh, Susanne, ' "A Space for Me": Jewishness, Memory, and Identity in Julia Pascal's *Holocaust Trilogy*', in Behlau and Reitz: 29–40.

— 'Stages of Memory: Imagining Identities in the Holocaust Drama of Deborah Levy, Julia Pascal, and Diane Samuels', Tylee, '*In the Open*': 210–28.

Grenville, Anthony, *Continental Britons: Jewish Refugees from Nazi Europe* (London: The Jewish Museum, 2002).

Grimwood, Marita, *Holocaust Literature of the Second Generation* (Basingstoke: Palgrave Macmillan, 2007).

Gross, Jan, *Neighbors: The Destruction of a Jewish Community in Poland* (Princeton: Princeton University Press, 2001).

Hacker, Melissa (Producer/Director), *My Knees Were Jumping: Remembering the Kinder-transports* (1995; New Video Group, 2003).

Halberstam, Judith, *Skin Shows: Gothic Horror and the Technology of Monsters* (Durham: Duke University Press, 1995).

Hammel, Andrea, 'Between Adult Narrator and Narrated Child', *Holocaust Studies* 11:2 (Autumn 2005): 62–73.

Harris, Mark Jonathan, and Deborah Oppenheimer, *Into the Arms of Strangers: Stories of the Kindertransport* (London: Bloomsbury, 2000).

Harshav, Benjamin, *Chagall and the Lost Jewish World* (New York: Rizzoli, 2006).

Hartman, Geoffrey, *The Longest Shadow: In the Aftermath of the Holocaust* (Basingstoke: Palgrave, now Palgrave Macmillan, 1996).

Hepburn, Allan, *Intrigue: Espionage and Culture* (New Haven: Yale University Press, 2005).

Hirsch, Marianne, 'Surviving Images: Holocaust Photographs and the Work of Post-memory', in Barbie Zelizer (ed.), *Visual Culture and the Holocaust* (New Brunswick: Rutgers University Press, 2001): 215–46.

Hirsch, Marianne, and Susan Suleiman, 'Holocaust Representation, Material Memory: Holocaust Testimony in Post-Holocaust Art', in Hornstein and Jacobowitz: 79–96.

Hoffman, Eva, *Shtetl* (New York: Houghton Mifflin, 1997).

Holmes, Colin, *Anti-Semitism in British Society 1876–1939* (London: Edward Arnold, 1979).

Homberger, Eric, 'W. G. Sebald', Obituary in *The Guardian* (1 December 2001) (<http://books.guardian.co.uk/news/articles/>).

Hornby, Richard, *Drama, Metadrama, and Perception* (Lewisburg: Bucknell University Press, 1986).

Hornstein, Shelley, and Florence Jacobowitz (eds.), *Image and Rememberance: Repre-sentation and the Holocaust* (Bloomington: Indiana University Press, 2003).

Horowitz, Sara, 'Mind, Body, Spirit, and Contemporary North American Fiction', *Journal of The Association for Jewish Studies* 30:2 (November 2006): 231–54.

— *Voicing the Void* (Albany: State University of New York Press, 1997).

Hulme, Alan, '*Theresa*', *Manchester Evening News* (14 March 1992): n.p.

Iganski, Paul, and Barry Kosmin (eds.), *A New Antisemitism?: Debating Judeophobia in 21st Century Britain* (London: Profile Books, 2003).

Isaacs, Esther, 'Surviving the Survial', review *The War After, Jewish Book News and Reviews* 12:1 (February 1997): 4–5.

Jaggi, Maya, 'Recovered Memories', *Guardian* (22 September 2001): 14.

Jewish Museum, *The Last Goodbye: The Rescue of Children from Nazi Europe* (London: Jewish Museum, 2004).

Jewish Women in London Group, *Generations of Memories: Voices of Jewish Women* (London: Women's Press, 1989).

Jones, Sian, Tony Kushner, and Sarah Pearce, *Cultures of Ambivalence and Contempt: Studies in Jewish-Non-Jewish Relations* (London: Valentine Mitchell, 1998).

Julius, Anthony, 'Anti-Semitism and the English Intelligentsia', in David I. Kertzer (ed.), *Old Demons, New Debates: Anti-Semitism in the West* (Teaneck, New Jersey: Holmes & Meier, 2005): 53–80.

Kalman, Matthew, 'Julia's Journey', *New Moon* (October 1995): 26.

King, Nicola, *Memory, Narrative, Identity* (Edinburgh: Edinburgh University Press, 2000).

Kingston, Jeremy, 'Rats in the Attic', *The Times* (11 September 1996): n.p.

— 'Theresa', *The Times* (30 November 1990): n.p.

Klienman, Susan, and Chana Moshenska, 'Class as a Factor in the Social Adaptation of Kindertransport Kinder', *Shofar* 23:1 (Fall 2004): 28–40.

Korte, Mona, 'Bracelet, Hand Towel, Pocket Watch: Objects of the Last Moment in Memory and Narration', *Shofar* 23:1 (Fall 2004): 109–20.

Kremer, S. Lilian (ed.), *Holocaust Literature*, 2 vols. (New York: Routledge, 2003).

Kuhn, Jonas, 'The Pied Piper Homepage' (<http://www.ims.unistuttgardt.de/~jonas/piedpier.html>).

Kushner, Tony, *The Holocaust and the Liberal Imagination* (Oxford: Blackwell, 1994).

— 'The Paradox of Prejudice: The Impact of Organized Antisemitism in Britain during an Anti-Nazi War', in Tony Kushner and Kenneth Lunn (eds.), *Traditions of Intolerance: Historical Perspectives on Fascism and Race Discourse in Britain* (Manchester: Manchester University Press, 1989).

— 'Remembering to Forget: Racism and Anti-Racism in Postwar Britain', in Cheyette and Marcus: 226–41.

LaCapra, Dominick, *History and Memory after Auschwitz* (Ithaca, New York: Cornell University Press, 1998).

— *Writing History, Writing Trauma* (Baltimore: Johns Hopkins University Press, 2001).

Lang, Berel, *Holocaust Representation: Art within the Limits of History and Ethics* (Baltimore: Johns Hopkins University Press, 2000).

— 'Second-Sight: Shimon Attie's Recollection', in Hornstein and Jacobowitz: 22–30.

Lasdun, James, 'Books and Writers', *Encounter* (October 1984): 51.

Lassner, Jacob, *Demonizing the Queen of Sheba* (Chicago: University of Chicago Press, 1993).

Lassner, Phyllis, *British Women Writers of World War II* (Basingstoke: Palgrave, now Palgrave Macmillan, 1998).

Lathey, Gillian, *The Impossible Legacy: Identity and Purpose in Children's Literature Set in the Third Reich and the Second World War* (Bern: Peter Lang, 1999).

Lawson, Peter, *Anglo-Jewish Poetry from Isaac Rosenberg to Elaine Feinstein* (London: Vallentine Mitchell, 2006).

— 'Karen Gershon', in Kremer: 415–19.

— 'Karen Gershon', in Sicher: 105–10.

— 'Lore Segal', in Sicher: 304–9.

Lefkovitz, Lori Hope, 'Inherited Memory and the Ethics of Ventriloquism', in Epstein and Lefkovitz: 220–30.

Lehrer, Natasha, 'Coming of Age', *Jewish Quarterly* (Summer 1998): 74–5.

Leverton, Bertha, and Shmuel Lowensohn (eds.), *I Came Alone: The Stories of the Kindertransports* (Sussex, England: Book Guild, 1990).

Levi, Neil, and Michael Rothberg (eds.), 'Introduction', *The Holocaust: Theoretical Readings* (New Brunswick: Rutgers University Press, 2003): 1–24.

London, Louise, *Whitehall and the Jews, 1933–1948* (Cambridge: Cambridge University Press, 2000).

Luckhurst, Mary, 'The Case of Theresa: Guernsey, the Holocaust and Theatre Censorship in the 1990s', in Edward Batley and David Bradby (eds.), *Morality and Justice: The Challenge of European Theatre*, European Studies 17 (Amsterdam: Rodopi, 2001): 255–68.

Lyndon, Sonja, 'Speaking Out: An Exchange between Four Women in Theater', *Jewish Quarterly* (Autumn 1994): 19–25.

Lyotard, Jean-François, *Heidegger and 'the jews'*, trans. Andreas Michel and Mark Roberts (Minneapolis: University of Minnesota Press, 1990).

McLaine, Ian, *Ministry of Morale: Home Front Morale and the Ministry of Information in World War II* (London: Allen & Unwin, 1979).

Malcolm, Cheryl Alexander, *Unshtetling Narratives: Depictions of Jewish Identities in British and American Literature and Film* (Salzburg: Poetry Salzburg, 2006).

Marcus, Laura, *Auto/biographical Discourses: Theory, Criticism, Practice* (Manchester: Manchester University Press, 1994).

Marrus, Michael, *The Holocaust at Nuremberg* (Toronto: Faculty of Law, 1996).

Meyers, Helene, *Femicidal Fears: Narratives of the Female Gothic Experience* (Albany: State University of New York, 2001).

Montague, Alan, 'Guernsey Says No to Holocaust Play', *Jewish Chronicle* (14 December 1990): n.p.

Moorehead, Caroline, 'In Enemy Terrritory', review *The War After*, *Times Literary Supplement* (30 August 1996): 36.

Morris, Abigail, 'Beware the Treadmill', *Jewish Quarterly* (Winter 1994/95): 4.

Morris, Leslie, and Jack Zipes (eds.), *Unlikely History: The Changing German-Jewish Symbiosis, 1945–2000* (New York: Palgrave, 2002).

Neumeier, Beate, 'Kindertransport: Childhood Trauma and Diaspora Experience', in Behlau and Reitz: 61–72.

Ofer, Dalia, and Lenore J. Weitzman, *Women in the Holocaust* (New Haven: Yale University Press, 1998).

Parry, Ann, 'The Caesura of the Holocaust in Martin Amis's *Time's Arrow* and Bernhard Schlink's *The Reader*', *Journal of European Studies* 24:3 (1999): 353–68.

— '"Lost in the Multiplicity of Impersonations?" The Jew and the Holocaust in Post-War British Fiction', *Journal of Holocaust Education* 8:3 (Winter 1999): 1–22.

Patraka, Vivian M., *Spectacular Suffering: Theatre, Fascism, and the Holocaust* (Bloomington: Indiana University Press, 1999).

Peter, John, 'No Escaping the Horror', *Sunday Times* (6 September 1996): n.p.

Petrovsky-Shtern, Yohanan, '"We Are Too Late": Ansky and the Paradigm of No Return', in Gabriella Safran and Stephen Zipperstein (eds.), *Between Two Worlds: Ansky and Russian-Jewish Culture* (Stanford: Stanford University Press, 2005): 83–102.

Polonsky, Antony (ed.), *From Shtetl to Socialism: Studies from Polin* (London: Littman Library of Jewish Civilization, 1993).

Pratt, Rob, 'Future Past' (<www.metroactive.com/papers/cruz/09.08/99/taylor-9936 html>).

Reisz, Matthew. 'Lollipops and Broken Glass: A Conversation with Lucy Ellman', *Jewish Quarterly* (Summer 1998): 16–17.

Reiter, Andrea, 'Kinds of Testimony: Children of the Holocaust', *Holocaust Studies* 11:2 (Autumn 2005): 1–10.

— *Narrating the Holocaust*, trans. Patrick Camiller (London: Continuum, 2000).

Rittner, Carol, and John K. Roth (eds.), *Different Voices: Women and the Holocaust* (New York: Paragon House, 1993).

Rokem, Freddie, *Performing History* (Iowa City: University of Iowa Press, 2000).

Roland, Neil, 'Guernsey's Nazi Collaboration', *Manchester Jewish Gazette* (6 March 1992): n.p.

Rothberg, Michael, *Traumatic Realism: The Demands of Holocaust Representation* (Minneapolis: University of Minnesota Press, 2000).

Sage, Victor, and Allan Lloyd Smith (eds.), *Modern Gothic: A Reader* (Manchester: Manchester University Press, 1996).

Sanchez, Maria C., and Linda Schlossberg, *Passing: Identity and Interpretation in Sexuality, Race, and Religion* (New York: New York University Press, 2001).

Sanders, Paul, *The British Channel Islands under German Occupation 1940–1945* (Jersey: Jersey Heritage Trust, 2005).

Sanyal, Debarati, 'A Soccer Match in Auschwitz: Passing Culpability in Holocaust Criticism', *Representations* 79 (Summer 2002): 1–25.

Schlossberg, Linda, 'Rites of Passing', in Sanchez and Schlossberg: 1–12.

Schneider, Hans, Review: *Into the Arms of Strangers: Stories of the Kindertransport*, *Shofar* 20:4 (Summer 2002): 116.

Schumacher, Claude (ed.), *Staging the Holocaust: The Shoah in Drama and Perfor- mance* (Cambridge: Cambridge University Press, 1998).

Seidler, Victor J., *Shadows of the Shoah* (Oxford: Berg, 2000).

Seller, Maxine S., *We Built up Our Lives: Education and Community among Jewish Refugees Interned by Britain in World War II* (Westport: Greenwood Press, 2001).

Sharples, Caroline, 'Reconstructing the Past: Refugee Writings on the Kindertransport', *Holocaust Studies* 12:3 (Winter 2006): 40–62.

Shatzkes, Pamela, *Holocaust and Rescue: Impotence or Difference? Anglo-Jewry 1938–1945* (Basingstoke: Palgrave, now Palgrave Macmillan, 2002).

Sherman, A. J., *Island Refuge: Britain and Refugees from the Third Reich 1933–1939* (London: Frank Cass, 1994).

Sicher, Efraim (ed.), *Holocaust Novelists, Dictionary of Literary Biography*, Vol. 299 (Detroit: Gale Publications, 2004).

Silberstein, Laurence J. (ed.), *Mapping Jewish Identities* (New York: New York University Press, 2000).

Smith, Andrew, and Jeff Wallace, *Gothic Modernisms* (Basingstoke: Palgrave, now Palgrave Macmillan, 2001).

Smith, Hazel R. Knowles, *The Changing Face of the Channel Islands Occupation* (Basingstoke: Palgrave Macmillan, 2007).

Smith, Paul, Review of Angus Calder's *The Myth of the Blitz*, *Times Literary Supple- ment* (13 September 1991): 28.

Snowman, Daniel, *The Hitler Emigrés: The Cultural Impact on Britain of Refugees from Nazism* (London: Chatto & Windus, 2002).

Sonin, David, 'An Unusual Twist to a Classic Tale', *Jewish Chronicle* (June 1992): 26.

Spencer, Charles, Review of Charlotte Eilenberg's *The Lucky Ones*, *Theatre Record* (9–22 April 2002): 491.

Stier, Oren Baruch, *Committed to Memory* (Amherst: University of Massachusetts Press, 2003).

Suleiman, Susan R., *Crises of Memory and the Second World War* (Cambridge, Massachusetts: Harvard University Press, 2006).
— 'The 1.5 Generation: Thinking about Child Survivors and the Holocaust', *American Imago* 59:3 (2002): 277–95.
Swale, Jill, 'Feminism and the Jewish Novel: A Cross-Cultural Comparison', *Jewish Quarterly* (Autumn 1992): 47–52.
Tatler, Maria, *The Hard Facts of the Grimms' Fairy Tales*, 2nd edn. (Princeton: Princeton University Press, 2003).
Turner, Barry, *...And the Policeman Smiled* (London: Bloomsbury, 1991).
Tylee, Claire, 'Community and Harmony in Charlotte Eilenberg's Post-Holocaust Play *The Lucky Ones*', in Aránzazu Usandizaga and Andrew Monnickendam (eds.) *Back to Peace: Reconciliation and Retribution in the Postwar Period* (Notre Dame, Indiana: Notre Dame University Press, 2007): 180–95.
— 'Diane Samuels', in Kremer: 1082–5.
— 'Elaine Feinstein', in Kremer: 328–31.
— *'In the Open': Jewish Women Writers and British Culture* (Newark: University of Delaware Press, 2006).
Van Alphen, Ernst, *Caught by History* (Palo Alto: Stanford University Press, 1997).
— 'Caught by Images: Visual Imprints in Holocaust Testimonies', in Hornstein and Jacobowitz: 97–114.
Vice, Sue, *Children Writing the Holocaust* (Basingstoke: Palgrave Macmillan, 2005).
— 'Trauma, Postmdernism and Descent: Contemporary Holocaust Criticism in Britain', *Holocaust Studies* 11:1 (Summer 2005): 99–118.
— 'Writing the Self: Memoirs by German Exiles, British-Jewish Women', in Tylee, *'In the Open'*: 189–209.
Walker, Jeanne Murray, 'High Fantasy, Rites of Passage, and Cultural Value', in Glenn Edward Sadler (ed.), *Teaching Children's Literature* (New York: Modern Language Association, 1992): 109–20.
Warner, M., *From the Beast to the Blonde: On Fairy Tales and Their Tellers* (London: Vintage, 1995).
Wasserstein, Bernard, *Britain and the Jews of Europe 1939–1945* (Oxford: Clarendon Press, 2001).
Watson, Denise, 'Scant Reward for Top Drama', *Evening Chronicle* (26 April 1990): 7.
White, Hayden, *The Content of the Form: Narrative Discourse and Historical Representation* (Baltimore: Johns Hopkins University Press, 1987).
Whiteman, D. B., *The Uprooted: A Hitler Legacy* (New York: Insight Books, 1993).
Wolf, Janet, 'The Iconic and the Allusive: The Case for Beauty in Post-Holocaust Art', in Hornstein and Jacobowitz: 153–74.
Yerulshami, Yosef Hayim, *Zakhor: Jewish History and Jewish Memory* (Seattle: University of Washington Press, 1982).
Young, James E., *Writing and Rewriting the Holocaust* (Bloomington: Indiana University Press, 1990).
Zemel, Carol, *'Z'chor!* Roman Vishniac's Photo-Eulogy of East European Jews', in Epstein and Lefkovitz: 75–86.
Zipes, Jack, *The Brothers Grimm: From Enchanted Forests to the Modern World* (New York: Palgrave, 2002).
— *Fairy Tales and the Art of Subversion: The Classical Genre for Children and the Process of Civilization* (New York: Routledge, 1991).

Index